Award-winning *US*
Lindsay has alway
the real world. Mar
with two adult chil
stories of her hear
with her nose firmly in someone else's book.

Niobia Bryant is the award-winning and nationally
bestselling author of more than forty works of romance
and mainstream commercial fiction. Twice she has
won the RT Reviewers' Choice Best Book Award for
African American/Multicultural Romance. Her books
have appeared in *Ebony*, *Essence*, *New York Post*,
The Star-Ledger, *Dallas Morning News* and many other
national publications. One of her bestselling books was
adapted to film.

Also by Yvonne Lindsay

Honour-Bound Groom
Stand-In Bride's Seduction
For the Sake of the Secret Child
Tangled Vows
Inconveniently Wed
Vengeful Vows
Seducing the Lost Heir

Also by Niobia Bryant

A Billionaire Affair
Tempting the Billionaire

Discover more at millsandboon.co.uk

SCANDALISING THE CEO

YVONNE LINDSAY

ONE NIGHT WITH CINDERELLA

NIOBIA BRYANT

MILLS & BOON

First Published in Great Britain 2021
by Mills & Boon, an imprint of HarperCollinsPublishers,
1 London Bridge Street, London, SE1 9GF

Scandalising the Ceo © 2021 Dolce Vita Trust
One Night with Cinderella © 2021 Niobia Bryant

ISBN: 978-0-263-28281-8

0121

MIX
Paper from
responsible sources
FSC® C007454

This book is produced from independently certified FSC™ paper to ensure responsible forest management.

For more information visit: www.harpercollins.co.uk/green

Printed and bound in Spain
by CPI, Barcelona

SCANDALISING
THE CEO

YVONNE LINDSAY

To the amazing and wonderful
Kim Standridge Boykin.
Thank you for sharing your insights and
pictures of your exquisitely beautiful home.

One

"This is where you'll be working. Take a seat."

Begin with the end in mind, Tami told herself as she settled at the desk she'd just been shown to by the HR staffer who had greeted her on her arrival at Richmond Developments this morning. It was a policy that had led her to start many projects, not all of them successful, but she'd always maintained it was a good stepping-off point.

Tami tugged at the unfamiliar skirt she was wearing. More into jeans or leggings and a T-shirt, herself, the suit she'd donned today screamed corporate chic at the same time as she'd screamed internally at the cost of it. Not because she couldn't afford it, but because of the meals that amount of money could have provided at the shelter for displaced families that was run by the charity where she used to work. Her stomach clenched hard at the memory and the reason why she'd been forced to leave. The same reason she was here now.

When her father had made his demands clear, her mom had smoothly stepped in and ensured she had the appropriate props for her new role. Clothes, shoes, makeup, manicure, hair—even a new smartphone. The list was endless. The end would justify the means, she reminded herself, and she could always return the Chanel suits to her mom to add to the collection for her next charity auction. The same could be said for the silk blouse she was wearing today, which was the same hue as Tami's hazel eyes.

The impeccably groomed HR staffer smiled but Tami noticed it didn't so much as crinkle the skin at the corners of the woman's cold blue eyes. Was everyone here like that? Remote and unfriendly? This job might be harder than she thought. Then another thought occurred to her. Was this woman the mole her father had within Richmond Developments? The one that had assured her of her own position here so she could spy on one of the joint CEOs? It wasn't as if she could actually ask her, though, was it?

"We try to run a paperless office in as far as it is possible here, so any note-taking will be on your issued device or your computer. You'll be given your passwords by IT in the next half hour or so. Guard them carefully and share them with no one. Is that understood?"

Tami felt the words like a punch to the gut. No one knew about the event that had driven her here—well, no one except her, her dad, the charity that was stripped of its bank-account contents and the pond-scum-sucking lowlife who'd stolen the funds. Okay, so *some* people knew. But with that very basic, common-sense admonition, Tami had again been reminded of exactly how stupid she'd been allowing her boyfriend to use her laptop. *Ex-*

boyfriend, she corrected silently. She swallowed against the lump that had thickened her throat.

"Don't worry. I take security very seriously," she answered. *Now.*

She'd learned her lesson the hard way when her ex-boyfriend, Mark Pennington, who was the director of Our People, Our Homes, the charity they both worked for, had borrowed her laptop, accessed her banking code for duplicate authorization and then subsequently cleaned out the bank accounts. The bitter truth of his betrayal, the absolute abuse of her trust, still made her feel physically ill. And, while Tami was the kind of person who could forgive a lot, she'd never forgive Mark for stealing from those so much less fortunate, or for making her go to her father for help. She felt a personal responsibility to the charity and had offered to repay the missing two and a half million from a trust fund her grandmother had established for her. The trouble was, her father was one of the trustees administering the fund and he'd made it clear to the other trustees that she was incapable of taking control of it as an adult—all because of a few rebellious choices when she was a teenager. But he'd agreed to distribute the necessary funds to her if she did what he asked and spied on his biggest rival.

"Good," Ms. HR continued. "Mr. Richmond will be here shortly. He mostly sees to his own needs in the office, but be ready to attend any meetings immediately. He'll need you to take notes and load them to the cloud that you will share with him alone. Is that clear?"

"As glass," Tami answered, resisting the urge to add a salute and heel click at the same time.

As if the woman could sense her irreverence, she gave Tami another cold, hard stare before nodding. "If you need me, you can reach me by telephone or email. My details are in the company directory in your computer."

"Thank you, I'm sure I'll be fine."

The woman cocked a perfectly plucked and outlined eyebrow. "You'd need to be better than fine. Mr. Richmond delivers the best at all times and that's exactly what he expects from his inner circle, too."

"Duly noted. Is that all?" Tami said as officiously as she could. No small feat for someone who'd rather be handing out meals to families or calming a confused child while her mom got some sleep on a cot nearby.

"For now. Have a good day."

The moment she was alone, Tami sank down into the chair at her desk. At least it was comfortable, she noted as she gave it a spin.

"'Mr. Richmond delivers the best at all times and that's exactly what he expects from his inner circle, too,'" she muttered as she looped around a second and a third time. "Well, how's this for a circle?" She spun once more for the hell of it.

There was a sound behind her and she rapidly put her expensively well-shod feet in their boringly practical pumps down to the carpeted floor, bringing herself to a halt as she turned back around. A man, in what was clearly a bespoke dark suit, stood in front of her. Impeccably dressed, from his perfectly shined shoes all the way up to his immaculately groomed hair. Even the light beard on his face had not a whisker out of place.

"Ms. Wilson, I presume?" he said in a deep, well-modulated voice that turned her insides into molten honey.

Wait, that wasn't supposed to happen. She was off men for good, maybe even forever, wasn't she? Especially after the last one. But, despite having been caught out, quite literally, fooling around on the job, and despite that weird reaction to the tone of his voice, Tami managed to gather her wits and stand up to greet him.

"Yes," she answered with the smile she'd been practicing in the mirror all weekend as she offered her hand. "Please, call me Tami. And you're Mr. Richmond?"

He looked at her with clear gray eyes that felt as though they were staring right through her. He hesitated a moment before taking her hand. The second he touched her, Tami felt a quiver of highly inappropriate interest ripple through her body. One that intensified into a distinct tingle that headed to her lady parts as his lips spread into a smile of welcome. He let go of her hand and Tami fought the urge to rub hers down over her thigh. That man needed to license that smile, she thought privately.

"I'm Keaton. There are two Mr. Richmonds here in the office and we're identical twins, so you'll need to figure out how to tell us apart. You'll be reporting to me, and only me. Is that understood?"

She fought the urge to roll her eyes. What was it with everyone here with all the rules? It was going to make her job so much harder. These people needed to lighten up. Although, given the well-publicized drama when Keaton's father suddenly died last Christmas and it was revealed that he had a whole secret life on the other side of the country, including another wife and kids, maybe she could understand their need to be sticklers for convention.

"Ms. Wilson?" he prompted.

"Oh, yes, sorry. Of course," she said, feeling totally flustered at being caught not paying attention, again.

Heat suffused her cheeks and she just knew her skin had gone all blotchy. Way to go on making a good first impression, she told herself.

* * *

Keaton watched as his new EA changed color. Judging by their interchange so far, he was beginning to wonder if he'd done the right thing in leaving the appointment solely to Monique in HR. Perhaps she hadn't been quite as meticulous in her vetting procedures as usual. Or maybe it was merely an indication of the caliber of person now applying to work here at Richmond Developments, that Tami Wilson was the best of the bunch. Since the scandal involving his father's second family and the damage the publicity had done to their family name, not to mention the company stock, morale had been low at the office. Several key staff had left, hence the recruitment of the woman standing in front of him doing her best impression of a beet.

"Perhaps you could come in to my office and we can go over a few things together."

"Do you want me to make notes?" she asked.

He watched as she caught her lower lip between her teeth. His gaze locked on to the lush fullness of that part of her and he was momentarily transfixed. Keaton gave himself a mental shake and dragged his eyes upward to hers. Hazel. He couldn't remember the last time he'd met someone with precisely that shade of green-brown, nor with such thick dark lashes. Natural? he wondered. None of his business, he reminded himself firmly and gathered his thoughts to answer her question.

"Unless you have a perfect memory, it would probably be a good idea. At least until we get a better grip of how we're going to work together."

Or even if they were going to continue to work together, he realized. She was distracting. Far prettier than the male assistant he'd had previously, and wearing a suit and shoes that were definitely not straight off the rack.

She was worse than distracting, to be honest. He did not need or want distraction. He and his siblings, Logan and Kristin, were fighting to keep Richmond Developments going, and with what he was about to tell Tami, he wondered if he shouldn't just assign her elsewhere within the company because the idea of spending the next week alone with her sounded like his worst nightmare.

He moved into his office and after a short while, Tami followed. He settled behind his desk and gestured to her to sit down in one of the chairs opposite him. She did so, unconsciously hitching up the hem of her skirt just a little. Try as he might, he couldn't help but appreciate the shapely thigh, highlighted by the sheerest of black stockings, that she exposed with the action. She tapped a stylus against the phone device she'd brought in with her. Like her outfit, it was sleek and expensive-looking. Clearly, Ms. Wilson wasn't short of a penny. He only hoped she worked as hard as she obviously shopped.

But, it occurred to him, it also wasn't the standard issue to Richmond Developments staff. Since pretty much everything in their offices was conducted electronically and maintained within a strictly operated company cloud, he could only assume she hadn't been allocated her own device yet and that the phone was her own. He'd have to ensure that she understood that the moment she began to record company information electronically, it became the property of Richmond Developments. They couldn't afford to have any of their property, intellectual or otherwise, inadvertently shared with the outside world. Their business rivals were circling like sharks, waiting for them to crumble in what was a difficult and highly competitive market.

He decided to tackle the issue of the phone immediately, so he picked up his own tablet from the desk and logged in to a blank page. It wasn't strictly protocol to share his device, but the document would upload to their shared cloud and she'd be able to access it from her computer and her own company-issued device once she had been given her passwords from IT.

"Here, rather than clutter up your personal phone with company information, use my device," he said firmly, handing it over the desk toward her. "If you scribe in that window, it'll convert your handwritten notes to text and we'll both be able to access them after our discussion."

"Oh, okay, sure. My previous role was with a charity and we were a lot less strict on note-taking procedures."

She smiled as she said it, but he saw the question in her eyes. It surprised him.

"We used to be less careful, but we recently decided to tighten everything up here. Anyway, tell me a little about yourself," he began. "Exactly where were you working before you came here and what made you want to work for us?"

"Oh, um… I was working for a charity that specifically assists displaced people. We not only provide kitchens and shelters, but also work toward placing our people in actual homes. It was challenging and rewarding work and I enjoyed it, but—" She swallowed and took in a deep breath. "It was time to change. As to working with Richmond Developments, it's a well-established company with a strong reputation for integrity and an eye for detail. Who wouldn't want to work with you? While my work with the charity allowed me a lot of diversity within my role, I see this as an opportunity to hone my talents in organization and project development, while bringing my personality and interpersonal skills to the table."

They were fine words, but Keaton couldn't help feeling there was a lot there that she didn't say. Like, if she enjoyed the charity work so much, why had she left?

"And what do you do with your spare time?"

She laughed then. A charming chuckle that sent a flurry of warmth spiraling through him. Keaton found himself involuntarily smiling in response.

"Oh, spare time isn't something I indulge in often. The work at the charity took up much of my spare time and I like to volunteer where I can, as well. Overall, I like to be useful and offering support to those in need is deeply fulfilling. But, during the evenings I'm not helping at the shelter, I find it relaxing to knit. Again for charitable causes like the homeless shelters and animal rescues."

"Knit? Isn't that something older people do?"

Tami arched a brow at him and a pitying smile quirked at the side of her mouth. "Older people? Isn't that a little ageist, Mr. Richmond? I thought your company prided itself on inclusiveness."

It was gentle, but she was definitely chiding him and he had the grace to acknowledge her censure.

"I'm sorry, yes, it was inappropriate of me. And, please, do call me Keaton. To be honest, I don't think I've ever known anyone who knits. It's certainly not a skill my mother possesses."

"It's wonderful," she said, her eyes lighting with enthusiasm. "You get to work with color and texture, and see something grow from a straight line into a garment that can be worn, enjoyed and be functional at the same time. What's not to love about it?"

"Well, when you put it that way…" He laughed in response.

She was different, that was for sure. If he wasn't careful, he had no doubt she'd be giving him knitting lessons— she was so animated about it. He was impressed that she hadn't been afraid to call him out on the ageist comment. There weren't many employees here that would do that, be it existing or new. And she hadn't hesitated. That was a good sign as to her personality, despite the fact he'd caught her fooling around on her chair when he'd arrived. Maybe she would be a breath of fresh air in the place. Goodness knew they needed something.

But they weren't there to have fun and games, he reminded himself. They had a business to bring back to its former strength—and beyond—which meant that he had to focus on the tasks at hand.

"Okay, well, if you slide the stylus from the top there," he said, gesturing to where she could extract the tool that would help her write on the screen, "we can get started."

He waited until she'd done so before continuing.

"You may be aware that Richmond Developments has been in a state of flux since the death of our CEO, my father, Douglas Richmond. His sudden passing and the revelation of a second family gave the media way more fodder to create bad press against the company. We can't afford any additional slanted reporting against the company or those working within it."

An uncomfortable expression crossed her face and she nodded carefully before speaking. "I had read about your father's death. My condolences on your family's loss. It must have been very difficult for you all."

Keaton felt every muscle in his body tense and let go again. So she'd obviously read the newspapers or heard the gossip. At least he didn't have to revisit that again by explaining the situation in further depth to her.

"We are currently in a rebuilding phase," he said firmly. "Part of that phase is strengthening relationships. First, within our company, then subsequently, with our suppliers and clientele."

"That sounds like a very good plan."

He allowed himself a smile. "Thank you for your approval."

And just like that, she colored up like a beet all over again.

"I didn't mean to sound condescending," she said, obviously flustered.

"You didn't," he reassured her before continuing. "We are in a unique position, you and I. We don't have a working history together, which is problematic in some ways, but in others it offers us a blank canvas from which to build. On the recommendation of the consultant we hired to target boosting staff morale, we are running structured team-building experiences across the company. As you and I are a team of two, we will be conducting ours together and using that time to ensure the wilderness experience that was chosen will meet our requirements as a team builder for both Richmond Developments and DR Construction. We are working to build a strong working relationship between the two companies and that starts with its employees. The other teams will be larger, obviously, based on their department sizes."

A small *V* pulled between Tami's dark eyebrows as she frowned. "A team of two. Just us. Together," she repeated.

"Yes. I agree it's not ideal, as we don't even know one another, let alone know how we will work together, however, as one of the CEOs I have to be seen to be doing the right thing so we will embark on our team-building experience first thing tomorrow. It's a good opportunity for us to discover one another's strengths and weaknesses, while testing out the experiences the course has to offer. Another two groups will meet us there on Saturday morning and we'll complete aspects of the course with them."

The frown deepened. "Tomorrow? Isn't that rather

soon? I don't even know what this will entail. What if I don't feel comfortable with this idea? As you so rightly pointed out, we don't even know one another. And you mentioned wilderness?" Her voice raised several octaves on that last word. "I'm a city girl. I don't have any wilderness experience at all."

"Nor I. Which makes it the perfect opportunity for us to rectify that. As I said, we leave tomorrow. I'll arrange a driver to collect you from your home at oh-five-hundred hours."

Tami squeaked a sound of shock. "That's five a.m., right? Don't you think that's a bit early?" She gave a nervous little laugh. "I'm really not my best until at least eight."

"Tami, I'm sure I don't need to remind you that as a new employee, you are on a trial period, per the terms of the contract you signed. Either of us can terminate that contract. If you're telling me you don't wish to work here then please feel free to leave."

She looked at him then, her green-brown eyes widened in shock. "No!" she blurted, before composing her features. "I'll be ready at five a.m., as required. Do you have a packing list?"

"I do, as it happens." He slid a sheet of paper across the desk.

"I thought you preferred a paperless office," she commented before covering her mouth with her hand. "My apologies again. I sometimes tend to speak before I think."

"Well, then, that should make our time away very interesting, because I, too, have been accused of that. Sounds like it's something we can work on together, right?"

She nodded and picked up the list. He watched as she skimmed the items.

"Hiking boots? Backpack for luggage, day pack for

day trips? Evening wear? That's an interesting list. Exactly where are we going?"

"Sedona."

"But that's—"

"In Arizona. About a three-hour flight, which we'll undertake in the company jet, and then I understand we have a forty-five-minute drive to our destination."

"Well, okay. I can make sure I have all of this by tomorrow."

"I'm aware that you may not have everything required immediately at hand, so I suggest you spend the balance of this morning on orientation here at the office, then leave at midday to purchase whatever supplies you don't already have. Make sure to forward your receipts to Accounting. They will reimburse you."

She nodded and looked at him from under her lashes. Those eyes. They were intensely staring at him as if she was trying to read his mind and through to the very essence of him. It made him uncomfortable and he didn't like that she could have that effect on him. He shifted his gaze so he was looking at a point just past her ear, inwardly shocked that he could be unsettled by something as innocent as a look. Was it that he was too suspicious these days? That he now saw villains at every twist and turn of each day?

He knew Tami Wilson would have been thoroughly vetted by HR before her appointment, so why did he feel this prickle of unease about her? Was it because she was so attractive? However she looked, it should make no difference to him whatsoever. He'd done the whole office-romance thing once before and been badly burned when his then-fiancée had slept with his twin brother. Granted, she'd initially thought Logan was him, but the fact remained their relationship had been destroyed, and while all three of them continued to work together, there was an element of strain there now that affected everyone around them. He sure as hell wasn't going to set foot on that road again, no matter the appeal of the person working with him.

He bent his head to his desk and clicked a few buttons on his keyboard, then looked back up to her again.

"Any questions, Ms. Wilson?"

"Please, do call me Tami, and no. I think I have everything I need here."

"Good, then if you'll hand me back the tablet, I'll ensure that any notes you made are sent to our cloud. You'll be able to access that from your desktop and from your own tablet when it's issued."

She passed his device back to him. Their fingers brushed. It was the slightest of contacts, but it made everything inside his body clench tight. Instinctive fight-or-flight reflex, he told himself as she withdrew her hand and rose from her chair. Attraction, another more insidious voice whispered in his ear. He rid himself of the suggestion instantly, even though he couldn't help but watch her as she walked from his office to her desk. The fit of her skirt enhanced the sweet curve of her backside and her jacket was nipped in enough at the waist to showcase a perfect hourglass figure. And he was being all kinds of fool looking at her and noticing these things, he reminded himself. He swiveled his chair to gaze out the window at the rain streaming down the glass, all but obscuring the cityscape beyond.

The outdoors course was going to be tough enough without the added complication of Ms. Tami Wilson. He wondered how they'd cope having to rely on each other through each demanding day…and night.

Two

As their plane began its descent to the airport, Tami sat as far from her window as her seat belt would allow. While she was quite certain the stunning view of the cliffs, some distance from the mesa where the airport was situated, was incredibly beautiful, she didn't need to see them from above—or from the side—as their plane raced toward the ground.

The journey in the Richmond company jet had been a comfortable one, except for the proximity of her boss sitting directly opposite her for the journey, and the uncomfortable fact that she hated flying. It had become unsettling to find his eyes on her a couple of times. It wasn't as if he was staring—it was more that she was so hyperaware of his presence that if he turned in her direction she knew it instantly. She'd never thought that good peripheral vision was a problem, until now. Now she wished she wasn't as keenly attuned to his every movement, or the sighs of frustration that came from deep within him as he scanned whatever was on his tablet screen.

"I thought we weren't supposed to bring work away on this jaunt," she commented.

"I'm trying to get as much completed as I can before we land. Once we're on the tarmac this will be locked away on the aircraft and we are to be incommunicado with the outside world as much as we can. Even mobile-phone coverage is going to be patchy."

"That sounds…" She struggled to find the right word. She suspected that *antediluvian* would not be particularly well-received. "A challenge," she said lamely.

He snorted a small sound that might have been indicative of humor, but it could as easily have been derision. A sudden drop in the aircraft's altitude made her hands tighten on the armrests.

"Don't worry, it's just a downdraft," Keaton quickly assured her. "Quite normal for this runway, I'm told."

"Normal. Right."

He gave her a quick smile. "It'll be okay. We only hire the best at Richmond Developments, and that includes our pilots."

The best? Did he think that included her? A pang of guilt tugged at her ever so slightly, but she clamped down on the thought. She felt the plane drop farther, and with the unwilling compulsion of someone facing certain doom, she turned her attention to the window just as the wheels hit the tarmac. Her knuckles went white as she tightened her grip on the armrests and she forced herself to recite the mantra she'd trained herself to use when flying. Bit by bit, she willed her body to relax back into her seat as the plane rapidly slowed. When she looked forward again, she saw Keaton's eyes firmly fixed on her. No looking away this time.

"You didn't mention you're a nervous flyer," he said with a note of compassion in his voice she hadn't heard before.

"It's not something I'm proud of and I've come a long way in recent years. There was a time I couldn't even set foot in an airport without turning into a wobbly lump of jelly."

"Then you've come a long way. If I hadn't been watching you, I would never have noticed."

So he had been watching her—she knew it. Thinking it and knowing it were definitely two different things. And knowing it made something pull deep down inside her.

He continued. "My mom is a nervous flyer, too. Perhaps, when we return to Seattle, you could spend some time with her and explain the techniques you use."

Tami swallowed back her anxiety as the plane taxied toward the airport terminal. Helping others was what she loved to do most of all. Maybe it was her nature, but sometimes she suspected it had more to do with focusing on other's needs so that she didn't have to consider her own.

"Sure, I'd love to share my coping techniques if I can. No guarantees that what works for me will work for her, though."

"Understood," he responded with a nod.

The aircraft came to a complete halt and the pilot informed them they were free to disembark when they were ready. Tami watched as Keaton shut down his tablet and rose to stow it in a neatly hidden cupboard beside his chair.

"That's nifty," she said, gesturing to the hidden compartment.

"One of the perks of being able to customize your corporate aircraft. You can make the most of the nooks and crannies the shape of the fuselage provides. Come on, let's go. Once we have our packs we can pick up our rental and head out to the camp."

Tami felt a frisson of nerves. She'd never been camping, although the list of items she'd been told to pack suggested they weren't doing it rough the whole time they'd be away. She looked across at Keaton and saw a light of determination reflected in his eyes.

"You look as though you're looking forward to this," she commented as they made their way to the exit.

He turned and flung her a brief smile. It was so fleeting she almost wondered if she'd seen it at all.

"I always enjoy tackling a new challenge," he said.

Tami felt another ripple of trepidation. "So this is going to be really testing? Like, physically?"

"Worried you're not up to it?" he said as he gestured for her to precede him on the stairs from the plane.

"Oh, I'm up to it." Then she muttered under her breath, "Even if it kills me."

She'd faced far greater challenges than those she expected to be presented by an outdoor-experience course. Like the ones she'd faced at school, where her learning style did not fit the prescribed criteria of any one of the charming boarding schools her parents had sentenced her to during her childhood. Not to mention the ones she'd faced as a child of a very privileged family, when she finally managed to get her parents to accede to sending her to the local high school in their district. A kid learned a lot about challenges in those environments. Granted, none of those required swinging from trees or navigating rapids, but there were distinct similarities.

"Good to know," Keaton said, dragging her attention back to her current situation.

Her feet touched the tarmac and she felt a surge of relief course through her to be on solid ground again. She stood back as Keaton and the pilot opened the luggage compartment of the plane and removed the packs they'd stowed earlier. The two men hefted the packs as though they weighed nothing, but Tami knew hers was around forty pounds. She probably should have packed lighter, maybe stuck to the list Keaton had given her yesterday, but a girl always needed contingencies, didn't she? And while her knitting hadn't taken up that much room, it was possible the five skeins of yarn she'd added to her bag was a little excessive.

Keaton dropped her pack at her feet. "Is there anything in there you'd like to remove before we head out? It's on the heavy side."

"No, I'm fine," Tami stubbornly insisted.

"Really, we can send anything you don't need back on the plane and they can keep it at the office for you until our return."

"I'm fine," she said adamantly.

"I won't be carrying it for you."

"I'm perfectly aware of that," she said, and to make her point she hoisted up the pack and slung one strap over her shoulder. "See? Fine."

He looked at her again and for a moment she thought he might argue, but then he firmed his lips and nodded. "Come on then. We'll go collect the car."

By the time the rental agent had shown them to the SUV he'd had ready and waiting in the parking lot, she could feel the pack beginning to rub on her shoulder. It was one thing to carry it around the house, quite another to have to lug it everywhere in a far warmer climate than back home. Maybe she should have unpacked it and left some things behind. She gave herself a mental shake. Nope. She'd made her decision and she'd stick to it. It was all part of being the new, improved Tami Wilson. And no more using the words *maybe* or *should*, either. They reeked of regret, and regret was something she didn't want in her life ever again. At least, not until she'd cleared her debt with her father.

She unslung her pack from her shoulder and shoved it firmly into the back of the SUV with a great deal of relief, then went to the passenger side of the vehicle and climbed in. She looked around at the countryside, finally allowing herself to appreciate the raw, natural beauty that surrounded them on all sides. They were atop a mesa. Below she could see the civilization that stretched before them, and all around they were bordered by the amazing rock formations and cliffs she'd so assiduously avoided looking at from the air.

"It's breathtaking, isn't it?" she said as Keaton settled in the driver's seat.

"Let's hope we both still think so when this is all over."

She wasn't sure if he was joking or not, so decided to let that one slide. Tami watched as Keaton keyed in a few details to the GPS, then she fastened her seat belt as he put the car into gear and they drove away from the airport.

"A forty-five-minute drive, you said?" she asked as they negotiated their way out of the parking lot and onto the main road, away from the airport.

"Thereabouts," Keaton responded.

"Do you mind if I put on the radio?" Tami asked, reaching for the power button on the center console.

"That will depend on the music you choose."

"I'm pretty easygoing. I listen to most things. Tell me what you like and I'll see what we can find."

"How about you find something and I'll tell you if I don't like it."

She shrugged. "Works for me."

After a few minutes she settled on a classic rock station, and as the SUV began to eat up the miles she felt the last of the tension she'd experienced on their flight ease from her muscles. She hadn't realized she'd fallen asleep until she felt Keaton shake her by the shoulder.

The woman certainly could sleep. She'd dropped off about two minutes after finding that radio station and hadn't so much as twitched since then. Still, if she was a nervous flyer, she probably was already feeling pretty tired. Add that to the early start this morning and the weight of lugging her pack around into the equation, and it was no wonder she'd dozed off.

He'd flung her the occasional glance. Just to check that she was breathing, he'd told himself, but he knew it was more than that. Knew it and didn't like it. He wasn't in the market for a girlfriend. Not now and maybe not ever. Trusting someone enough to want to spend all your free time with them was something he didn't know if he'd ever feel comfortable doing again. Logically, he knew he probably wouldn't be alone forever, but now, with the brutality of Honor's betrayal with Logan, on top of his father's web of lies, he certainly planned to be alone for a good while yet.

Keaton looked again. She wasn't conventionally beautiful. Not in the polished way the women who moved in his family's circle usually were, anyway. But Tami Wilson certainly was striking, and there was a quality to her skin that made her look almost as if there was a hidden glow from inside her. He shifted his attention back to the road ahead and growled at himself. This was not someone to stare at. She was staff and he didn't engage with staff that way. Not ever again.

By the time he pulled up at the outdoor center he was beginning to feel a little tired himself. Always an early riser, he hadn't balked at the early start today, but that, teamed with another sleepless night and driving in unfamiliar territory, made a nap look mighty promising right now. If he did naps, which he didn't. He could see his sister, Kristin, roll her eyes at the very thought of him napping. She was often telling him to slow down, to take time out, but she didn't understand how driven he was, or why.

And now, here he was, in the middle of nowhere, somewhere in Sedona, about to spend far more time with a total stranger than he'd ever anticipated. Oh, sure, he did believe in the benefits of the team-building strategy he, Logan and Kristin had all agreed upon as a strong initiative to pull their staff together again. But that was before he'd realized he'd be having his own intimate twosome for part of the trip.

"Tami, wake up. We're here," he repeated with another gentle shake of Tami's shoulder.

The woman slept like the dead.

Her eyes shot open and for a moment her pupils remained fully dilated and her gaze unfocused, but she snapped out of her daze in an instant.

"Oh, heck, I'm sorry. I didn't mean to fall asleep. That wasn't very companionable of me."

"I'm not looking for a companion," he snapped, before he could stop himself.

She looked startled for a second and then composed her features into a mask of indifference.

"Of course, you're not," she said smoothly.

In fact, it was the most professionally she'd spoken since he'd met her and he had the feeling that her instant shutdown was a facade. As if it was something she was used to doing to protect her feelings. He gave himself yet another mental shake. Why on earth was he even worried about her feelings? They were here to do a job and to learn to become a more cohesive unit...working unit, he corrected.

He alighted from the car before he could say anything else potentially volatile and extracted their packs from the back of the vehicle. Hers really was far too heavy, especially for the trekking they'd be doing in a few days' time. But she'd been adamant and he wasn't about to enter into an argument with her. *Not my circus, not my monkey,* he told himself. But she was his employee and he had a duty to her, he reminded himself. And she had a duty to him, too. They needed to build themselves into a team, and that's where his concern began and ended.

So why, then, were his eyes caught by her as she got out of the car and stretched, before bending deeply from her hips and reaching down to the red soil at her feet? And why did that fluid movement make his body tighten uncomfortably?

"Oh, it feels so good to move," she said. "I'm not used to being inactive for so long."

He cast her what he hoped was a friendly smile but he suspected more resembled a bare-toothed grimace. "I'm sure you'll have plenty of opportunity to move while we're here. We both will."

And he would need to make a note to be in front of her wherever possible. Not because he felt he was better than her. Not because he was her boss, or even because he was a natural-born leader. It had far more to do with self-preservation, because he had no doubt that if she walked ahead of him, he'd end up face-first in the red dirt of the trail because he knew he wouldn't be able to keep his eyes off that shapely butt.

Three

Keaton turned as a tall, slender man came down the stairs of the large two-story cabin, which he assumed was the accommodation block. The man stretched out his hand in welcome and a warm smile spread across his face.

"Hi, and welcome! You made good time. I'm Leon, one of your hosts and guides."

Keaton made the introductions. "Hi, I'm Keaton Richmond, and this is my assistant, Tami Wilson. The advance guard, so to speak."

Leon grinned in response. "It's a cool thing your company is doing. Come on in and I'll show you where you'll be staying until the weekend, when the others join you. It'll give you a head start on getting used to the elevation here."

"Does that mean you'll take it easy on us the first couple of days?" Tami asked.

"Perhaps a little less strenuous than what we've got planned for farther down the track," Leon said with a wink.

He turned as another man came down the stairs from the cabin. Slightly shorter than Leon and with a sturdier build, he bounded down the steps with unrepressed energy.

"Ah, here's my husband, Nathan. At the moment he's our chief cook and bottle washer until we're back to full staff for the beginning of our season. That will coincide with when the rest of your teams arrive so don't be put off by how quiet it is right now."

"Quiet is good," Tami said with a small smile. "And all too rare these days."

"I think you will enjoy it here then," Leon said before introducing Nathan to Keaton and Tami.

"Come on inside," Nathan said. "Leon will show you to your rooms and then bring you down to the kitchen. I have a late breakfast set up for you because I'm sure you're starved. You must have been up since before the birds woke today."

"It was an early start," Keaton admitted, beginning to really feel the weariness he'd tried to ignore earlier pull at him a little harder.

He stumbled a little as they picked up their packs and followed the men to the house.

"You okay?" Tami asked, a worried crease appearing between her eyebrows.

"Fine," he said shortly. "We didn't all get a nap on the way here, is all."

He didn't mean it to come out the way it did, but he saw his words found their unintentional target. Her cheeks colored up a little and she ducked her head.

"Maybe it's the altitude," she said quietly. "You don't

strike me as the kind of person who suffers from a lack of sleep."

Nathan turned and looked back at them. "Don't under-estimate the elevation here. We're about four thousand feet higher than what you're used to. While I don't expect you guys to suffer true altitude sickness, you may feel a little—" he paused while he searched for the right word "—hungover, for want of a better description."

"Great," Keaton muttered. "All the punishment with-out the fun getting there."

Leon laughed. "Oh, you'll have fun all right. Just give yourself a little time to adjust. And keep drinking plenty of water. We restock the bottles in your room fridges twice a day. Staying hydrated is probably one of the most important things you can do to cope."

After being shown to his room, Keaton took the time to have a quick shower, then returned downstairs. He followed the sounds of voices and laughter to the mas-sive kitchen at the back of the cabin. There, Tami was perched on a barstool at one end of a large kitchen island. She looked happy and relaxed, right up until she spied Keaton standing in the doorway.

"Everything okay?" she asked. "Can I get you a cof-fee?"

"Fine. Everything's fine." At least it had been until he saw her again. He'd thought the time alone to get his thoughts back in line would have inured him to the ri-diculous reactions he'd been having to her, but no. "And, yes, coffee would be great. Thanks."

"Black and sweet?"

He cracked a half smile. "You remembered that from yesterday?"

She shrugged. "What can I say? My mind has a cast-iron ability to remember small details."

Keaton pursed his lips and nodded. "That could definitely come in useful. As long as you never lose sight of the big picture."

Again he realized he was the direct cause of her losing the animation on her face, replacing it with that expressionless—almost subservient—look she'd worn earlier. And, dammit, he felt guilty. He needed to learn to temper his remarks. This was as much about him learning how best to work with her as it was about her working with him.

"Sorry," he said gruffly as he accepted the steaming mug of coffee she'd poured for him. "I get a bit intense at times."

"Accepted and noted," she answered with a small smile. She gestured to Nathan, who was at the wide stove. "Nathan's finishing off huevos rancheros. I keep trying to peek over his shoulder and learn his secrets, but he shooed me back to my chair. Doesn't it all smell divine?"

Keaton realized, with some relief, that he hadn't repressed her excitability completely. "It does, indeed," he agreed.

He was hungry and the food did smell great. Hungry? Hell, he was starving. Last time he'd eaten was a quick snack at the office late last night. By the time Nathan turned around with two heaping plates of steaming food, Keaton was just about drooling.

"There you go. Have at it. You'll need the energy," he said with a short laugh. "Just kidding. Leon is going to take it easy on you guys today."

"Should we be worried?" Tami asked.

"Nah, I mean it. I'm just kidding."

"I don't want to let anyone down. Especially on our first day," she said quietly.

"You'll be fine," Keaton said, feeling an uncharacteristic urge to reassure her. While this experience was supposed to test its participants, it wasn't supposed to strike fear into their hearts. "You can set the pace, okay?"

Leon arrived in the kitchen as Keaton spoke. "Sure, today's just a bit of a walk to get used to the terrain, that's all. When you've both eaten, get your hiking boots on and make sure you have day packs with a couple of bottles of water each. And wear light layers. It's going to get warmer, so you'll probably need to peel off at a certain point."

"Certainly not like the weather we left behind at home, is it?" Keaton said to Tami before sitting down beside her and tucking in to his breakfast.

"No, it's not."

While she was agreeing with him, he couldn't help but feel she had some other concerns she wasn't expressing. All in good time, he told himself. Right now he needed to apply himself to his plate. He allowed the taste explosion of the beans, eggs and salsa to fill his mouth. Beside him, Tami moaned in what was clearly an expression of extreme delight. It was an expression more suited to a bedroom than a kitchen, he mused. And just like that he felt a very unwelcome tug of desire.

Tami felt Keaton stiffen beside her. Should she have done that? She was a spontaneous person and it was only natural to her to express pleasure in something, especially something as delicious as the food on her plate. This wasn't going to be a lot of fun if she couldn't be herself. She'd spent her entire childhood being firmly reined in, and she wasn't going to permit any unnecessary restrictions in her world now, not from anyone. Keaton Richmond would just have to get used to the fact that she was open in her appreciation of the finer things

in life, be they food or otherwise. And if it made him uncomfortable, then he was going to have to learn to deal
with it. But thinking about her childhood and her father
reminded her of why she was here in the first place, and
suddenly the food in her mouth took on a bitter flavor.

She forced a smile toward their host.

"This is really good, Nathan. Thank you."

"My pleasure. Always good to see our guests enjoying our efforts."

"Are we the only ones here right now?" she asked,
pushing her remaining food around her plate.

"Until the rest of your staff and those from DR Construction arrive on Saturday. Your two companies have
booked us out, exclusively."

Tami looked at Keaton. "Exclusively? Wow, that's
quite a commitment. To the adventure center and your
staff."

Keaton shrugged. "When we do something, we like
to do it right. This is all about helping all of us to work
better as a team." He gestured to her now-empty plate.
"Are you done? If so, we should probably get ready to go
meet Leon. Remember your water."

He rose from the bench and took their plates to the
deep sink on the other side of the kitchen.

She returned to her room, grabbed her day pack and
stocked it with sunscreen, a light waterproof jacket in
case of rain—although the sky this morning was such a
clear blue she doubted it would be necessary—and three
bottles of water. Tami hesitated about putting her phone
in the side pocket of her bag, but remembered her father's
admonition to keep it near at all times in case he needed
to call or text her. She had to remember that, right now,
she was operating under his instructions and, no matter
how much she wanted to rebel against him, she needed

to glean the information he wanted. She made sure the phone was turned to silent, then slid it in the pocket and zipped the pack closed. The last thing she wanted was to have him attempt to call her during the hike with Keaton. How on earth would she explain that? She threw on an extra layer over her long-sleeved T-shirt and jeans, laced her hiking boots and shoved her favorite hand-knitted beanie on her head, then bounded back down the stairs.

The air outside was brisk, but not quite as cool as it had been when they'd touched down at the airport earlier. The men were waiting for her as she walked outside to meet them. She groaned inwardly. She'd been quick, she knew she had, but it seemed Keaton had been quicker, and by the casual glance he made at the gold-rimmed watch on his broad wrist, he didn't like being kept waiting.

Her father had always been the same. In fact, he'd been such a stickler for time it had made her a very nervous youngster, until she'd learned that it made no difference if she was on time or not. She always disappointed him in one way or another. Even if she was on time, he wouldn't approve of what she was wearing or how she'd done her hair. After that, she'd made every effort not to be on time, knowing how much it would annoy him.

Tami sighed. She may as well grab the bull by the horns, she decided. This wasn't the time for petty games and she had a new boss to impress. And draw secrets out of, she reminded herself grimly.

"Sorry I kept you both."

"Not a problem, Tami," Leon said. "Keaton just arrived a minute or two ahead of you."

Ha! she thought with a private smirk. *So much for checking your watch and making me feel bad.* Instead, she merely smiled.

"Shall we go then?" she asked cheerfully.

"What's that on your head?" Keaton asked with a be-mused expression on his face.

"This?" She gestured to the glaringly bright pink beanie. "It's so you can find me easily if I get lost. Do you like it? I can probably knit one up for you tonight if you want one?"

"Um, no, thank you. I don't think pink is my color," Keaton said with a spark of humor in his gray eyes that she found most gratifying.

It was good to bring other people joy. It was something she always strived to do and it was one of the driving reasons why, as an adult, she'd had next to nothing to do with her parents, who were manipulative, emotional vampires at the best of times. Not seeing them was one thing but she'd taken the further step of changing her surname from Everard to Wilson when she turned eighteen to help increase the emotional distance between them. Plus, it helped her avoid the need to make excuses for not using her family connections to give other people entry into her father's world or, through her, access to his money. She'd had enough of that as a kid.

"No?" she responded with a gurgle of laughter. "I have a nice lime green that might do the trick. I was saving it for a puppy jacket but I'm more than happy to knit it up for you."

"A puppy jacket," Keaton said solemnly, then raised a hand as she started to explain. "No, thank you for the offer, but I'll be fine with my cap. Far be it from me to disadvantage an abandoned puppy." He tipped the brim of the baseball cap that was crammed over his dark blond hair and turned to Leon. "How far are we going today?"

Leon gestured to a peak that looked awfully far away to Tami's untrained eye.

"Nathan's gone on ahead on a quad bike to take our lunch supplies and extra water. We'll probably hike about an hour and a half before we get there. Maybe two hours, depending on how you're both feeling. And as to getting lost, it wouldn't be much of a team builder if we let that happen, would it? You'll be safe with us." He smiled reassuringly at Tami.

Tami wasn't sure she'd be hungry by then after the massive breakfast they'd consumed and an hour-and-a-half-to-two-hour hike seemed like an awfully long time to be traversing the terrain. Still, she was here to do a job and she needed to do it. She adjusted the straps on her day pack and hitched it onto her shoulders.

"Well, I'm as ready as I'll ever be," she said as brightly as she could.

The hike wasn't too arduous and she found it interesting to watch Keaton as he applied himself to every aspect with a quiet, calm intent. He appeared unflappable, even when a family of javelinas crossed their path partway through. For herself, the moment the odd-looking creatures that reminded her of wild boar pictures she'd seen in a *National Geographic* had appeared on the trail, she'd been ready to climb the nearest tree, but Leon had hastened to reassure her that the beasts were herbivores and were unlikely to eye her up as a potential meal. Keaton had shown interest in the creatures, but barely batted an eyelid at their long, sharp-looking, almost canine teeth that protruded from their jaws. Was he like that with everything? A lake of serenity? Or did those still waters run deep?

By the time they'd stopped and had lunch, then done the loop back to the cabin, she was beginning to wonder what her father had hoped to gain by her being with Keaton Richmond. So far they hadn't discussed work at all. In fact he appeared to be assiduously avoiding the topic. Maybe it was because Leon was with them and he was being ultracautious, but then maybe he really just wanted to stop and enjoy the scenery, too. Whichever reason, she couldn't keep bringing up work without it starting to look weird, so she opted for focusing on her breathing as they walked and enjoyed the magnificent scenery around them.

She'd grown very warm during the walk and had ended up wearing only a tank top with her jeans on the way back. A very snug tank top that hugged her body intimately.

Back at the cabin they were told they had free time to enjoy before a candlelight dinner on the enclosed deck at seven o'clock.

"Seems as though all we do here is eat," Tami remarked with a grin and a pat of her tummy.

She noted Keaton's gaze follow her movement and focus on her stomach, then lift slowly to her breasts before tracking up to her throat and her face. A prickle of awareness made every cell in her body go to full attention. Unfortunately, that included all the cells that made up her nipples and darned if they didn't stand to attention as if it wasn't just Keaton's gaze that was on her. Her own eyes dropped to his hands. Strong, capable, long-fingered hands. Hands that right now were clenched into tight fists at his sides.

She prayed the fabric of her bra hid her reaction, but a quick glance downward confirmed her prayer had gone unanswered. Wow, like this wasn't awkward?

Tami shrugged off her day pack, with the intention of pulling out her long sleeve T-shirt and putting it back on to cover the wayward behavior of her body, but the movement made the shoulder strap of the pack catch on the straps of both her tank top and her bra, and tug them off her shoulder completely. Mortification sent heat flooding to her cheeks. Could this get any worse?

"Here, let me help you with that," Keaton said in a slightly gruff voice.

Damn, she'd annoyed him. She'd be lucky to still have a job if she kept this up, and if he sent her home she'd be out on a limb when it came to her father. Her bare skin tingled when Keaton's fingers brushed against her shoulder as he lifted the day pack off her and set it down by her feet.

"I'm not normally this clumsy," she said by way of apology. "Thanks for your help."

"No problem."

Keaton was making every effort not to make eye contact with her.

"Well, if you don't need me for anything, I'll go grab a shower and knit for a while before we meet for dinner. Okay with you?" she asked.

He gave her a curt nod. As she bent and grabbed her pack, then started up the stairs toward the house, she could feel his eyes burning on her back. She wouldn't turn around, she told herself firmly. She absolutely wouldn't. But when she got to the top of the stairs she couldn't help herself. She turned and looked at him. Keaton was still watching her, his face set into tight lines of disapproval.

She felt her stomach sink to her feet. He was regretting bringing her on this venture, she could tell. Tami gave him a small, pathetic wave, then went inside and up to her room, all the while scolding herself for giving him any opportunity to find fault with her. Under normal circumstances, his displeasure wouldn't have mattered. She'd have cut her losses and simply moved on. But she had two and a half million very important reasons to get this right and she was determined to ensure that every last dollar Pennington had stolen would be replaced in the Our People, Our Homes coffers. Then, her promise that she would make full restitution for her stupidity would be fulfilled and she could remove herself from her father's influence again. Hopefully permanently this time.

Could she really keep the promise she'd made? She had to. There was no other choice.

Despite the directive to keep mobile-phone use to a minimum for the duration of the team-building exercise, Keaton couldn't resist the downtime available to him to check on the office. Kristin answered his call on the first ring.

"Hello, brother. Missing us already?"

He could hear the teasing smile in her voice.

"Just ensuring everything is okay."

"And why wouldn't it be?" When he didn't answer, she continued. "Everything is running just as smoothly as when you left the office last night, okay? No one else has resigned."

"Yet."

He heard her snort of derision. "Yet," she confirmed. "How's the new assistant working out? Talk about baptism by fire."

"What do you mean?"

"Well, you can hardly have gotten to know one another in just one day, although it's nearly two now, isn't it?"

"She's fine," he said succinctly.

Too damn fine, his inner voice reminded him.

"Pretty?"

"Kristin, that's unprofessional of you."

"I agree. But is she?"

Keaton rolled his eyes. His sister might be a whiz kid

with financial matters and a more-than-competent joint-CEO, but at times she remained that annoying baby sister she'd always been.

"Pretty enough but not my type." *Liar.* "Besides, I'm not going that route again. Once bitten…"

"Keaton, I'm sorry. I shouldn't have been so asinine."

"It's okay. And, like I said, she's fine. Not what I was expecting, though."

"In what way."

"She offered to knit me a beanie."

"She what? How old is she?"

"Not sure. Although I'm guessing late twenties."

He heard his sister tapping on her keyboard. "She's thirty. And she knits beanies?"

"Puppy jackets, too. And don't say anything about her age and knitting in the same sentence or you'll be given a dressing-down on ageism."

His sister's laughter bubbled down the telephone line and filled his ear with unrepressed humor.

"She did that to you? She sounds amazing—I can't wait to meet her. You do know that knitting is a very popular pastime, for people of all ages, and that's not anything new. You could learn a thing or two from Miss Wilson. Now hang up and get back to retreating."

"It's not a retreat. It's a team-building exercise."

"Whatever, go build your team, then. For what it's worth, I'm really impressed with the enthusiasm and engagement the staff are showing with the concept. They're already beginning to discuss what strengths they can bring to the exercise and wondering which departments from DR Construction they'll be teamed with, not to mention the challenges they might have to face. This was a really good idea."

"They realize this is not a them and us situation, don't

they? We're not competing with DR Construction. This is all about creating a stronger corporate bond between both companies."

"Yes, and I was talking with Lisa about the team building today," Kristin continued, mentioning their half-sister in Virginia. "All the discussion was very positive. Although apparently her mom thinks the whole thing is a waste of time and has reiterated her advice to her kids to stay well clear of us. I'm so glad Mom hasn't been like that."

Keaton grimaced. All along Eleanor Richmond, as she continued to insist on being called despite her marriage to Douglas Richmond having been proven to be void, had been a thorn in their sides. Rather than gracefully accept the truth that had been exposed about her bullying her parent's housekeeper into signing a permission for her to marry, when Eleanor was still underage, she still maintained that Douglas's intention all along had been to marry her and as far as she was concerned, that was all that mattered. Her reluctance to form any kind of bond with Douglas Richmond's other family was not mirrored by her children, thank goodness, and Fletcher, Mathias and Lisa had proven to be both professionally and personally open to the new family dynamic.

After their call ended, Keaton paced the covered deck feeling like a caged mountain cat. Kristin might see this as a good idea, but as far as he was concerned, this was shaping up to be a less-than-stellar one. Spending almost two weeks with a total stranger to build a team? It was irresponsible. He could still can the whole thing. In the face of what Kristin had said, if he pulled the plug now he'd end up doing more damage than ever. Staff were counting on this to work to rebuild the camaraderie they'd enjoyed before they'd felt their world tilt with the sudden death of Keaton's dad and the subsequent discovery of a mirror family and company on the East Coast. And not just staff, his family was counting on it, too. Which left him with only one option. To keep going.

Which meant dinner, alone with Tami tonight. He already knew their hosts wouldn't be joining them and a quick peek at the enclosed porch before he'd made his call to Kristin had shown a rather intimate setting of a table for two, together with fine silver and china, as well as flowers and candles. He forced his jaw to relax, the ache in his teeth evidence that he was clenching too tight, then, bit by bit, attempted to relax the other muscles of his body. Trouble was, there was one part of his body that seemed determined not to relax when Tami Wilson was around.

Well, it was something he'd just have to learn to deal with, he told himself. And quickly, because there were many days and nights ahead, and at the end of it, they had to have a strong working relationship because the most important thing right now was keeping Richmond Developments on an even keel.

Four

Later that evening, Keaton adjusted the collar on his suit and the knot on his tie as he checked himself one more time in the mirror. Quite a change from the outdoor gear they'd been wearing all day. Even his wind-ruffled hair was slicked back into submission and he'd trimmed his light beard to a controlled stubble. He'd wondered about the necessity to dress for dinners, but this entire exercise was about getting to understand people in all types of situations. A formal dinner party, even if it was for only two people, was a situation, after all.

He went downstairs and let himself out onto the porch. Tami had beaten him to the porch and as she turned to face him, he felt all the air leave his lungs in a giant whoosh. Dressed in a killer gown in an iridescent amethyst purple and with her hair drawn up into an updo that exposed the slender lines of her neck, she was nothing like the imp he'd caught spinning around on her office chair whom he'd met yesterday. Nor was she anything like the determined hiker who'd gamely trailed along behind him and Leon for the better part of the afternoon even when he'd sensed she was tiring. No, this vision of loveliness was another person entirely and every cell in his body responded with appreciation.

"Is something wrong?" she asked, looking hesitant. "Is this too much?"

A sackcloth and ashes would be too much.

"You look stunning."

A hint of color stained her cheeks. "I wasn't sure if it would be over-the-top, but the list you gave me did say formal dress for some meals and this is the most formal dress that I own."

"It's perfect."

Too perfect, he thought as he noted the way the fabric dipped between her breasts and skimmed the rest of her body like a second skin before elegantly flaring softly from her hips to drape at her feet. Feet that were in glittering silver sandals that added a good three inches to her height. Realizing he was staring, Keaton forced himself to walk toward the sideboard that was set up on the wall against the house. He reached for the bottle of wine that was chilling in the ice bucket. Next to it, warmed silver chafing dishes exuded delicious aromas.

"Wine?" he asked, lifting the bottle from the ice.

"Thank you, that would be nice."

Glad for something to do, he opened the wine and poured them each a small serving of the wheat-colored liquid. He passed her one of the glasses and held his up in a toast.

"To good working relationships," he said.

Inwardly, he shuddered. Man, he sounded so darn

pompous. But wasn't that what this was all about? Building stronger work-based relationships?

"To working relationships," Tami murmured, then took a sip of her wine. "Mmm, that's nice. I don't usually drink chardonnay but this one is very good."

He looked at her with a little surprise. She could have seen the label and known what variety of wine it was, but he'd met few people who could tell from one sip what type they were drinking, as she'd just done.

"You know a lot about wine?"

"It was one of the few things my parents tried to educate me on that actually stuck."

"You were clearly a good student."

She snorted inelegantly, the sound in total contrast to the polished appearance of the mesmerizing creature that stood in front of him.

"I was anything but a good student." Then, as if she realized that might reflect badly on her ability to do her job, she added, "But I am very good at plenty of other things. I found, at an early age, I need to be hands-on to learn best. Theory was never one of my strong points."

Keaton found himself laughing at her self-deprecating tone. "I'm sure you have plenty of strong points to balance out your lack of application to theory."

"I like to think so. So, how about you? A good student? No, let me guess." She leaned back and studied him carefully before giving a sharp nod. "I'd say straight A's, class valedictorian and a highly competitive athlete as well. Cross-country champion—am I right?"

He nodded in amazement. "You can tell that just by looking at me?"

"Oh, I can tell a lot by looking at you," she said. "Shall we sit down?"

They sat at the small round dining table and he

watched as Tami picked at her salad before she set down her fork and lifted her wineglass again.

"Well, won't you look at that. My glass is empty. Can I top you up, too?"

"Sure, but let's not go wild. Leon left me a message to say we're under our own steam for a lot of tomorrow. Some orienteering, I believe, and then an additional activity tacked on toward the end of the day. He'll meet us at that one."

She looked startled. "He's letting us out there on our own? I mean, I love the outdoors and stuff, but navigating the wild with only a map and compass sounds like it's out of my comfort zone."

"You can always wear your pink beanie in case we get lost," he teased.

"Yes, there is that," she answered with a quick smile that eased the worried line that had appeared between her brows. "Ah, well, we'll just take it all as it comes. Right?"

"Is that how you approach everything in life? Take it as it comes and see how it turns out?"

"Mostly," she acknowledged with a graceful dip of her head. "But I can make plans when absolutely necessary, too. And you? I'd wager a guess that you plan everything down to the minutest detail, and that you don't like surprises—for you, it's about the preparation and the execution, not the destination."

Again, she had him thoroughly pegged. What was she? Some kind of mind reader? Feeling a little uncomfortable at how accurate her summation of his character was, he turned his attention to the silver chafing dishes set out on the buffet against the wall. He rose from the table and went over to check what was on offer for their meal.

"You hungry?" he asked as he lifted the lid off the first one.

"I'm starving. That walk back here this afternoon burned off every last morsel we had for breakfast and lunch." She rose to join him. "Are those baby potatoes in butter and parsley sauce? My taste buds are going to think they've died and gone to heaven. What's in the next dish?"

He lifted the lid, exposing boneless chicken thighs in a rich, mushroom gravy. The unadulterated groan of anticipation that came from her next made even the hairs on the back of his neck stand to attention, along with another regrettably more visible piece of his anatomy. If she could elicit this kind of response from him just by lusting after some meat and potatoes, what would she be like when it came to more physical pleasures? Keaton slammed his thoughts closed on that question before he could get himself into serious trouble. Only a few months ago he'd been engaged to be married. His reaction to Tami had to be purely physical because he certainly didn't know her well enough to have formed any kind of connection the way he had with Honor. But then again, he'd never reacted to Honor this way, either. There'd never been that rush of arousal like he'd just experienced. And that had been exactly what had driven Honor into his brother's arms, he reminded himself.

Thankfully, Tami was busy inspecting the final chafing dish, which was divided into two sections—one with honey-and-garlic-glazed carrots, judging by the smell, and the other with steamed broccoli florets.

"This is all for us, right?" she said with a wicked gleam in her eyes.

"We are the only ones here right now."

"Then let's do it justice."

She took two plates from the warmer and began to dish up vegetables for the two of them. He took the hint and did the same with the meat and potatoes. Soon, their plates were equally laden. How on earth would she put all that away? he wondered. Actually, more to the point, how was he going to put it all away? He shouldn't have worried. It seemed he was as starving as she'd professed to be.

Keaton found himself mesmerized by the way she ate, with neatly proportioned mouthfuls on her fork being drawn to her mouth with elegant movements. From what he could tell, she applied herself to everything with care and attention to detail as well as a fair dose of enthusiasm.

When she looked up, she caught him staring. Her eyes flared slightly and a tinge of pink touched her cheeks.

"Do I have gravy on my chin?" she asked. She picked up her napkin and dabbed at her mouth.

"No, no. Sorry, I didn't realize I was staring," he said apologetically.

"Is the meal not to your liking?"

"It's great."

"Then why are you letting your food grow cold?" she said with a teasing note to her voice. "Didn't your father ever warn you not to let your meal get cold?"

"No," he said with a chuckle. "Did yours?"

Tami nodded. "And if I didn't eat every bite, he made the housekeeper serve it to me again at my next meal. One learns a certain level of compliance at an early age when faced with that."

While her words were uttered lightly, as if her childhood had been some kind of joke, she'd given him an unwitting insight into her background. Clearly discipline had been a feature in her childhood. Was that why she was so determinedly carefree now? Keaton found himself wanting to know more but schooled himself to keep his curiosity in check. Theirs was a working relationship. He didn't need to understand everything that made her who she was. He just needed her to do her job. That was all.

Once they were done, Tami pushed her plate to one side and leaned back in her chair.

"That was so good, I feel like I could climb a mountain tomorrow."

"Don't joke, we may well have to."

She leaned forward and gave him a reassuring pat on the hand.

"And if we do, we'll do it. Together, okay?"

The moment her fingertips touched him he felt a zing of electricity up his arm. *Note to self—avoid touch*, he thought. As fleeting as it was, the contact unsettled him. Maybe it was just all the stress of everything else that was going on. *Or maybe it was just Tami*, that little voice whispered.

But then his rational mind asserted itself. His reactions to Tami were an aberration. That's all it was. He was under a lot of stress with the company and with the need to rebuild trust within that company, not to mention within his own mind. He needed to cut himself some slack on his physical reaction to a woman who appealed to him. It was an instinctual response—that was all. Nothing he needed to worry about or act on. And he needed to know he could trust her. If completing this course of activities in the next few days would make that clear, it would be worth every last second of physical torture.

Wouldn't it?

Tami watched Keaton from across the table. His face, normally devoid of emotion, currently appeared to reflect a major internal battle. Today she'd discovered he was a firmly closed book when it came to sharing thoughts and feelings. Even tonight, he'd let her do most of the talking. Not that she had a problem with that—after all, jabbering on came all too naturally to her. But sometimes it was important to listen, too, and from that, to learn.

Clearly, her touch just now had unsettled him. She made a mental note to hold back on her instinctive need to physically connect with other people. She was a toucher—she hugged, she patted, she kissed. It was part of who she was, but that would have to change, especially around her new boss.

If she could hazard a guess, she'd say he'd been badly hurt somewhere along the line, and as much as she barely knew him, it made her heart ache to think that someone would close themselves off that much to the possibility of receiving warmth from another human being. She suspected that beneath the closed-door vibe Keaton gave off all the time that he was, deep down, a really nice guy. Tortured, very probably, but she suspected that he had a good heart even if he acted as if nothing really touched him deep down.

People like Keaton Richmond were a challenge and she like nothing better than to draw wounded souls to the lighter, more joyful side of life. Everyone deserved happiness, right? Well, maybe not the pond-scum-sucking douchebag who'd abused her trust and stolen the charity's money. But Keaton Richmond looked as though he carried the responsibility of the entire world on his shoulders. She wished she could have met him under other circumstances and not as a spy planted in his camp because, as things stood now, she would end up being yet another reason for him to remain cautiously shut down and that hurt. And beneath the hurt lingered a burning anger, too. If it wasn't for men like Mark Pennington and her father, people like her could simply *be*, and not be abused as tools for others' advancement. She was being forced to act contrary to everything she'd sworn to stand for and it hurt, not just on a moral level but on a deep emotional level, too. The sooner she got through this, the better.

From this point on she'd do her best to keep things businesslike. No more probing questions about him personally. Just take every opportunity to probe for information her father would find useful. Which reminded her, she needed to touch base with him tonight. He'd be expecting her call. Suddenly the meal she'd just eaten sat very heavily in her stomach.

Tami startled as she realized that Keaton was talking to her.

"I'm sorry, I was away with the fairies for a moment there," she apologized. "What did you say?"

"I was asking you if you'd like some dessert."

The last thing she wanted right now was more food, but if they didn't continue eating right now, they had very little reason to stay here at the table and talk—and she'd have less opportunity to probe him for information about Richmond Developments, too. Maybe dessert would sweeten up Keaton and encourage him to open up a little more. Maybe then she might learn something that could be useful to her father.

With her stomach groaning in protest, she answered, "I never say no to dessert."

Keaton rose from the table and cleared their plates.

"Oh, wait, let me do that!" she blurted, rising from her seat.

"It's no bother. My mom always taught us to do our share. I'll be back in a moment," he said, and disappeared through the double doors to the kitchen.

When he returned, he held two servings of tiramisu centered on plates artfully decorated with perfect balls of vanilla ice cream and shavings of chocolate. Despite her earlier reservations about consuming more food, her mouth watered at the sight of her favorite dessert.

"They really go to a lot of effort, don't they?" she commented.

She lifted her spoon and sliced into the dessert, then brought it to her mouth to taste it. She closed her eyes and moaned in delight.

"Oh, my. That's so good."

Tami looked across to Keaton, who sat frozen with an odd expression on his face.

"Are you okay?" she asked in concern. "Don't you like tiramisu?"

"I do, in fact," he said in a stilted way. "But perhaps not as much as you apparently do."

She gurgled a laugh. "Oh, the moan? I'm sorry if that unsettled you. I spent my entire childhood being forced to conform to other people's expectations. I resolved that from the moment I was responsible for myself I would embrace everything without reservation, at least once. You should try it. It's very liberating."

He stared at her for a moment before tasting his dessert.

"Mmm, very nice."

She laughed again. "Is that the best you can do?"

He tasted another spoonful and added a sliver of ice cream sprinkled with shaved chocolate, then nodded.

"It's good. What can I say?"

"Well, I guess it's a start," she conceded. "But to be honest, I wasn't just talking about trying the dessert. I meant embracing life and to heck with what others think."

He gave a derisive snort in response. "I don't have that privilege, Tami. I have a business to run and many egos to pander to."

"Does that make you happy?"

"What, pandering to other people's egos?"

She nodded.

He looked out the window for a moment, clearly formulating his answer. "I do what I have to, to get the results we need. Sometimes I even succeed. Success gives me pleasure."

She had no doubt he was playing down his level of achievement. It seemed to her that it was important to him to deliver on his promises, and that his striving for perfection drove him harder than was probably healthy. But she'd noticed he didn't answer her question.

"But does it make you happy?" she persisted.

"Of course it does." His answer was short, almost snappish, as if he didn't really like having to face the truth about whether something gave him joy or not. "Not everyone has the luxury of pursuing happiness with every breath."

Tami blinked in surprise. "You think it's a luxury?"

"Isn't it?"

"No, of course not. It's what we do anything for. It's intrinsic to our well-being."

"I think we'll have to agree to disagree on that."

"Okay," she ceded, then decided to take the bull by the horns. She'd felt her phone vibrate in her antique beaded evening bag, which she'd kept in her lap while they'd been at the table. No doubt her father was growing impatient. "How about we talk about work, then. That's why we're here, after all."

"What do you want to know?"

"Well, if we're going to work together, I think you need to open up a bit more, to be honest. I know Richmond Developments is primarily involved in construction and that you've recently begun to explore repurposing old buildings in ecofriendly ways to create microcommunities within a larger area. It sounds like a very interesting field to be involved in with the juxtaposition between old and new. Tell me more about what's coming next. What's the first project we're going to be working on together?"

Keaton played with his napkin before refolding it meticulously and placing it back on the table.

"Okay, since you're determined to discuss work, I'll do it, but I don't have to remind you about the confidentiality agreement you signed on starting with us, do I?"

Hot color flooded her cheeks. "Of course not," she spluttered, hoping he'd take it that she was insulted by his insinuation, rather than internally squirming with guilt.

She was no Mata Hari, that much was clear. To her relief, Keaton didn't seem to notice her reaction. He leaned back in his chair and began to talk, outlining a prospective contract the company was relying on to drive them through the next five years. By the sound of things, it would be huge, involving both housing and commercial interests, and for the first time it would amalgamate both arms of the businesses his father, Douglas Richmond, had established. In fact, from her research, it seemed that DR Construction and Richmond Developments had historically been rivals and she got the impression that the two families and companies merging effectively hinged on the success of winning the project.

Tami leaned forward, resting her elbows on the table, as he expanded on the plans the company had for the development.

"That sounds incredible," she enthused. "But what about low-income families? Do you have anything to offer them?"

He frowned a little. "Generally our complexes cater to upper-middle and high-income families. It's where the money is, to be blunt. And if we develop the commercial interests around the housing complexes the right way, it's where they'll continue to spend their money, too."

"I can see the logic in that, but don't you think you have a duty of care to those who aren't as fortunate?"

"Richmond Developments, through our charitable trust, is an active supporter of several charities. Giving back to the community is something my mom has always been passionate about and it's something we take very seriously."

He looked affronted and Tami hastened to smooth the waters again.

"Yes, I'd heard that. You know my last role was with a charity and we worked in conjunction with other charities, some of which I know Richmond supports generously. But throwing money at a problem is only one aspect of solving that issue. Everyone is entitled to some pride. A lifetime of handouts is galling to a lot of people. I know—I've worked with them. Sure, there will always be those that take the easy ride, but there are more that genuinely want to get ahead, but life keeps treating them like some kind of Whack-A-Mole, keeping them in the dirt all the time. If there were better employment opportunities, childcare, low-rent accommodation and low-cost housing with low-interest finance available to more people, there'd be a chance for them to genuinely take charge of their lives and get ahead. And it's an opportunity for these families to show their kids that life's not all about hard graft and still failing."

"It's a good point, but it's not what Richmond Developments is known for."

"You've already shown you can diversify your portfolio with the renovations you're doing so successfully now. Why not become known for even more things that help build communities and pride in those communities at the same time. There are plenty of people out there who'd jump at the opportunity to work on a home that they could eventually buy for their family. You'd not only be providing homes, but job security along with a huge dose of goodwill for the firm."

"Right now we're sticking to what we know while we work to rebuild confidence in our business."

He shut her down so effectively, she knew that to belabor the point any longer would be a waste of time. But she couldn't resist one more poke at the tiger.

"Maybe it's something Richmond Developments could consider for the future?"

"Perhaps."

She looked at the half-eaten tiramisu on her plate. She really couldn't force down another bite, as delicious as it had been. An unexpected yawn caught her unawares and she covered her mouth with her hand.

"I'm sorry," she apologized. "It seems as if I've hit my limit for today. If you don't mind, I think I'll head up to bed."

"No problem. We have an early start and a full day tomorrow. I'll be heading up shortly, too."

She rose from the table and clutched the beaded bag in her hand. It vibrated again, letting her know she hadn't yet responded to however many messages had been left on there.

"Okay then, I'll see you tomorrow morning at breakfast. Six?" she asked.

He inclined his head slightly in acknowledgement and turned his attention to the darkness outside. Tami turned and walked away. She stopped at the door and hesitated. Looked back. He was still in the same position, and in that brief unguarded moment he looked so very lonely. So isolated. It made her heart ache. Every nerve in her body screamed at her to stop and go back, but her brain very firmly instructed her that would not be a good idea. He wasn't ready to let down his defenses and he wouldn't welcome her probing behind them. That much was very clear.

Five

"No! I won't do it."

Tami was emphatic and on the verge of tears, something that made Keaton feel intensely uncomfortable. He didn't do tears. Not his mom's, not his sister's, not anyone's. Tears were a reflection of unbridled emotion and that made him squirm.

"Come on, it's perfectly safe," he coaxed.

She shook her head, crossed her arms and took several steps away from the platform erected at the edge of the sandstone outcrop.

"No."

"You came on the plane," Keaton reasoned. "We flew far higher than this."

"With metal tubing all around us, and engines propelling us forward and we had seat belts and a pilot. This," she said, flinging her arm out toward the zip line that extended from their location to some point in the distance they could barely see in the foliage on the other side of the canyon. "This is sheer madness."

Keaton looked at her. She was genuinely frightened. No, judging by the fresh perspiration that soaked the armpits of her T-shirt and her rapid breathing, *terrified* was probably a better word for it. To be honest, he was surprised. She'd been so intrepid on their hike to get to this point on the cliffside. Her interpretation of the instructions had occasionally been a little offbeat, but they'd made it to their destination in good time and, on the way, it had been an interesting insight into how her mind worked. He felt his lips twist into a rueful smile. Worked? Bounced around like a high-density rubber ball, more like.

His first impression of her in the office a couple of days ago had not been a great one. Seeing her spinning on her office chair with reckless abandon had felt like an affront to him, an indication that she wasn't prepared to take her role as his executive assistant seriously. But the past couple of days had shown him that she wasn't quite the flighty character she appeared to be on the surface, and her deep compassion for those less fortunate—something she'd volubly demonstrated last night—exhibited a clear understanding of their plight.

He hadn't been able to stop thinking about it after she'd gone up to her room, and he'd emailed Kristin and Logan to ask if they could look in to the logistics and viability of including some lower-cost housing into their plan. It was only after he'd done that that he'd been able to drift off to sleep somewhere around midnight.

But right now, his biggest challenge was getting Tami on that zip line, and her adamant refusal to even step into the harness was something he hadn't anticipated.

"There's lunch at the other side," he said in an attempt to cajole her.

"I figure if I climb back down and start walking it'll only take me another hour. I can wait that long."

Her stomach rumbled loudly.

"Or we can be there in a couple of minutes."

Her stomach rumbled again.

Keaton tried again. "C'mon, I've seen little kids do this with their parents. How bad can it be?"

"Have you seen how high we are? Do you understand anything about terminal velocity and the laws of physics?"

Keaton couldn't help it. He laughed. In fact, he laughed so hard, he felt tears spring to his eyes.

"Actually, yeah, I do. Physics was one of my better subjects at school."

"Of course it was," she muttered and turned away from him in disgust.

"Tami, please—trust me. You'll be completely safe. How about this—why don't we go in tandem? Would that make it easier for you?"

She turned back to face him, her lower lip caught between her teeth and a nervous expression on her face.

"We could do that?"

Keaton looked across to Leon, who had met them here at the zip line launch point and who was waiting patiently to harness them up. He must have seen this kind of reaction many times before, Keaton realized, because he made no move to rush them along. The fact they were the only ones there probably helped, too.

"Leon? Would we be able to go across in tandem?" Keaton asked.

"Sure," Leon answered. "Just give me a few minutes to change the rigging."

Tami's eyes were wide when Keaton looked at her.

"There, see? Problem solved."

"I think you're forgetting one thing," Tami insisted.

"What's that?"

"Me. I can't do it. I. Just. Can't."

"Of course you can. Look, you conquered your fear of flying. This is way more fun. And like I said before—lunch."

"Flying took me years, Keaton. Years!"

"Well, we don't have years. We have now. C'mon. Where's your adventurous spirit. I know I don't know you all that well yet, but you strike me as the kind of woman who usually gives anything a go, right? And didn't you tell me last night that you'll try anything once?" he paraphrased in reminder.

She begrudgingly nodded.

"Then let's do this."

She sighed heavily, then uncrossed her arms.

"Okay. But if I throw up all over you, it'll be your own fault."

Keaton fought the urge to fist-pump the air in triumph, but reminded himself quickly that they weren't there yet. And then there was the vomit thing. He really didn't want that to happen. He held out his hand.

"Look, I'm with you every step of the way. I trusted you to get us here during the orientation and you can trust me to keep you safe on the zip line. Okay? Let's go get harnessed up."

She tentatively accepted his hand, her smaller fingers curling around his and sending a trickle of warmth up his arm. Trust. It was such a simple concept, yet the weight of it was huge. He could feel the tremors that rocked her body as they walked toward Leon, but she didn't balk. He honestly hadn't considered what pushing her to do this might cost her in emotional terms until he held her hand right now. The sense of responsibility that put on his shoulders was huge.

"All ready?" Leon asked, looking carefully at them both.

"We are," Keaton said firmly. "In tandem, okay?"

"Yep, I've got the harnesses all set. Tami? Are you sure you're okay with this?" Leon asked her directly.

She nodded. "Let's just get it over with."

Leon moved quickly and efficiently to get them into their harnesses and gave them simple instructions on what to do and what to expect when they reached the other side. They positioned themselves at the end of the platform and Tami emitted a small moan that was as different from her delight in good food as chalk was from cheese. She was absolutely terrified—he could feel it in every quake of her body.

"Any last requests?" Leon said cheerfully as he smiled from his position at the other end of the platform.

Keaton laughed and looked down at Tami. Her arms were wrapped firmly around him and her eyes were scrunched shut. And were those tears squeezing out from under her lashes?

"We can do this. C'mon, Tami," he said firmly. "We'll go on three, okay? One, two, three!"

And then they were flying. Tami's eyes sprung open the second they launched, but she didn't so much as scream or say a word. In fact, Keaton wasn't even certain she was breathing. He was so busy watching her, he hardly noticed the journey himself, and it was over all too quickly. Nathan was waiting on the landing platform at the other side.

"So, guys, how was it?" he asked with a beaming smile on his broad face.

Keaton looked at Tami, who was as white as a ghost. Would she need medical attention? he wondered worriedly. But then a transformation took place and a massive grin pulled her lips wide. Excited energy poured off her in waves and she danced a little jig as she shrugged out of her harness. Tami looked back along the zip line they'd traveled on before turning toward him and Nathan.

She closed the short distance between them and grabbed his hand, then reached up and planted a kiss on his lips.

"That was a-mazing! Thank you so much for making me do it. Can we do it again?"

Keaton looked at her in absolute shock, his lips tingling from the unexpected contact. His face must have reflected his surprise because the joy in her eyes dimmed instantly and she took several steps back.

"Oh, heck, I'm sorry. I overstepped the mark, didn't I? That was really inappropriate."

"It's okay," he said stiffly. "I'm glad you enjoyed it in the end."

"And you? Did you enjoy it, too?"

"I think I was too concerned for your safety and state of mind to even be aware of what was happening, to be honest."

She gave him a smile. "Thank you. I really mean it. Without your support, I would never have attempted anything like that. I guess that's a tick in the box for teamwork, right?"

He barked a short laugh. "Yeah, that's a tick in the box, all right."

While they'd been talking, Nathan gathered up all their equipment and packed it away. When he was done, he joined them and asked them to follow him to a lookout, where they'd be enjoying lunch. The whole way there,

Keaton tried not to think about that kiss. It had been spontaneous. Something born of her sheer joy in conquering a fear. He compressed his lips more firmly together in an attempt to rid himself of the memory of the soft, sweet pressure of her mouth on his.

It had meant nothing, right?

Right. It couldn't mean anything. He wouldn't let it. These were extreme circumstances and they'd just taken part in an extreme event together. Emotions, especially hers, had been running high. There. He'd managed to compartmentalize it. Fold it neatly in a box and shove it into the darker recesses of his mind. Where it would stay. And he wouldn't think about how it had felt to have her arms tightly wound around his body as they'd swung along the zip line, or how her hands had clung to him as if he was the only thing between her and certain death. Nope, not at all.

Tami stood outside in the cool morning air and watched the sun begin to rise. Her fingers were wrapped around a hot, steaming mug of coffee and she listened to the sounds of the desert waking around her. The past few days had been a challenge. Not physically—at least, not too much—because with each day she felt stronger and fitter and more capable of the tasks that had been set before them. But mentally things had been tough. She'd let her exuberance cross personal boundaries after the zip line and that was not a good thing. Keaton had been very distant with her since then. Sure, they'd enjoyed their dinners together, and by mutual agreement had continued to discuss work over the table, but there'd been nothing personal. In its own way that was a relief. Tami wasn't about to race to reveal her own past, but she couldn't help being more curious about Keaton's. It was one thing to probe his plans for Richmond Developments, moving forward, and he was opening up more and more about that, but her dad had made it clear in last night's text message that he wanted all the information she could get on the family members themselves. It turned her stomach to think her father would use the information she passed him against the Richmonds but, as he had reminded her again last night, she was here to do a job—for him and no one else.

At least they wouldn't be forced to spend as much time alone together from today. Two new groups would join them today, one headed by Fletcher Richmond, from Virginia. Apparently, he was the eldest Richmond brother and from the secret family Keaton's dad had maintained on the East Coast. The other group was headed by Logan Parker-Richmond, the long-lost twin. She'd met him, and his fiancée, Honor Gould, very briefly on her first day with Richmond Developments. She'd been struck by just how identical the twins were. But where Keaton had a simmering intensity and a very driven attitude, Logan appeared to be a little less intimidating. Maybe it was because when he'd found his family, he'd also been lucky enough to find love with Honor at the same time. Or maybe it was just the way he'd been raised.

Tami remembered hearing a little about his situation and how he'd been abducted from the hospital nursery as a newborn and then spirited away to New Zealand, where he'd been brought up by his abductor and her family. From what she'd heard and seen of New Zealand in the media and from friends who'd visited the country, the lifestyle there was relaxed and less frenetic than many other parts of the world and the few Kiwis she'd met had an easygoing way about them. Even in that brief introduction she had to him, Logan certainly appeared to be more laidback than Keaton. It would be interesting to see how the two brothers interacted together.

What she had noticed even in her brief stint in the office on her first day, was a distance between Logan's fiancée and Keaton. She wondered if there was something to that or if she'd just imagined things. Obviously things were strained in the office with all the turmoil they'd been through, and with Tami being the newbie on the floor, it wasn't as if she'd been privy to the details of what had been going on prior to her starting there.

Ah, well, she told herself. The next few days with the new teams would give her plenty of time to get to know others better. And to hopefully find something to get her father off her back. She'd tried ignoring his text messages but that had only encouraged him to try phoning her, which had not been at all convenient. In the end, she'd told him she'd check in, by text, each night. Though she'd taken notes on her phone each day after dinner, she didn't really share the details, only sending her dad the briefest of messages before she went to bed. If he wanted more than that, he would just have to wait until she returned to Seattle and made her full report.

And while making that statement clearly in her head should have made her feel as though she was in control, she'd never felt less so in her life. Over her head still hung the obligation she had to somehow repay the money Mark had stolen. She'd given her word she would, and it was only on that promise that the administrators at Our People, Our Homes had agreed not to go to the police… yet. The whole thing made her stomach crunch in a tight knot. She sighed heavily.

"Everything okay?"

She spun around as Keaton came across to join her.

"Yes, sure."

"You just looked as if something was bothering you. Or maybe it's just that you're supposedly not your best until eight a.m.," he said with an injection of levity.

The man was too astute for his own good. Tami forced a smile to her face. There'd be distraction enough to keep her mind off things very soon.

"No, I'm fine. Kind of wondering how we're all going to work together when the new teams arrive, I guess."

"Well, in the initial couple of days we'll each be pairing up with someone from Virginia. DR Construction run on very similar lines to us and have experienced similar fallout from my father's deceit." His mouth twisted harshly on that last word. "Anyway, we're all committed to making this work, going forward. The sooner we get used to each other, the more easily we'll work together. After breakfast, let's go through those pairing lists before everyone else begins to arrive."

"Yes, good idea. I see Leon and Nathan's extra staff have begun to arrive, too."

Keaton looked back at the main cabin and surrounding buildings, which were starting to light up with new activity. "Yeah, it's going to feel quite different, but I'm glad we had this time to work out the kinks ahead of time."

"Not that there really were any," she commented.

"True. The guys run a well-oiled machine here." He went over to the coffee carafe on the hot plate and poured himself a mugful. "Shall we go in for breakfast?"

"In a minute. I just wanted to watch the sunrise. It's something I don't take time to do at home."

He stood beside her in the stillness as they faced east and watched the myriad shades of gold and orange as they unfurled into the sky. There was a calmness that came from being alone with Keaton that she'd never experienced with anyone else. Despite what he'd said when she'd started at Richmond—about speaking without thinking—she'd noticed he was happy to be silent, which was something she never did enough of. After a few more minutes of watching the sky, she tipped the last of her coffee into the bushes and turned to the cabin.

"I guess we'd better go in and start preparing for the day," she said stoically.

"You don't sound keen. Is there a problem I need to know about?"

"No—no problem. I've just enjoyed it being just us here. More than I thought I would, to be honest. It's going to feel strange being surrounded by a whole lot more people again, even if it is the purposes of the whole exercise."

"Yeah," he said with a slow smile. "I get what you mean. But we'll adjust. C'mon. Let's go eat."

After breakfast, Keaton got up and helped himself to more coffee from the perpetually brewing pot on the countertop.

"More for you, too?" he asked.

"Any more and I'll be jittering, so, no thank you. I guess I'd better go and get ready. I have the printed name lists in my pack. I'll bring them down in a few minutes."

She got down from her stool and headed for the door.

"Good, thanks. Oh, and Tami?"

She hesitated and faced him. "Yes?"

"I just wanted to say I've been really impressed by how you've tackled the challenges we've been set. I think we're going to work really well together when we get home."

"Was there ever any doubt?" she asked flippantly.

"Well, including spinning around on office furniture, you've managed to surprise me every day with your strength and resilience."

"A girl's gotta do what a girl's gotta do," she said, suddenly feeling awkward.

He cracked a grin that just about made her knees melt. "Yeah, something like that. Anyway, I just wanted to say that I'm really glad you're on my team."

"Me, too."

She would have said more but her throat had choked up on the swell of guilt that pummeled through her with the pace of a freight train. On his team? She hadn't been on his team from the minute she'd set foot inside Richmond Developments. He was beginning to trust her, which was exactly what she'd needed, but she was going to take that carefully wrought trust and exploit it. Use it against him in the cruelest way imaginable. Remembering that fact made her feel sick in her soul. She liked Keaton. Was attracted to him, too, to be totally honest. Knowing that she was merely a tool of her father's making—being used to bring Richmond Developments down another notch—made her the worst kind of person and totally undeserving of Keaton's praise. But she couldn't tell him any of that, could she?

Tami swiftly turned and went back upstairs to her room. Once there, she locked her door behind her and took out her phone. Yes, there was another message from her father.

Remember your promise to me.

She blew out a breath and composed a text reply.

Going off grid for a couple of days. Will text on return.

She pressed Send and waited for his reply. She didn't have to wait long.

You'd better have something good for me by then.

His disapproval was loud and clear. Tami checked the phone was fully charged and turned off all mobile data before tucking it away in her pack. Not for the first time she wished she'd been born into a different family. Even a family like the Richmonds, who'd had their fair share of trouble, but still remained tightly knit despite everything.

She couldn't remember a single time her father had told her he loved her, or was even proud of her. And for as long as Tami could recall, her mother had made it clear that she needed to conform if she wanted to be loved. She'd tried—oh, how she'd tried. But conformity had never been her style and never would be. She was the child, at junior ballet, who happily skipped in the opposite direction to everyone else—the one at gymnastics who preferred wildly executed somersaults on the mat to carefully performed balance-beam routines. As far as her family was concerned, she was a rough, square peg in a smoothly round and highly polished hole. But whether she liked it or not, they were the only route out of her current predicament.

A wave of rage against Mark Pennington and his deceit and greed poured through her. She breathed her way through it, allowing it to fill every nook and cranny of her mind before letting it, and all the tension that gripped her body with his memory, go. She'd permitted him to woo her—welcomed it, in fact. But, just like every other bad decision she'd made in her life when it came to men, she'd been blind to his faults and all too trusting. How ironic, she thought, as she went to the bathroom to finish getting ready for the day, that she should now be on the other side of the coin. She was the one who shouldn't be trusted right now. She was the danger. And she'd never been more miserable about anything in her life.

Keaton's words downstairs had rammed it all home to her. When it was discovered that she was a deliberately planted mole, and she had no doubt it would come out one day, he'd hate her. And that prospect made her hurt to her core. Not so much because she'd have breached her employment agreement and the confidentiality clauses she'd signed with the fingers of one hand crossed behind her back, but for the fact that she'd won Keaton's trust and would stomp it into the ground like sand before this was all over. But she had two and a half million reasons to see this through. More than that, she had the expectations and the needs of every beneficiary of Our People, Our Homes weighing on her shoulders at the same time.

Tami blew out one more breath and, after grabbing the team lists, headed back downstairs. Time to face the day.

Six

Keaton watched as everyone hoisted their packs and prepared for the hike toward the river. So far everything seemed to be going well, although he still found it hard to accept Fletcher Richmond was his half brother. Seemed there was barely a moment when there wasn't another sibling popping out of the woodwork, he thought with a large dose of cynicism.

Logan was on the other side of the group, Honor never far from his side. He'd caught a sideways glance from her earlier, not long after their arrival, and felt a twinge of something he really didn't care to examine too carefully. Was it envy? Granted, Honor had mistaken Logan, his identical twin, for him and had thought she was sleeping with Keaton that night before Christmas last year. It rapidly became obvious that the two of them were inexplicably drawn to one another and as far as he and Honor were concerned, on a personal level at the least, the writing had been on the wall.

He'd been the one to end their engagement. What else could a man do when he'd been cuckolded by his own twin? But it hadn't taken long for him to realize that he wasn't heartbroken by the event. Angry, yes. Cheated, definitely. But when push came to shove, his disappointment in Honor's betrayal had been just that. Disappointment. Not heartrending sorrow. Not vengeance-seeking fury. It was galling to admit to himself that the woman he'd planned to spend the rest of his life with really didn't matter as much to him on an emotional level as he'd once believed. It didn't make seeing her with Logan comfortable just yet, but in time that would come. It had to. He would not be responsible for creating any further divisions in a family already torn apart by his father's actions.

He shifted his gaze to where Tami was completing her duty of letting everyone know whom they'd be pairing with. At least he could rely on her. It was a rare feeling to know he could depend on someone, especially after these past three months.

"Okay, everyone," Keaton called out. "Follow Tami and our guide, Leon, down to the river and he'll allocate us to our two-man inflatable kayaks. Nathan and I will bring up the rear. If anyone has any problems or issues on the hike, we all stop. Is that clear?"

After a cavalcade of assents, Keaton nodded to Tami and Leon to lead off on the trail. During the hike, he heard more than a few grumbles, but it wasn't long before everyone settled into a steady stride and appeared to be enjoying the clean air and crisp, clear weather. Once they were by the river, Fletcher came up alongside him. He wouldn't have been his first choice of partner in this exercise. For all that he barely knew his half brother, he'd have preferred someone he didn't know at all, but then again maybe this would help cement a better relationship between them.

"This exercise was a good idea. Not exactly comfortable, but a good idea nonetheless," Fletcher said with a grin that reminded Keaton all too much of their father.

"Thanks, but it wasn't just mine. We all worked on it."

"But you undertook the logistics of putting it in place. It'll be interesting to see how everyone mixes together. Nice new assistant, by the way. She seems capable."

"Yeah, she is."

"You two seem to work well together."

"It would have made this difficult if we didn't. Did you have much pushback from any of your staff about the venture?"

Fletcher grimaced. "A few of the older staff in senior management—Dad's die-hards. Not so keen to step out of their comfort zones, especially with who they still see as the opposition, y'know?"

"Yeah, I know. It was the same for us," Keaton said with a grin at his half brother. "Not that we have many die-hards left, to be honest."

"Same. Dad's actions betrayed a lot more people than just his immediate family. But we'll get through it. And we'll be stronger for it, too," Fletcher said emphatically.

In that moment, Keaton felt an odd sense of kinship with his half brother. Something he hadn't anticipated, given the way their two families had been drawn together. Meeting for the first time over the grave of their dead father hadn't made the familial connection a sweet one, he reminded himself sardonically. Maybe things would be better all-around after this exercise.

At the river, everyone assembled in their pairs, and amid much laughter and a few squeals and much rocking of the kayaks, they all went on the river. Their packs were loaded into small trailers that were being towed by ATVs by some of Leon and Nathan's additional staff to the campsite farther downstream. Keaton found Tami in the group and watched her carefully as she paddled with her partner well ahead of him and Fletcher.

"She's doing okay," Fletcher said from behind him.

"Who?"

"Your assistant, Tami."

"What makes you think I'm keeping an eye on her?" Keaton said defensively.

"Man, you can barely look anywhere else."

Had he really been that focused on her? "I'm just keeping tabs on all my staff. Aren't you?"

"Yeah, sure."

But Keaton could hear the faint humor threaded through his half brother's response and decided to make a concerted effort not to keep watching out for Tami.

In all, they spent just over an hour on the river. Several areas were low-grade white water, and required more concentration than others, but overall the journey was quite serene. Keaton realized that this was the first time he'd actually begun to relax and unwind in many months. And he and Fletcher worked well together on the water, their strokes even and well-matched. Better still, Fletcher didn't seem to feel the need to fill the relative quiet with inane chatter. Maybe he and his half brother were more alike than he'd ever considered.

By the time they made it to the campsite, there were a few complaints about blisters and sore butts from sitting in one position so long, but overall the mood was buoyant. Everyone began erecting their sleeping quarters for the night, still in their matched pairs. Tami and her partner appeared to be struggling a little, not having pegged the base of the tent down first, but amid much laughter they eventually got there and were the last to complete their setup. He found it fascinating watching her. She appeared to be able to find common ground with everyone she spoke to and did so effortlessly. He envied her that talent.

"Still watching her, bro," Fletcher said quietly from behind him. "But I can see why. She's quite the package."

Keaton wheeled around. "If I'm watching her it's only out of concern, not anything else. I've been down the route of an office-based relationship before. I'm not heading on that road again. Intimacy does not belong in the workplace."

"Noted." Fletcher rubbed his chin with one hand, looking speculatively in Tami's direction. "Do you think long-distance would work?"

"No, I don't," Keaton said before he realized the other man had deliberately baited him. "And stay away from my assistant."

Fletcher laughed as he walked away and Keaton felt his lips twitch into a smile.

Over the next six days the groups completed high-ropes courses and a mountain bike trek, and spent a day rock climbing—the latter affording them incredible views across the heart-stoppingly beautiful vista of towering red-rock towers and cliffs amid more hiking and another stretch of kayaking on the river. Keaton felt renewed and invigorated by the time they started the hike back to the cabins. He and Fletcher had forged a much stronger friendship during their team challenges against other small groups, and for the first time in what felt like forever, Keaton was looking forward to what the future brought.

Tami, however, appeared to become more tense with

each day. He'd wondered if it was all the aerial work
they'd had to do, but she'd applied herself to everything
with far more enthusiasm than she had the zip-lining. But
something was clearly bothering her. Maybe he'd be able
to coax it out of her tonight, after the dinner and party
they were going to have in celebration of the end of the
exercise. And then again, he reminded himself, maybe
it was none of his business.

Leon and Nathan and their staff had coordinated a
spectacular meal and festivities, with their own special
set of awards for people they'd thought had come the
furthest in terms of development, both personal and as
groups of two or more. Keaton was pleased to see one
of the older members of Fletcher's team win an award.
The guy had really come out of his shell, transforming
from an impatient and reluctant piece of work to someone who'd shown compassion and leadership in a group
challenge the day they'd had to find a way to bridge a
fast-moving section of water. And then there was Logan
and Honor. Keaton had had little to do with them during
most of the challenges, but he was pleased to see them
given a commendation for the way they'd not only worked
together when pitted in direct opposition to one another,
but also how they'd encouraged their teams.

Overall, everyone appeared to have had a great time
and it was interesting to see both sides of Richmond Developments and DR Construction mingling freely. On the
surface, the exercise had achieved the sense of camaraderie Keaton knew they'd need moving forward. There
was only one fly in the ointment. Tami. She still had an
air of distraction around her and her smiles were few and
far between. Something was definitely bothering her.

Tonight she was dressed again in the stunning purple
gown she'd worn on their first night here, and Keaton

wasn't oblivious to the admiring glances that were sent her way by many of the people gathered there. He wanted to tell them all not to look at her that way, that she wasn't a piece of meat to be hungered after, but then drew himself up short. What was it to him, anyway? Maybe she'd be happy for the attention. Besides, it wasn't as if he had any kind of claim on her.

By the time the evening wound down, with everyone exhausted and heading off to their allocated cabins and beds before the early start back home in the morning, Keaton decided now was the time to check on Tami's mood. She'd been going from table to table, ensuring no one had left anything behind. She hadn't seen him approach her and he saw her flinch a little when she realized he was standing right there beside her.

"Everything okay?" she asked. "I didn't forget anything, did I?"

Keaton shook his head. "No, everything went perfectly. In fact, with you only having started with us the day before we embarked on this thing, you were exemplary with how you hit the ground running. I'm glad you were here, Tami."

A small smile pulled at her lips. He'd expected her reaction to his praise to be more enthusiastic, but perhaps she was just tired, too.

"Thank you," she said softly. "Was there anything else?"

He was about to tell her to go on up to her room, but that worry about her demeanor prodded him again.

"You don't seem to be yourself, tonight," he said. "Is something wrong?"

Tami looked at him in shock. She'd thought she'd hid it well, but then again, given the type of man she'd discovered Keaton to be, maybe it wasn't such a surprise that he could read her better than everyone else.

"I guess I'm just wondering how I'm going to do once we're away from here and back in the office," she hedged.

It was a poor excuse for an explanation, but she could hardly tell him that she was terrified by the fast-approaching deadline that awaited her. She forced herself to smile.

"I know," she continued, "it's silly, right?"

"Yeah, it's silly. You'll be fine. *We'll* be fine."

"I've enjoyed the time here. It's made me realize I can do so much more than I'd ever believed I could do."

Keaton nodded. "I know what you mean. It's been an eye-opener."

She heard him sigh a little and followed his line of sight. Outside the dining room, Logan and Honor walked arm in arm toward their cabin. Seeing the two of them so engrossed in one another made Tami's heart ache for Keaton. From a conversation with another Richmond Developments staffer, Tami had heard that Honor had been previously engaged to Keaton until his twin came out of the woodwork. She'd noticed that Keaton had had very little to do with the couple during their camping trip and that his interactions with Logan had been stilted. Did Keaton still harbor feelings for Honor? It couldn't be easy to see the woman you loved transfer her affections to your mirror image.

Tami took a step closer to Keaton and put a hand on his shoulder. She wanted to draw his attention away from something that was a very painful reminder. It made sense that Keaton would keep himself shielded from emotional harm, and Tami's nature made her want to protect him from that, too. Her nature? she asked herself. No, she had to be honest. She was becoming more and more attracted to her boss. An unfortunate truth, when she forced herself to look at it under a microscope, because wasn't that exactly what had gotten her into the financial trouble she was now in? But Keaton was nothing like Mark. He was honorable and true. He'd never abuse another's trust and then cut and run, leaving someone he'd professed to love to face the music all alone, not to mention setting them up to look complicit in the bargain.

Keaton reacted to her touch and turned to her with a face that could have been carved from granite.

"Keaton?"

She watched as his eyes focused on her and as the cold expression that had been there a moment ago dissolved into something else. His pupils flared and she heard the slight hitch in his breath before he reached for her and dipped his head to take her lips in a kiss that seared away any thought of anything or anyone else.

Heat blossomed through her body, coalescing deep inside her as his mouth teased hers open and his tongue swept her own. She felt her knees grow weak and she clung to him with both hands as he angled his head and deepened their kiss. He tasted of something sinfully, delightfully decadent. It took her a second to realize that it was purely him, and she wanted more. She kissed him back, tasting him as he tasted her, her fingers stroking the back of his neck. His strong hands pulled her even closer and she felt the hard evidence of his arousal against her lower belly. The embers at her core flamed higher as she shifted against him, first one way, then the other.

She wanted to feel him everywhere—she wanted to learn every inch of him in return. Just then, a clatter of pots from behind the kitchen door at the far end of the dining room echoed through the space around them. They sprang apart, creating a yawning distance between one another that left her feeling bereft until she realized she'd just been kissing her boss.

"I—" she began, but Keaton put a hand up to stop her.

"No. Don't apologize. Don't say a word. The fault here was entirely mine. I overstepped my position as your employer and I took advantage of you when you were obviously in need of support. That was wrong of me. It won't happen again."

"Keaton, I—"

She tried to speak but he simply acted as if she'd said nothing.

"Obviously, if my actions have left you uncomfortable about continuing to work with me, I won't hold it against you. I can find you another position within the company or make sure you receive the appropriate assistance until you find another role somewhere else."

What? What was he saying? Did he want her out of Richmond Developments? No! She couldn't let that happen. And who was this stranger standing in front of her now, anyway? He was nothing like the man who'd drawn her into his arms and kissed her just now as if their very existence depended on it. Tami's entire body hummed with suppressed energy, burned with molten desire. With sheer need for him. She took a step forward, but hesitated as his eyes once again grew cold and distant. His breathing might be a little faster than normal, but he'd managed to get himself back under control a whole lot quicker than someone who'd genuinely been invested in what they'd just shared.

Had she been a convenient outlet for his frustration over his doomed relationship with Honor? Was that all it had been? She dragged her scattered wits together and pushed away the hurt that now lodged deep in her chest.

"No need to apologize. It was nothing," she said with

all the dignity she could muster. "We've had a challenging time and we needed an outlet. Don't worry, I don't hold you responsible for something we both clearly wanted at the time. And, please, don't worry that it will cause a problem for us at work. I'm sure we can get along just fine without hashing this out any further."

"Tami, I—"

"Good night, Keaton," she said firmly.

She deliberately turned her back and paused by her table, then collected her evening bag and exited the room. She held herself together through the dining room, out the door and up the stairs, but the moment her door was closed and locked behind her, she lost it. Her entire body shook as tremors took her over and the tears that she'd so staunchly kept in check until she was alone began to track down her cheeks.

She'd done it again. She'd fallen for someone who didn't want to love her. Was she so desperate for affection that she'd just accept whatever emotional bone was thrown in her direction? No, she deserved better. And Keaton, too—he deserved to know that life wasn't always about rigid control. Sadly, she accepted she wouldn't be the one to show him that.

Seven

The flight home was quite different from the one to Sedona. Every seat on the private jet was taken and other Seattle-based staff had boarded a charter aircraft that was leaving just after the Richmond jet took off. The Virginia-based group were heading back on another charter flight shortly after. There was a hum of conversation around them that filled the awkward silence that persisted between Tami and Keaton.

Tami had barely slept a wink last night and, judging by the look of him, Keaton hadn't, either. Logan and Honor were on the flight with them, seated opposite, and she couldn't help but notice the number of times Keaton glanced at them both, then looked away equally quickly. More and more she wondered if Keaton was still in love with Honor. It had to be tough, working with the woman you were going to marry and watching a man who was a virtual stranger to you, and yet your mirror image at the same time, sweep her out right from under you.

Poor Keaton—he'd been through so much. She could understand why he wouldn't want to pursue another office-based relationship. She didn't, either, as her last liaison had turned into a complete disaster, too. A disaster that had planted her firmly in the Richmond family's path, where she was supposed to be the instrument of their next failure. The whole idea twisted her stomach in knots. Hadn't the Richmond family all been through enough already?

She didn't want to be the one responsible for making Keaton's life even more difficult than it had been in the past three months, but she was committed to doing so if she was going to get out of the hellhole Mark had left her in. And her dad would only keep his end of the bargain if she gave him a scoop on whatever Richmond Developments was planning. And until she'd gone through all her notes, she wasn't even sure she'd have anything he'd consider important enough. The very idea that she'd have to betray Keaton, the entire company and all its employees—many of whom she'd now struck up firm friendships with over the course of the trip—it all made her stomach pitch and heave. She swallowed hard.

"Tami? Are you feeling okay? You've gone very pale," Honor asked from where she sat across from Tami.

"I'll be fine."

Honor summoned a cabin-crew member and requested some sparkling water for Tami to sip on. She also reached into her bag and passed Tami a small packet of crystalized ginger.

"Chew on one of those. It'll help with your stomach."

Tami smiled gratefully at Honor's consideration, but she seriously doubted that a cube of ginger and some fresh water would fix what ailed her. Either way, she did as she was told and then sought refuge in sleep for the balance of the journey. It was only when a strong male hand clamped on her shoulder and gave her a little shake that she realized she'd slid across in her chair and was snuggled up against Keaton. She moved back instantly.

"I'm so sorry, I didn't know I'd—" she spluttered.

"It's okay. Don't fuss. We're preparing to land."

His voice was brusque, his words clipped. Of all the stupid things she could have done, sleeping on top of him was nearing the top of the list. Of course, kissing him after the zip line ranked right up there at the very top, alongside kissing him back like a wanton woman, as she had last night. And while Keaton's unbridled passion had taken her by surprise, she'd loved every second of it. Clearly, he did not feel the same way, and she had to accept that. Maybe she'd just been a convenient vessel to vent his frustrated yearning for Honor on. And like that wasn't a slap in the face?

But Tami felt like there was more to it. Yes, he'd been watching Logan and Honor as they walked by the windows last night, but she'd been getting a vibe off Keaton over the past several days that he was fighting with something internal. Was he attracted to her? Well, it had certainly felt that way last night. Was he prepared to do something about it? She pursed her lips slightly, remembering exactly what he'd done and how thoroughly. So while her first two questions had returned a positive response, that left her last question. Was he prepared to pursue this further? And to that she could only hear an empty, echoing *no* in the back of her mind.

She sighed and shifted her position. All of the above meant that to keep moving forward, she needed to remember to keep her physical distance and simply try to do her job to the best of her ability. There was no room to relive the embrace they'd shared. There was no way she could ever hope to explore that attraction, and that was for the best, wasn't it? Because, no matter how much she was attracted to Keaton Richmond, or how likely she would have been to fall into his arms and bed last night, if he'd offered them, she wasn't here to fall in love, or lust, or anything like that. She was here for one purpose only, and that was to feed information back to her father.

Her stomach pitched again as she made sure her seat was upright and her seat belt tight. At least she wasn't by the window on this trip. Keaton had offered to take the window seat when it had been clear they were going to have to sit together. He'd assiduously avoided brushing against her, right up until she'd fallen asleep all over him.

They'd no sooner landed when Keaton switched his phone from plane mode to regular service. The instant he'd done that, it began to ring. Tami tried to give him a little privacy while he answered, but it wasn't easy while they were still expected to be seated during taxi to the terminal.

"Hello? Yes, who?" He grimaced. "From which media outlet? Really?" He paused and listened for a few minutes. "That was the Everard pitch? Interesting." He paused again. "My comment on the Tanner project going to Everard Corporation? I have no comment."

He severed the call abruptly and looked across at his twin.

"What the hell was that all about?" Logan growled, looking fierce.

"It seems that Everard Corporation have preempted our offer for the Tanner project—and won—with a near identical pitch to our own."

Tami's stomach rolled.

"What do you mean they've gone with Everard Corporation? The tender wasn't due to close until tomorrow. And an identical pitch? What the hell?"

Logan sat up sharply and stared at his brother. His face was wreathed in lines of concern. Honor, too, looked worried.

"That bastard. Everard has to have a spy in our camp," Honor said in a shaking voice. "How else could he have done this?"

Keaton swore a blue streak. "This is going to play out very badly for us in the media. They're going to assume, like we do, that we have a mole, and that's going to damage all the work we've been doing to restore our company's name and reliability after Dad's double life was exposed. The fallout is going to hurt us far more than just financially."

Tami scrambled for the packet of ginger Honor had given her and popped another piece in her mouth to try and combat the rising bile that boiled up from inside her stomach. How had her father anticipated the Richmond bid so accurately? Keaton had only told her about it at dinner their first night in Sedona. She knew everything about the bid was being kept under wraps—in fact, it was being so closely guarded she hadn't heard anyone even discuss it during the team outdoor experience at all, and had only caught murmurs here and there between Fletcher Richmond and the three people sitting with her here.

And, more to the point, she hadn't told her father about anything she and Keaton had discussed during their intimate dinners together. Another sobering question flared in her mind. If her father had somehow acquired the information he needed without her help, where did that leave her with respect to the two and a half million he was supposed to be releasing from her trust fund?

Keaton ended the call, only to have his phone ring again immediately. He looked at his twin and grimaced.

"It's Mathias. Do you think he's heard the news? Fletcher will still be airborne for the next hour or so."

Tami had learned that Fletcher's younger brother, Mathias, together with their sister, Lisa, ran the east coast construction company Douglas Richmond had set up. It was almost an exact mirror in every way to the company that Logan, Keaton and Kristin operated in Seattle.

"Yeah, Kristin will have told him, I'm sure. Better deal with his call now. It's only going to get worse the longer you leave it," Logan said somberly.

"Yeah," Keaton agreed.

He answered the call. The words exchanged between the men were pithy and few.

"I promise you, I'll be conducting a full investigation starting the minute I'm back in the office. I suggest you do the same at your end."

Tami could hear the protest on the other end of the line.

"I don't believe any of my staff could be culpable, either, but someone had to have leaked the information to Everard. He's a sneaky bastard, but we will root out the traitor and there will be legal ramifications. Don't worry, we will make them pay. Corporate espionage will not be tolerated."

The plane had come to a full stop and the doors were being opened by the time he ended the call.

"We need to get straight to the office," he said to his brother and Honor. "When Fletcher hears the news, we need to be prepared. Mathias was mighty pissed off, but Fletcher is going to be apoplectic."

Tami was shaking. She couldn't be responsible for

this somehow, could she? She had to talk to her father. She had to find out how he'd gotten the information he needed to preempt the Richmond offer with an identical one of his own.

It was late when she left the office. Keaton and his brother and sister were still locked in discussions in the boardroom, along with the head of IT, who had instigated a forensic investigation into the computer activity of all staff to see where any of the information may have been accessed and disseminated.

The anticipated blowup from Fletcher Richmond had been exactly what they'd expected. In the video call in the Richmond Developments boardroom, his fury had been incendiary and the relationship between the half siblings had become tenuous, with accusations about carelessness from one camp or the other being flung back and forth. Kristin had become the voice of reason, halting the flow of angry words between the four half brothers and their two half sisters, and reminding everyone they were all in this boat together. The only trouble was, with this development, the boat was rapidly sinking.

Tami had done her best to support them, but there'd been little she could do, aside from coordinate fresh water, hot beverages and food at regular intervals and take screeds of notes on her tablet. They were going to be at this for hours, and eventually Keaton had told her to head home. There was nothing more he needed her for.

While she knew the words weren't meant to be another blow to her already fragile state of mind, she couldn't help but feel them as such. She got into her car and sat there, exhaustion pulling at every part of her. As much as she wasn't looking forward to it, she still needed to meet with her father. She headed straight for her parents' home, relieved that even with the Friday night traffic, she could be there in half an hour.

Her parents' mansion, in the suburb of Magnolia, was lit up like a Christmas tree. There was no conserving power or anything like that in Warren Everard's world. No, he wanted everyone to see, carbon footprint or no, just how powerful and successful he was at all times. Tami spoke in the speaker box at the entrance and waited as the heavy wrought-iron gates, embellished with her father's initials in gold leaf, swung open. She drove through, and in the rearview mirror, watched as the gates swung closed again.

The burning sensation in her stomach, which had started on landing at SeaTac midday, ratcheted up a few notches, and after she pulled up by the ornate portico at the front door, she reached in her bag for the crystalized ginger. The packet was empty. It had been that kind of day. She was going to have to do this without the benefit of anything to help settle her stomach.

Tami forced herself from the car and went to the front door. Her father's butler, an anachronism in this modern age, waited in the open doorway for her.

"Good evening, Sanders. I need to talk with my father rather urgently."

"He's expecting you. You'll find him in the den."

Tami's stomach burned that little bit more fiercely. Her father was waiting for her? How did he even know she was back? Had his spies at Richmond Developments told him? This was worse than she'd anticipated. She crossed the black-and-white marble-floored entrance, her footsteps echoing in the two-story foyer, as she made her way to her father's den.

She hesitated a moment at the door, remembering the

many times she'd been summoned to this room to be castigated over her latest failure. But, she reminded herself, she wasn't that cowed child anymore. She was an adult who'd been independent of her parents since she was eighteen—well, independent until she'd needed two and a half million dollars, she reminded herself. And that gave her two and a half million reasons to face up to her father and demand to know what he'd done. She knocked sharply and pushed the door open before her father could respond.

He was seated in a wingback chair in front of a burning fire. Not for the first time, Tami saw every aspect of him and his life as one cliché after another. Aside from her coloring, she'd inherited very little of the man sitting there with a smug expression…and she was painfully glad of it. She never wanted to be anything like him.

"I see you got what you wanted with the Tanner development," she said bluntly.

"I did. I imagine they're a little upset at Richmond Developments and DR Construction right now."

He laughed. It was a nasty sound that grated on Tami's ears. How could he take so much joy in this? His actions had been underhanded and would cost jobs and livelihoods for so many people who were already in shaky circumstances.

"How did you circumvent the tender process?" she demanded.

He waved a meaty hand in the air. "A minor detail. The thing is, I won."

"Yes, you did. That means you can release my trust fund to me now."

"Oh, how so?"

"It was what we agreed. When you got the information you wanted—which you obviously did somehow, because from what I understand your pitch was identical in virtually every way to what the Richmond pitch was going to be—I'd get access to my fund."

"Ah, but you're forgetting something."

"What?"

"*You* didn't specifically give me the information I asked for. In fact, if I remember correctly, you ignored most of my messages and calls requesting updates, and only replied in a series of painfully short and noninformative texts, did you not?"

She swallowed and nodded. It was no use telling him now that she'd planned to write up all the notes she'd made on her phone.

"Then you didn't deliver on your side of the deal, did you?" He shook his head with a sardonic smile pulling at his lips. "Tami, Tami, Tami. You'll never learn, will you? To survive in this world you have got to be more cutthroat. You won't win anything by being a doormat."

"I'm not a doormat," she argued.

No matter how hard she tried to ignore her father's baiting techniques, and he had many of them, she always rose to them, giving him the satisfaction of winning every darn time.

"You're both a doormat and a disappointment. And you can forget access to your fund. Your grandmother did the right thing appointing me as your trustee. Obviously, you lack the clarity of foresight and wisdom required to manage such a sum of money." He made a derogatory sound. "Giving it all to a charity, what the hell were you thinking? No, wait, don't bother telling me because we both know you never think things through and it's because of your failings that you got yourself in this situation."

"I was used," she protested.

Used by someone as scurrilous as your father, a little voice jeered in the back of her mind.

"Yes, used because you're too darn trusting for your own good. You can leave now. And don't bother showing your face here again until you develop some backbone."

"Just because I don't choose to stomp all over people doesn't mean I don't have a backbone."

"Sure, you keep telling yourself that. And while you're at it, ask yourself why, when you encountered a problem, the first person you came running to was me."

He got up from his chair and walked past her and out of the den, leaving her standing there, seething in silence. She refused to let the cruelty of his words sink any deeper. She had enough worries on her plate now. Our People, Our Homes had a fiduciary duty to report the theft of the money from their coffers to their donors and to the necessary authorities. Even though she'd been the innocent dupe, she *had* made her computer password available to Mark, and by doing so had given him access to the file where she'd kept the charity's banking password and access code, as well. Both those actions had been in breach of her user agreement, which had been designed precisely to protect that kind of data.

Tami turned and made her way out of the house, barely even acknowledging Sanders's polite "good evening" as he let her out the front door. What on earth was she going to do? For now, she still had a job to do at Richmond Developments, but in all honesty she couldn't keep her initial intentions secret from Keaton anymore. If he knew the lengths to which her father was prepared to go to win whatever it was that he'd set his sights on, even going so far as to use his daughter, then maybe he could find out exactly how her dad had finagled their tender details so precisely. She had to tell him about the person her father had positioned in HR for a start. And who knew how many other spies he'd positioned within the company?

And then there was Our People, Our Homes. She had to tell them she couldn't make good on her promise. Suddenly, the meeting she'd just had with her father seemed like child's play compared to what she had yet to face.

Keaton was at his office long before the sun began to rise as he had been every day for the past week. He cradled his mug of coffee in both hands and stared out the window at the awakening city. He loved this place—the city, the state, the country. But most of all he loved Richmond Developments and he hated to see it crumbling on his watch. It didn't matter that the responsibility was shared between himself and his siblings. It didn't matter that it was circumstances beyond their control that had started the downward slide—it mattered that it was happening while he was at the helm and he was going to do whatever it took to make things right again.

And it mattered that they were still no closer to discovering exactly who had been behind the leaked information that had rocked them to their very foundation. As anticipated, the media had been having a field day with speculation about what had gone so wrong here at Richmond Developments.

He heard a sound in the outer office. It would be Tami. He wasn't surprised she'd come in early. She'd been in early every day this last week, even over the weekend. At least that shell-shocked look she'd worn the day they came home from Sedona had finally left her, and each day she had done her best to offer as much support as she could. He thought about the way he'd spoken with her lately. He'd been abrupt on most occasions, which had been unfair. It wasn't her fault that things had gone pear-shaped. He turned away from the window, set his mug on his desk and went through to the outer office.

She was settled at her desk, looking immaculately groomed in the dark navy suit she'd worn on her first day here. Corporate Tami was quite a change from the jeans and casual tops he'd grown accustomed to seeing her in while they were in Sedona, but no less attractive from his point of view, either. He snapped his mind back to attention. He was not going down that route. They'd drawn their line in the sand. Regrettably, his body hadn't gotten the memo.

Even from the back, she stirred him. She'd swept her hair up into a tight roll at the back of her head, which exposed the slender, elegant line of her neck—a neck made for nuzzling, his libido teased him. A neck made to be ignored, his more pragmatic brain responded promptly. It would be best to face her, he decided, so he walked quickly around her desk. She looked up immediately.

Keaton felt as if he'd been punched in the gut. She looked terrible. Her skin was pale and there were violet shadows beneath her hazel eyes that spoke of yet another rough night. She was taking this hard. Guilt tore at his chest. Or had he done this to her?

"What can I do for you, Keaton?" she asked.

Even her voice sounded weary, and although she smiled there was nothing of the vibrant, cheerful character she'd demonstrated as they'd tackled challenge after challenge during their outdoor pursuits.

"Are you well, Tami?"

"You mean, I look like something the dog dragged in, right?"

There was a sardonic twist to her mouth that was out of keeping with the woman he'd come to know. The woman he'd kissed. The woman he'd wanted with every cell in his body, but denied himself.

"I won't lie—you've looked better."

This time her lips curved into a more genuine smile and a snort of laughter escaped her.

"Well, thank you, I think. I had a bad night is all," she said, glossing over her shattered appearance. "Now, I imagine we have plenty of work to do today. Where do you want me to start?"

He was both relieved and disappointed that she was all business. The practical side of him started dictating a list of orders. Contracts that they needed to follow up on, tenders they were awaiting responses on, suppliers they needed to woo to ensure they received the best prices. By the time she got through the list he would hopefully have a stronger handle on where Richmond Developments would be heading in the next few weeks.

"Oh, and Logan and Kristin will be in shortly. Can you get someone to rustle up some coffee and breakfast bagels for us?"

"Of course. Is that all for now?"

He blinked. Wow, she was all business all right. "Yes, thank you. That will be all for now."

Feeling as if he'd missed a golden opportunity, but unsure exactly as to what that opportunity was, he returned to his office and closed the door. She was different. Untouchable. No, that wasn't the right word, she was eminently touchable, but there was a fragility about her right now that made him feel as though if he did touch her, she might shatter into a million tiny shards.

Surely, she wasn't this invested in Richmond Developments already that losing the Tanner project had impacted her to this degree? Or maybe she really was. She'd certainly been interested about expressing her ideas when they'd discussed it during their first dinner in Sedona.

But all that bright enthusiasm had very thoroughly been quelled. Was that his fault? Had he been too harsh when he'd stepped away after that kiss? Of course he had. He'd been angry at himself for not resisting the temptation she offered—angry, even, at her for simply being there and tempting him in the first place. All of it had been unfair and unreasonable. They'd kissed. No one died. He could have handled it way better. He should be pleased about her obvious professionalism, given the fact that he'd been the one to reach for her and kiss her like a man starved of a lifetime of affection.

He picked up his coffee mug again and took a sip, then twisted his mouth in disgust at the now cold brew.

He'd been the one to pull back. He'd been the one to say he'd overstepped and that it wouldn't happen again. She'd agreed. That was that. Done, dusted, over before anything could begin.

So why did he feel like he'd lost something special now? He had exactly what he wanted. Didn't he?

Eight

Things were beginning to show promise, aside from the fact that they'd lost several more key staff members in the aftermath of losing the Tanner project. There was always more work to pitch for, even in a depressed market, and while things weren't as buoyant as they would have been if they'd taken on the Tanner job, they weren't exactly heading to the financial wall, either.

The main fly in Keaton's ointment these days was the complete lack of so much as a thread of information to lead him to whoever had fed their tender details to Everard Corporation. And that lack of information made Keaton edgy. Who could be trusted? It didn't create the best working atmosphere, no matter how many teams they'd sent to Sedona. That said, at least they'd managed to patch up the wrenching hole that had opened up between them and their half siblings. And that had put them in an even stronger position when it came to pitching for projects nationwide. Their joint reputations counted for a lot and Keaton was eternally grateful that, for all that their father's deception had destroyed, his children had had the grace and strength to pull everything together cohesively.

He and Tami were working late, again. Each day he'd given her the opportunity to leave on time, but she'd been dogged in her determination to match him hour for hour at the office. The shadows under her eyes remained, but were slightly less noticeable these past couple of days, but something still clearly troubled her. In those moments when she wasn't one-hundred-percent focused on her work, it was as if her mind would drift somewhere else and she'd get a deeply worried expression on her face. If he asked her if anything was amiss, she'd merely cover it up, smile and say everything was okay.

But everything was very definitely not okay. With every day they worked together, he only wanted her more and that knowledge was like a thorn in his side. Other people made office romances work, but Keaton didn't want to lay himself bare like that again. Trouble was, no one but Tami interested him in that way. Not a single other woman drew him to her, as she did. And when he thought about it, he hadn't even felt this way about Honor. Their relationship had been convenient on every level, but not passionate. Not spontaneous. It had been structured and balanced and about as boring as a spreadsheet, now that he came to think about it.

Oh, sure, they'd have made things work, if they'd stayed together, but seeing her glow under Logan's care and attention showed Keaton exactly how little they'd offered each other. He was glad for Honor now, even though it had meant her cheating on him for them to discover they weren't right for each other. Occasionally, watching Honor and Logan together, it still stung just a little, but that was more a matter of pride than anything else.

With Tami, however, he'd struck a wall he had no idea of how to get through. A wall of his own making, he reminded himself as he looked up to see her enter his office. Keaton cast a look at the ornate hanging clock and was shocked to see it was already 9:00 p.m.

"Here's that data analysis you and Fletcher asked for. Would you like to go over it first, before I send it through to him?"

"No, send it to me and I'll go through it with him tomorrow. It's late, we both need to call it quits for the day."

"Are you sure? I still have those figures to run on the—"

"Tami," he interrupted. "Stop. Sit." He waited until she sat down in the chair opposite his desk. "Now, take a breath."

"I take breaths all the time."

"But you, and I, have been working double time in this past week. I think we both need to think about cutting back to normal hours."

"Seriously, Keaton, that report will only take me a minute to—"

"Tomorrow," he interrupted again. "Now, how about we go and grab something to eat together somewhere. I know you haven't had dinner yet and I'm starved. How about it?"

For a moment he thought she'd refuse, but then she nodded.

"You want to go now?"

"It's as good a time as any," he said with a shrug.

"I'll just go freshen up and I'll be back in a couple of minutes."

She was true to her word, and on her return he escorted her down in the elevator and out the front of the building.

"Good night, Stan," he called to the late-shift security guard at the main counter.

"Good night, sir, Ms. Wilson."

Tami smiled and gave the man a slight wave before turning to Keaton. "Are we going somewhere in walking distance?"

"No," he answered and gestured to the car waiting outside. "I made a booking and called a ride. We deserve to go somewhere special after how hard we've both been working."

"Okay," she answered warily. "But I'm not dressed for anywhere too high-end."

"It's not, don't worry. It'll be good food in a great setting."

When they pulled up outside the lakeside restaurant, he saw Tami's lips curl up in a smile of approval.

"Oh, I love this place!"

"Yeah, it's one of my favorites, too. I love Asian fusion. The best of everything."

They went into the restaurant and were quickly shown to their table. It was cramped quarters, but the glittering view out over the lake was second to none, and if the aromas from the kitchen were anything to go by, they were in for a treat. They didn't waste a lot of time on the menu—both of them were hungry and ready to order the moment their server returned. Both of them eschewed wine, opting instead for mineral water.

"You've been working really hard, Tami," he said as he leaned back in his chair as they waited for their dishes to arrive. "I really appreciate how quickly you've settled into your role."

"I try my hardest to fit in."

There was a hint of sorrow in her eyes and he hastened to assure her that she was doing great.

"Seriously, it was a lucky day for us when you started as my assistant."

She didn't hold his gaze, but fiddled with her napkin as if it was the most important thing on the planet right now.

"I can't help noticing that you're not yourself, though. Is everything okay?" he pressed.

As he expected, her lips lifted in an approximation of a smile. But he could tell that while she assured him everything was fine, something was still bugging her. Was it the kiss they'd shared that last night in Sedona? Or something else?

"Tami, you'd tell me if there was something bothering you, right? I mean, I know I can come across as a bit single-minded about things, but you can always approach me if you need to."

"I know. And everything's fine, just fine."

If she said it often enough, maybe it would be true, right? The investigation had begun into the missing funds from Our People, Our Homes, and she'd been given an appointment time to go into the police station and answer questions. It wouldn't be long before the news got out that she was involved, and once that happened, she'd no doubt be fired from Richmond Developments. It was strange, she thought. She'd been so nervous about her role working for Keaton, and thought she'd miss her work with the charity much more, but she found the cut and thrust of Keaton's work fascinating from a peripheral perspective. And her support role was something she enjoyed and knew she excelled at.

Watching Keaton work was something in itself. He

attacked things with purpose and with a clear result always in sight, and he wasn't afraid to change direction if something wasn't working. The support of Logan and Kristin in their roles as joint CEOs made the three of them even stronger and their style was so different to anything she'd witnessed before. Success-driven, but always with an eye to the social benefits their work would produce. She could see Richmond Developments and DR Construction rising from their current funk and reassuming their position among the strongest players in the construction and development markets. It felt great to be a part of that and she wanted to remain there. And the fact it was a metaphoric middle finger to her father gave her no small amount of satisfaction.

There was also the fact that working there paid very well and with limited savings and no other income to speak of, she needed the funds. She knew it wouldn't last forever. Not when the truth came out, and as much as she wasn't looking forward to it, she knew she had to come clean. Even if she hadn't been the person who'd actually given her father the information, she had intended to. Living each day on tenterhooks was taking its toll on her, but she also knew that if she'd just up and left immediately when they'd returned from Sedona it would have made her look even guiltier. No, she would tell him the truth, in her own time.

Her attention returned to the man sitting opposite her. She admired Keaton on so many levels and felt herself drawn to him more every day. It was all she could do to keep her head down and focused on her work each day, when all she wanted to do was relive that kiss they'd shared, right before he'd rejected her. No, that wasn't fair. Even then, he'd done the noble thing and taken all the blame for their kiss. A kiss that lived in her subconscious and plagued her fractured sleep with the memory of his touch, his taste, his warmth. At least by doing her job to the best of her ability, she was making herself indispensable, proving she was capable of being an adult about their embrace and that she could carry on as if it hadn't totally rocked her world. And that way, his suggestion that she either leave or take on another role within the company, away from him, would not come to pass.

And when he found out that her father had been responsible for her appointment? She swallowed against the fear that threatened to close her throat. She hoped that when she eventually told him that he'd listen to the truth that she never wanted to be a spy and that she wasn't the cause of the loss of the Tanner project. But when her involvement with Our People, Our Homes became public knowledge…? She swallowed again. Living with the fear of him discovering her secrets was just about giving her a stomach ulcer. She could only hope that her diligence would speak volumes as to her dedication to both her job and to him.

Thankfully, their dishes began to arrive at the table and she was saved from further discussion as they started on their meal. Conversation fell away as they began to sample the dishes. Keaton ate the same way he kissed, with great attention to detail and savoring the minutest aspects. A swell of desire flowed through her, making her shift a little in her seat. She had to stop thinking about him like that, she growled at herself as she bit into a succulent shrimp and let the flavors dance along her taste buds. He'd made it clear there could be nothing between them, and given what had happened with Honor Gould, she wasn't surprised.

She, too, should be more wary of office romances, especially after the way Mark Pennington had used her before disappearing and smearing her name in the process. And yet, she could barely take her eyes off Keaton as they shared the platters of food. Wariness be damned, she thought. Every now and then, life threw chances your way and if you were too scared to reach out and grab them, you deserved to get nothing in the end. With that in mind, she decided to force Keaton to talk—really talk—about their time in Sedona, especially that kiss. She felt as if it was an elephant in the room every day at work and she wanted to deal with it head-on and get it out of the way for good.

"This is good, huh?" she asked, opening the conversation again.

"So good. I didn't realize how hungry I was. I imagine you're just the same."

"Are you referring to my obscenely huge appetite back in Sedona," she said with a smile.

There, she'd done it. She'd injected Sedona into the conversation. Now, to keep it on track.

"Hey, nothing obscene about a healthy appetite," he said, helping himself to more of the shrimp dish.

"I really enjoyed the trip there and meeting some of the DR Construction team. Making those connections has really helped with sharing information these past couple of weeks. What would you say your favorite part of the whole experience was?"

She stared at him expectantly.

"I'd say the kayaking on the river. I know those rapids were child's play in the grand scheme of things, but it was fun. I bet your favorite part was the zip lining, am I right?" He grinned at her and waited for her reply.

"No, actually. While that really ranked up there, there's another moment that meant a lot to me."

"Oh, what was that?"

His fork halted halfway to his mouth and he watched her, waiting for her to explain.

"It was when you kissed me."

She felt the air between them thicken and Keaton slowly lowered his fork to his plate.

"Tami, I—"

She raised a finger to silence him. "Please, hear me out. I know you felt as if you went too far—I can understand that. I also know why you probably don't want to enter into a new office romance."

"Ah, so the office grapevine has been working as efficiently as ever, I see," he said with no small amount of irritation.

"That aside, I feel like the whole situation has put some kind of invisible wall between us. And it's one that needs to come down if we're to be able to continue to work efficiently together. I don't want you to feel as if you have to walk on eggshells around me. I won't deny that your kiss totally blew me away. It did. And if I had the chance to repeat it, I'd grab it with both hands." She smiled. "Kind of like the way I'd like to grab you. I can and do accept that you feel it's inappropriate for us to have a relationship, but can we at least have some semblance of friendship? You know, figure out a way to accept we're attracted to one another and work around it, anyway?"

Keaton leaned back in his chair and took his time responding. She was beginning to worry she'd gone too far with her honesty, but then he leaned forward again and, to her surprise, he took her hand from where it rested on the table and held it in his.

"I don't want to be friends with you, Tami. I want more than that, way more, but by your own admission you can see why that wouldn't work for us."

She curled her fingers around his and squeezed gently. "I know, but we can do much better than we've been doing, can't we?"

"Of course we can," he agreed and let go of her hand.

It was a start, she conceded. Maybe not quite the start she'd hoped for, but he'd admitted he wanted more than friendship. It was his own stubborn personal rules that were holding him back. Okay, she could respect that. It wouldn't be easy, but at least they had it out in the open.

When their meal was done, Keaton booked a ride share to take them home. As they waited in the cold outside the restaurant, a chilling wind blew off the lake and Tami shivered a little. She was startled when Keaton put his arm around her and drew her closer to his body.

"We don't both need to freeze," he said by way of explanation. "Why don't you snuggle into me a bit more. We've still got a few minutes before the car will be here."

"Or we could wait inside the restaurant lobby?" she suggested perversely.

She turned into him so they were chest-to-chest, and could already feel the heat of his body permeating her suit and seeping in to her skin to warm her up. He looked back and the movement caused cold air to filter in between them.

"Not with that massive line of people waiting for tables," he said. "Looks like you'll have to make do with me instead, or freeze. Friends, remember? We have to look out for each other."

"I…" She hesitated a moment, afraid that all her longing would coalesce into whatever she said next. "I'll make do with you."

He laughed, and the movement of his chest made her nipples rub against the cups of her bra and stand to attention. Mortification filled her. What if he noticed? Her blouse and suit were designed for a climate-controlled office, not a cold March Seattle night. At least she could always put it down to the cold, right? Even though her body's reaction had nothing to do with the temperature and everything to do with him.

He checked his phone again. "Hmm, our ride must be stuck in traffic. Looks like we'll be waiting a while longer. You okay with that?"

His breath was warm against the top of her head and she nodded, barely trusting herself to speak.

"Why don't you wrap your arms around my waist?" he suggested.

"Are you sure?" she asked, surprised.

"Hey, it's cold. I'm doing the right thing by my employee in keeping her warm, aren't I?"

"Whatever you say, boss," she said as lightly as she could, but her voice broke on the last word.

Even though every particle of her body urged her to take him at his word, she took her time hugging more deeply into his body. He was right, though. Their shared warmth made a difference. Keaton slipped his phone back into his jacket pocket and closed his arms around her, too. To anyone watching, they'd look like any other loving couple on the side of the road, but Tami was all too aware that they were not a couple, no matter how much they'd cleared the air at dinner.

After another few minutes, she realized that she was not the only one being physically affected by their nearness. There was a distinct pressure against her lower belly. She must have moved slightly because she felt a puff of air escape Keaton's lips.

"Sorry," he said in a strangled voice. "Can't help nature."

"Would you like me to move?" she asked, leaning back a little and angling her head up to look at his face.

Trouble was, her movement saw her pelvis press in a little more firmly against his lower regions and the contact sent a spiral of longing deep to her core.

"Tami, I…" He sucked in a harsh breath. "It seems that no matter how hard I try, I just can't resist you."

He looked down at her and she watched as a tumult of emotions crossed his face. First, helplessness, then a little frustration, and finally, acceptance, which was quickly followed by what she privately called his decision expression. When he bent his head toward her she knew what was coming. Knew it, ached for it, welcomed it.

His lips closed on hers, the pressure at first soft and gentle, then she opened her lips in response and kissed him back with all the longing she'd bottled up since they'd left Sedona and with deeper demand. Her fingers tightened on the fine cotton of his shirt and beneath them she felt the muscles of his back. His strong hands pressed her more firmly against him and she relished the heat of his body against her torso. His tongue stroked hers and right now, everything about her focused on that point of their bodies. It all began and ended with Keaton in that moment. It was only when a car horn sounded beside them that she remembered where they were.

Keaton was breathing heavily as he wrenched his lips from hers.

"It's our ride."

She started to pull away, but he stopped her.

"Before we get in the car, I just want to say something. I won't apologize for that kiss and I won't pretend it didn't happen. These past two weeks have been torture and I haven't been able to stop thinking about the last time we kissed. I've tried to fight it, but it's a losing battle. In fact, it's a battle I want to cede. The hell with being friends. I want you, Tami. I want to make love to you, I want to lose myself in you, and see you lose yourself in me, so we can forget for a while. I won't hold it against you if you say no. I will respect whatever decision you make, but when we get in that car, do I give the driver both of our addresses, or just mine?"

She hesitated a few seconds, her insides jumping with a weird combination of heated desire and a healthy dose of caution. If they did this, it would change everything about their working relationship. Everything about *them*. It was a line she had told herself she would never cross again, and she believed Keaton had felt the same way. And now they felt the same about each other. She took a deep breath.

"Yours."

"Thank you," he said, and kissed her fiercely on the top of her head.

Keaton took her hand and led her to the car, opening the door for her and following her into the back seat. Their driver wished them a good evening, then focused on his route while Tami and Keaton sat, fingers entwined and bodies humming with anticipation, as they traveled the dark streets to his apartment building on the other side of the lake. The journey didn't take long, which was just as well, Tami told herself. She wasn't certain if it was because she was grasping this opportunity with both hands to show Keaton how much she felt for him, or because if the journey had taken any longer she might have changed her mind.

But she'd spent too much time regretting her choices and her actions in life, and she was determined to take this night to express how her feelings for him had developed. Even if she never said the words, she would show Keaton with every breath, every touch, every thought she was capable of, how much she admired him and how much he meant to her. She knew he was an honorable man—the way he conducted himself at work was a prime example. That she was less honorable was something she'd have to sweep under a metaphorical rug for now and hope against hope that their lovemaking tonight would show him the real Tami. The one who wanted to belong. The one who wanted to love freely. The one who would be loyal without question if only given the chance.

Tension vibrated off Keaton in waves as they traveled up in the elevator to his penthouse suite. The minute they were through the door, he pressed her against the wall and hungrily kissed her again. Tami tangled her fingers in his hair, holding him to her, not wanting to let him go. She felt his hands at the lapels of her jacket and let go of him only long enough for him to peel the garment from her shoulders and down her arms, and then she was touching him again. His fingers were nimble on the buttons of her blouse and it fell open, revealing the simple balconette bra she wore beneath it.

Maybe she should have splashed out on something more elaborate, indulged herself, but judging by the expression on his face as he looked at her creamy skin swelling above the pale pink cups rimmed with the merest froth of lace, she knew it wouldn't have made any difference.

"I want to touch you," he said in a voice that had grown deep with longing. "Everywhere."

"I want you to touch me, too," she answered.

He bent to press his lips against the swell of one breast and inhaled.

"You smell so damn good," he murmured against her skin.

"Why am I still wearing too many clothes?" she said with a small laugh.

He snorted in response and she felt his hands move around her ribs to the fastening of her bra. In seconds, he had it loose and he tugged her blouse and bra free of her breasts, exposing them to his hungry gaze. Tami felt her nipples tighten in response and an ache filled her, an ache that she knew would only be assuaged by his touch, his possession. And she ached to touch him, too.

"We're both wearing too many clothes," Keaton murmured with a smile as he straightened to his full height. "Come with me. We're not doing this in my entranceway."

This turned out to be a slow disrobing of one another in the dimness of his bedroom, while outside the city lights glittered below them. Tami felt goose bumps rise on her skin as he divested her of her last item of clothing and she stood naked in front of him. Her eyes roamed his naked form. She'd already known he was beautifully chiseled from watching him while they rock-climbed, with strong arms and a flat stomach and powerful legs, but seeing him completely naked was enough to rob her of coherent thought.

His erection jutted proudly from a nest of dark blond hair and she stepped forward, feeling the heat of him against her bare body before they even touched.

"You're beautiful," she whispered, lifting one hand to trace the muscles of his upper arms, then his chest, then lower.

"Beautiful…no. That word is reserved for you," he said gruffly.

He lifted his hand to her hair and slowly pulled out each pin that held it in the tight roll that she wore for work every day. He filtered his fingers through her locks, shaking them loose from the confines of the brutally tight twist, and massaged her scalp.

"There, that's better," he said.

Then his hands dropped to her shoulders and he carefully edged her back toward the bed. They stopped when the back of her legs made contact and he coaxed her down onto the broad surface, letting his fingers drift softly over her, back and forth and back and forth, until she was squirming with need.

"Come to me," she said. "I want to touch you, too."

"Next time," he answered. "For now I want to revel in you. Let me make you mindless. Let me chase away the shadows I see in your eyes every day."

His words were a balm to her soul and she allowed him his wish. His hands were gentle and soft at first, then sure and firm as he explored her shoulders, her arms, her breasts and then, finally, her hips and upper thighs. She was wet with longing and let her legs drop open as his touch skimmed her mound. The palm of his hand brushed against her clitoris and it was as if he'd set off an electrical surge through her body. She felt her hips lift off the bed as she sought the release she so desperately wanted.

"You like that, huh?" he murmured softly. "Let's see if you like this more."

He skimmed her again before shifting his touch to between her legs. His fingers probed her, and then, slick with her wetness, he slid one finger inside her body. Her inner muscles clenched on the welcome invasion, but still it wasn't enough.

"More...of you. I need more," she begged.

"Your wish is my command."

She felt the mattress dip a little as he shifted over her and heard the tear of a foil packet as he took care of protection. Tami reached for him as he positioned himself between her legs.

"I had planned to take a little longer over this," he said with a rueful smile.

"Next time," she said. "Now, please—now."

He maintained eye contact as he guided his erection to her entrance. She moaned as he teased her by nudging her with his swollen tip.

"More," she demanded, her voice guttural with need.

And then he gave her more, and more, and more. Over and over until she lost all sense of being and plummeted over the edge of here and now and into a realm of pleasure the likes of which she'd rarely known before. She hooked her legs around his hips, not wanting him to stop even as the pulsing waves of her climax pounded through her. When Keaton came, his entire body went rigid, his muscles straining as he groaned in relief, his hips surging against her as if he could never get deep enough, be part of her enough, before easing to a halt.

He collapsed against her and she relished the weight of his body on hers, the scent of his skin, the throb of his heart as it beat in unison with hers. Tami clung to his shoulders as though he was the only thing keeping her anchored at this point in time. And maybe he was. Her world had been in turmoil for weeks and this moment with him had been the most real and grounding experience of her life. He might have suggested it as respite, but Tami knew that, for her, at least, it was so much more than that.

Keaton rolled to one side, taking her with him. His gray eyes were solemn as he stared at her.

"This changes everything, Tami, you know that."

"Shh," she said, placing her forefinger on his lips. "Let's not analyze this. Let's just take tonight...for us. Everything else can wait."

He was silent a moment, then nodded. "Okay. Let's take tonight. I'll be right back."

He rolled off the bed and walked through to what she assumed was an en suite bathroom. When he returned she let her eyes roam over the contours of his body. He truly was magnificent. And, for tonight, he was hers and she didn't plan to waste a minute of it.

Nine

Tami watched as the digital clock changed from 4:59 to 5:00. She'd been watching each minute roll over for the past hour and no matter how much she thought and worried and obsessed, nothing had changed.

Trust meant everything to Keaton, and she'd taken all he could give her and she was about to throw it all back in his face. It had been selfish to accept his lovemaking, she knew that. And the truth she had to share with him would shred any chance they had of having a relationship or any kind of future together. She had to do it—she had to tell him. She couldn't go forward with the ugly truth of her reason for working for him being kept hidden away.

But how to start? What to say?

Keaton was lying on the mattress, deep in sleep. The sheets were tangled around his waist and Tami took every care not to disturb him as she slid from the bed and tip-toed around to pick up her clothing, including going out to the entrance of the apartment to retrieve her bra, blouse and jacket. She let herself into the half bath off the entrance and gave herself a quick wash, then dragged on her clothes.

Her hair was a mess, her throat pink in patches where Keaton's beard had left its mark. She touched her throat with trembling fingers. She'd relished every moment of last night, but she was terrified now that the memories would be as fleeting as these reminders of Keaton's passion. She swallowed and blinked back the burn of tears in her eyes.

No one had forced her to do this. She could have just let Our People, Our Homes commence their investigation right from the start. But she'd taken personal responsibility for what had happened and seen it equally as her responsibility to make restitution. But her ability to do that had been hindered by her father the way he'd tried to block and stifle every single thing she'd ever tried to do. She should have known he'd do whatever he could to see her fail again.

She stared at her face in the mirror. She was every bit as weak as her father had always said she was. She was the one who'd approached him for an easy out instead of facing the consequences of her choices. And she was the one who'd agreed to his conditions without any consideration as to the effect of her actions. She'd put Keaton and his family's businesses at risk. And even though she'd wanted to make everything right and she'd ended up making everything wrong instead.

She knew now, she loved him. Deeply, completely. And, feeling as she did, she couldn't continue to live the lie she'd agreed to perpetuate for her father. It was past time to take ownership of what she'd done. This thing with Keaton couldn't go any further with her deception lying like a coiled snake between them. Even though it meant she'd be getting into a whole world of trouble— trouble that would likely double as the investigation into the missing funds at Our People, Our Homes deepened. She had no doubt that Richmond Developments would take legal action against her. She couldn't hide from any of it. Not even the anger she knew she'd see on Keaton's face when she told him the whole truth. She deserved it, and as much as it would flay her heart, she had to take this step.

Tami squared her shoulders and turned out the light before making her way to the living room. There she sat, staring out the window until the gray light of dawn began to streak the Seattle skyline. A movement in the hallway alerted her to Keaton's presence and the fierce burning sensation in her stomach ratcheted up another notch.

"You're up early," he commented with a yawn. "Couldn't sleep?"

She watched as he rubbed his jaw with one hand, heard the rasp of whiskers on skin. She would take each of these memories and tuck them away, because she knew once she told him what she had to, that they would be all she had left.

"Keaton," she said on a sigh. "We need to talk."

All signs of slumber disappeared from his face and his eyes sharpened instantly.

"Talk? Why do I get the feeling I'm not going to like what you have to say?"

"Because you won't. I should have been upfront with you before we got to this."

Despite the fact that he wore nothing but a pair of pajama bottoms and his hair was still tousled from her fingers running through it, his demeanor changed instantly to that of the corporate warrior he truly was at heart.

Somehow, that made it easier. Seeing the expression on his face and the closed body language was all so much easier to face than the sexy man, warm from sleep and still bearing the marks of her fingernails on his shoulders from when he'd driven her mad with desire and pleasure and all the things she didn't deserve.

"Well, spit it out," he said sharply.

"I think I need to go to the beginning. To when I started at Richmond Developments. You see, my appointment there wasn't everything it seemed."

He raised one sardonic brow and crossed his arms across his bare torso. "Carry on."

"My father is Warren Everard."

She could see a muscle working in Keaton's jaw, but he remained silent. His eyes, however, flashed with barely repressed fury. The burn in her stomach increased.

"You don't go by your father's name," he said bluntly.

"No, I don't. I changed my name twelve years ago when I decided I no longer wanted to be associated with him."

She took in a shallow breath, then another. She could guess what Keaton would say next and he, true to form, didn't disappoint.

"And yet you became his puppet?" His voice seethed with repressed fury.

"I, um, asked him a favor. In repayment, I agreed to be positioned in your employment and to feed him information."

"That was you? You're responsible for us losing the Tanner project?"

Keaton's voice had reverted to being flat and clipped, but she had no doubt as to the emotions behind his words.

Loathing.

Disgust.

Anger.

"I have no idea how he got the information, but it wasn't from me," she said in a level voice that didn't betray the near overwhelming flutter of nerves in her chest.

"You seriously expect me to believe that?"

Tami rose on shaking legs and stood her ground. "Believe what you want—I know what's true."

He sneered. "True? Really? You have the gall to say that when you were your father's spy?"

She swallowed back the bile that threatened to flood her mouth. "I know you're mad at me—"

"Mad? You think I'm mad? Oh, I'm way past mad. You're going to regret this. I will use all the legal might I have at my disposal to make you pay for your treachery. Your actions cost us millions—worse, you've cost *decent* people their livelihoods."

"Keaton, please. Hear me out. My father has at least one other person positioned in the office that I know of. Someone in HR. That's how I got the role. I'm not certain who it is, but I suspect it was the woman I met on my first day—Monique. If she's working for my father, she could have filtered a lot more people into Richmond Developments who are reporting back to him, too."

"You can be sure there will be a thorough audit of staff, but out of everyone, you were the one outside of our family that I talked to about the Tanner project. Not anyone else. Just you."

"Keaton, I'm sorry. I never expected—"

"Never expected what, exactly? To lie? To deceive? To deliberately earn my trust with that sweet little speech at dinner last night and then shove it back down my throat? To see my company potentially crumble into dust while allowing your father's firm to scoop up business that we'd all but won? Interesting, when that's exactly what you set out to do.

"Congratulations, you are truly your father's daughter. I hope he's proud of you. You've not only betrayed me, but you've betrayed every honest person working for my family. I don't know how you can live with yourself. You no longer hold a position at Richmond Developments and you are in gross breach of your employment contract. Expect to hear from our company lawyers on Monday. Now, get out of my home."

She knew there was nothing left to say or do so she grabbed her handbag and started to leave. Keaton's voice stopped her as she reached the door.

"Why now?"

"What?"

"Why tell me now?" Keaton demanded.

There was a note of anguish in his voice that made her insides coil in a knot. She'd done this to him. She'd betrayed him, hurt him and ruined everything.

Tami drew in a deep breath and let the truth fall from her lips. "Because I realized that I've fallen in love with you and I couldn't keep working for you with that between us. I only wanted to do what was right, Keaton."

There was more, so much more she ached to tell him, but she knew if he now heard about what had happened at Our People, Our Homes, he'd never believe she had been an unwitting pawn in that disaster. As it was, the expression on his face grew even darker.

"Haven't you told enough lies already? I don't need to hear your clichés," he said, his lips twisting in a bitter line. "Leave. I don't want to see you again."

The security guard was waiting for her when the elevator got to the ground floor.

"Miss, I've been instructed to see you off the premises," he said firmly.

It was all Tami could do to nod in acknowledgement and then put one foot in front of the other as she left the building. Inside, her heart was slowly being torn into a million pieces. Somehow she had the presence of mind to call a cab and get home, where she stripped off her corporate clothing and made it into the shower. But as hard as she tried, she couldn't scrub away the sense of utter desolation that filled all the empty spaces inside. She'd brought this on herself. Her decisions. Her responsibility. Her mistakes.

After the shower, Tami wrapped up in her robe and curled in a ball under her bedcovers. Even then she couldn't escape the enormity of what she'd done. The vastness of her betrayal. Keaton's words continued to echo in her mind—*you are truly your father's daughter.* And it was true. In trying her hardest not to be like him at all, she'd allowed herself to become a tool for his use, and in doing so, had caused damage equally as bad as anything he'd ever done.

The weekend passed in a haze of nothingness. There was no one she could turn to. Early on Monday morning she was roused from her bed by the doorbell to her apartment. She peered through the peephole to see a courier standing there, and she opened her front door.

"Ms. Wilson?" he asked, holding his digital scanner toward her with a stylus at the ready.

"Yes," she answered.

"Parcel for you. Please sign on the screen."

She did as he asked and he bent to pick up the box at his feet and passed it to her.

"Have a great day!" he said cheerfully as he raced off down the hall.

Tami was beyond words. She recognized the logo on the address label of the box. Richmond Developments. Inside her apartment, she ripped open the lid and saw her personal effects from her desk nestled inside, together with a white envelope printed with her name on it. Inside was a statement from the legal department outlining the terms of the cessation of her employment, including, in detail, the alleged breaches of her employment agreement and the steps they would be taking against her to seek compensation.

Compensation? Knowing what the Tanner project would have been worth to them, she would need to live a hundred lifetimes before she could even scratch the financial surface of what she'd owe. And that wasn't even considering what she'd tried to repay to Our People, Our Homes. A sound erupted from her mouth. It should have been a hysterical laugh but it was more like a howl of desolation. She had never felt more wretched in her life.

Keaton paced the office. It had been three days since Tami's revelation and the sense of betrayal was as raw today as it had been back then. How had he been so stupid? Hadn't he learned his lesson with Honor? He'd called his brothers and sisters over the weekend and told them he'd let Tami go because she'd admitted to acting for Everard Corporation. They'd been equal parts shocked and angered at her duplicity. He hadn't quite been able to bring himself to tell them she was the old man's daughter. For some reason, he felt like it was his fault that he hadn't known sooner. Either way, it made no difference, she was gone and he and his siblings had agreed to start an internal investigation using an independent company so as not to alert any other potential plants within Richmond Developments as to what they were doing.

So far, only Monique in HR had been brought up for further investigation and she'd been arrested for facilitating corporate espionage, although it appeared there might be another infiltrator in the contracts division of the finance department. Kristin had been hot under the collar about that eye-opener and it had taken all her self-control not to face up to the guy and accuse him outright.

Honor had gently reminded them that there was a process to follow and that while it would take time, and they'd all hate the idea of knowing there were moles within their organization, it was better to do this methodically and in accordance with employment law.

But nothing took away the hurt that dwelled deep inside him that Tami had, from the outset, planned to spy on their company. And how, despite everything, he'd allowed her behind his carefully constructed walls and let her into his heart. Was he that poor a judge of character? He'd fought the feelings she'd engendered in him. He'd put the attraction down to being purely physical and congratulated himself on his ability to rule with his mind. But having kissed her that last night in Sedona, he'd honestly lost his battle with himself. The next week had been hell, knowing he'd probably hurt her with his rejection that night. And none of that had dimmed his need to reach out for her. Even now, he couldn't stop thinking about her, and that, more than anything, made him angry at himself and, unfortunately, everyone around him.

Even news from Fletcher that they had the lead on a new proposal that might help turn things around on the lost Tanner project was little comfort. Especially when, on a video call to discuss the various aspects they wanted to push where their company created a point of difference with others who might be pitching for the tender, he realized he was incorporating some of the suggestions Tami had made back on that first night in Sedona. Her suggestions about offering low-interest loans to allow low-income families into homes in better areas, and to bring affordable social housing into the project, had germinated in the back of his mind, and all his siblings had caught on to the idea and were expanding it with a financial team to see how it could be blended into the overall plan.

So how did someone like Tami, who'd turned out to be a total snake in the grass, have such a strong social conscience? To all appearances, she'd been good at her job and wasn't afraid to pitch for the underdog. And yet, that didn't gel with the fact that she'd deliberately walked into her role with the express purpose of feeding information back to her father. Keaton shook his head. He couldn't make sense of it and he'd allowed her far too much real estate in his mind already. It was time to shelve his feelings about her and let the legal department take care of the rest.

He turned as there was a knock at his office door and he saw Honor hovering there.

"You're looking rather fierce. Is it safe to come in?" she asked.

"Sure. I was just thinking."

Honor gave him a gentle smile. "That's definitely you. Always thinking. Sometimes overthinking, too, though. Am I right?"

He automatically smiled in response but there was no humor to it.

"You know me too well," he said bluntly.

Honor sat down in one of his guest chairs and he took the one opposite her.

"I do know you well, Keaton, and I have to admit that I'm really worried about you. You're not yourself."

"We're dealing with a lot here."

"We've been dealing with a lot here since December last year," she pointed out. "But that's not what I'm talking about. It's you, in here." She leaned forward and tapped him on the chest. "Something's not right. Talk to me. Tell me what's troubling you."

"Look, I really don't have time for—"

"Don't give me that, Keaton. If you don't make time to talk to me now, when will you? And if not me, then who? Kristin? Logan? Your mom?"

He must have pulled a face because she carried on.

"See? Then it's me. Look, I know I hurt you, but I thought you were okay with Logan and me now. At least tell me if that's what is still upsetting you," she pressed.

"No, that's not what's upsetting me."

"There! So you admit you're upset about something."

Keaton groaned. "Of course I'm upset. We lost a major contract."

"But we're on the verge of winning another, so I know it's not that. Hmm, but I think it's tied to that somehow, isn't it?"

"Fine. Tami is Warren Everard's daughter. Satisfied now?"

Honor reeled back a little in shock. "His *daughter*?"

"His own personal spy."

Honor shook her head slowly. "Wow. I was shocked when you'd told us she'd been let go for spying. I have to be honest, from what I learned about her while we were in Sedona and in the days after we came home, for me at least, it just didn't ring true to her character. But now you're saying she's Everard's daughter? Do you think her father coerced her?"

He snorted a laugh but then became serious again as he weighed up telling Honor the rest of it. He had to tell someone. It was eating him up.

"We slept together." Okay, so maybe he hadn't meant to be that blunt about it, but those three words pretty much summed it all up. "Do you think her father told her to do that, too?"

"You what?" Honor asked incredulously.

"You heard me."

"But you'd only known each other a couple of weeks."

"Three and a half, actually. Seriously, Honor, is there a statute of limitations on when a couple can have sex when they're attracted to one another? I would have thought you'd be the last person to cast judgment in that regard."

"No, of course not, and I'm not passing judgment," Honor said, with that same incredulous expression on her face. "But I know you—you don't rush into that kind of thing. She must have felt very special to you. No wonder you're hurting."

Tami had felt special to him. It's why the betrayal of finding out exactly who she was had made him so angry. Yes, and hurt, too.

"Keaton…" Honor leaned forward and stared earnestly into his eyes. "You know that sometimes people are driven to do things they would never normally do because of extenuating circumstances."

"Circumstances like you and Logan, last year?" he asked with a tinge of acrimony.

Honor's expression turned sad and he saw the shimmer of tears in her eyes. "I never wanted to hurt you, Keaton."

He felt something ease in his chest. "Yeah, I know. We weren't right for each other, no matter how hard we tried. And I'm sorry for that comment. It wasn't fair of me. I hold no bitterness toward you or Logan anymore. Don't feel guilty about it. Now I understand what it's like to be so drawn to someone that you go against your own common sense. I think I comprehend even better why you couldn't resist your attraction to Logan."

Honor bowed her head and wiped away an errant tear. "Thank you. That means a lot—and it'll mean a lot to Logan, too. But it doesn't solve the current issue, does it?"

"With Tami? It's solved. She's gone and Legal are preparing a case against her for breach of her employment contract."

"You're actually going after her?"

"She cost us millions of dollars, Honor. I can't just let that slide. Logan and Kristin are with me on this. Besides, it's not like her daddy can't afford to pay her damages, especially now he has the Tanner project."

Honor firmed her lips and shifted in her chair before answering. "Will it make the hurt go away?"

Keaton looked squarely at her. Trust Honor to cut straight to the chase.

"No, it won't, but it'll send a message to anyone else lurking in the shadows that we won't tolerate disloyalty of any kind."

"I can see that is necessary, but Tami really didn't seem the type to be into subterfuge and corporate espionage."

"Do those people ever broadcast what their true intentions are?"

"No, of course not, but you know what I mean, don't you? She was just too… I dunno…" She waved her hands in frustration. "Too nice. She was passionate about the things that make life good for people. Tami never struck me as the kind of person who made a single decision based on personal gain."

"She was clearly very good at her role as her father's pawn then, wasn't she?" he said cynically.

"I honestly don't think that was all an act. It makes

me wonder what circumstances drove her to work for her father in that way. Maybe, if you can understand what those circumstances are, you can get a better grasp of why Tami did it."

"Do we really need to know why?"

"Keaton, you're an intelligent man with a compassionate heart, when you let anyone else see it. Can you honestly tell me you don't still care about her? That you aren't driven to figure out the why behind her actions?"

She got up to leave and gave him another long, concerned look before turning and heading for the door. Honor was asking too much. Figuring out why Tami spied on them was not on his agenda. The reason was obvious—money. It drove her father and it obviously drove her, too. But she'd been the one to come clean to him and she'd insisted that she hadn't passed any information on to her father. Keaton hadn't believed her then and he didn't feel inclined to believe her now. So where did that leave him? Was it Monique from HR or the snake in Kristin's department who'd passed on the information?

He weighed them up in his mind and rejected Monique almost immediately. She wouldn't have had clearance to access the information Everard wanted and IT had already scoured her computer and found no track back. And while the guy who'd been suspended pending an investigation in the finance department had a higher clearance, unless he was an extraordinarily skilled hacker, he wouldn't have been able to access the secure network where Keaton and his siblings had discussed the new venture. No, it all came back to Tami. She was the only person, outside of the family, he'd even mentioned the project to.

But what if Tami's father had gotten the information more indirectly from her somehow? He thought about when he and Tami had discussed the company's plans back in Sedona. She'd mentioned she'd made notes on her phone. Was that how Everard had found out? Did he have access to her phone? And, if he did, was she complicit or was she as innocent as she claimed?

Keaton huffed a sigh of frustration. However Warren Everard had gotten his data, the damage had been done and Tami was out of Richmond Developments and out of his life, even if he couldn't quite dislodge her from the back of his mind.

Ten

"I'm so glad you could come with me tonight," Nancy Richmond enthused as she led Keaton through the throng of heavily perfumed and expensively clad attendees at the charity dinner she'd coerced him into attending with her.

She'd been slow to get back out among her peers after the scandal and fallout from her husband's death last December, so he'd been pleased to be able to escort her this evening, to be honest.

"Me, too, Mom. You look exceptionally lovely tonight," he said with genuine feeling.

"Oh, you!" she said with a blush and patted his arm lovingly. "You always know how to say the right thing."

He placed his hand over hers and pressed her fingers in response. His mom had been an integral part of the management team at Richmond Developments for longer than he could remember, but with his father's sudden death, she'd withdrawn from almost every aspect of her life that had taken her outside her home. She'd grieved for far more than the man she'd loved intensely for over thirty years. Discovering their entire marriage had been mirrored with another woman and family on the other side of the continent had done a huge amount of damage to her confidence. Especially when it initially appeared that Nancy's marriage had been the bigamous one. By the time it was discovered that Douglas Richmond's first marriage had not been legal, the fallout had already been widespread. Keaton would have done anything to get her back to her old self, and if coming along to this two-thousand-dollar-a-plate dinner for a veteran's charity put a smile back on Nancy Richmond's face, then that's what he'd do.

"How's that lovely new assistant of yours doing?" Nancy asked after they'd been shown to their table. "I didn't tell you, did I? I popped into the office when you returned from Sedona. You were all locked in one of your meetings and Tami looked after me. We got to talking and she mentioned how she'd overcome her fear of flying and was super understanding about how I feel about it. Her suggestions on how to manage my anxiety made such good sense to me. So much so, Hector and I are thinking of a spa retreat to Palm Springs in a few weeks."

"That's great, Mom," Keaton said, equally surprised that Tami hadn't mentioned the time she'd spent with his mom and thrilled that his mother was beginning to think about taking steps away from home on her own. But hang on a minute… Hector was their family lawyer. He'd been a great support to Nancy, but a trip together? His father hadn't been gone that long.

"Oh, look at your face," Nancy said. "Don't worry, we don't plan to sleep together…yet."

Keaton blanched. Thinking about his parents that way

was something he'd never done, but his mom and Hector? He really didn't want to go there.

"You're an adult in charge of your own choices," he said stiffly. "And, as to Tami, she has left us already."

"Oh, she didn't work out in the end? That's a shame."

"Actually, Mom, I had to let her go. She's Warren Everard's daughter."

"Really? Goodness! And she never told HR about the potential conflict of interest."

"We had reason to believe she was instrumental in us losing the Tanner project. It seems that an HR senior staffer was also on the Everard payroll and assisted in planting Tami in my office."

Nancy gasped in shock. "Well, I never. Still, if her father was behind it, it should come as no surprise. That man would stoop to anything to get what he wants. He and your father went head-to-head several times. Warren Everard always was a bastard—excuse my French."

"That's something I've always loved about you Mom—you like to call things as you see them."

"We have that in common, my darling boy," she said with a proud motherly smile. "But getting back to Warren and Margot Everard, everyone always said they were very difficult and demanding parents. They said they'd cut ties with their daughter once she turned eighteen but you know how people gossip. Many said it was more the other way around. Either way, I couldn't imagine doing that to one of my children, no matter how difficult their upbringing, but then again, Margot always was such a cold fish. Appearances meant everything to her. They still do.

"You know, given their situation, I can't imagine Tami ever wanting to work for her father. If there'd been a familial reconciliation I'm sure the gossip lines would have been buzzing. Why on earth would she do something like spy on you for him when they haven't spoken in years?"

"Who knows?" Keaton said with a shrug. "The fact remains that she admitted her relationship with Everard and what he'd asked her to do."

"Such a shame," Nancy said.

Keaton couldn't help but agree.

He had just returned from a run the next morning when his mom called, her voice throbbing with excitement.

"Keaton, you'll never believe what I've just heard!"

"Good morning to you, too, Mom. It was a lovely night last night, thank you."

"Oh, yes, all of that," she said offhandedly. "But listen. One of my girlfriends phoned me for a chat today and she said that she'd heard from Bitsy Tyler, whose daughter is married to that guy who works in the prosecutor's office. I never liked him, you know, he's got snaky eyes and a fidget that makes you wonder what he's thinking all the time. Anyway, Bitsy said that Warren Everard's daughter was under investigation by the police for her involvement in a rather large sum of missing money from the Our People, Our Homes charity."

Keaton stood still and gripped his phone so tightly the plastic squeaked. "Just how much money are we talking here?"

"Their entire operating capital. Two and a half million dollars."

He let out a long, low whistle. "And she's accused of taking it?"

"No...well, not directly, anyway. Apparently she was dating her boss—he was the director of the charity and now neither he, nor the money, are anywhere to be found.

One of my bridge-club ladies apparently asked Margot Everard to her face about it yesterday and Margot said they have no contact with their daughter and she had nothing to say on the matter."

Keaton barely heard her after the part where Nancy told him that Tami had been dating the charity's director. It raised all sorts of ugly questions in his mind. Did she make a habit of sleeping with all her bosses?

"Do you think she was an active party to it, Keaton?"

He dragged his attention back to her question. A part of him wanted to say an emphatic yes, but there was a tickle at the back of his mind that urged him to look beyond what had been presented on the surface.

"It's hard to say without knowing more, Mom. And it's not our place to discuss it, to be honest. If she's being investigated we have to trust that they will uncover her involvement, or establish her innocence."

"I can't accept that the lovely girl I met in your office would be capable of such a thing."

On the surface, Keaton would normally have agreed with his mom, but then he had his own experience of Tami's ability to appear to be one thing when she was very definitely another.

"Appearances can be deceptive, Mom. We all learned that the hard way with Dad."

His mom went silent on the other end of the phone and he cursed himself for his insensitivity.

"Mom, look, I'm sorry, I shouldn't have said that."

"No, darling, you're right. Appearances can be deceptive, but I've had a lot of time to think about my situation and for all that your father cheated on me the entire time I knew him, he still managed to provide me with a very good life and three children I love to the moon and back. What he did was wrong on so many levels I still can't bear to think of them all. But I've learned to move past that and, in my own way, find forgiveness for him for what he did to us because if I hadn't been able to do that, I would forever be a victim of his circumstances, and that I refuse to do."

"You're an incredible woman, Mom. I'm so proud of you."

"And I'm proud of you, too. I'll let you know if I hear any more about Tami. I'm sure there's more there than meets the eye."

Keaton ended the call and went to take a shower. He leaned his forearms against the tiled wall of the shower stall and set the jets of the shower to a penetrating pulse down the back of his neck and his shoulders. A part of him continued to seethe with fury over the betrayal he believed Tami was responsible for, especially in light of her apparent involvement in the theft of funds from the charity she'd worked at before. But that niggle in the back of his mind continued to urge him to push harder and look deeper.

As to his mother's forgiveness for his father, he wasn't prepared to rejoin the Douglas Richmond fan club just yet. He'd idolized his father his entire life. Had dedicated every breath in his body to making his father proud. Everything he'd done or achieved had been because he'd given twice as much effort, as if he could somehow make up for his missing twin. He'd worked damn hard for everything he had achieved. He'd made sacrifices and not stopped to count the cost. And for what? To be overthrown the second Logan had turned up. As the older twin, his brother had taken over everything that Keaton had worked for his entire life, even his fiancée. Then, to add further insult to injury, to discover he, Logan and Kristin were not Douglas's only children? Well, that had been a shock too far. Keaton didn't think he'd ever be capable of thinking about his father without the deep sense of betrayal that had infiltrated pretty much everything in Keaton's life in the past four months.

Keaton snapped off the faucet, stepped from the shower and grabbed a towel. As he dried off, he accepted he was going to have to talk again with Tami. The gossip his mom had shared with him raised more questions than provided answers.

Once he was dried off and dressed, Keaton checked the personnel file he had in his laptop for Tami and typed a note in his phone with her address. They were going to have this out, right now.

Keaton did a quick check on the address he'd entered into his GPS. Yes, this was definitely the one. There was certainly no evidence here that Tami was the daughter of one of Seattle's richest men, nor that she'd had any benefit from the two and a half million dollars that was reportedly missing. This suburb was everyday, middle America—nice, certainly, but not what he'd been expecting for Warren Everard's daughter.

The clapboard home was small and set back on the lot. A small garden looked as though it struggled to survive out front and the path to the door showed signs of weeds coming through the cracks in the path. He went up the shallow stairs that led to the front door and knocked hard, still unconvinced he had the correct address. It wasn't long before he heard movement behind the door.

"Who is it?"

That was definitely Tami.

"It's Keaton. I need to talk to you."

He heard the sound of a chain being slid off the door before the lock turned and the door slowly opened. His eyes roamed her instantly, taking in the dark discoloration beneath her eyes, which lacked any of their usual sparkle, and the paleness of her face. She wore a pair of yoga pants and an oversize woolen sweater that dwarfed her frame. And yet, despite all that, his body reacted instantly to her. He clamped down on the urge that spiraled through him and of all the memories of their lovemaking—of how she sounded, tasted, smelled—that his mind seemed determined to revisit.

Tami could barely take her eyes off him. Dressed in a good pair of casual trousers and a finely knitted sweater, Keaton looked as if he'd just stepped away from a designer photo shoot. Even his hair was its trademark perfect. His cool gray eyes looked straight back at her and she shifted slightly under his scrutiny, suddenly self-conscious of her appearance. She knew she didn't look good and hadn't cared, right up until this moment.

"May I come in?" he asked, his voice a little more gruff than usual.

"Of course," she answered in a small voice and stepped back to allow him into her hallway.

As he stepped past her, she caught a trace of his cologne, the woodsy scent reminding her of what it had been like to be close enough to him to feel as though they'd been one unit, working together. But she'd ruined all that, hadn't she? She dragged in a breath and closed the door behind him.

"I'm sorry, I wasn't expecting anyone. Please, come through to the kitchen. Can I get you anything?"

"Coffee would be great."

As she moved about the kitchen, she felt his gaze on her, even watching her every movement as she measured out beans into the coffee grinder, as if he didn't trust her to do even that right. Her hand shook and she dropped some beans on the countertop. She was turning into a clumsy wreck. She cleaned up and put the coffee on, before turning to face him. The sooner he cut to the chase, the sooner he'd leave.

"You said you needed to talk to me. What about?"

He must know she'd already received the document from the legal department of Richmond Developments outlining her responsibilities under her employment agreement and then listing her breach of the same, and that they would be seeking damages. Surely, he hadn't needed to come to her door to discuss that further? Faced with the other disaster in her life—the investigation into Our People, Our Homes—dealing with Richmond Developments was peanuts in comparison.

She was surprised when Keaton began to outline the investigation into the charity and her alleged involvement in it. A sour taste rose in her mouth. It seemed the grapevine had been well and truly busy.

"The business of embezzlement at Our People, Our Homes. Is it true?" he asked.

"What exactly are you asking? Did I steal the money? No, of course not! It is true that I let Mark use my password-protected computer—he was my boss and my boyfriend. I had no reason to believe he'd abuse my trust. It's also true that he filtered the money through our joint bank account before immediately transferring it all out again."

Keaton looked squarely at her. "Were you involved in that?"

It was as if she hadn't even spoken. Hadn't he listened to a word she'd just said? Tami closed her eyes, counted to three, then opened them again.

"Only in that I let him use my computer. In itself,

that was a breach of the user agreement I signed when I started at Our People, Our Homes."

The coffee machine hissed and spat its conclusion and Tami grabbed two mugs and began to pour the coffee. Her hands were still shaking and she hissed under her breath as a few droplets of the steaming-hot brew splattered onto her hand. Thank goodness Keaton hadn't noticed or he'd probably see her nervousness as some kind of admission of guilt.

"And you're adamant that's the extent of your involvement?"

"Look, I don't see that it's any of your business, Keaton, but, yes. That is the extent of my involvement. And that's what I told the police over four hours of questioning yesterday afternoon and six hours the day before, when they came to my house. The only thing I'm guilty of is giving Mark access to my computer.

"We were cosignatories on the charity accounts and it never occurred to me to distrust him. I thought I loved him, so why wouldn't I trust him? He kept talking about the future, about what we'd do together. For the first time in my life, I thought I'd found someone who loved me for myself and not for what advantage I could give them because of the family I was born into. Yes, being in a relationship together and being cosignatories was probably not wise. I should have requested to be removed from the signing authorities when things got serious between us. But it never occurred to me that he was using me. Even when I was faced with what he'd done I could barely believe it.

"Now, looking back, I can see that he groomed me, wooed me, then manipulated me to get ahold of that money. And, in doing so, he set me up to look equally as guilty and left me as the fall guy to take the blame.

Even though I knew it looked as if I was complicit in the whole thing, I took it straight to the board. I laid everything bare to them and I presented them with a solution."

It was a far-fetched story, but she hoped the truth rang clear in her words.

"A solution?"

He was dogged, she'd give him that.

"Because I was responsible for the loss, I offered to make full restitution so we could continue to operate. I should have known it was a stretch and that I should have just allowed them to follow the correct procedure from the start when the loss was exposed. But I went to my father for help. I don't know why I thought that anything might ever have changed between us, but at the time going to him was the only avenue I could see to make things right again. He's a trustee of a fund left to me by my grandmother. I asked him for access to the fund to repay the money Mark had stolen. He agreed, but had conditions."

Keaton grunted, then went silent a while before speaking again.

"If you didn't take the money, why did you attempt to refund it? Why aren't the authorities chasing this Mark guy down and making him pay it back?"

Tami felt her throat tighten. How many times did she have to say it before he'd believe her?

"He is under investigation, now, but he's left the country. As to me wanting to return the money–I gave Mark the access and I ignored the safeguards set in place to prevent exactly that from happening. Me. No one else. I felt it was my responsibility."

"He still had to make the choice to abuse your trust. Where is he now?"

"From what I understand, the money was traced to an

offshore account, and Mark…well, the police believe he's enjoying the tropical climate of Nauru. And, of course, there is no extradition treaty between the USA and the islands of Micronesia." She sighed heavily. "He did his research all right. And all the time he was doing that, right under my nose, I believed him when he said he was planning a vacation for us. I guess I was so wrapped up in the idyll of being loved for myself, that I didn't see the signs that I was being exploited. The police aren't fully convinced that I'm not just biding my time, either, waiting to join him."

"Are you?"

"No! Of course not. And to prove it I voluntarily surrendered my passport before they asked for it and I'm cooperating fully with the investigation."

"And this business with Everard. Exactly what did he expect from you?"

Tears sprang into Tami's eyes and her fingers tightened around her coffee mug. She blinked fiercely and took a long sip of the brew before answering.

"He expected me to find out what you were working on and report back to him. The outdoors experience set his plans back a little, I think. He messaged me several times a day while we were away."

"And you told him what we'd discussed on our first night?"

She shook her head vehemently. "I told him absolutely nothing about that. When we arrived back here in Seattle, I went to see him. He told me in no uncertain terms that I wouldn't see a penny of my money because I hadn't personally given him the information he'd needed, and then he basically kicked me out of the house." She swallowed another sip of coffee, the burn of it in her stomach reminding her that she probably should have eaten at some stage in the past twenty-four hours. But then again, the idea of putting food in her mouth had made her stomach lurch uncomfortably.

"Look, Keaton, I don't know what you want from me, but I never told my father anything about the Tanner project. I know that I don't exactly look like the innocent party in any of this, but I wish you could believe me."

"I wish I could, too," he said quietly.

His words excoriated her heart and she knew, in that moment, that in his eyes she was damned no matter what she said.

"I'd like you to leave now," she said firmly.

"One last thing," Keaton said as he rose to leave. "The phone you used while we were away. Had you had that long?"

"No, why?"

"May I ask where you got it?"

"My mother gave it to me when she organized my new corporate wardrobe," Tami said. "Which reminds me, I need to donate those clothes somewhere. She said that Dad insisted I have the best technology available so I would at least look the part in my new role as your assistant."

Even then her father hadn't believed in her enough to think she could do a job well.

"Would you mind loaning the phone to me? I'd like to have our IT people look at it. I promise we'll get it back to you."

"Sure. I don't use it now, anyway. I'll grab it for you on your way out."

Tami led the way down the hallway and opened the front door for him, leaving him standing in the hallway as she ducked into her bedroom and retrieved the phone from where she'd tossed it to the back of a drawer in her dresser. She handed it to Keaton and their fingers brushed, the warmth of his skin instantly permeating hers. The sensation robbed her of breath, but the moment he took the phone he severed their contact almost instantly.

"Keaton, I'm really sorry. I wish I could go back and undo all the harm I've caused."

He looked at her, his eyes sharp and clear, before nodding abruptly.

"We'll courier it back to you," he said as he moved out the front door.

"Don't bother. I don't want anything to do with a single thing from my father."

And in the next second he was outside and on the path heading for his car, as if he couldn't wait to be clear of her. Tami rubbed her hand down her thigh, ridding herself of the sensation of his all-too-brief touch. And, as she watched him drive away and closed the door behind her, a shocking sense of loss billowed from deep within and drove her to her knees. She'd never felt so alone in her entire life.

Eleven

Keaton read the report that had come with the returned phone. That niggling suspicion of his had been confirmed. Tami's phone not only had a remote-access function that had allowed a third party to listen in on calls and conversations, but everything she'd done, from photos she'd taken through notes she'd made on a notetaking app on the phone, had also been backed up to a cloud that was registered to an anonymous user.

He had no doubt that if they explored further, they would discover the anonymous user was most likely a company sheltering under the umbrella of Everard Corporation. Keaton made a sound of disgust and tossed the report to his desk before getting up from his chair and striding over to the window. He heard the office door open, but was too absorbed in anger at the magnitude of what Tami had unwittingly done to bother turning around to identify his visitor.

"Problem?" Logan's voice came from behind him.

"Read that," Keaton said, half turning and gesturing angrily to the printed report on his desk.

Logan let out a long, low whistle. "So that's how the old bastard did it. Do you still think she was complicit?"

Keaton's initial reaction was to utter a sharp affirmative, but in light of the information he'd received from his mom and what Tami herself had told him, she either had to be the best actress and liar in the history of womankind, or she'd been cruelly duped. Not once, but twice. And each time by the men she should have been able to trust would love and protect her.

"Not fully, no. She did mean to spy, but didn't know she was being duped by her own father at the same time."

"So what now?"

"What do you mean, what now? Even if it was inadvertent, she still gave Everard the information he needed."

"Are we still going to bring a case against her?"

Keaton swung around to face his twin. It was still slightly disconcerting to feel as though he was looking at himself in a mirror. Aside from a chicken-pox scar above Logan's right eyebrow, it would take someone who knew both men extremely well to be able to tell the difference between them. And, after a lifetime of believing he was an only son, and now discovering the twin he'd developed with in utero was still alive, it had been a hard road to accepting his brother into his life.

"Y—" Keaton couldn't say it. While he was still furious she'd come under their umbrella with every intention of spying, she hadn't completely followed through. Was it enough that she'd been fired? Probably. "I'll think about it."

Logan sat down in one of the chairs opposite Keaton's desk and crossed one leg lazily over the other.

"What are you doing?" Keaton asked.

"Waiting for you to open up and admit you have feelings for that girl."

Keaton threw himself back into his chair and stared back at his brother. "Honor's been talking to you, hasn't she?"

"Of course she has, but, honestly, even a blind man could see you're hurting and it's not just the loss of a contract that's made you more prickly than *kina*."

"*Kina*?"

"Sorry, I forget. You guys call 'em sea urchins, I think. You know, a squat round shell with spines about this long—" he gestured with his fingers "—and meaty flesh inside. It's a delicacy back in New Zealand."

"If you say so," Keaton answered uncomfortably. He wasn't sure if he was comfortable about being likened to a sea creature, especially one with spines.

"I do. So talk to me about Tami."

"I don't know where to start. She arrived and somehow inveigled her way into pretty much every thought I've had since."

"Sounds like love to me."

"No. I've been in love." He stared at the brother who was currently engaged to his own ex-fiancée.

"Be honest. Did you feel for Honor the way Tami makes you feel?"

"We barely know each other," he protested.

"Yeah, you do. In here." Logan pointed to his chest. "Even if you're fighting it in your head, your heart knows. Take it from me. Trust your heart."

"I don't know if I can."

"Sure you do. You just need to take the leap. Metaphorically speaking, of course." Logan got up from his chair and flung his brother a smile. "See you later at dinner at Mom's."

Logan left him ruminating on his thoughts. Keaton picked up the report and read it again. Tami could have consented to all of this spyware on her phone, but if she was telling the truth, she'd been thoroughly tricked. Knowing how passionate she was for the underdog, it just seemed wrong that others could have used her this way, especially her family. He stared at the doorway his brother had just exited. Yes, there'd been a time when he'd wished Logan had never come back to the States. But, for all their banter, imagining a life without him now was impossible. Keaton knew it would destroy him if he was alienated from his family the way Tami was.

He thought back to something Tami had said when he'd gone to visit her. *For the first time in my life, I thought I'd found someone who loved me for myself.* With what little he knew about her upbringing, he could imagine that when people knew she was Warren Everard's daughter they might have formed sycophantic relationships if they thought it would gain them access to the Everard money. Even he and Kristin had faced that through school, and to a lesser degree in college. Some kids gravitated to those with privileged backgrounds for reasons other than genuine friendship. Some adults, too. Was that all Tami's life had been? No wonder she'd been so eager to please her boyfriend.

Keaton knew there was obviously very little love between her and her parents. Even that he found hard to comprehend. For all his own father's faults, Douglas Richmond had loved his family—families, Keaton corrected himself—deeply, and within those families, they'd been brought up to love and respect one another, too. Despite all she'd been through, Tami had grown into a warm and compassionate woman. Someone who deserved better than to have her faith in people violated by the very ones to whom she should always be able to turn.

So what, exactly, was this creep she'd imagined herself in love with like? Keaton wondered. What had she called him again? Mark? He pulled up the name of the charity on his computer and searched for their website, then any reference to the people running the charity. There was only one person who fit—a Mark Pennington was still listed as the director of the organization. Keaton opened a new search window and keyed in the guy's name. There wasn't a lot to be found about him, even through social media. Just a couple of references to college sports and some public appeal he'd headed for the Our People, Our Homes charity. It was as if he'd deliberately wiped as much personal information as he possibly could from the internet, which was no small feat.

But there had to be a way to track him down and make him face the law for what he'd done. Keaton put a call through to their head of security—Janice May, who'd spent many years on the Seattle police force—and asked her for a meeting. After an intense hour of discussion, Keaton had a plan to move forward. Clearly Mark Pennington was a man motivated by easy money. If he could dangle a sufficiently enticing get-rich-quick scheme in front of him, it might just be enough to get Pennington to leave his tropical-island sanctuary and set foot on home soil. The minute he did that, the police would be ready to pounce. Janice had already spoken with an old colleague who'd confirmed there was a warrant out for Pennington's arrest.

He would have loved to be the person baiting the trap for Pennington himself. But there were a couple of reasons why he couldn't. The first was his desire to likely pulverize the guy for being such a lowdown dirty cheat.

The second was that he was needed here. He couldn't afford to take his eye off the ball here at work. Janice had suggested a private firm that would be able to assist him—all he needed to do was dream up a suitable scheme to bait the trap with enough money that would appeal to Pennington. The guy was a greedy slimeball, so Keaton didn't think that would be too difficult.

Careful planning was all it would take and Keaton was nothing if not careful. Two days later, his representative was on a series of flights to Nauru and the sting was in place. Now it was merely a waiting game.

"Why don't you answer your phone!" Warren Everard demanded from the front porch of Tami's house. "You'd have saved me the trouble of coming to this dump!"

"Well, if you called my phone, I would answer it," she said, blocking her doorway and refusing to let him in.

Keaton had sent her an express envelope, which had included a copy of the report from the IT people at Richmond Developments. She'd been shocked to see how easily her father had manipulated her and accessed information she'd thought was private. There was no way she was letting him inside her modest home. It might not be much, but it was her sanctuary and she'd worked hard for it.

She reached into the back pocket of her jeans and checked the screen on her old, outdated mobile, then held it up to him.

"See, no calls, no messages."

"Not that piece of junk," he sneered. "I mean the phone I gave you when you started at Richmond."

"Oh, that phone. That would be the one you planted spyware in so you could keep tabs on me and renege on the agreement we made?"

He didn't even have the grace to look shamefaced.

Tami sighed wearily. "Why are you here, Dad? I thought you said you were done with me."

"I wish," he muttered with a sour expression on his face. "I want to know if you knew that crowd at Richmond damn well set me up!"

There was an unusual gray cast to Warren Everard's skin that was at odds with his normally ruddy complexion. And his breathing was labored, as if he was under great physical stress.

"Are you okay, Dad? You don't look well."

"Of course I'm not well," he snapped. "Now answer the damned question!"

"No need to shout at me. Knew what, exactly?"

"About the contamination?"

"What contamination?"

"Don't play games with me. I know precisely how cozy you got with Keaton Richmond. Did he set the whole thing up just to see me fall?"

Tami paled. Keaton's covering letter had told her the spyware her father had had installed on the phone could pick up conversations and phone calls, as well as back up notes to where he could access them. Did that mean he'd heard *everything* between her and Keaton? Even their lovemaking?

A hot flush of embarrassment began to flood her body, but it was rapidly followed by an anger that she'd never felt before. This was a violation that went beyond corporate espionage. She had no cause to feel embarrassment. She should feel nothing but pity for the man who'd fathered her. He was so driven that he considered nothing private. So driven that he thought he had the right to win at all costs and to hell with anyone who stood in his way.

"What…contamination?" she said deliberately.

"The Tanner project. The entire thing is stalled because of land contamination due to illegal toxic dumping in the area thirty years ago. Bastards falsified reports and hid the truth so deep even my lawyers didn't find the details until it was too late. When I sent out my people they began ground testing, which subsequently raised so many red flags I'm surprised the land doesn't glow at night. Keaton Richmond knew about it, didn't he?"

Tami shook her head slowly. "Dad, he was privy to the same information you were before making the pitch. He knew nothing."

"I don't believe you. I'm suing everybody involved with this. The vendors, the realtors and if I discover Richmond Developments knew any of this I'm going to damn well sue them too. We're going to be tied up in court now for so long I'll probably never live long enough to see the conclusion. This is going to cost me millions!"

He turned sharply and stomped his way down the path to the road, where his driver waited patiently beside the car. She watched as he got in and the car then drove away. A tiny smile curled her lips.

She shouldn't feel so satisfied when this was clearly making her father ill, she told herself. But the fact was, he'd used subterfuge to steal that contract out from under Richmond Developments and he was now reaping his just reward as far as she was concerned. That it had led to a very lucky escape for Keaton's team was a monumental bonus. She doubted, given the struggles the company was experiencing at present, that they'd have weathered the fallout her father now faced from the Tanner project without major losses.

Tami also wondered how her father would feel when he received the correspondence she'd directed her newly appointed lawyer to send him. She'd approached a law firm to act on her behalf in the Our People, Our Homes case and the Richmond Developments matter. While there, she'd mentioned her father restricting her access to her trust fund and her lawyer had made the appropriate enquiries. The information requested had confirmed her father had blocked her late grandmother's wishes regarding Tami's access to the fund, citing Tami's instability and unreliable character.

While he had, judging from the balance sheet provided, managed her trust fund very well since her grandmother had passed away ten years ago, she couldn't see him being fair going forward, not after the way he'd abused his position as the trustee of her fund, or with the Tanner project. It was past time for her to take more control into her own hands, to have a say in how the fund was handled. Her father's actions had weaponized the fund that was rightfully hers to manage. And, given the way he'd treated her recently, there was no way she had any reason to ever be in contact with him again, or have him control a single aspect of her life, so her attorney had been instructed to take steps to see to Warren Everard's removal as a trustee.

She turned and went inside, feeling freer than she had in a very long time. After what had happened with Mark, and then her father's manipulation of her, she knew she couldn't be that person anymore. She needed to take charge of the things that were important to her. Making everyone around her happy was all very well, but she needed to take care of herself, too.

Would Keaton have heard the news about the Tanner project yet? It was possible her father had only just found out, and when he couldn't reach her had driven straight to her house. Should she call Keaton, or maybe go and see him? Tami grabbed her mobile phone and began to key in his number but the phone beeped three times and then the screen went dark. The battery was dead. Since phoning was now out, that meant she had to go see him. She doubted she'd be permitted back into the Richmond tower, but maybe she could try to catch him at home.

Before she could talk herself out of it, she grabbed her car keys and bag and headed out the door. Keaton deserved to get the news on the Tanner project now, and not through some other intermediary source. When she got to his apartment tower, however, she hadn't counted on the security guard being the same guy who'd been on duty when she'd left the last time.

"But this is important—I must see him," Tami insisted.

"No, miss. It's more than my job is worth to let you upstairs. Send him a letter."

Tami groaned and started to turn away, but caught sight of the very man she needed to see coming in through the main doors from the street.

"Jeffrey, is there a problem?" Keaton asked as he drew near.

"I'm sorry, Mr. Richmond. I've told her she's not permitted on the premises, but she refuses to leave. Would you like me to call the police?"

Tami wheeled around to face Keaton. "Please, I won't be long. It's really important or I wouldn't be here. I promise."

Keaton looked at the security guard. "It won't be necessary to call the police." He shifted his gaze to Tami. "Come with me."

He led her to the elevators and they ascended to his floor. Through the short journey, he didn't make eye contact, nor did he say a word. Maybe this hadn't been the greatest of her ideas, Tami thought as she watched the numbers count inexorably up. She let out a breath as the elevator pinged and the doors slid open, then followed Keaton down the thickly carpeted hall to his door.

Inside, she was assailed with the memory of her last visit here. Of how they had barely made it past the entrance foyer, so strong had been their hunger for one another. It sent a shiver of longing through her body.

"Cold?" Keaton asked.

"No," she answered, staring straight into his eyes.

She noted the exact moment his pupils flared and his sharp intake of breath as he understood exactly where her thoughts had been.

"Take a seat in the living room," he said. "I'll be back in a minute."

She did as he said, and was again lost in the memory of the state she'd been in the last time she'd sat here. Sated, yes, but tied up in a hundred knots for the truth she'd had to deliver. And now? Well, she was just tied up in knots.

She started when Keaton returned. He'd changed out of his suit and into a pair of trousers and a finely woven sweater that looked like it had cost more than her monthly house payments. A look at the subtle logo on his breast confirmed her suspicion.

"Can I offer you anything to drink?" he asked.

"No, thank you. I meant it when I said I wouldn't be long. I wanted to tell you the news myself, before it makes headlines tomorrow, which I'm sure it will do."

"And that is?" he said, sitting down opposite her.

"It's to do with the Tanner project," she began.

Keaton stiffened in his chair. "Go on."

"The land is contaminated. My father came to see me about an hour ago. He accused me of setting him up." She uttered a bitter laugh. "Ironic, isn't it? He used me and now he blames me. Anyway, that's not what I'm here to say. I just wanted you to know that I'm glad he beat you to that contract. Apparently a large tract of the land was an illegal toxic dump site and the records were purged somehow. If the past is any example, I'm guessing the land will need be left empty until testing levels show it is safe for development. Given my father's reaction, I'm guessing that will be a very long time."

Keaton leaned forward, his forearms resting on his thighs and his hands clasped together. "You're certain of this."

"Oh, yes, he came to my front door and told me himself. To be honest, he looked physically ill over it. And I'm not surprised. A part of me does feel some compassion for what he must be going through—I wouldn't be me, if I didn't. But overall I'm just so relieved that Richmond Developments has dodged a bullet. Anyway, I wanted you to know first. Before it makes the news."

Keaton leaned back again in his chair and blew out a long breath. "Wow, I was not expecting that. But thank you for coming to tell me. The rest of the family will be thrilled."

Tami let her eyes roam over him and felt that familiar tug of need deep in her chest. She wished things could have been different between them, but wishes weren't reality. She knew that only too well.

"Well," she said as she slowly rose to her feet. "That's all I wanted to say. Thank you for hearing me out. Don't bother getting up. I'll let myself out."

She felt his body heat behind her before she even got to the door.

"Tami?"

She hesitated, turned. This close she could see the silver striations in his eyes. She swallowed. There were bare inches between them. All she had to do was close the distance and she could kiss him. But that could never happen again. She'd betrayed him. He'd never want to build again on the camaraderie they'd shared during the outdoors experience, nor repeat that night they shared almost two weeks ago. Trust was all-important to him and he didn't believe he could trust her, even when she'd shown him that she wasn't the bad guy here. But she had entered his business with the intention of stealing information, and for that she would forever be filled with regret. She'd never counted on feeling like this about him. Never counted on wanting to love him.

"Yes?"

He took in a deep breath. Every part of her yearned to hear him ask her to stay. To say he'd forgiven her for her intentions. To say his feelings for her mirrored her own.

"Thank you for coming here today. I appreciate that you brought the news to me in person."

She deflated like a pricked balloon.

"Yeah, well, it was the right thing to do. I might have made some stupid decisions in my life, but I do always try to do good. Maybe you'll be able to find it in your heart to believe me and, in time, forgive me. Goodbye, Keaton."

Tami turned and fumbled for the door handle, then flinched as Keaton reached past her to open the door for her. She mumbled something that might have sounded like a thank-you, before heading back down the hall and to the elevator. She kept it together until she reached her car, and once she was inside, key in the ignition and doors locked, she let go all of the nerves and tension and, yes, even the tiny flicker of hope that had bloomed for an infinitesimal moment, and sobbed at the empty future that now faced her.

Twelve

Keaton couldn't get Tami out of his head. A part of him knew he needed to put this whole business behind him and take a stride forward into his future. Another part of him hung back, telling him he wasn't done here yet. And that part questioned his every thought and every decision. It was an unhealthy obsession, he told himself, and yet he couldn't stop the snippets of memory that would pop into his thoughts at any given time of the day or night. Even at his apartment, she invaded his thoughts. Not even his bedroom felt the same anymore.

If he was to be totally honest with himself, his life felt empty and he didn't like it one bit. He should be on top of the world, he told himself. They'd dodged a flaming arrow with the Tanner project and the new bid for the job Fletcher had initiated had been accepted. Everything was on the up. Logan and Honor had set a date for their wedding this coming summer, while his mom had booked the Palm Springs retreat with Hector. Even Kristin seemed marginally happier these days.

He'd thought it would be easy to move on without Tami in his sphere—after all, they'd only known each other a very short time—but somehow she'd inveigled her way into every nook and cranny of his mind. And, yeah, his heart, too, if he was going to be totally honest. It seemed Logan actually knew him better than he knew himself—in relation to Tami, at least.

He paced the floor with nervous energy. Today Mark Pennington was due to arrive on a flight from New Zealand to Los Angeles, and then catch the next available flight to Seattle. It turned out that the offer of a very lucrative contract to appear to manage the dispersal of twenty million dollars through several charities, but to filter the money instead into an offshore account and eventually distribute it between himself, Jones and Keaton, had been just the right enticement to get Pennington to risk his safe position in Nauru. Sure, he'd tried to avoid actually returning to US soil—saying he could do all that remotely— but an offer of an additional bonus apparently sweetened the deal enough for him to hop on a plane. Jones, the guy he'd hired from the private investigation firm and who'd visited Pennington in Nauru, would collect him from the airport and take him to a restaurant, where Keaton would join them as part of the sting. Keaton would be wired so everything Pennington said in their meeting could be recorded and, where possible, used to bring any additional charges against him.

Keaton checked his watch for the umpteenth time and realized it would be a good idea to head to the restaurant now. He'd be wired up there before the investigator and Pennington arrived. He used a driver to get him to the destination in Renton. The restaurant would have no other patrons this evening aside from a few plainclothes officers who would be involved in the arrest.

Security buzzed from downstairs to let him know his car and driver were waiting. Keaton was glad to finally be moving and became filled with a sense of purpose. He was doing this for Tami and for the charity that had been ripped off. Maybe once this was done he'd be able to draw a line under the whole experience and start afresh.

The restaurant was dimly lit and the offerings from the laminated menu leaned heavily on fried food. The tablecloth was none too clean, either, Keaton observed as he sat down at the table after being prepped by the technician with the trace equipment. One of the officers from the three small groups scattered around the restaurant rose and joined Keaton at the table.

"Jack Hima, pleased to meet you. Thanks for helping us out here," the man said, extending his hand.

Keaton took it and smiled. "Feels very cloak-and-dagger, doesn't it?"

"Sometimes you have to think like a rat to catch one."

"And this guy really is a rat."

Hima nodded. "We've done a little poking into his past. There are warrants for him under another name. He's a greedy bastard, all right. Likes the high life on other people's money. But don't worry, we'll get him this time and once we're done with him in Washington, he'll be facing charges in Oregon and Idaho as well."

It sounded like Pennington was a professional thief. It irked Keaton intensely that he hadn't been caught up until now. But his reign of abuse would end today and it gave Keaton no small amount of pleasure to know that. Tami hadn't stood a chance against a man like Pennington. She was the most open and accepting person Keaton had ever met. He only wished she hadn't agreed to spy on him for her father.

Hima slid his phone from his pocket and checked the screen. "Looks like they're almost here. I'll go back to my seat. Just remember, keep it business, as we coached you. A guy like this has a big ego. Hopefully, he'll trip himself up and give us more to hold against him before we make the arrest. If not, we'll take him down, anyway."

Keaton nodded and took a deep breath to calm the nerves that had begun to flutter in his stomach. He really wasn't cut out for this undercover stuff. He vastly preferred the cut and thrust of business to this kind of thing, which belonged in the shadows. He saw a movement at the main entrance to the restaurant and two men entered. The hostess, another plainclothes officer, he'd been told, showed them to his table. He rose, and even though it went against every honorable notion that had been drilled into him by his parents, he offered his hand to Pennington.

"Glad you could make it," he said.

He stared at the guy. Obviously he'd been traveling a long time, probably the better part of twenty-four hours not counting layovers. His clothing was disheveled, his eyes red-rimmed, and his hair stuck out as if he'd been running his hands through it several times. He kept looking around nervously, as if expecting someone to jump out of the woodwork at him. Which they would do, eventually, Keaton thought with satisfaction.

"Yeah, well, you made an interesting proposition. Let's get down to business."

He and the investigator sat at the table with Keaton, then the hostess came over with menus and filled water glasses.

"You hungry?" Keaton asked as he saw Pennington eye the menu thoroughly.

"Starved."

"Go ahead, order. It's on me," Keaton said with as much munificence as he could muster.

"Thanks, I will."

Pennington raised a hand and gestured for someone to come and take his order. He ordered a double order of fries and a triple decker burger with cheese sauce on everything, together with a beer.

"You ordering?" Pennington asked Keaton and the other man.

"No, I'm good. You?" Keaton asked the investigator.

"Just some coffee, thanks."

When the waitress had gone, Pennington sat forward on his chair and stared at Keaton.

"How did you find me?"

"You were hiding?" Keaton asked, avoiding the direct question.

Pennington grinned and Keaton got a glimpse of what he must look like when he wasn't jet-lagged. Yeah, the guy had a certain charm, which was obviously what had appealed to Tami. That and the fact they'd been working together for what she'd believed was the common good would have made him all the more likable as far as someone like her was concerned. An unexpected anger boiled up deep from inside Keaton and he forced himself to tamp it down. Pennington would get his just deserts.

"You could say that. I might have pissed off a few people."

Keaton smiled in return, remembering Hima's comment about trapping a rat by being like one. "That'd be the Our People, Our Homes board and management, I imagine."

"Oh, you heard about that?"

Pennington cast a considering look at Keaton and

looked uncomfortable for a moment. As if he was debating getting up and leaving. But Keaton kept his expression as bland as he could.

"I have my spies," Keaton said with a conspiratorial smile. "Nice work on that one."

The words tasted like sawdust in his mouth but they did the trick and Pennington relaxed in his seat again. A smug expression formed on his face.

"Yeah, that was a good one. With some interesting side benefits along the way," Pennington said with another grin, this one definitely heavy on the sleaze.

Side benefits? Was that how Pennington had viewed his relationship with Tami? Keaton forced himself not to make two fists and give the guy what he had coming to him.

"So, the side benefit. That would have been the woman you worked with?"

"Yeah. Nice enough, good body, but a bit too heavy on the good works and kindness for my liking. I prefer my women with a bit of mean in them."

"But mean is less malleable and a whole lot less trusting, right? You wouldn't have been able to fool a woman unless she trusted you."

"Sure, sure. Tami was a sweetheart. Enough to make your teeth rot, to be honest."

Again Keaton had to fight the urge to smash the guy into the next century. The way he spoke about Tami, the way he denigrated her. She deserved so much better than that.

"So she knew nothing about what you were doing?"

"Nah, of course not. If she'd had any idea she'd have gone straight to the police. What's it to you, anyway? That doesn't have anything to do with us."

"True, I was just wondering if you'd had help pulling

that off. If you had, I'd be withdrawing my offer. I don't want someone who needs someone else to make them successful. So tell me, with all you took from that charity you'd have been nicely set up in Nauru. What made my offer so attractive to you?"

Pennington shrugged. "Money is money, right? Can't ever have enough."

"And you have no scruples about how you get it?"

"None whatsoever."

The creep even looked proud of that fact.

"Sounds like you're just the kind of man I thought you were," Keaton said sardonically.

"I'm the man you want for the job, that's for sure. You give me those banking passwords and I can work wonders. Even split between the three of us, you said?"

Out of the corner of his eye, Keaton saw Hima and his partner rise from the table near them and walk over to Pennington. Hima put his hand firmly on Pennington's shoulder.

"Mark Pennington?"

"Hey, what's this?"

Pennington tried to rise from his seat but was firmly pushed back down by Hima, who was removing a set of cuffs from his belt.

"I'm arresting you in relation to the theft of two and a half millions dollars from the Our People, Our Homes charity." He continued to read Pennington his rights then helped him from the chair.

Pennington turned to Keaton, his face feral. "You bastard! This was a setup?"

"It was," Keaton said with no small amount of satisfaction. "And your disgusting greed allowed you to fall for it hook, line and sinker."

Hima's partner began to escort Pennington to the front

door, the other officers following in support. Hima stayed back a moment.

"Richmond, thanks for your help, and you, too, Jones." He shook both men's hands. "Let me get that gear off you and I'll be on my way."

Hima helped remove the wire from under Keaton's clothing.

"What's going to happen to him?" Keaton asked.

"He'll be charged and held pending a hearing. He's a flight risk so bail will be set high. A lot higher than what he'll have access to, anyway."

"And the money?"

"Steps are being taken to recover it as we speak. Eventually it'll be returned to the charity, but that'll take a while."

"Good, I'm glad to hear it," Keaton said.

After thanking Jones, he called a ride and traveled back to his apartment. By the time he arrived there, he was still pumped from the encounter. While not having actively enjoyed himself, there was an echoing sense of satisfaction in knowing he'd helped bring that thieving piece of work to justice. He hoped they threw the book at him. Stealing was bad enough, but stealing from a charity? That took a whole new level of low. And the way Pennington had unscrupulously used Tami was a burr under Keaton's skin. She deserved better than that. At least he'd helped clear her name with Our People, Our Homes.

That brought him to wondering how the charity would be able to continue to function without its operating capital until it was returned. He had no idea how long that would take. At least he knew that Tami would be cleared of any involvement. Pennington's words had fully exonerated her. And she'd know in due course. The police would be able to officially strike her from the investigation.

He wondered if that meant she'd stand a chance of getting a job back with them. Yes, she had breached their security process but it hadn't been a willful act and the funds would be returned, eventually. Maybe he could find out. Not that it was his business, but he wanted it to be. And he wanted to ensure that the charity didn't miss out, either. From his mother's work he knew how hard it was for these organizations to remain afloat unless they received grants. An idea began to percolate and he reached for his phone. It was time to pull out the big guns. His mom would know exactly what to do.

Tami set down the skein of lime-green yarn she'd offered to knit up for Keaton with a heart that felt as though it was made of lead. Try as she might, she couldn't bring herself to knit it up into a puppy jacket, despite that being her original intention. Keaton would have looked cute in one of her beanies, especially lime-green, she thought with a poignant smile.

Beside her, her mobile phone began to chirp. She recognized the number on the screen immediately. Our People, Our Homes. Who would be calling her from there, and why? She answered the call, surprised to hear the voice of the chairperson of the board on the other end.

"Tami, is that you?"

"Yes, Philippa. What can I do for you?"

"Well, actually this call is more about what we can do for you. First up, now that due processes have been followed with the investigation into yourself and Mark Pennington, we have reconsidered the termination of your employment."

"Reconsidered? We both know I was in breach of my employment and user agreements when I let Mark use my laptop."

The other woman made a shushing sound on the other end of the phone.

"That's true, your judgment regarding Mark Pennington was flawed, as was ours. However, we've received information from the police that clears you of any involvement in planning the theft of our operating funds."

"Seriously? That's fantastic!" Tami couldn't believe her ears. "How? What happened? Have you got the money back?"

Her questions tumbled one over the other and she heard Philippa laugh.

"I see you're still the same. It's good to know. We've missed you here. In answer to your questions, Mark was arrested three days ago and charged with theft. He's in custody. His statement to the police has cleared you from any wrongdoing."

"He came back? Why?"

"They didn't go into the exact details with me but they did say he was lured back in a sting operation. He had an ego, that man. He thought he could make it into the country and out again without the warrant for his arrest being activated."

"An offer?"

"Look, I don't know all the details, but suffice to say he's where he belongs, behind bars, and let's hope they keep him there for a very long time. Now, as to your last question, no, we don't have the money back, but we've been assured that after due process most of it will be returned to us. In the meantime, we've been granted a windfall from another source."

"How much of a windfall?"

"Five million dollars."

"Five—"

Tami's voice choked on the rest as emotion began to

overwhelm her. She blinked back the tears that burned in her eyes. This was incredible. What they could do with this would make such a difference to so many people. But then she remembered, she was no longer a part of Our People, Our Homes. She would be forced to watch from the sidelines rather than be a true participant in the many great projects they could fund with this much money.

"It was totally unexpected," Philippa continued, "but there was one condition attached to it."

"A condition?"

"That you be reinstated to your previous position. Obviously that would be without the banking access you previously held, but your role would essentially still be the same."

Tami stiffened. Who would make such a stipulation, and why? Having been used not once but twice, recently, Tami was wary of the offer.

"Who made the donation?" she asked carefully.

"We don't know. It's been handled by a legal firm and the donor does not wish their name to be known. We're not about to look a gift horse in the mouth, however, so I would like to formally and officially invite you back, Tami."

Would they have invited her back if that condition hadn't been attached to the donation? she wondered. She'd accepted they had to fire her before, when she'd looked guilty, but this offer to return being tied to a large donation put her between a rock and a hard place. She didn't want to go back if it meant her earlier mistake would mean they'd constantly be monitoring her over her shoulder. Trust, once broken, was hard to win back, as she knew only too well.

And then there was her trust fund to consider. She'd been considering transferring it to Our People, Our

Homes, anyway. She didn't need the money and she'd always wanted to do good with it rather than spend it on things that had no meaning to her. Just because she'd been exonerated from involvement with Mark's deception hadn't changed her desire to put that money to use where it would be most helpful.

"Tami?" Philippa prompted.

"I'd like to take a few days to think it over, if you don't mind."

"I understand," Philippa said. "Will you call me as soon as you've made your decision?"

"Of course."

Tami ended the call. She had a lot of thinking to do.

Thirteen

This was the kind of work that left her most fulfilled, Tami realized as she helped serve at the shelter she'd continued to volunteer at three nights a week. This was hands-on genuine support. All the administration she used to do had its purpose, but here she could really see and feel the difference she could make to someone else's life.

It was as different to her role at Richmond Developments as chalk was from cheese, and she didn't have to dress up in ridiculously expensive suits, either. Still, it had felt good, sometimes, to make that extra effort, especially when she'd seen a gleam of approval in Keaton's eyes. She clamped down on that thought as quickly as it hovered in the periphery of her mind. She couldn't allow herself to go down that road. She'd been doing so well in terms of getting on with her life. And, while she hadn't made her decision yet about whether or not to return to her role at Our People, Our Homes, she'd managed to keep busy with her volunteer work. By day she'd helped at the animal shelter, losing her heart to each and every abandoned dog or cat who'd been brought in. It was a no-kill shelter, but even so it was still, at times, heartbreaking work. And her evenings were either spent here or at home furiously working her needles and yarn into garments to donate.

But Tami knew all of this was merely a stopgap. She'd have to make a decision soon. She focused her attention back to passing out bread rolls to go with the stew that was on offer for dinner tonight. It was simple fare, but hearty. Tami smiled at the man in front of her. She only knew him as George, and knew he slept in doorways at night. Recently, he'd developed a hacking cough that worried her deeply. He'd refused medical help, but she was determined to try again to persuade him to attend a clinic. She was about to say something, but all of a sudden she felt a shift in the air. Several heads turned to the newcomer at the door.

All the hairs on the back of Tami's neck stood to attention and she slowly followed everyone's gaze. Keaton. She blinked, as if, after thinking about him and conjuring him out of thin air, she thought she could rid herself of his image on her retinas, but no, there he was and he was walking toward her.

"Expecting company?" George asked.

"No, I'm not."

"Looks like he's here to see you," the old man said with a raspy chuckle that set him off on another bout of coughing.

"George, you really need to let me take you to the clinic to get that cough seen to."

"Nah, I'll be fine."

He took his tray and turned away from her to join a group at one of the tables. Tami watched him as he settled down to eat. At least he still had an appetite, she observed. She turned back to the line of people waiting to be served and was shocked to see Keaton standing square in front of her.

"Why haven't you taken your old job back?" he demanded.

"What? No 'hello'? 'How are you, Tami?'" she responded and directed her attention to the young girl standing next to him and offered her a roll.

"Tami, please. Answer the question."

Slowly, it dawned on her that he must be behind the five million dollar donation. But why? A whole lot of questions burned on her tongue but she couldn't deal with this right now.

"I'm busy right now. If you want to talk to me, see if you can find yourself something to do and when my shift is ended, if you can wait that long, we'll talk."

"Fine," he answered in a clipped tone. "What can I do?"

Tami looked around, spying a small family who'd appeared with the newcomers this evening. They were seated against the wall, as if trying to be as inconspicuous as possible.

"Over there," she said, and nodded. "Jerome and his daughters need a hand. He can't feed both of them and himself at the same time. Go help him."

She was surprised when Keaton did just that.

"Miss, may I have a roll, please?"

An older lady, whose well-fitting fine woolen coat suggested she may have known better times, interrupted her and drew her attention back to her duty here. It grew busier from then on and it wasn't until the kitchen closed and she'd gone out back to help with the cleanup that she thought about Keaton again. When she came back into the main room, there he still was sitting by Jerome and with a sleeping one-year-old nestled in his arms. A group of men and women had gathered around them, all listening intently to whatever it was he was saying, but the instant he looked up and saw her standing in the kitchen doorway he said something to Jerome and handed off the baby back to her daddy.

Tami watched him as he walked toward her and she felt a frisson of awareness track down her spine. There was a lean, confident, animal grace to the way he moved and she wasn't the only one noticing it. There were appreciative glances from several of the people there.

"Are you free to talk now?" he asked.

"Thank you for staying with Jerome. It's his first night at the shelter. His wife died of influenza this winter and he lost his job because he had to stay home and care for the kids. And with the loss of his job they lost their accommodation, too. The baby, Lucy, has asthma and he's terrified she'll get sick."

"Do you know everything about all the people here?" he asked, cocking his head slightly.

"It's my business to know their business, Keaton. How can I best help them if I don't understand where they're coming from?"

"Good point. And, as to Jerome, I've offered him work on a small local restoration project that Logan's team is managing. Did you know he's a cabinetmaker by trade? He showed me photos of some of his work on his phone. We're always looking for craftsmen of his caliber. There's a reputable day-care facility nearby where he can leave the girls and I've offered him an advance on wages so he can secure accommodation for them all somewhere near to the project."

She was stunned. All that in one evening?

"Did he accept?"

"He did—he seemed excited about it. From what he's saying, it's the first time in a long time they've had something to look forward to." He looked back at Jerome, who was talking and smiling with the people around him. "I see what you mean about not just throwing money at a situation. You were right. People need the opportunity to take ownership of their lives."

"Not everyone wants assistance," Tami said softly, seeing the light of zeal in Keaton's eyes that was common in those new to volunteering. "But it's wonderful you could offer constructive help to someone who really needs it to get back on his feet."

"Which takes me back to my original question to you. Why haven't you taken your old job back?"

"That donation is from you?"

"Not me, personally, but our foundation, yes."

"Why put strings on it? If you were so moved as to make such a huge contribution to Our People, Our Homes, why put all the responsibility of whether they receive the money, or not, back on to my shoulders. To be honest, a donation with a condition is not a donation at all, is it? It's a manipulation and I won't be manipulated. I've been there, I've jumped through other people's hoops and I don't like it. I'm my own person. I make my own decisions. I will not be coerced."

She realized the shelter had grown silent as her voice had grown louder and everyone around them was staring. It didn't matter, she thought, as her cheeks flamed. The words needed to be said. A slow clap started at the back of the room, soon joined by more and more people applauding. The tips of Keaton's ears turned red and he turned to raise one hand in acknowledgement and silent apology for what they'd overheard.

"Look, can we talk somewhere that's a little more private? You've misinterpreted my intentions."

"Really? And tell me, what were your intentions?"

"Please, Tami. Somewhere private?"

"Go on, Tami, give the guy a break. He looks pretty and he smells nice," one of the older female regulars said from behind Keaton.

"You think so?" Tami answered with a wry grin. "You can have him if you want him, Sally. He's single."

The woman cackled in response. "Hell, no. Too high-maintenance for me!"

Tami saw Keaton's shoulder sag in relief and she couldn't help but grin. To give him credit, at least he hadn't run for the door, yet.

"Okay," she relented. "There's a coffee shop around the corner. Would that do?"

Keaton looked at her. "Are you all finished up here?"

"Yes, why?"

"How were you planning to get home?"

"Parking here is difficult so I took a bus. I was going to call a ride to get home."

"Why don't I see you home? We can talk there."

Tami mulled over his suggestion. What difference did it make, in the long run? She'd say what she had to say, and he'd hopefully listen. Then he'd go away again. She wondered how many more times her heart would have to be torn apart by this man, by either leaving him or watching him leave her.

"Fine. Let's go then."

She grabbed her coat and followed him out the door after bidding everyone good-night. They walked a short distance in the dark, wet streets to where he'd parked his car under a streetlight.

"You were lucky to get a spot here," she commented as he held the door open for her.

"I had to drive around the block a few times, but I was prepared to wait. I needed to see you."

Tami merely grunted a noncommittal response and busied herself putting on her seat belt as Keaton closed her door and got in on the other side. They didn't speak as they drove out to her home on the outskirts of town, and after they alighted from the car Keaton followed her down the path to her front door. Once they were inside she led him to her small sitting room and gestured for him to take a seat.

"Can I offer you anything? Tea? Coffee?"

"No, thank you, please just sit with me." When she'd settled on an easy chair he continued. "Look, you got me all wrong on the donation. I know you lost your position at Our People, Our Homes because of Pennington and your involvement with him. I just wanted to ensure that they made your job available to you again now that your name is cleared."

"How did you know that my name is cleared?" she asked.

He firmed his lips a moment before speaking again. "I was involved in the sting that brought Pennington back to the States. A man like that is motivated by money, lots of money, so with the help of the police, I dangled an obscene sum in front of him as bait and he fell for it."

"But why would you do that? You had nothing to do with him, or the charity. What did you stand to gain?"

"Nothing, personally. But you stood to gain your reputation back. You deserved to have your name cleared of all and any guilt or suspicion."

She looked at him in surprise and shook her head slowly. "That's not what you thought a short while back. May I remind you of the damages claim your company has against me?"

"Our lawyers have been instructed to drop it. You should get confirmation on that from your lawyer tomorrow. I was so angry with you for what you'd done to us at Richmond Developments I was determined to make you pay. That said, it was unfair of me to treat you the way I did and not to listen or try to understand why you were forced to do what you did. I understand that now and I plan to try harder to listen first before jumping to conclusions. I hope you can help me with that and that you'll find it in your very warm and generous heart to forgive me for my behavior."

"Warm and generous?"

"I've watched you, Tami. I know that at your core you are the most incredible, beautiful, loving woman I think I've ever known. And you're like that with everyone you meet. Whether it's the people at the shelter, or your work colleagues, or even a total stranger in the street. You exude warmth and caring. You deserve far better than the way Mark Pennington treated you, or the way I treated you. That's why I wanted you to get your old job back and I wanted them to have sufficient motivation to ensure they took you back. I understand how shaky things were there financially after the money was stolen and while most of what Pennington stole will be returned to them, it's going to take time. Time they probably did not have. So the Richmond Foundation took up the slack. That's all. Putting a proviso on the donation was for your sake, not to manipulate you, but to give you back what was taken from you."

"Five million dollars is a lot of slack, Keaton."

"We looked further into the charity. It does really good things, but like all charities they're hamstrung by financial constraints. We think we've found a way forward where we can possibly use some of our construction as a method of providing the low-cost, low-interest housing you discussed with me in Sedona, and provide jobs for skilled workers on hard times. Working with Our People, Our Homes is a viable way for us to do this."

"That's really great news, and I'll give serious consideration to resuming my old role. I miss it. But I'm not sure it's the right thing to do."

"Well, you could always come back and work with me," he said with a smile.

"No, I couldn't. I don't want to go anywhere where people will always be second-guessing my integrity."

Keaton looked at her as comprehension dawned. For the first time he really understood the toll this entire chain of events, started by that lowlife Pennington, had taken on her. She was right. Because of Pennington, her integrity had been grossly undermined, and he'd added to that.

"Tami, I'm so sorry."

"Don't you see, Keaton. In forcing Our People, Our Homes to take me back, I'll never know whether I'm there because I'm worth it, or because you made them do it. I know you think you were trying to help, but you've only made it worse for me."

"I was trying to help," he insisted. "And we can certainly make the donation unconditional."

But he knew it was too late. The damage was done. And, considering the way Pennington and her father and who knew who else had treated her, he knew why it was so important to Tami to feel valued. Another idea took shape in his mind.

"I have a suggestion and I want you to consider it carefully before giving me an answer."

"More manipulation, Keaton?" she asked wearily.

"No, an opportunity for something new. The Richmond Foundation, Our People, Our Homes and Richmond Developments will need someone to act as the coordinator for the new affordable-homes initiative. I don't see why that shouldn't be you, if you wanted the role. It would give you the opportunity to expand on the organizational skills you've already proven you excel at, while allowing you the hands-on involvement with the people you're so passionate about caring for. You're far better-suited to that position than anyone we could appoint internally from Richmond."

Her expression changed and he saw a glow of hope light up in those beautiful hazel eyes of hers.

"You'd offer that to me?" she asked, still sounding unsure. "But you have no reason to trust me. We both know that."

Keaton sat forward in his chair and reached for her hands, holding them both in his, then stared directly into her eyes.

"I understand why you did what you did, Tami. And I forgive you, totally and absolutely. I'll admit, it took me a while—too long a while, to be honest—but I know now it was your compassionate heart that led you to take the steps you did. I'm sorry you were forced to do that. I'm sorry your father used you that way and I'm sorry that a man like Pennington put you in a position where you felt you had to turn to your father for help."

"None of that was your fault," she said, pulling back.

He felt the loss of her touch as if she'd slammed a door in his face, but he wasn't going to give up. Not yet, maybe not ever.

"No, but my reaction to the situation could definitely have been better. I did what I could to bring Pennington to justice, for you, Tami."

"But, why?"

"Because…" Keaton took her hands again. "I would have done the same thing for any person that I loved. I had to bring Pennington back to the US no matter the cost because of what he'd done to you and to Our People, Our Homes. He had to pay for what he's done and he will pay, dearly. You weren't his first mark, Tami, and you wouldn't have been his last. He had to be stopped. Anyway, that's what I needed to say. I'll go now. But, please, think about my offer, okay?"

He got up and began to walk toward the front door, but stopped when he felt Tami's hand on his shoulder. He turned around. There was an incredulous expression on her face.

"Did you just say you love me?"

He smiled. "Well, yeah. I love you, Tami Wilson. More than I'll ever be able to express in words, so I had to do it with actions. Will you forgive me for being so arrogant about everything? For not listening? For not trusting what my own eyes had told me about you? For not trying to understand you better?"

"Of course, I forgive you, Keaton, not that I believe I have anything to forgive you for—you are exactly who you are and I love you for all of it. I think I've loved you since you were so patient with me on the tandem zip line and taught me then to trust you. Knowing what my father wanted me to do to Richmond Developments tore me up inside, all the more so because I continued to learn about what an incredible man you are. Intelligent, mostly patient, strong and kind. And, I have it on good authority that you smell good, too," she said with a chuckle.

"Mostly patient?" he asked with a crooked smile.

"You know what I mean," she said.

Tami slipped her arms around his waist and cuddled in close for a moment before stepping back and taking his face in her hands and gently pulling him down toward her. He needed no encouragement. He'd been craving her taste, her touch, from the second he'd woken on the morning after they'd first made love. The morning he'd sent her out of his life. Their lips met, sealed and ignited a conflagration of need inside him. Her also, judging by the enthusiasm with which she returned the embrace.

He pressed her up against a closed door and lifted her hands above her head, stepping in so close to her that his hips met with hers. He pressed against her and felt her groan into his mouth. He dragged his lips from hers and burned a trail of kisses from her mouth to her jaw, then down her neck.

"Bedroom," she growled in a hoarse voice. "Behind me, the door, open it."

He didn't need to be told twice. Keaton twisted the doorknob and pushed open the door to the darkened room, then turned around so she could walk him backward toward the bed. As he did so, she began to reach for the buttons on his shirt, the buckle of his belt, his zipper. By the time they reached her bed, he was more than half-naked and he kicked off his shoes and shucked off the last of his clothing before helping her off with her jeans and the soft sweater she wore.

There were no niceties about their urgency. Only need, demand, give-and-take. She pushed him back onto the bed and straddled him. He reached for her breasts, cupping them in his hands and squeezing gently. Her thighs tightened around his and he felt the wet heat of her body against his skin. He squeezed her breasts again, this time pulling gently at her nipples with his thumbs and fore-fingers, and was rewarded with a moan that seemed to come from deep inside her.

Tami bent down then, and began a thorough explora-tion of his body. Taking her time to nuzzle and lick and kiss and, yes, bite her way from his neck to his abdomen. When she got to his belly button, she looked up at him with a wicked grin.

"Sally's right. You do smell good. *All* of you smells good."

He laughed but it was a strangled sound. "Can we please leave Sally out of the bedroom?"

She chuckled again and Keaton decided he could very well get drunk on the sound. "I will if you will."

She bent her head again and took his erection into her mouth. His entire body started in reflex to the warm, wet shock of her possession of him. He forced himself to relax, to enjoy, to give in to the sensations she wrought from him, and when he climaxed, she took that from him, too. Taking her time to give him the deepest of pleasures while he ached to give her her own.

She shifted again so her body was over his and he wrapped his arms around her tight. Right now, he never wanted to let her go, ever again. He knew that this was more than a fleeting kind of love. This was something he wanted, with her, forever. They stayed together like that until he felt his heart rate return to normal, until he felt his body stir to life again. He rolled her over and hovered over her, returning the pleasure she'd given him, taking his time to savor the very special taste of her skin, the heat of her body, the texture of every inch of her.

Tami was squirming beneath him when he felt her reach for the top drawer on her bedside cabinet. She dragged it open and grabbed a foil packet from inside.

"Now, Keaton. Please. No more playing around. I want you, inside me. Filling me. Loving me."

"Of course. Whatever you want. Always."

He sheathed himself and positioned himself at her entrance, then forced himself to take it slowly, entering her body and feeling her welcome him, inch by slow inch. When he was buried to the hilt he stopped, allowed them both to relish the depth of their connection. Her arms were up, her hands beside her head, and he laced his fingers with hers and bent down to kiss her. A long, wet, thorough kiss that left them both breathless.

"I love you, Tami Wilson. I'm going to love you for the rest of my life," he promised solemnly.

And then he began to move. At first slowly and then, as his movements stoked the flames of their desire, faster and faster until, in a swoop of pleasure, they reached their peak together. Exhilaration flooded him and he felt her body's reaction to the joy they'd just given one another. Felt the pulse that beat through her, felt her shake and buck gently beneath him until her body suddenly relaxed and he allowed himself to settle into her before gently rolling them both onto their sides.

He looked at her in the semidark. The room lit only by the light from the hallway. Both of them panting. He could feel the light sheen of perspiration on her body and tracked the shape of her face with one hand.

"I mean it, Tami. I love you more than I ever knew was possible. Will you help me to grow our relationship into something that will last both our lifetimes?"

She reached a shaking hand to cup his face and closed the small distance between them to kiss him.

"Keaton Richmond, I'd be honored to do that with you. Yes, my answer is, yes. To everything. To spending the rest of my life with you, to loving you forever. To being the example to our children that they will deserve."

"Our kids, I like the sound of that." He kissed her back. "The day I saw you in the office for the first time, I wondered what the hell I was letting myself in for. Now I know. Thank you for remaining true to who you are and I promise I will remain true to you every day I draw breath."

"Oh, Keaton, thank you. I will treasure your words, and you, for the rest of my days."

"I never realized it until you came into my life, that you're all I ever wanted," he said solemnly. "I guess I should thank your father for that."

She laughed and he felt her whole body shake.

"Yeah, I don't think so. I'd like to imagine we'd have come to each other eventually."

"Yeah," he agreed and tightened his arms around her some more. "I can't wait to see what our future brings."

"It's going to be like our zip line ride," she murmured, snuggling into his chest and inhaling deeply. "Challenging, a little bit terrifying, but overall it's going to be absolutely amazing."

And it was.

* * * * *

ONE NIGHT WITH CINDERELLA

NIOBIA BRYANT

For all the romance readers who have supported
my career these last twenty-one years.
Cheers to a new romance!

One

"One day I hope I'm as rich as I look right now."

Monica Darby turned this way and that in the full-length, wood-framed mirror leaning against the wall of the spacious walk-in closet. The bright crimson of the couture gown she held in front of her body was so different from the dark tones she normally wore. With her free hand, she gathered her ponytail atop her head and sucked in her cheeks as she struck a dramatic model-like pose.

She felt like a little girl playing dress-up.

In the reflection, she caught sight of the price tag dangling from the sleeve. She checked it, not surprised to see it cost nearly a fourth of her annual salary. It was one of five extravagant garments delivered that morning. Each more glamorous and decadent than the last.

Monica imagined what it would be like to own such

beautiful clothing, live in a luxurious home and jet all over the world at a whim.

Only in my dreams.

She reached up to hang the dress among the other expensive gowns, fearing being caught having a brief moment of folly into a lifestyle in which she lived on the fringe as the housekeeper to the powerful Cress family—a position she cherished because, in their home, she had found the stability she lacked growing up in foster care. With one last glance back at the closet to ensure it was pristine and in order, she turned and left the space, closing the French doors behind her.

Her sneaker-covered feet barely made any noise against the herringbone pattern of the polished hardwood floors as she crossed the suite to retrieve the caddie of her cleaning supplies. "Eight suites down and the kitchen to go," Monica said to herself before leaving the room and entering the spacious den that centered the top-floor hall of the five-story town house in the prominent and historic Lenox Hill section of Manhattan's Upper East Side.

The ten-thousand-square-foot home was quiet as she made her way to the elevator. She was the only in-house staff. The chef was out shopping, and all of the Cress family members were gone for the day. She had the peace she needed to clean without intrusion.

When the lift came to a stop, she opened the wrought-iron gate and stepped on, pulling the rolling caddie behind her before pressing the button for the finished basement level, where the items not sent out for dry cleaning were awaiting laundering. Her bedroom was located there, as well.

Ding.

She frowned when the elevator slowed. She thought she was alone and clearly, she was wrong. Her eyes widened

as it came to a stop on the fourth floor and she was looking through the bronzed wrought iron at Gabriel Cress,
known to everyone as Gabe. The middle son of Phillip
and Nicolette Cress was busy looking down at his iPhone.
She licked her lips as she stepped back until her spine was
pressed to the wall and lowered her head. Her heart raced
and thundered inside her chest so crazily that she feared
he would hear it.

He looked up briefly and nodded his head at seeing her.
"Mornin'," he said, his voice deep and obligatory, as the
wrought-iron gate squealed a bit at being opened.

Her pulse pounded. "Good morning, Mr. Cress," she
said, her voice soft as she kept her eyes on the tip of the
sensible black sneakers she wore.

This gorgeous man made her so *very* nervous.

Monica wished she could fold herself into a much
smaller version or fade into the woodwork lining the walls.
Not that it mattered. She chanced a fleeting look up. He
stood off to the side in front of her with his attention still
focused on the screen of his phone. He barely noticed her.
She was used to that. Men such as Gabe Cress—strong,
handsome, sexy, wealthy and confident—were drawn to
women so very unlike Monica the Housekeeper, with her
all-black uniform and face free of makeup.

She let her eyes study his profile.

He was a handsome man with a strong resemblance to
the actor Jesse Williams. Shortbread complexion. Grayish-
blue eyes. Square jaw and high cheekbones. Soft mouth.
Short haircut with just the shadow of a beard. Tall—over
six feet—with an athletic frame that was well defined and
perfectly dressed in a crisp navy shirt tucked into dark
denims with a cognac belt and polished handmade shoes.
It was his signature outfit, seemingly simple but still stylish and tailored.

It had been five years since she was hired by his mother, Nicolette, but she still had not got used to him. Or the scent of his cologne. The warm and spicy scent reached her without being loud and cloying. It made her tingle.

All of the five Cress sons were handsome, but it was only Gabe that sent her into a tizzy. Only him.

Grab a hold of yourself, Monica.

For her, being enclosed with him in the elevator was like standing in the open doorway of a plane before spreading her arms wide and leaping to feel that quick shift from nervous anticipation to the sweet glory of free-falling through the air.

He was overwhelming without even trying to be so.

The elevator slid to a smooth stop and he slipped his phone into the back pocket of his denims before opening the gate. He offered her a brisk, congenial nod as he strode away.

She released the breath she must have been holding, finding it shaky as she closed her eyes and lightly bit down on her bottom lip as she awaited recovery. She was used to it. The man just did *it* for her. She couldn't explain it. It was quite unfamiliar. And she didn't even want to want him.

But there *it* was.

That spark.

"Gabe and Monica sitting in a tree. He's I-G-N-O-R-I-N-G me," she said dryly before allowing herself a self-deprecating little chuckle as the elevator continued its descent to the basement.

Not that she wanted the attention of him or any other man. As far as she was concerned, love spelled nothing but a bunch of trouble.

She enjoyed her life of solitude. She spent her days keeping the family's home organized and tidy before retiring to her maid quarters and enjoying a night of television or reading. She felt safe from the disappointment and hurt she'd felt all her life growing up in the foster care system, never feeling at home or fitting in...and wondering why her parents didn't want her for themselves.

Monica pushed away the all-too-familiar pain she felt at being abandoned, thankful time had dulled it to just an ache. She shook her head a little as she stepped off the elevator into the basement, moving past the wine cellar, storage room and utility closet—every area grander than the next. She refused to give her unknown parents that type of power over her life—just as she had the numerous social workers, case managers and foster families she encountered as she was shifted from various group homes and foster families throughout her childhood.

She did not emotionally invest in anyone.

Love had let her down one time too many.

Look how my last relationship turned out.

As she rolled the caddie into the closet where she kept some of her cleaning supplies, she paused with her hand on the door. Remembering him.

James.

She rolled her eyes and shook her head, wishing life had rewind and delete buttons.

Once she aged out of the system at eighteen when the government deemed her an adult, Monica had been lucky enough to attend a community college and acquire a studio apartment, relying on school grants, loans and a part-time job to pay her way. Times had been tough and lean. Never had she felt so afraid that she wouldn't be able to make it on her own but also so determined to enjoy her freedom. She had been a student there for two years when she'd met and fallen in love with James Gilligan, a handsome travel photographer who convinced her to drop out of college and go RVing across the country with him as he documented his adventures on his popular blog. Leaving school had been a huge choice, but she felt she finally had someone who loved her and hadn't dared to risk losing him. Their travels and nomadic lifestyle lasted five years, filled with fun and spontaneity, until they traveled back to New York for a brief visit and she awakened one morning to discover he had left her behind to search for his next quest without her.

Monica grunted at her foolishness, hating how heartache and betrayal had left such an imprint. It'd been five years since she'd had to gather her wits, put aside her tears and make a new plan for her life. The advertisement for an in-house staff position had seemed like an answer to her prayers, providing a job and a place to stay. She applied and then thankfully accepted the position when it was offered.

Once she had work to focus on, she resolved to never give someone the chance to hurt her and leave her behind again.

Like her parents.

Like so many foster parents.

Like James.

Monica sighed as that poignant ache of bitter disappointment radiated across her chest. His treachery still affected her. She hated that so much.

She closed the door to the supply closet and moved over to open the door to the stylish and brightly lit laundry room, where she loaded two high-capacity washers with bed linen that she changed every day. While the machines quietly went to work, she walked to the other end of the basement to her quarters. It was a lovely little suite comprised of a bedroom, adjoining bathroom and small sitting area. She'd decorated the area in shades of yellow to give it more warmth, make it feel a little bit like her own, since it was the longest she'd ever been in one residence.

She pulled a small stack of envelopes from the front

pocket of her apron to put on the side table near the recliner to sort through later. The family's mail was left on an ostrich leather tray in the foyer, as was customary. Leaving her room, she closed the door and retraced her steps until she reached the stairs to make her way up to the modern and brightly lit kitchen on the first level. The space, with its dark wood against light walls, chrome appliances and bronzed fixtures, was as beautifully designed as the rest of the town house.

The family's chef, Jillian Rossi, was out doing her daily shopping, and Monica always used that time to clean the kitchen from what little mess was left over from the family's breakfast dishes. Before loading the dishwasher, she opened it to find the high-end cutlery she knew belonged to Jillian from the initials engraved on the handles. She spotted the chef's leather carry case on the granite counter and retrieved it, undid the clasp and unrolled it.

A handwritten note was inside.

"'The taste of you still lingers on my tongue,'" she read aloud.

Well, well, well, Jillian...

Monica furrowed her brow as she rolled the carry case back as it had been, wishing she'd never seen the note—or the embossed gold Cress, INC. logo at the top. In such a large, affluent family, whose members chose to do business *and* live together, secrets weren't scarce. She'd seen and heard plenty in her five years. Hidden safes. Vices. Stubborn grudges. Business deals. Promises made. Promises broken. Even two of the brothers unknowingly dating the same sexy socialite. Discovering that one of the Cress men was enjoying a secret tryst with Jillian the Chef—complete with a handwritten note in this day and age—was light work in comparison.

It was none of her business, but Monica couldn't help but wonder which one.

Phillip Jr.? Or Sean? Cole? Maybe Lucas?

She winced as she pictured Gabe passionately kissing Jillian. She had no right to the jealousy warming her stomach. If Gabe and Jillian were secret lovers then it was no concern of hers.

Right?

Right.

Still, at that moment, it was feeling easier said than done.

Gabe stroked his chin as he stared at the waterfall fountain at the end of the paved garden area. Winter was just truly beginning to break and the air was crisp and refreshing instead of biting and chilly. He sat at the long concrete table beneath the arched framework that covered the full thirty-two-foot length of the area with the leaves of bamboo trees offering the family privacy and shade when they were outdoors. The sounds of New York on the adjacent busy Lexington Avenue reached him, but it was vague background noise as he focused instead on his thoughts.

Serving as the president of the restaurant division of Cress, INC. made him responsible for making decisions that produced results. Phillip Cress Sr., his stalwart father and the company's chief executive officer, expected nothing less and made that fact clear with all of his sons. Gabe was a strong-willed man with his own vision and ideas, but he had little patience. He was finding it tiresome proving himself worthy to a domineering father who expected nothing but blind allegiance.

Gabe wished his father knew his loyalty to his family existed because he loved his parents and his brothers above all and would do anything to see them happy. Making sacrifices wasn't new. Gabe had always tried so very hard to be unproblematic for his parents. With five rowdy boys and a busy professional life that had led to stellar careers, his parents hadn't needed an extra hassle. Another child to discipline. Another child to worry about. It had become his custom to keep his head tucked down, stick to himself and never disappoint the parents he admired. The accomplishments of his parents could not be overlooked or disrespected.

Phillip Cress Sr. and Nicolette Lavoie-Cress loved cooking second only to their five sons. Over the past fifty years they had established themselves as acclaimed and well-respected chefs, won Michelin stars and James Beard Awards, established many successful restaurants, and written more than two dozen bestselling cookbooks and culinary guides. As they began to slow down, the couple increasingly focused on growing the powerful culinary empire of Cress, INC. and diversifying their business to nationally syndicated cooking shows, cookware, online magazines, an accredited cooking school, which Nicolette operated, and a nonprofit foundation.

The couple had also passed their love of cooking on to their sons, who were all acclaimed chefs in their own right. Each son also played a role in the business. Gabe headed up the restaurant division. His oldest brother, Phillip Jr., ran the nonprofit, the Cress Family Foundation. Sean supervised the syndicated cooking shows. Cole oversaw the online magazines and websites. And their baby brother, Lucas, had just been appointed head of the cookware line.

But now Phillip Sr. was looking to one of them to groom as his successor to the Cress, INC. throne, and each of the Cress sons wanted the coveted prize of leading the family business into the future. And to have their father, who they all respected, give such a nod would be the ultimate testament and acknowledgment of their abilities. Still, it made for competitiveness and minor flare-ups among the brothers, which Gabe was finding tiresome. They had always been raised to be loving and loyal to one another. With each passing day, sadly, he saw less of that allegiance.

At times working and living together was a handful. Thus, his day of working from home and not at their corporate offices in Midtown Manhattan. He needed a breather. Of everyone in the family, he hated useless confrontations and arguing the most. He found it tedious.

His stomach grumbled, and he picked up his phone from where it sat atop his open files on the table. It was nearing lunch and he had skipped breakfast. Rising, he slid his phone in the front pocket of his tailored shirt, moved down the length of the garden and opened the sliding door of the glass wall of the dining room.

Across the dining room he spotted their housekeeper, Monica, closing the dishwasher and pressing the buttons to turn it on before she briskly walked over to the pantry. He hadn't seen her moving about the kitchen when he was in the garden, but he wasn't surprised. She was a great housekeeper, who they all trusted with their home and possessions, but she also made sure not to intrude on their lives. She barely spoke and rarely made eye contact. She was…skittish.

This morning in the elevator, if she had pressed her body back against the wall any more, she could have melded with it. It's why he hadn't bothered with much conversation. He hadn't been sure she wouldn't jump out of her own skin if he said too much.

Five years, and he doubted he'd spoken more than a dozen words to her in all that time.

Reaching the kitchen, Gabe opened the Sub-Zero to study the many contents for something to feed his hunger. He was almost tempted to prepare his own favorite dish of homemade ravioli stuffed with a mixture of wild mushroom, ricotta and parmesan cheese served in a bisque. Almost. It had been nearly three years since he departed his role as the head chef of the Midtown Manhattan CRESS restaurant. Cress, INC. came first. Gabe hardly ever cooked that much anymore. In fact, no one in the family did. There wasn't time. Thus, the need for a family of chefs to have a chef on staff to cook for them.

With the release of a deep breath he acknowledged how much he missed being a chef. That alone was the clearest example of his loyalty to his family and his desire to help his parents further their dreams of a culinary empire.

"Oh. Sorry."

He closed the door a bit and looked over his shoulder at Monica, standing in the entry to the pantry. Her eyes were wide with surprise before she looked down at the cleaning supplies she held in her hands.

"Jillian's not here, Mr. Cress," she said, her words rushed. Awkward.

He frowned. "Jillian? Do I need her permission to enter the kitchen?" he asked sternly, giving her an odd look before turning back to the fridge and removing a container of leftover ginger-lime carrots and another of seared scallops.

"No…no. Of course not. I just thought you were looking for her. Just…never mind," she said, shaking her head as she set the supplies on the counter and began walking out of the room.

Annoyance sparked in him. *This is ridiculous.*

"Have I done something to offend you or make you so uneasy around me?" he asked, feeling as if she saw him as a wolf about to jump on his prey.

Of that, she shouldn't worry. This shy and reserved woman unable to look him in the eye was hardly his type.

He was tempted by fire and confident sex appeal. She appeared afraid of her own shadow.

Monica whirled, her face filled with her surprise. "Of course not, Mr. Cress," she insisted.

Gabe was surprised by the sudden knot in his gut as he eyed the rare show of emotion she displayed. The first he'd seen in five years. It opened her face. Brought life and light to it. And interest. For the first time, he noticed she was pretty. If by instinct his eyes quickly took in all of her. A man studying a woman.

She favored Zoe Saldana. Medium brown complexion. Long dark brown hair pulled into a loose ponytail that emphasized her high cheekbones and doe-shaped eyes with long lashes. Beneath her black T-shirt and pants, he could tell she was tall and slender but curvy. He even found the flat mole near the corner of her left eye intriguing.

He wondered just what other emotion she hid beneath the surface. Passion? Desire? Pleasure? Satisfaction?

How would her face be transformed during her climax? Dazed eyes? Gaped mouth?

The thought of that caused his heart to skip a beat, as temptation rose with a quickness.

Easy, Gabe. Easy.

"I just wanted to make sure I've never done anything to make you uncomfortable with me," he said, setting aside the allure of a subdued woman with hints of fire beneath the surface—a taste in women he had never known himself to have before.

She looked at him and visibly swallowed over a lump in her throat. "No. Never," she assured him, her voice soft.

No. Not soft. Husky. Throaty.

Well, well, well. Who knew?

"I don't want to interrupt your schedule," Gabe said, crossing the kitchen to retrieve a plate from the glass-paned cabinet she stood beside. "I'm just getting some lunch because I'm working from home today."

She stepped back from his sudden nearness.

He frowned a bit as he looked down at her. Their eyes met for a brief moment before she looked away. She had to be close to his age of thirty-two, so her nervousness piqued his curiosity. "Monica," he said, his voice low.

She looked up at him. "Sir?" she said, wringing her hands together in front of her.

Oh.

Her truth was in the depths of her doe-shaped eyes.

Gabe was a man quite familiar with women. As a chef he was a connoisseur of wine, needing the right accoutrement to the food he created. His experience with women reached the same expert level. Standing before him was a woman made nervous because she liked him. Was aware of him. Desired him.

Of *that* he was sure.

His body warmed over at the thought of her interest. He cleared his throat and moved back across the kitchen to plate his food before warming it in the microwave.

Bzzzzzz.

He reached for his vibrating phone and checked the caller ID. It was an old acquaintance calling. Felicity. He thought of the tall and shapely beauty with big eyes, lips and thighs, but didn't answer the call. It had been weeks since they'd spent time together, and he wasn't interested in striking up a new round of their on-again, off-again dalliance. She'd wanted nothing more than access to his upscale lifestyle, and he'd been satisfied with beautiful arm candy who was very eager to do nothing more than keep a smile on his face. Her first not-so-subtle hint of marriage had cooled his ardor.

Gabe was as adamant about his success in business as

he was about avoiding a serious relationship. His romantic history had proven he was unable to balance the expectations of love and the duties of his career without someone suffering, so he chose the latter, enjoying the prestige, the challenge and the admiration of a father who, like himself, expected nothing but the very best.

Felicity had unknowingly served as a reminder of the sophisticated and sexy women he favored. Very unlike Monica.

Not that it mattered. She was a part of the family staff and off-limits.

He looked over to where she had stood and wasn't surprised to find the spot now empty.

That's for the best.

The last thing he wanted was to encourage her and then have her be disappointed when nothing came of her crush. He was more interested in her skill at organizing and cleaning his private bedroom suite than having her in it beneath him on his bed as he sated her desire.

Our *desire*, he admitted to himself.

Had things been different—time and place—and had she had a little more flash and sass about her, Gabe knew he would've gladly satisfied the craving he saw in her eyes.

Two

One week later

Gabe loosened his black silk tuxedo bow tie, leaving it to hang beneath the collar of his black shirt as he leaned in the doorway of the newest CRESS restaurant. It was the tenth such venture of Cress, INC., and as the president of its restaurant division, this was a personal celebration. He'd overseen every stage of its creation from its high-end modern design to its menu of French cuisine, and the selection of the head chef and staff.

His entire family was gathered in one of the four private rooms of CRESS X, celebrating its grand opening. The champagne had been drunk. The meal savored. The compliments shared, along with some business talk about current plans for the Cress, INC. empire.

He took a sip of vintage champagne as he looked over the rim of the crystal flute at his brothers.

Phillip Jr., the eldest son, pressed a warm kiss to the neck of his wife, Raquel, as she rubbed the back of their very sleepy toddler, Collette, stretched across their laps. Whatever he whispered in her ear brought a slow smile to her face.

Gabe could only imagine, and that made him chuckle into his glass.

His next eldest brother, Sean, moved about the room with his brandy snifter in hand, in full-charm mode. He hosted several culinary shows produced by Cress, INC., ran with high-profile celebrities and had snagged a spot as one of *People*'s Top Ten Sexiest Chefs last year. Thankfully his smile and culinary skills were as big as his ego.

His two youngest brothers, Cole and Lucas, both glanced over at a pretty server moving around the table, touching up everyone's drinks, before they shared a wolfish smile that revealed they both appreciated her appeal, even though they didn't dare to act upon it. Although Gabe wouldn't put it past Cole to defy the rule and enjoy a night in her bed. He seemed to love going left just because everyone else went right.

Lucas was the youngest Cress son and, hands down, his parents' favorite. They all knew it and accepted it. These days it wasn't clear from his chiseled frame that he used to carry an extra fifty pounds from his mother's indulgence.

Everyone had long since been assigned a role. Phil, the responsible one. Sean, the star. Cole, the rebel, and Lucas, the fave. Gabe knew he was the good one. The nonproblematic middle child.

He flexed his shoulders and took another deep swig of his drink.

Ding-ding-ding.

The blend of voices and cutlery hitting plates silenced as everyone turned their attention to his father, just hav-

ing stood and now tapping a fork against his flute. Gabe
eyed the tall solid dark-skinned man with broad features
and a bright smile.

"We've shared forty years together, my love," Phillip
Sr. began, his English accent thick and his eyes locked on
his wife, Nicolette, an olive-skinned beauty whose silvery
locks held a hint of her past blond color. "Together we have
accomplished so much and we did it with love. Of each
other. Of our family. Of enjoying life. Of food."

Gabe smiled as his mother reached to slide her hand
into his father's and softly stroke his palm with her thumb.

"And we passed that love on to our children—our sons.
Five," he stressed, patting his chest in pride.

The room filled with chuckles.

From the time they were small, the Cress boys had
learned firsthand about food and the best way to cook
it. To appreciate its nuances and how varying techniques
brought out different results—all delicious. Each of them
had trained in their parents' restaurants and attended culinary school, then traveled different paths to become chefs.
All were skilled culinary experts with a love of food that
their parents had passed to them through their genes and
home training.

"Tonight, we celebrate yet another success for Cress,
INC.," Phillip said, eyeing his adult children. "An empire
that is the greatest manifestation of our two greatest loves.
Food and family."

Nicolette rose to stand beside her husband. *"À la nourriture. À la vie. À l'amour."*

His mother's favorite saying in her native French tongue.
To food. To life. To love.

It was painted on the wall above all of her stoves—personal and professional—on the base of every pan in the
Cress line of cookware, in the watermark of every letter

from the various editors of their culinary magazines. It was
also branded on all their online presences and the saying
at the end of the cooking shows produced by Cress, INC.'s
television division.

"À la nourriture. À la vie. À l'amour," they all repeated
in unison as they raised their flutes in toast.

Phillip Sr. and Nicolette shared a kiss and then a few
more until they stopped with a reluctance that was clear.
He took her hand in his and led her to the small area in the
middle of the room, designed in shades of linen and bronze,
before pulling her close to him to dance as he softly sang
a French love song in her ear.

Gabe looked at them. He was single and mingling to his
heart's content without a thought of the lasting love his parents shared. Life had long since proven to him that he was
a failure at balancing love and his ambition.

He stopped the pretty server with a polite and distant
smile before setting his empty flute on the tray she held.
"Thank you," he said, unbuttoning the single button of his
tailored black tuxedo jacket before turning to leave the
room unnoticed.

For him, the night and the celebrating were over.

He made his way down the hall and then through the
front of the house, barely taking note of the contemporary
design, high ceilings and lush decor as he left the Tribeca
restaurant and made his way to his waiting SUV. The driver
left his seat and came around the front of the polished black
vehicle to hold the rear passenger door for him.

Gabe thanked him with a nod and relaxed against the
plush leather as soon as he'd folded his body onto the seat.
The combination of champagne and the premium cuts of
perfectly marbled and aged Miyazaki A5 Wagyu strip steak
had been delicious but tiring. He was ready for a little soli-

tude and self-reflection before the family returned from the restaurant and the festivities most likely continued.

Upon reaching the town house, under the cloak of darkness broken up by towering streetlamps, Gabe jogged up the stately steps and pressed his thumb to the biometric sensor to unlock the wrought-iron door and enter the marbled foyer. The length of the entire first floor was dimly lit with small pockets of light, breaking the darkness of night. With long strides he made his way across the wood floors of the living room through to the spacious chef's kitchen.

On top of the island counter awaited a case of champagne and a dozen flutes.

Whistling, he grabbed a bottle and a flute to carry over to the elevator in the corner. He paused as he stepped on the lift and eyed the rear wall. He remembered that day when he'd walked in and barely noticed Monica standing there with her back pressed against it, as if trying to blend into it. A day like so many others. What was different was later that day, in the kitchen, he saw her—really saw her—for the first time.

And he had liked what he'd seen.

Still do.

He frowned, turning as he held the bottle and glass between the fingers of one hand and pressed the illuminated button for the rooftop with the other. The elevator gently shifted upward as he remembered the look of desire in her eyes and how his heart had raced at the awareness that quiet, reliable Monica had a hidden desire for him.

The thought of her made his gut clench.

Her beauty was subtle. Quiet. But once recognized? Not to be denied.

He released a breath and shifted back and forth in his stance.

What was most important about Monica Darby was her

aptitude at her job as their housekeeper. How she kept her head tucked down and completed her tasks without disturbing their lives or breaking their trust in her. Many times his mother had raved that she was integral to their busy lives, even going above and beyond what was asked. The house ran like a well-oiled machine because of her quietly completed tasks.

That mattered more than her doe-shaped eyes, heated by the fire of desire.

Ding.

The elevator slowed to a stop. With his free hand he opened the gate and stepped out onto the rooftop terrace that spanned the twenty-two-foot width of the building. The air was calm, not too hot, and the sounds of the city echoed as he moved past the open seating area and around the glasshouse.

At the sight of Monica leaning against the wrought-iron railing, looking over at Central Park, he paused. A spring wind blew and caused the hem of her floor-length cotton robe to lift a bit. Her hair was loose down her back. There was a hint of a smile at her lips, and the moonlight cast a sweet glow upon her profile as the fairy lights adorning the pergola seemed to twinkle behind her.

It was a little endearing and magical.

Like one of those romance movies his sister-in-law, Raquel, loved to watch.

Monica looked toward him just as he was about to turn, leaving her to her solitude.

"Oh, I'm sorry, Mr. Cress," she said, shifting to face him. "I thought the family was out for the night."

Her robe and the high neck of the gown she wore beneath it was all very prim and proper. Very sedate. Very reserved. Very Monica.

"They are. I'm not. Well, not anymore," he said, holding

up the bottle and flute. "Wanted to enjoy a moment alone before everyone got back."

She nodded in understanding. "I'll leave you to it," she said, tucking her hair behind her right ear as she walked toward him.

"We launched our newest restaurant, CRESS X, tonight," he said, surprised at the need to fill the silence.

Monica glanced up at him with an impish look. "I know," she said. "Congratulations."

Of course she knew. He doubted there was much she didn't know about everyone in the family. Thus the non-disclosure agreement she was required to sign when she was first hired.

There was a sudden squeal of car tires from down below.

They both quickly moved to the railing to look at the street. A bright red sports car swerved to the right of a blue convertible before racing away.

"The aftermath of a near collision," Gabe said, glancing over at her, standing beside him.

"Hopefully everyone will get home safe," she said.

Gabe took in her high cheekbones, the soft roundness of her jaw and the tilt of her chin. The scent of something subtle but sweet surrounded her. He forced his eyes away from her and cleared his throat. "Hopefully," he agreed as he poured a small amount of champagne into the flute.

"I'll leave you to celebrate," Monica said.

With a polite nod, Gabe took a sip of his drink and set the bottle on the roof at his feet, trying to ignore he was so aware of her. Her scent. Her beauty. Even the gentle night winds shifting her hair back from her face. Distance was best. Over the last week he had fought to do just that to help his sudden awareness of her ebb. Ever since the veil to *their* desire had been removed, it had been hard to ignore.

She turned to leave but moments later a yelp escaped her as her feet got twisted in the long length of her robe and sent her body careening toward him as she tripped.

Reacting swiftly, he reached to wrap his arm around her waist and brace her body up against his to prevent her fall. He let the hand holding his flute drop to his side. Their faces were just precious inches apart. When her eyes dropped to his mouth, he released a small gasp. His eyes scanned her face before locking with hers.

He knew just fractions of a second had passed, but right then, with her in his arms and their eyes locked, it felt like an eternity. He wondered what it felt like for her. Was her heart pounding? Her pulse sprinting? Was she aroused? Did she feel that pull of desire?

He did.

With a tiny lick of her lips that was nearly his undoing, Monica raised her chin and kissed him. It was soft and sweet. And an invitation.

"Monica?" he asked, heady with desire but his voice deep and soft as he sought clarity.

"Kiss me," she whispered against his lips, hunger in her voice.

"Shit," Gabe swore before he gave in to the temptation of her and dipped his head to press his mouth down upon hers.

And it was just a second more before her lips and her body softened against him as she opened her mouth and welcomed him with a heated gasp that seemed to echo around them. The first touch of his tongue to hers sent a jolt through his body, and he clenched her closer to him as her hands snaked up his arms and then his shoulders before clutching the lapels of his tux in her fists. He assumed she was holding on while giving in to a passion that was irresistible.

* * *

Monica was lost in it all. Blissfully.

The taste and feel of his mouth were everything she ever imagined.

Ever dreamed.

Ever longed for.

She was lost in a heady mix of surprise and excitement as she raised slightly trembling hands to stroke the back of his head. A moan from deep within her escaped. His grunt quickly followed. Somewhere in the heat of it all, she heard the flute crash against the roof as he released his hold on the drink to drag his hand up the back of her thighs.

He tasted her lips before pressing heated kisses down to her throat where she felt him deeply inhale her scent before suckling that little dip above her clavicle. She gasped and cried out as she flung her head back giving him more of her neck to taste. She clung to him, lifting and bending her leg to the side of his solid body and being rewarded by his hand gripping her buttocks through the cotton, feeling the heat of his touch.

"Gabe," she whispered into the air, saying his first name aloud for the first time ever.

And what a time to do so.

When she'd noticed him standing there, looking so sharp and handsome in his black tuxedo with a bottle of champagne in his hand, he'd seemed to have stepped straight off the pages of a high-fashion magazine or some cologne ad. With his shirt open at the neck and his tie undone, she'd felt pushed over the edge of reason, no matter how well she'd covered it. Just tempting. Strong, dark and sexy. Devastatingly so.

Her heart had pounded with both surprise and a desire that took her breath away.

And now he was kissing her. And touching her. And pressing her body against his.

Am I dreaming?

Her mouth sought his and he accepted her boldness when she offered him her tongue. With a grunt of pleasure, he sucked the tip into his mouth. Deeply. And then did it again. And again. She trembled. Her pulse raced and she ached deep inside her womanhood.

Don't wake me up.

Monica pressed her hands to the sides of his face, enjoying the feel of his shadow against her palms as she gently played with his earlobes and the soft skin just behind them. She felt the slight tremble of his body and knew she had happened upon his hot spot. Maybe one of many.

Against her thigh she felt the length of his hardness.

Breaking their kiss, she leaned back just a bit to look at him as she panted.

Their eyes locked and something happened between them. A current. A spark. A vibe. She felt it and shivered.

This was desire, and in it, they were equal.

"Monica?" he whispered into the small break between them.

It had been so long since she'd given in to pure carnal pleasure, but she couldn't remember ever feeling the thrill *his* touch brought her. Her entire body felt electrified. He was seeking approval to give her even *more* pleasure. When in her entire life had *more* ever been an option? After a lifetime of so many disappointments. So many dreams she never dared to give hope to. How could she deny herself *this*?

"Yes," she acquiesced, giving both him and herself permission.

Gabe swung her up into his arms and took long strides to reach the flower-covered pergola. There, beneath its cover, he pressed her down onto one of the round, double chaise longues, and the thick cushion welcomed her. He removed his jacket and flung away his bow tie. The shirt clung to the hard definitions of his body.

He got sexier?

Monica leaned against the pillows as the fleshy bud between her legs swelled to life. She watched him remove a condom packet from his wallet before undressing as she slowly untied the belt of her robe and opened it to fall at her sides. Her trembling hand paused at the top button of her nightgown as she took in the first sight of Gabe Cress—*the* Gabe Cress—standing before her gloriously naked.

Oh. My.

He was sculpted. Plain and simple. But then not simple at all, because the all of him was everything. Broad shoulders, narrow waist, eight-pack abs and strong thighs. The hair on his chest lay flat before narrowing to an arrow down the jagged middle line of his abs and connecting with the curly dark bush that surrounded the base of his smooth, thick and long hardness. It curved away from his body in a darker complexion than the rest of his light brown skin. Like milk chocolate. Decadent.

Gabe massaged the length of his inches before covering his hardness with their latex protection. He bent his body to crawl up the chaise. She hitched her matronly floral-print gown up her thighs as she opened her legs to him. She assumed he was going to press his body down upon hers, but instead he reached to undo each tiny pearl button running down the front of her gown. Somehow each one being undone seemed to send a jolt through her as more and more of her naked body was exposed to his. And when he reached the last one and flung the gown open, she arched her back and released a hot gasp as the spring wind floated across her body and hardened her nipples even more.

Gabe stroked and massaged her inner thighs before lying flat and then giving her a heated look as he lowered his head.

He couldn't. He wouldn't.

But he did.

The first feel of his clever tongue stroking against her bud was her undoing. Monica cried out and reached to grip the sides of his face as she rotated her hips while he sucked the all-too-sensitive bud into his mouth. As he pleasured her, she wished she had followed her instinct and done the same to him. Just imagining the feel of his hardness against her lips and her tongue as he tasted of her in the most intimate fashion, she felt breathless. She was lost in her passion but finding a piece of herself that she had locked away in her loneliness over the last five years.

It was a wonderful hello to her femininity. Her sexuality. Her being.

An awakening.

"Gabe, Gabe, Gabe," she gasped into the night air as she clutched at the pillows with her nails and dug in for control as she felt herself spiraling into an explosive climax that made her entire body feel so raw and exposed. So alive. In the best way. Ever.

Just as she was on the brink, Gabe quickly shifted his body atop hers and probed her wet and quivering core with the tip of his hard inches. She tilted her chin up and licked at his mouth as their eyes met. "Just this once," she said.

"Just once," he agreed with a nod, his eyes so dark and intense in his handsome face. "Then I better make it damn good."

"Please," she begged, wrapping her legs and arms around his body almost desperately as he used his hips to fill her with one swift thrust.

They cried out roughly.

They were united.

Connected.

Monica closed her eyes as she winced at the feel of him so tightly sheathed by her core. Every pulse of his dick seemed to pound against her walls. She knew he was fighting for control. Trying his best not to climax. She was glad her own peak waned off. For now. She wasn't ready for their wild night atop the roof of the beautiful Victorian town house to end.

"Look at me."

She did as he bid.

Their eyes stayed locked on one another—lost in each other—as he began to stroke inside her. She felt it. From base to tip. Hardness. Thickness. Heat. Over and over again.

Feeling emboldened and lost in the carnal pleasure, she matched each thrust with a slow wind of her hips that tightened her walls down upon his shaft.

He pursed his lips at the move and then swore.

She knew she pleased him and she smiled, tilting her head to the side, her mouth agape, as she continued to match his stare. He dipped his head to kiss her and she tasted herself. It thrilled her as she sucked his tongue into her mouth with a low purr.

Their eyes were still locked. It was intense. And heady. And powerful.

His strokes deepened and he sped up the pace. She gasped as her eyes widened, and she could do nothing but give in to his passionate onslaught as she broke their stare and buried her face against his neck to muffle her cries of pleasure. He slid his hand beneath her to grip her bottom. She looked over his shoulder at the up-and-down motion of his buttocks as he stroked away. His muscles clenched with each movement. A trickle of sweat coursed down his back and disappeared in the deep groove between his hard buttocks.

It was a glorious sight to see.

He lightly bit down on her shoulder as his body went stiff.

"What's wrong?" she whispered in between pants.

He replaced his teeth with a kiss. "I don't want this to end. Not yet," he said, his own breathing labored as he waited for his orgasm to recede.

"No. Don't. Not yet," she agreed, turning her head to the side to face his.

They shared a soft laugh as they looked at one another.

Monica stroked the side of his face and was surprised when he turned his head to kiss her palm. She gave him an inquisitive look at the tender move.

"You're beautiful," he admitted.

She made a face of disbelief. "No, you are," she said, stroking his buttock with her heel as she massaged his back with her fingertips.

He chuckled.

She tightened her walls against his hardness.

He stopped laughing and shifted his arm around her waist to hold her close before turning both their bodies so that she was atop him. She looked down into his silvery-blue eyes that seemed to blaze against his light brown complexion. Her gaze searched his face. Missing nothing. Not even the small scar on his chin that was barely hidden by the shadow of his beard.

Feeling bold and confident, she removed his arm from around her and slowly sat up straight as she drew her hands up his sides and across his chest to press against his pecs. She flipped her hair back over her shoulder to have a clear view of his face as she began to ride him. His eyes seemed to fill with wonder as he watched her move her body like a snake, her one hand held up in the air.

Gabe ran his hands up her thighs to her belly and up to cup a breast in each hand.

"Aaaaaaah," Monica cried out, letting her head fall back so that the tips of her hair tickled the top of her buttocks as he eased one hand up to press against her throat with his index finger near her mouth.

She turned her head to suck the tip into her mouth and was rewarded when she felt him get harder inside of her. The base of his inches stroked against her bud, fueling the slow and steady rise of yet another climax. She was anxious for it to explode.

She moaned with a wince of pure anticipation.

Gabe sat up to draw one taut brown nipple into his mouth as he gripped her hips to slam down as he thrust his own upward, sending his hardness against her fleshy bud with slight force. Again. And again. And again.

The combination of him licking her nipples and her swollen and aching bud being plucked like a chord was earth-shattering. She quickened her pace, back and forth on his length, as he matched her speed. "Yes," she sighed. "Yes."

"I'm with you," he moaned against her cleavage before moving to her other breast to suck and lick it as if starved.

"Yes!" she exclaimed, her throat dry from her panting and gasps of pleasure. Her entire body felt heated as she exploded with the first sweet wave of her release.

Gabe roared with his own release as he held her tightly and continued to taste her nipples.

Monica was lost as she rested the side of her face atop his head and bit down on her bottom lip as she succumbed to her climax and felt a wave of pure pleasure made all the more electric by Gabe free-falling into the abyss with her.

Their rough cries filled the air, blending with the drone of late-night traffic as their sexual haze came to a shuddering end that left them both sweaty, panting and fighting for control of the rapid pounding of their hearts.

As he lay back and she shifted her body on top of him, her head on his hard chest, she marveled at what they'd shared. She wondered if he had experienced such pleasure, such invisibility of inhibitions and such electricity before. Because she hadn't. Not ever. And wondered if she would ever again.

Just this once.

That had been her request, and she knew it was for the best. Even as they lay in each other's arms weakened by their explosive climax, regret was settling in. She nibbled at her bottom lip as reality returned. Gabe Cress, as beautiful and sexy as he was, and having far surpassed her seductive dreams, was one of her employers. She couldn't afford to lose the job she loved nor did she want encounters like this to be a regular occurrence. It was all so typical of upstairs-downstairs relationships.

Tonight had been just for me, but no more.

She hated the insecurity she felt even as she lay in his arms. "Just once," she reminded him in a soft whisper as she listened to the pace of his heart begin to slow.

He nodded, and for moments she didn't count, he continued to hold her before he pressed a kiss to the top of her wild hair and rose from the chaise. A goodbye to their rendezvous.

Three

Two weeks later

Monica wiped her sweaty brow with the back of her hand before she rose from her knees and dropped the large sponge into the bucket of sudsy water.

"Thank you," Raquel said from her seat on one of the two custom-made, light gray velvet sectionals in the sizable den centering the fifth floor of the town house, where there were three bedrooms, each with their own attached bathroom.

"No problem, Mrs. Cress," she said, picking up the bucket from atop the silk Persian carpet in the same shades of gray and steel blue as the stylish decor throughout the entire town house.

"Apologize to Miss Monica for your mess, Collette."

Moments after she heard Raquel's request to her and Phillip Jr.'s daughter, Collette, Monica felt a gentle tug on

her pants leg. She turned and looked down at the preco-
cious three-year-old with dimpled cheeks and bright yellow
spectacles that made her all the more adorable.

"I'm sorry I spilled my milk, Miss Monica," she said.

"No worries, Colli," she said with a soft smile, using the
child's pet name. "No worries at all."

With her absolution, the little girl went running back
across the room to sit at her mother's feet where she'd been
playing with her iPad.

Monica made a mental note to have the rug removed for
professional cleaning. Once done dumping the bucket, she
used the wrought-iron staircase running along the north
side of the house to go back down to the fourth floor where
she had been cleaning the bedroom suites before being
summoned upstairs to attend to the spill.

She crossed the den that was the exact same design as
the one upstairs, with the glass letting in so much spring
light to shine against the hardwood floors and elaborate
woodwork of the custom shelving and doors. She retrieved
her cleaning caddie and pulled it behind her to Gabe's bedroom suite on the far end. Her steps faltered a bit. This was
his sanctuary, and after their lovemaking, entering it felt
all the more nerve-racking.

At the door she took a long breath and wet her lips before
finally opening it and entering his spacious suite decorated
in stylish shades of gray, from charcoal to smoke. Her eyes
fell on his unmade king-size bed and she envisioned him
lying there nude as he slept.

"Just once. Then I better make it damn good."

Closing her eyes, she shook her head to erase the hot
thought and the memory of his words *that* night. Two weeks
later and it was still scorched into her memory. She looked
down at the goose bumps on her arms, brought on at the
very thought of him.

Get it together, Mo.

She forged ahead, swiftly crossing the room to open gray suede curtains, exposing the glass wall that gave him a view of the city landscape in the distance. She used the leather ties to secure them back before moving over to the bed to take up the coverlet, the blanket folded across the foot and the crisp white cotton sheets. With them gathered in her arms and pressed against her chest, it was hard to ignore the scent of him rising from the bed linens.

Like a silly schoolgirl with a crush, she allowed herself to press her nose against the sheets for a deep inhale that took her back in time to that night.

"Oh. My apologies, Monica."

Frightened, she released a squeal and dropped the covers to the silk rug as she looked at Gabe, standing in the now open doorway of his en suite bathroom. Her eyes dipped to avoid his bare chest but then fell to the towel barely clinging to his hips. She gasped and turned from him, wishing the sound of her harsh breathing didn't echo so loudly in the air.

"Um. Sorry, Mr. Cress. I thought you were already gone for the day," she said, moving quickly toward the door.

"Monica. Wait. I didn't know you were here either," he called behind her in explanation.

"I'll wait outside," she said, her words rushing together with the same quick pace of her heart.

As soon as she closed the door, she stepped over to press her back against the wall and looked up at the tray ceiling with the brocade design, a nod to the Victorian era in which the home was first constructed. *So delicate and ornate*, she thought, trying to focus on anything but the sight of the plush towel wrapped around Gabe.

Monica remembered that night on the roof so very well.

She shook her head, now focusing her gaze outside the glass to the swaying emerald leaves of the towering tree in the backyard. She and Gabe had fallen back into their cordiality, but her awareness of him had not been lessened by the coupling. If anything, it made it all the worse. Simple touches—as she handed him something or passed him in a hall—sent her pulse racing. Her dreams at night were consumed by him and their passion.

In a perfect world—where she was not an employee and had lineage and wealth of her own—she would more than gladly have him as her lover. But that was not her truth, and although it hurt her pride and stoked insecurities, she knew that one night had been all Gabe Cress would ever desire from his family's housekeeper.

So move on, Mo the Maid. Move on. There is nothing but heartache for you at the end of this road. Just like before.

She winced. Thinking of her ex, James, at a time like this was insult on top of injury.

The door to Gabe's bedroom opened. She pushed off the wall to stand tall, clasping her hands and pasting a blank expression on her face.

He exited.

And, of course, he looked handsome in a lightweight tan suit that was perfectly tailored to his frame.

"Thank you, Monica," he said, his tone indicating nothing more than the cordiality one would give a stranger. "Have a good day."

"You, as well, Mr. Cress," she said, matching his politeness with a nod.

She made the mistake of looking up to find his grayish-blue eyes resting on her.

Their gazes locked.

She felt drawn to him and felt the now-familiar hum that gave voice to their chemistry. She knew he felt it, as well. Several times over the last few weeks, she had looked up to find his gaze *just* shifting away from her.

Setting a trap, whether he meant to do so or not. Fueling her longing.

Monica forced herself to look away.

Moments later, the sound of his Italian leather shoes tapping against the hardwood floors as he walked away was a relief to her senses. Rubbing her hands against the front of her black uniform pants, she walked over to the glass wall and looked down at the backyard. She squinted and leaned in to better see Lucas walking away from Jillian, who stood by the garden of fresh herbs in her white chef's coat.

Was the youngest Cress brother Jillian's secret lover, who wrote the note?

The taste of you still lingers on my tongue.

She looked on as Jillian watched Lucas's retreat, shook her head and bent her frame to pick herbs to place in the basket at her feet. Bitten by curiosity she knew she should resist, Monica rushed across the wide den to the stairwell, where her feet ate up the steps like she was trying to win a race. Reaching the first floor, she paused upon seeing Gabe and Lucas reaching the front door and didn't move until they exited.

Monica had just reached the dining room at the rear of the first floor when Jillian entered with her basket on her arm. Monica eyed the tall and slender bronzed beauty with her auburn curly hair pulled up into a topknot. The chef's tortoiseshell spectacles didn't hide the long and thick lashes framing her round brown eyes. Her cheekbones were high and her chin narrow, giving her face a heart shape that brought emphasis to her full pouty mouth, which was painted crimson.

Jillian was pretty. And smart. And talented.

Just which of the Cress men had found it hard to ignore her appeal?

"Good morning, Chef Jillian," Monica said with a warm smile. "Busy?"

Jillian chuckled. "Good morning. And yes. Always," she said. "Lucas just threw a last-minute, picnic-lunch request at me for him and a date."

Well, that answers that.

"But what can I do for you?" the chef asked as she moved around the long dining room table for ten, topped with charcoal leather and surrounded by steel blue suede armless chairs.

"N-nothing," Monica stumbled. "Just taking a little break and thought I'd check on you."

Jillian gave her a polite smile. "I'll be honest, Monica, I'm too swamped for much girl talk today," she said with another a look of regret before swiftly walking into the kitchen to set the basket on the island.

"No problem. Another day," Monica said, already turning toward the elevator to ride back up to the fourth floor.

Lucas wouldn't make a lunch date and then ask his secret lover to prepare the food? Would he?

"Hmm," she said aloud.

Monica thought of the youngest Cress brother's steady merry-go-round of beauties since he'd lost fifty pounds and gone from chubby to chiseled in the last year. In fact, she remembered seeing him sneak one woman out of the house early one morning and catching him sneaking another in later that night.

He had only wiggled his eyes in mirth at her wide-eyed shocked expression as he hurried his "date" into his suite.

With *him* anything was possible.

Back in Gabe's suite, she was able to finish making his bed with fresh linens and tidy the sitting area and walk-in closet only by forcing herself to focus, pinching her wrists anytime her mind became occupied by naughty thoughts of the man with the name of an angel.

Monica rolled her cleaning caddie behind her to take the elevator to the third level, entirely devoted to Phillip Sr. and Nicolette. To her, it was the most beautifully luxurious space of the entire town house. As always, she paused in the doorway and took in the pure elegance of the massive bedroom, sitting room and office space, all flowing seamlessly from one room to the next, with elaborately carved wooden doors that blocked the views of the en suite bathroom and walk-in closets. The decor, flowers and plants, elaborate accessories, and the light streaming through the glass wall made for a stunning look.

It was like the glamorous set of a 1940s movie.

For a moment she pictured herself dressed in a satin gown with perfectly coiffed hair, large diamond baubles and painted with elaborate makeup, smoking from a long and slender cigarette holder as she blew perfect rings in succession.

The idea made her chuckle.

Allowing herself a quick stretch, Monica pulled on a fresh set of gloves and set about putting the room back to showcase status. She smoothed out any wrinkles in the gray coverlet before she folded it down to the edge of the king-size bed. She turned and noticed the edge of a folder sticking out from the mirror-trimmed antique nightstand. Normally she didn't venture inside private spaces, but she didn't want it to appear that she ignored her duties. She pulled the drawer out just enough to ease the folder back inside but found resistance when she tried to close it. She tried twice more with a frown. It felt off track.

Monica pulled the drawer out again to get it back on track. An inadvertent glance down revealed a typed sheet atop the file. She gasped as it registered just what she was seeing, and she rushed to ease the drawer closed. But then she thought one of the Cress parents would know she'd seen the file, and that could lead to her dismissal, so she quickly took the drawer back off track and tried her best to place the file peeking out just the way she'd found it.

She'd rather be admonished for overlooking the drawer than fired and kicked out on the street for seeing that one of the Cress parents—maybe both—currently had their family under surveillance by a private detective.

They were wealthy and powerful but still human, and there was no such thing as a perfect human being. Nor perfect parents. Or family.

Not that she had much experience with one of her own.

But she knew she would rather tackle her loneliness than be in a family that was slowly shifting as the sons all vied for their father's position as Cress, INC.'s CEO. In the six months since Phillip Sr. had first alluded to stepping down, the closeness she'd witnessed between the five brothers was beginning to fade. That troubled her, but she was a hired employee and said nothing about the more frequent arguments, the sly observations of another brother's missteps or failures whenever they were in their father's presence, or the decline in family events over the last few months.

Even the night of the celebration, Gabe had left the rest of the family behind to party alone.

It is none of my concern. It's my job to clean up their physical messes. Not the emotional ones. I just hate they don't know how blessed they are to have each other. I wish I had—

She pushed away that long-held regret, refusing to give any more energy to her grief over her parents not wanting her for their own.

Quickly, Monica finished her duties and was glad to

leave. She had just peeled back a veil to the Cress family that she could not unsee. With that, she no longer viewed them as a loving, close-knit family.

"Gabe, Gabe, Gabe."

The memory of that night and his name tumbling from Monica's lips with a passion she couldn't hide had him in a trance. So much so that he didn't even see the Manhattan skyline outside the floor-to-ceiling windows of his office in the Cress, INC. headquarters in Midtown. Instead, in the reflection, he visualized a scene of him making love to Monica playing out before him.

And that had been nearly a constant during the last three weeks.

Monica had surprised him that night and left him impressed with her ardor. The passion.

Still, no matter how delicious their tryst, it had been a one-time treat. He wasn't interested in anything more with the shy beauty and her hidden hunger. Nothing could ever be between them but hot sex, and he was willing to honor her request for a one-night stand.

"Just this once. Then I better make it damn good."

"Please."

Gabe had learned long ago the leap from good sex to love was easier for some women than most men. And his gut told him Monica Darby was that type. He had no love to give, and he would never want to lead her on when he knew he was just as adamant about his success as he was in avoiding a serious relationship. His romantic history had proven he was unable to balance the expectations of both love and his career without anyone suffering.

Most important, he was fully aware his mother would fire Monica if she discovered their tryst. Common sense said Monica needed her job, and he'd much rather have the trustworthy and efficient woman as their reliable house-keeper than his temporary bedmate. Anything else was selfish on his part.

I can't believe I almost messed it all up, he thought.

Not that it hadn't been one hell of a night.

They'd both agreed that they should put the night behind them and move on as if it had never happened.

It's for the best.

Still, he was quite tired of waking up from erotic dreams of her and taking cold showers to ease his desire.

Bzzzzzz.

Gabe cleared his throat and turned in his chair to face his ebony-wood desk. He pressed the intercom button. "Yes," he said briskly, flexing his agile fingers before turning to type his password to access his laptop.

"Your brother Phillip Jr. is here," his assistant said, her voice echoing through the speakerphone of the system.

"Gabe, Gabe, Gabe."

"Send him in," he said, ignoring the sultry memory that seemed akin to the enchanting whispers of one of Homer's Sirens. Although he didn't want to admit it, he was thankful to his brother for intruding on thoughts of Monica he knew he had no right having.

Phillip Jr. opened the door and strolled in, closing it behind him. "I heard you and Lucas went to look at a new factory for the cookware line," he said, his deep voice booming.

It matched his tall muscular frame. He lived up to the comparison to former wrestler turned actor Dwayne "The Rock" Johnson. To tease him, the brothers would all mimic The Rock's signature wrestling line: *Can you smell what The Rock is cooking?* Tongue wiggle and all.

"Yes. He wanted my advice," he said, going to the website of the James Beard Award to scroll down to announced nominees in the categories for restaurants and chefs before briefly glancing over at his brother.

"After he asked me for it first and then left me hanging? Or were you two plotting against me?" Phillip Jr. asked, coming to stand behind one of the chairs lined in front of the desk and gripping the back of one of them so tightly Gabe feared his fingers would burst through the leather.

Gabe leaned back in his chair and eyed his brother. "In what way, Philly?" he asked, purposely reverting to his brother's childhood nickname.

It served his purpose to disarm him.

Phillip Jr.'s stance softened. "Maybe the two of you think you stand a better chance at Dad's favor as a team," he said.

Gabe shook his head. "I don't like to share anything. You know that," he said.

"And I don't like being the eldest—his damn *namesake*—and being overlooked," Phillip volleyed back, once again voicing his opinion that he should automatically inherit the throne.

Gabe remained quiet. He wanted to be named CEO, but he refused to fight with his brothers to obtain the title. It was a horrible use of time, intelligence and energy.

Phillip released a derisive chuckle filled with his frustration before turning to take long strides to the closed door to jerk it open. He paused in the frame. "Good luck on the nominations *next* year," he said before taking his leave.

That last shot did cause Gabe to shift in his seat. None of the Cress restaurants had received a nod.

In the past, the family used to gather together for the announcement of the nominees to celebrate or commiserate together. Now he didn't know if his brother truly wished him well the next time or if he'd let his blind ambition make a loss a reason to gloat to their father as proof of Gabe's inability to lead the empire.

Sad times.

Gabe wiped his mouth with his hand as he closed his eyes and released a long breath. He wanted to win the coveted seat, as well, but to what end? This wasn't a nighttime soap opera where hurt and misdoings could be erased or lessened with the stroke of a writer's pen.

What was happening to the *family* in their family empire?

Bzzzzzz.

He glanced at his watch and his body tensed, even as he reached over to hit the intercom button once more. "Yes?"

"Lunch is served, Mr. Cress."

Gabe drummed his fingers atop his desk. "Thank you," he replied, wishing he had anywhere else to be.

Absolutely *anywhere.*

He eyed his stocked bar and contemplated a double pour of brandy but decided against it. He needed to be sharp. The verbal daggers were about to fly.

Cress, INC.'s corporate offices occupied the entire fortieth floor of the towering building, and there was a test kitchen nestled among the dozen offices and conference rooms. It had become tradition when his mother wasn't busy at her acclaimed cooking school for her to fix lunch for the family and support staff. Normally he looked forward to his mother's cuisine, but of late, the family gatherings could be a bit dicey and swing anywhere between loving and challenging.

The scent of tomatoes and seafood was heavy in the air. Admittedly his stomach rumbled, but he didn't quicken his pace to the family's private dining area that was separate from the one for the employees. Barbara, one of the company's office staff, gave him an appreciative eye as they came toward each other in the hall leading to the test kitchen.

"That's a beautiful tie, Mr. Cress," she said with a sly

smile as she came to a stop in front of him, effectively blocking his path.

Barbara had made it clear over the years that she was open to more than a work relationship, but Gabe had always maintained a professional distance. Today would be no different. "Thank you," he said with a polite nod that he knew was stiff. "Enjoy your lunch."

"Care to join me?" she asked.

Gabe opened his mouth.

"Sorry, Babs, but my big brother has a lunch date with me."

Gabe glanced back at his brother Cole, a near look-alike for the actor Michael Ealy, strolling up to them dressed in jeans, boots and a long-sleeved black T-shirt. Ever the rebel of the family, Cole ignored their parents' request for their sons to wear office attire. Just as his insistence on operating his food truck during the weekends was a thorn in their father's side.

"Another time, then," the petite and pretty woman said with another lingering look up at him before walking away.

As she passed Cole, he stopped to turn his head to watch her.

"Careful, little brother," Gabe warned and then silenced any further admonishments as he remembered his own recent tryst with an employee.

"Gabe. Gabe. Gabe."

Cole finally turned to reach his side and they continued up the hall together.

"Maybe she'll turn her attention to you," Gabe said.

"She can play with the fire if she wants," Cole said. "*I'm* not the good one who wouldn't dare break a rule."

The Good One.

His brothers had often teased him for being a Goody Two-shoes.

"Just once. Then I better make it damn good."

Funny. He'd been very good at breaking the rules that night.

Gabe bit back a smile at the memory.

"Hundred dollars, it's *fideuà*," Cole said as they reached the double wooden doors to the family's private dining room.

Gabe paused. "Paella," he said.

Cole nodded. "Bet."

They entered the brightly lit room of modern design to find everyone else already assembled around the large round set table.

"Damn," Cole swore at the sight of the big and wide frying pan of paella in the center of the table on top of a large trivet.

Gabe took the folded hundred-dollar bill from between his brother's index and middle fingers to slide into his pocket before claiming a seat in between Phillip Jr. and Lucas. The aromatic dish was filled with lobster, mussels, clams and shrimp. Steam still rose from it.

"The paella smells good, Ma," Sean said, removing the linen napkin atop his gold-rimmed plate and opening it across his lap.

"Ton père a préparé le déjeuner pour nous aujourd'hui," Nicolette told them, knowing her husband and sons spoke both French and Spanish fluently.

Their father had cooked.

The Cress brothers all paused and shared brief looks surreptitiously before watching their father's tall and solid frame move around the table as he filled everyone's goblet with a vintage white wine.

Gabe was sure their thoughts were in alignment with his own. There was no coincidence between their father cooking lunch at work—something he had never done—and the

James Beard Award nominations being announced and the family coming up nil in the journalism and restaurant-and-chef categories. In their separate careers as chefs, nearly all of them had been nominated or won as Outstanding Restaurateur or Best Chef. But as a collective under the umbrella of Cress, INC. the accolade had yet to be received.

Phillip Leonard Cress Sr. was not pleased by that fact.

And him cooking such a nuanced meal that took skill, knowledge and use of many techniques to create the Spanish dish correctly—perfectly—was an unspoken reminder that he expected nothing less from his sons than excellence. Earning prestigious awards for Cress, INC. would serve as a testament to the quality of the business.

Phillip Sr. served each of his family members before raising his wine goblet into the air. *"À la nourriture. À la vie. À l'amour,"* he said before claiming his seat next to his wife.

Everyone tasted the paella.

Gabe fought not to close his eyes in pleasure at the exquisite seasoning, the tenderness of the seafood mix and the perfect, crunchy crust at the bottom of the rice dish. It was divine.

Just as Phillip Sr. knew it to be.

Message received.

Four

Two weeks later

Monica trembled so hard that the letter she held clutched in both her hands rattled as if unsettled by wind. But she was secure from the spring breezes inside the posh Manhattan law offices. It was her nerves that caused the tremble. The shock of it all.

"Miss Darby?"

She heard the attorney, but his voice sounded distant instead of that of a man across the desk from her. She released small breaths as she looked down at the skirt of her print dress, remembering how much she'd fretted if it was the right thing to wear to an appointment with a high-powered lawyer.

Especially when I didn't know what it was about at the time. I hope it's okay.

Monica knew her random thoughts were a diversion from the truth she'd just been told.

"Do you understand what I've explained?" he asked. "You've been left an inheritance by Brock Maynard—"

"The actor?" she asked, although he'd already given her his name. She shifted her eyes to the bald portly man with thick, framed spectacles. "In all the movies?"

"Yes," he nodded. "Your father."

Monica's lip curled as she shook her head. "Not my father. He was a sperm donor," she said snidely, feeling overcome with all the years of sadness and loneliness she had felt. For so long she had wondered who her parents were and why they hadn't been able—or wanted to—raise her. And she'd thought of everything. Even their deaths.

Discovering that her father was a wealthy and famous actor was worse.

Had been an actor. Now he's dead.

She looked around at the high ceilings, upscale decor and the New York skyline so clearly seen out the windows. This was the world of the Cress family and those of that ilk. Wealthy and affluent. Smart and talented. She could easily see Gabe sitting behind the desk with all the confidence and bravado needed to control the room.

She felt out of place. Like an intruder into *his* world.

Gabe.

Why am I thinking about him right now? Why am I always thinking of him?

She bit her bottom lip at the memory of their encounter beneath the twinkling fairy lights entwined among the flowers of the pergola.

Because I can't forget that night.

"Miss Darby."

You're beautiful.

"Miss Darby?"

Monica cut her eyes back at the attorney. "Yes?" she

answered with a simplicity that made her wonder if she had lost her mind.

Yesterday afternoon FedEx had delivered a letter requesting her presence at the law offices of Curro Villar and Hunt. She'd looked them up, saw that they were reputable—and not attorneys hired as creditors—and called to make her appointment with Marco Villar as requested.

That's his name. Villar. Marco Villar.

And now, nearly five minutes later—maybe more than that—after being escorted into his posh offices in her inexpensive dress from a discount store, by a towering beauty who could be a model, Monica was still held fixated by a blend of confusion, shock and, yes, hurt.

"There is just one provision to receive the money," Mr. Villar said.

Something in his dark eyes behind the glasses let her know his next words would hurt. She stiffened her back and notched her chin.

"You must sign a nondisclosure agreement—"

Monica released a bitter laugh as she jumped to her feet. "The final insult," she said, her voice soft. "Not wanting to claim me even in death."

She turned and quickly walked across the wide breadth of his office.

"Monica!"

She turned, surprised by the feminine voice that called her name. A petite woman in an emerald green pantsuit was standing in the doorway of a room just off Marco Villar's office. She clutched her purse so tightly that her brown skin thinned over her knuckles.

"Now what?" Monica asked.

Mr. Villar rose to his feet, but the woman held up her hand and shook her head as she kept her attention on Monica. "We didn't mean to trick you or anything, Monica," she said loudly, her voice raspy as if she lived off cigarettes. "I am Brock's sister, Phoebe. Your aunt, if you will."

Monica stepped back with widening eyes and released a small gasp of surprise as the woman neared her. "We look alike," she said, her eyes missing no details of the woman, who was in her sixties or seventies.

Phoebe smiled. "Technically, you look like me," she said. *A famous father? A look-alike aunt? An inheritance?*

"Ladies, why don't you have a seat," Marco said, coming from behind his desk to wave them both over to his sitting area. "Help yourself to a drink from the bar and I'll give you a moment."

With that he left them alone.

Phoebe sat down and crossed her ankles as she patted the seat on the leather sofa beside her.

"What do you want with me?" Monica asked as she remained standing.

"I hate what my brother did to you, and had I known about you, I would have raised you myself," she said, her eyes filling with tears as she pressed a wrinkled brown hand to her chest. "He told me on his deathbed, and it took every bit of willpower I have in this small body not to reveal to my dying brother that his treatment of you angered and disappointed me. It forever changed my view of the man I thought him to be. I *swear* to you. I didn't know."

Her anguish was clear, and Monica did not have the heart to ignore that. She took the seat beside her and let the woman reach for her hands to clasp them tightly between her own.

"When Marco told me they located you, I begged him to let me hide here so that I could see you. I didn't know if you'd even want to meet me, once I learned of all the challenges you had to overcome in your life," Phoebe said. "But I couldn't let you leave and walk away from what he owes you, Monica. It is the least he could do, to give you an easier life than you've had these last thirty years."

"But even in death, he won't claim me," she said, her voice hollow. Her heart hurting.

"That money is yours to do with as you see fit," Phoebe said, her voice fiery and passionate. "If you sign those papers, collect that money and say to hell with all of us, I wouldn't blame you one bit."

"So *you* want me to sign the NDA, too?" she asked, easing her hands out of the woman's grasp.

Phoebe swiped away the tears with her hands. "I didn't know about it until Marco said it, but to get your money? Yes!" she exclaimed. "You may have to sign an NDA to get your money, but I don't. I can speak your truth even if you can't. Your presence will not be denied anymore. I promise you that! Hell, I would do it even if I lost the stipend he left me to maintain the beach house he purchased for me years ago in Santa Monica."

"In California?" she asked, still trying to process the entire thing.

"And guess what?" Phoebe said, reaching again for her hands. "He named you after one of his favorite places in the world."

"He named me?" Monica asked.

"A small gesture to appease his guilt, I guess."

Was I so hungry for love that such a small gesture mattered that much to me?

"And my mother?" Monica asked.

"I know the story of your birth but not her name. That, he wouldn't reveal," Phoebe said with obvious regret. "But I'm sure there must be a way to find her. Perhaps Marco and his team could help with it."

Was I ready to find my mother? I wasn't sure. It could be just more sadness and disappointment.

"We'll see. I need some time to process all of this," Monica said.

Her aunt nodded in understanding. "I hope you'll give me a chance to get to know you, Monica."

"Perhaps…in time. I can't make any promises," she said.

"I will leave my contact info with Marco and when—or if—you're ready, you can get it from him," Phoebe offered. "Just know there is no deadline on when you reach out to me. Be it a day or a year or a dozen—if I'm still alive, God willing—I will accept you with open arms."

Monica remained silent.

Phoebe rose to her feet to summon the attorney back to his office. "She's ready," she said.

Am I?

As Monica rose and moved across the spacious divide to the attorney's desk with her newfound aunt at her side, she longed for a moment of solitude to let it all sink in. She listened to his explanation of the NDA even as she continued to stare over his shoulder out the window.

She had so many more questions.

Do I have siblings?

Was he married?

What is this story of my birth?

When is the funeral? Am I invited to attend?

Who is my mother?

But she was not ready to absorb one more piece of info.

Not today. Except…

"Exactly how much is the inheritance?" she asked after Marco finished calling one of the clerks at the firm who was a notary public.

Marco looked to Phoebe briefly as he crossed his hands over the papers on his neat desk. "Fifty million dollars."

"Huh?" she asked, blinking so swiftly that it appeared to be rapid gunfire before her eyes. "Fifteen million?"

Both Marco and Phoebe chuckled.

"No. *Fifty* million, not fifteen," he said with emphasis.

She felt light-headed and willed herself not to faint to the floor and send the billowy skirt of her thin dress up over her head.

Gabe looked up at the top of the illuminated Eiffel Tower in the distance as he leaned in the doorway of CRESS V in the Champs-Élysées area of Paris. He was a Manhattanite who enjoyed the fast pace and urban flair of the city for sure, but the City of Lights, or *la Ville Lumière*, was a close second. It was where his mother had been born, where his parents had met and home to his favorite style of cuisine. He was staying at his parents' country estate in the village of Saint-Germain-en-Laye for the week while he scouted possible locations for a new Cress restaurant.

The flute of champagne he nursed was unrivaled in its quality and well worth its hefty cost. That evening though, the restaurant was closed for a private celebration, and because of the event the liquor was apropos.

Finishing his drink with a small grunt of pleasure, he turned and opened the glass door to step back inside the restaurant. The entire staff was gathered in celebration of the release of the tenth cookbook by its head chef and Gabe's best friend, Lorenzo León Cortez. He was well loved and respected by his staff and his peers.

"You look exhausted, friend," Lorenzo said, giving him a quick look over the rim of the bottle of beer he nursed as Gabe neared him. "Who is she?"

Monica.

Gabe shook his head, refraining from revealing to even his best friend that he'd slept with the family's housekeeper. "I'm on a little break from sex," he admitted.

Lorenzo scoffed. "Medical issues?" he joked.

He gave his friend a look that was reproachful before shaking his head. "A one-night stand has had me in a loop for the past month," he admitted.

"Ah. The one-night stand that's really not just one night," Lorenzo said, looking wistful. "I've had a few of those in my lifetime."

"Yes, but it was just one night," Gabe confessed.

Lorenzo winced and then released a short whistle. "Then at the very least have one more night, bro," he said.

One more wild night with Monica?

Maybe, just maybe, that would quench his desire for her. Or make him want her even more.

No. Monica Darby was off-limits. They couldn't risk it again. It was just the thing to get her fired.

And me hooked.

"Sometimes you make me very envious, Zo," Gabe said, purposely changing the subject.

"Why? Because I have three inches of height on you?" Lorenzo asked, shifting his bone-straight, waist-length hair back behind his broad shoulders.

Gabe chuckled. "I have the extra inches where it counts," he said before pouring himself half a glass of the golden champagne.

"*Way* more info than I needed," Lorenzo drawled. "But what's on your mind? Or should I guess?"

"We talk. It wouldn't be hard to guess. Not for you," he said, turning to face the large window into the kitchen, usually bustling with activity.

"You miss cooking," Lorenzo said with a brief glance over his shoulder.

Gabe nodded. "Sometimes more than other times," he admitted. "Don't get me wrong. I am so proud of the legacy we are building for Cress generations to come. These last three years at Cress, INC. has been eye-opening and challenging, *but…*"

"There is nothing like the adrenaline rush of heading a kitchen. Right, Chef?"

Gabe glanced over at his friend and then fixed his gaze back on the kitchen. "Correct, Chef," he returned.

A sudden surge in laughter caused both men to look over at the waitstaff having an impromptu dance contest.

"And what of the race for CEO, then?" Lorenzo asked him, leaving the staff to their fun.

"I want that, too," he stressed.

"In this not-so-perfect world, you can't always have everything you want, Gabe."

True.

Lorenzo nudged Gabe's arm and then slightly jerked his head in the direction of the double doors leading into the kitchen. As soon as they stepped inside the massive space, he grabbed two aprons from the stacks of clean ones on polished wooden shelves by the door. He tossed one to his friend with ease.

Gabe caught it with one hand and a curious look.

"If you could make any dish in the world right now what would it be?" Lorenzo asked as he tied the strings around his waist.

Gabe did the same. "You have an entire buffet of food out there."

"We are open six nights a week, and this is the first night I had time to celebrate my new cookbook, and tonight I would like Gabriel Cress, esteemed chef, my former head chef, two-time–James Beard Award winner and my best friend since culinary school, to cook a meal for me," Lorenzo said, waving his hand toward the huge walk-in cooler in the corner. "What can I get you, Chef?"

"And you'll be my sous-chef? Interesting," Gabe said as he moved to one of the sinks to wash his hands.

"Yes, but it will be like your mystery woman...one night only," Lorenzo said with a laugh as he gathered his hair at his nape with a black elastic band and then washed his hands, as well.

"Do you remember the dish that made Chef Roderick give me dish duties for a week?" Gabe asked.

"Do I!" Lorenzo said, shaking his head as he began retrieving pots.

For the next thirty minutes, Gabe allowed himself to think of nothing but his love of food, from prep to completion. Even as the music and the laughter of the staff filtered in to them, he was in a zone. It was an adrenaline rush, and his friend was the perfect sous-chef following every command and at times having the next item prepared for him even before he requested it. To Gabe it was the perfect symphony.

Soon the scent of his goat-cheese-and-roasted-butternut-squash bisque rose strong in the air. He used his hand to waft the aroma closer to his face and took a deep inhale. His cell phone vibrated in his back pocket, but he ignored it. With a plastic spoon he tasted the bisque before adding a large pinch from the bowl of pink Himalayan salt.

Moving with a rhythm that was fluid and precise, he cut the kernels from the cobs of corn Lorenzo grilled and added them, as well.

"Ravioli, Chef," Lorenzo said, sliding over the tray of handmade, dried ravioli he'd stuffed with ricotta, lump crab meat, parmesan and wild mushrooms.

Gabe gave him a brisk nod even as he focused on spooning the pasta into the boiling water. Ten minutes later, he ladled the bisque into a large family-style ceramic bowl before adding the ravioli using a long-handled skimmer. He shredded fresh parmesan and quickly chopped scallions to scatter across the top.

With a nod of satisfaction, he set the bowl before Lorenzo,

who at some point had poured himself a large glass of red wine. "Enjoy," Gabe said, stepping back and wiping his sweaty brow with the hand towel he had tucked inside the waist of his apron.

It was only then that he noticed the staff had wandered into the kitchen to observe him as he was cooking. He smiled as he saw the looks of admiration on many of their young faces. He had been so lost in his art.

"Well?" Gabe asked Lorenzo.

Everyone turned to him to gauge his reaction.

His friend took care to scoop an entire ravioli covered with bisque before spooning the steamy food into his mouth. He closed his mouth and released a little grunt of pleasure as he chewed. "I see you learned the lesson Chef Roderick taught you very well," he said. *"Es la perfección, amigo mío."*

"Gracias." Gabe thanked him with a nod as applause exploded around him at his friend saying the dish was perfection.

They all quickly moved to indulge themselves in consuming the dish, and he took time to watch the pleasure wash over their faces at their initial bites. It felt like the first time he knew he had the skill and the talent to make delicious food.

He retrieved a goblet and slid it over to his friend to fill.

"Here's to one night only," Lorenzo said with a wink.

Gabe toasted to that, thinking of another one-night stand that was unforgettable.

One week later

Life was surreal.

Monica awakened in her housekeeper's quarters as always. She showered and dressed in her uniform, prepared to begin her daily chores. In her all-white bathroom, she took a moment to study her reflection.

For five years this had been her life. Here with the Cress family. On the perimeter but still one among many. It was the most stability she'd ever known. What with growing up in foster care and then traveling with James, she had never had a chance to plant roots. It felt silly to worry about yet another new start when she had been blessed with so much money to do it with, but she did.

Same surroundings. Same tasks.

Different Monica.

She'd given her two weeks' notice to Mrs. Cress and was excited about the money, which was to clear her bank account the next day, but she was also nervous about leaving her home-that-wasn't-really-home next week, packing her personal items and forging ahead.

Alone again.

She saw the sadness and fear fill her eyes and turned away from it.

Was it silly that I'd rather have had my father back than his money now?

She made her way upstairs to the first level, and like any other day, the house was still and quiet. She took a moment to pause in the kitchen and slowly turn to take in everything in the early morning. Pockets of light from sconces and under-cabinet lighting gave it such a lovely glow. Even as she looked across the kitchen and adjoining dining room with its glass wall, the waterfall at the end of the garden was backlit and made the backyard appear magical as the sun began to rise in the metropolitan sky.

It was a beautiful home in an affluent neighborhood and she would miss it when she left.

What will Gabe think?

He'd been in Paris all week, and she didn't know if he knew her days at the Cress town house were nearing an end.

Pushing aside thoughts of him, Monica made herself a cup of coffee and had fresh fruit before moving throughout the entire first level ensuring no messes had been made by the family after she retired to her quarters last night. She chuckled, remembering during her first few weeks awakening to the aftermath of a late-night, spontaneous dinner party to top all dinner parties. Chaos had reigned and the empty plates and wine bottles had been abundant.

Thankfully all was well except for a random glass here or there, overturned pillows and a few filled wastepaper baskets that she emptied into a garbage bag. Lightly humming a tune, she carried that bag and those from the cans in the kitchen to the interior entrance and through the marbled vestibule to the outer door.

She paused halfway down the stairs and looked up the street at the rows of ornate townhomes. Next week, everything would change and she had some decisions to make. Home or condo. New York or New Jersey. Travel or…or…

Or what?

The sudden flash of cameras and raised voices caused her to turn her head. She froze and leaned back from the crowd advancing to surround the porch.

"There she is!"

"That's her!"

Monica's eyes widened in shock at the people pointing cameras up at her from the street. "What?" she asked, feeling her heart pound.

"Are you Monica Darby?" one of them yelled to her.

She climbed back up a step.

"How do you feel about the death of your father that you never knew?"

"Do you hate Brock Maynard?"

The bags dropped from her trembling hands.

"Why weren't you invited to the funeral?"

Their barrage of questions was rapid and overlapping. The flash of cameras and the steady beam of lights from the video cameras were shocking intrusions into her life.

"Were you mentioned in the will?"

"If you're not in the will, do you have plans to sue?"

"Move! Excuse me. Out of the way!" a male voice roared. Gabe pushed through the throng of paparazzi on the street with ease, holding his suitcase with one hand. She then noticed the family's SUV pulling off down the street.

He opened the wrought-iron gate to race up the stairs to her. She felt sweet relief when he slid his arm around her waist and turned her to guide her back up the stairs.

"How does it feel to go from being a maid to the daughter of an A-lister?"

Gabe ushered her into the vestibule, closed the door and set down his luggage.

"What is all that about?" Gabe asked as they entered the house. "What are they saying about your father? What's going on?"

Remembering her NDA, Monica pressed her lips closed and shrugged as she shook her head. Lines of annoyance filled his handsome face as he moved back to the door to look out the tinted glass panes at the photographers still there. She allowed herself a moment to take him in. To enjoy being near him for what was the last time. He looked so handsome in his denims and a crisp blue shirt that made his eyes all the more brilliant in his tanned shortbread complexion.

"I resigned from my position here last week and gave two weeks' notice," she began.

He turned his head to eye her. Confusion filled his face even as she gave him a brisk nod.

"But I think I should leave today," she said, enjoying

the subtle hint of his warm and spicy cologne. Fireworks seemed to shoot off in her belly.

"Today?" he said, his voice deep.

She nodded. Her nondisclosure agreement kept her from explaining even more. It was the price of her inheritance.

"Is it because of what happened between us?"

"No."

"Do you have a better position?"

"No."

They shared a long look before he extended his hand. "I guess this is goodbye," he said.

Monica slipped her hand into his. "I guess so," she agreed, silently taking note how his large hand easily engulfed her own.

And felt so warm. Especially his thumb resting against her sensitive inner wrist.

She broke the hold, choosing to focus on calling the police to get rid of the crowd outside. The Upper East Side address would speed up their arrival.

"Monica. Wait."

"Yes, Mr. Cress?" she asked, turning to face him.

He bent down in front of his monogrammed Vuitton case to remove an envelope from the side pocket. "The Cress Family Foundation's charity ball is next week. I'd like for you and a guest to attend. *Please*," he stressed.

"I don't think that would be appropriate—" she began but then remembered that in less than twenty-four hours she would be worth just as much as he was and she would no longer be his maid.

He eyed her.

"I'll consider it," she conceded, taking the thick and creamy envelope from him. "Thank you."

With one last smile Monica turned from him to finish out her last day and make plans for her tomorrow.

Five

One week later

The Cress family is as surprised as the world at the news that our beloved Monica is the daughter of Brock Maynard. Although we were saddened to lose her as an invaluable and dedicated employee no longer living in our home, we do ask that the privacy of the entire Cress family be respected at this time since we have no further information to add to this conversation. In closing, we wish Monica the very best.

Gabe didn't bother to read the rest of the online newspaper story about Monica after finishing the family's official statement, released through the publicity team at Cress, INC. The hope was to thin out the paparazzi still driving through the neighborhood at slow speeds in hopes of catching a photo of Monica, who had already moved out of the home.

"Now hopefully *that* is the end of *that*," Nicolette said with emphasis.

He shifted his gaze from a spot outside in the garden over to his mother, sitting at one end of the dining room table. She slapped the folded newspaper she held on to the leather top of the table, beside her plate of fresh fruit and a buttery croissant. He knew without asking that she was speaking of something to do with their ex-employee, Monica.

It was all she'd seemed to want to discuss over the week since the paparazzi had camped outside their house and the press had revealed that Monica was in fact the secret love child of a famous actor. The fact that she worked as a maid made the story even more salacious.

"Time heals all things," Phillip Sr. said from the other end of the table before taking a deep sip of his cup of coffee.

Will time make me stop dreaming of her?

"I read on the *Star Gazette* her mother was a maid for her father when she got pregnant, and they gave her up for adoption and she came full circle by becoming a maid," Phillip Jr. said just before Chef Jillian walked in carrying a fresh carafe of the fresh-squeezed citrus juice they all loved.

She paused midstep at his words and frowned a little before continuing into the room to set the container on the table among the serving dishes of steaming food she'd prepared for them.

Gabe squeezed the bridge of his nose between his fingers, wishing his brother had more tact and less tongue on the matter. "Websites like the *Star Gazette* are hardly the place to get news," he said with censure. "We know firsthand they deal more in fiction than facts."

All he could remember was the fright in Monica's eyes as she was assailed by the paparazzi that morning. As his car pulled up before the house, he'd taken in the people outside before realizing it was Monica frozen in front of them, her eyes filled with fear and confusion. The desire to protect her had flooded him, and the car had barely stopped before he'd climbed out and barreled through the crowd to rush her back inside the house. He'd had to fight the impulse to swing and connect on the faces of those in the crowd.

"True. It's to be entertained...not informed," Cole drawled, reaching for a croissant to tear and dip in the homemade honey butter on his plate.

"Whatever," Phil muttered.

"Want some, Uncle Cole," Collette said from where she sat on her knees in the seat beside him.

He winked and honored her request as if her plate wasn't already stacked with pancakes shaped like Mickey Mouse. She giggled and proceeded to lick the decadent honey butter from the croissant.

All of the Cress men chuckled, finding her, as always, adorable.

Nicolette playfully scowled, and her mother, Raquel, gave Cole a reproachful look as she took the croissant and cleaned butter from her child's sticky fingers.

"Right, the *Gazette* also claims she's hidden away, using psychics to try to reconnect with her deceased father," Lucas agreed, nibbling his fresh fruit as he steered the convo back to Monica.

Gabe remained silent, allowing them to continue speculating on their ex-employee, who the press could not locate to harass. He had thoughts and questions of his own. Like why she hadn't told him the truth that morning.

"I resigned from my position here last week and gave two weeks' notice. But I think I should leave today."

"Today?"

"Is it because of what happened between us?"

"No."

"Do you have a better position?"

"No."

Gabe didn't know why Monica did not reveal more about her departure, but it was clear it involved the discovery of her parentage. *Or...she felt it was none of my business.*

"I am curious about where she disappeared to," Raquel said with a one-shoulder shrug. "Maybe she knew all along and didn't want to be found and that's why she's MIA."

"Who would choose to be a maid when her father is a rich actor?" Cole protested. "Sorry, Raquel, but that's ridiculous."

"Hell, the whole damn circus about the mess is ridiculous," Nicolette said. "But hopefully our inclusion in the drama is at its end, especially with the charity event tonight."

Bzzzzzz.

Gabe wiped his hands with his napkin before pulling his phone from the front pocket of his shirt to check the incoming call. Felicity. He did not answer.

"Is it even necessary to say tonight is not the night for the ladies you would not bring home to meet me?" Nicolette asked, piercing each son with her steely blue eyes. "And especially not the type who would willingly sneak into someone's home to lie up all evening doing God knows what with one of my horny sons. Right, Lucas?"

Raquel rushed to cover Collette's ears as the brothers laughed.

Lucas gave his mother his most charming smile. "Of course," he agreed.

Bzzzzzz.

He looked down at the screen of his phone. Felicity again. He could block her, ignore her calls or answer. His curiosity was piqued by the back-to-back calls so he chose the latter. "Hello, Felicity," he said, rising to leave the table with his cup of coffee to step outside to the garden.

"Hello, stranger."

She was in full-flirt mode right out the gate. He could hear it in her husky tones. She wanted something and not just to catch up. "How can I help you?" he asked, hoping to push the conversation forward.

"So businesslike, Gabriel."

He took a deep sip of the brew. "I haven't heard from you in a while, so I know there's something you want from me."

"Maybe I was reminiscing on the good times and missing you," she said.

"Or…"

She laughed. It was soft. Meant to allure.

"Or?" Gabe asked again, his voice echoing inside the cup.

"Gabriel, did we end on bad terms?" Felicity asked.

"We didn't technically end at all. We both just stopped calling each other," he said, checking the time on his watch. "That's a clear sign we both moved on, but if there is something I'm able to do for you, just ask."

"A ticket to tonight's charity event would be nice."

Gabe looked up to the sky in exasperation. *And there it is.*

"I won't be able to do it, Felicity," he said.

He hadn't decided whether to bring a date or not, and the last thing he needed was an impetuous ex to ruin his evening out of spite.

"Besides, I gave away my last two tickets," he added truthfully.

"Ga-bri-el," she said in a singsong manner. "It's *your* family's event. Surely you can get another ticket."

"My brother Phillip runs the foundation and is running

the show on the ball. He told us over a week ago it was sold out," Gabe said.

"I think a ticket would just make me *sooo* grateful. I might lose my mind and do *anything* to show my appreciation," she said with a little moan. "You remember how I show my thanks, don't you, Ga-bri-el?"

He did.

Gabe cleared his throat. "Felicity, I can't help, but it was good hearing from you," he said.

"Was it?" she asked, her tone cool.

"Of course."

"Remember it well, because I doubt it will happen again."

She ended the call.

He finished off his coffee and reentered the house.

"Where in the world is... Monica Darby?"

His eyes followed that of his entire family to the sizable television over the fireplace in the den that was on other side of the chef's kitchen. A morning entertainment-news show was on, and the mention of the ex-housekeeper's name had caught everyone's attention.

He eyed the video of Monica on the television before reclaiming his seat at the table. Her eyes were round and wide as she stood frozen on the steps of their town house.

"There's our house on television! When will this madness end? Merde!" Nicolette swore in French.

"The secret love child of Academy Award–winning actor of stage and film Brock Maynard has not been seen since this day, leaving the Upper East Side town house of the Cress family who are well-known for their culinary empire...and their good looks. Take a look at this family!"

The family's publicity shot filled the screen.

Nicolette groaned.

Phillip Sr. frowned.

Sean smiled broadly.

Phillip Jr. released a heavy breath.

Cole laughed.

Lucas winced.

Gabe tightened his jaw as the image changed to the flashes of the cameras playing over Monica's face. He wondered about her whereabouts. Was she okay? Was she happy? He hoped so because she deserved it. She had been nothing but trustworthy and reliable as the lone regular employee in their home. He wished her nothing but the best. He thought of the tickets to the ball he'd given her and admitted that he hoped she'd decided to attend.

"We may not be able to zone in on Monica Darby's whereabouts, but we have recently learned from a trusted source that Maynard did indeed leave his estate, estimated to be worth more than fifty million dollars, to his daughter. Now, that's how you say sorry..."

That info stunned the entire Cress family.

The last week had been absolutely chaotic.

Monica sat on the foot of the king-size bed of her guest room of the luxury hotel on Fifth Avenue as she used the remote to flip through the cable channels. She paused at the sight of the video of her looking frightened that had been overused the last week, online and on television. "Now what?" she muttered.

"The secret love child of Academy Award–winning actor of stage and film Brock Maynard has not been seen since this day, leaving the Upper East Side town house of the Cress family who are well-known for their culinary empire...and their good looks. Take a look at this family!"

Monica's eyes went to Gabe's face in the photo. Nothing had changed in the week since she'd last seen him. The very sight of him still made her feel more alive than the moment before.

She looked over at the opened envelope on the dresser, holding the tickets to the charity event. An opportunity to see him once more. "Should I?" she mouthed.

"We may not be able to zone in on Monica Darby's whereabouts, but we have recently learned from a trusted source that Maynard did indeed leave his estate, estimated to be worth more than fifty million dollars—"

Click.

Monica tossed the remote behind her onto the bed after having cut off the television. "Trusted source?" she protested. "You mean Phoebe Maynard? Then just say that."

It was indeed her aunt that had planted the stories with the press because she refused to allow her brother to do in death what he'd done when he was alive—pretend he didn't have a daughter. And Monica appreciated the show of support from Phoebe, but it had sent the press into her life with the vengeance of bees whose nest had been knocked to the ground.

She was tired of being stung.

With a sigh she moved across the room to the dresser and picked up the invite and pressed it to her nose. With every passing day the scent of his cologne lessened and now it barely held a hint of the warm and spicy aroma. She shifted her eyes up to see herself in the mirror, dressed in the luxury hotel's plush white cotton robe, with her hair pulled up into a messy topknot, face free of makeup and her eyes bright with the light thinking about Gabe brought to them.

For the last week she had stayed cooped up in the posh hotel room in Midtown Manhattan, where the wealthy played, intending to remain until she'd made some final decision on where to start the newest chapter in her life. Every well-appointed detail of the room with its high ceilings, stylish decor and city view of Central Park was now imprinted on her brain.

No work. No guests. Nothing to keep her occupied. Nothing but her thoughts. And room service.

"Why let boredom be the death of me?" she asked, tapping the envelope against her chin as she decided it was time to have a little fun.

The next few hours were a whirlwind in Manhattan. Behind oversize shades, she ventured out of her room, and thankfully she faded into the fast-walking crowd with ease. Armed with advice from the concierge, she ventured to a nearby boutique, where she enjoyed trying on designer gowns until she found the one that made every eye in the shop stay on her. Diamond earrings from Van Cleef. Shoes from Bergdorf Goodman. Hair, makeup and manicure by the spa at the hotel.

Aside from the cost of the hotel, it was the first of her inheritance she'd dared to spend. And what felt trepid at first got a little easier with each swipe of the card connected to one of several bank accounts she'd opened. It felt odd to spend such an amount when before it would have taken weeks to earn that much, but it had felt good—for once—to treat herself. Not even a sales clerk asking her to provide photo ID to prove it was indeed her card had shaken her. She'd shown her identification and then left the store to spend her money elsewhere.

And now I'm here.

Monica looked out the tinted window from her seat in the rear of the chauffeur-driven Tahoe, taking in the entrance to the marina. It was beautiful at night with the moon's light reflecting on the gentle waves of the Hudson River. The lights from the towering buildings in the distance gave the perfect New York backdrop. When the SUV pulled to a stop in the parking lot, she forced herself to wait for the driver to leave his seat and come around to open the door.

"Thank you," she said, accepting the offer of his hand to help her from the sizable vehicle.

"Have a good night, Ms. Darby."

Ms. Darby? That flustered her for a moment. Everything felt new and different. Even experiencing a show of respect.

With a nod, she took a deep inhale of the scent of the river. Attendees clad in elegant evening wear were already making their way down the wharf toward the sleek two-hundred-foot navy megayacht docked on the other side of the marina. She smiled at their excited chatter—a clear sign of everyone's anticipation of the festivities.

A warm breeze blew in from the river as Monica stopped to look up at the yacht. The party was already in full swing and the music echoed from inside the three-tier vessel.

She knew from overhearing the family discuss the preparations that more than five hundred people were scheduled to attend the event. There should be a live band, open bar, decadent hors d'oeuvres, a silent auction of more than fifty culinary experiences with acclaimed chefs, a charity poker tournament, and a grand finale with a popular celebrity performing a miniconcert.

Aboard the yacht, with her heart pounding from excitement and a bit of nervousness, she went straight to the bar for a glass of champagne. Over the rim she took in the mingling crowd and the entertainers among them. Contortionists, magicians and jugglers performed for the crowd amid colorful decor, lighting effects and towering floral arrangements.

A uniformed server presented her a tray. She selected a small plate and used tongs to choose a bacon and chèvre tart, lamb lollipop and a mini potpie she soon discovered was filled with lobster. She was looking about the colorfully lit room when she spotted Gabe standing by the bar, looking devastatingly beautiful in an all-black tuxedo that fit him so very well. She nearly choked on her bite of food when she finally noticed the tall and shapely brunette in a strapless cerise jumpsuit beside him. *His date?*

The woman in red laughed as she stroked the velvet lapel of his tuxedo and removed the flute from his hand to press her crimson lips to the crystal for a deep sip of the golden champagne. Monica turned away from the sight so quickly that she felt loose waves of her hair tickle her spine. She hated how easy it was to notice how different she was in comparison to the woman. Even with the costly transformation that had given her confidence, Monica felt that familiar pang of being not good enough. A remainder of her broken and unstable childhood.

Needing to be out of Gabe and his sultry date's line of vision, Monica stopped another server to place her unfinished food and drink on his tray before she took her exploration elsewhere.

"Monica?"

A warm hand lightly wrapped around her wrist. She knew before she turned that it was Gabe. The goose bumps and soft hairs on her body standing on end were truth tellers. Facing him, she confirmed their accuracy. "Hello, Mr. Cress," she said, her heart racing as he eyed her from perfectly coiffed hair to painted toes.

Her black lace gown was delicate and sweet with its scalloped sweetheart bodice and bow-embellished straps, while still being sexy with her appearing to be nude underneath. The sheer A-line skirt showed hints of her thighs, and the lace border skimmed her ankles above the strappy heels she wore. Her hair was down in soft loose curls that passed her bare shoulders. Smoky eyes and a soft nude lipstick completed her look.

What does he think? she wondered.

"You...you look amazing," he said, his warm appreciation filling his voice.

She laughed softly. "You seem surprised," she teased.

"No. Not surprised," he said, easing his hands into the pockets of his slacks. "I've seen you even prettier than this."

That made her cheeks warm.

Monica tucked her hair behind her ears, revealing dangling diamond earrings. "I wasn't sure if the dress was too much or not enough," she confessed.

Gabe's eyes were intense. "It's perfect," he admitted.

Their eyes locked and held. Silence reigned, but there was a charge—a current—that fueled the air between them. She knew from the heat in her belly and in his eyes that he felt the same stir of desire as she did. "*Just once.* Remember?" she reminded him as her pulse sprinted.

"I thought you forgot that night," he said, his gaze searching hers.

She looked away from him, seeking relief from his unspoken temptation. "We were supposed to."

"I couldn't forget it even when I tried."

She shivered.

"Look at me, Monica."

With an audible swallow over a lump in her throat, she did. And at that moment, she remembered a dozen different things about that night, from the feel of his hands gripping her buttocks to the way she'd moaned from the back of her throat in pleasure at his deep strokes.

"Excuse us?"

They looked to find a couple behind them. They'd not realized they were blocking the stairs.

Gabe grabbed her hand and pulled her behind him. Several times people called out to him or attempted to step in his path, but he bypassed them all as he led her up the stairs of the next two levels to the sundeck. As soon as they came to a stop, he pulled her body close to his and weaved his fingers through her hair as she tilted her chin up and clutched at the lapels of his tuxedo blazer. He lowered his head to kiss her.

First, a soft press of their lips together. Then, lightly touching their tongues in that hot little moment before the kiss deepened with moans that were guttural. His head leaned that way and hers the other. Their bodies pressed closely together.

The seconds seemed infinite. Monica ended the kiss with reluctance, not sure of how much time had passed from the very first feel of his mouth. She felt tipsy. And as if in a dream.

Her Prince Charming looked too delicious in his tailored tux for her not to long to undress him and have him for another night of passion.

Is it midnight? Will the carriage change back to a pumpkin? Have I lost my shoe?

She smiled at the whimsy.

"Just once more?" he asked, his voice deep and thrilling.

Her eyes fell to his mouth before she swiped the gloss from his lips with her thumb.

He eased his hands down to her lower back to gently knead the spot just above the curve of her buttocks. "You don't work for the family anymore," he said.

"No, I do not," Monica agreed, before stepping back out of his embrace and walking over to the railing to look out at the waves highlighted by the glow from the moon. She enjoyed the feel of the breeze, but it was nothing akin to the heat of Gabe's body.

He walked over to close the gap between them. "I'm not built for a relationship," he admitted.

"And I wouldn't want one with you," she countered, tilting her chin up a notch as she turned to lean back against the railing as he came to a stop before her.

"With just me? Or with anyone?" he asked, his voice as deep as the river surrounding them.

"Anyone. Love is for fools."

He chuckled and gripped the railing on either side of her body as he leaned down to press kisses from her chin to her lips. She released a telling gasp of pleasure.

"This thing between us is going to happen again," he said near her ear before shifting his head to taste her mouth.

Anticipation nearly made her weak. "Just…once… more," she spoke against his mouth.

Gabe stepped back from her and extended his hand. "Then let's get the hell out of here," he said.

Monica bit her bottom lip and smiled as she slid her hand in his.

The sun rose over Manhattan with ease, casting the city with light streaked with crimson, pinks and orange. Monica eyed the beauty outside the window of her hotel room as Gabe pressed warm kisses from one shoulder to the other. It was how he awakened her after a night of the most electric sex of her life.

First round was in one of the private cabins aboard ship. That had been fast and furious, leaving them both sweaty and breathless.

Not done with each other, they used one of the family's cars to reach her suite, where the next round had been slow and passionate. Against the door. The floor. The sofa. The windowsill. And finally, the bed. At times he took the lead. Sometimes she was in charge.

Pure pleasure.

And now, from the length of his hardness against her buttocks, he was ready for round three.

She lay on her back, causing the sheet to twist down to her waist leaving her breasts exposed. She reached to pull it back up, now feeling shy under the light of day.

He shook his head before lowering it to suck one tight brown nipple into his mouth.

"It's morning," she gasped, even as her back seemed to arch up off the bed of its own accord. "We said just once more."

With one last delicious lick, Gabe freed her breast and looked down at her again. "Yes, but this part of me doesn't agree," he said, tightening the loose white sheet against his curving erection.

"She's regretting the deal we made, too," she said, giggling when he raised the sheet to look down at the smooth, flat hairs covering her vee.

Thank God for the waxing at the spa.

"Then maybe we need to do this again?" he asked, briefly locking his eyes with hers before he lay on his back and pulled her body so that she was atop him.

"Now?" she asked as she straddled him.

"And in the future."

She looked down at him, Gabriel "Gabe" Cress, and thought of all the nights over the last five years that she had only dreamed of having him naked and hard beneath her. She wasn't looking for love, because it was synonymous for heartbreak. But maybe she could just enjoy carnal pleasures knowing one day, when the heat cooled, they would just walk away and say a fond farewell? She had no doubt it would be very easy for him.

"No strings," she stated, mostly to let him know she was quite clear on the rules.

"None," he agreed, sitting up to lightly nuzzle her neck.

"The only thing I expect from you is great sex when I call," she teased, surprised at her boldness and liking it.

"And what about me?" he asked, his voice and his eyes smoldering.

Who have I become?

She felt naughty and flirty. Desirable and sexy. Was it her sudden wealth or the way she *knew* she made him feel? The only word for it was *powerful*.

Monica turned on his lap and then slid her body to all fours between his open legs. The bed dipped under his weight as moved to kneel behind her. She gripped the sheets and pressed her face against the bed as he eased his hardness inside her until nearly all of him filled her completely. They both hissed at the connection. With a wince and soft bite of her lip as Gabe reached around her to press his hand to her throbbing bud, she moved back and forth on his inches with a rotation of her hips when she reached the base. Such a sinful glide. Meant to build a slow explosion in them both.

Ten glides—maybe less—and she felt him tremble with his release. He swore with force as she felt him harden even more inside of her. Like steel. That plus the smooth circular motions of his fingers against her caused her to cry out into the mattress and pound the softness with her fist as she joined him in sweet, white-hot bliss.

Six

Two months later

The rules had been made. No long conversations on the phone. No official dates. No overnight stays. And they both held up their end of the arrangement. But that didn't stop the many hours they spent apart from being filled with thoughts of the other.

Gabe was consumed with constant memories of her at random spots of the day. The feel of her body. Her kisses. Her sighs against his mouth. And never knowing whether she would moan or release rough cries when she climaxed.

He made it his duty to get her yelling to the ceiling until her voice was hoarse.

That thought made him chuckle.

"What's funny, Gabriel?"

He looked up from the quarterly reports to find the entire board of Cress, INC. gazing down the table to where he sat, left of his father at the head. "A random thought," he explained.

"Care to share?" Nicolette asked from the other end of the oval-shaped conference table.

"Definitely not," he asserted.

The meeting carried on and Gabe was pleased. His family was blissfully unaware that their former housekeeper was his lover. His beautiful, smart, passionate and adventurous lover. Who he was ready to see. Smell. Touch. Taste.

"If there are no other new matters," Phillip Sr. began.

"Actually, is there an estimated date for when you will officially step down as chief executive officer and name a successor?" one of the board members asked.

Gabe looked on as his parents shared a glance across the length of the table. He also noted his eldest brother, Phillip Jr., seemed particularly pleased by the question. He twisted his favorite writing pen in his hand as he turned to his father for the answer to a question he was sure all of the Cress sons wanted to know. He certainly did.

"No, there is no estimated date, because I am not yet ready to step down," Phillip Sr. said.

Gabe frowned and fought the urge to shake his head as his grip on his pen tightened.

"Nor do I feel any of my sons are ready to step into my role," he added as he sat up straighter in his chair and folded his hands atop the table.

The frown deepened and Gabe gritted his teeth in a rush of annoyance and anger. Competing for the favor of their father in order to be appointed as successor to the "throne" of the Cress empire was in full swing, changing their family dynamic and pitting the brothers against each other. All to garner their father's approval. And now the goal line had been moved further out of their sights. Gabe was tired of it all, feeling more like a chess pawn than a respected grown man.

He glanced around the table and saw the same sentiments on the faces of his brothers.

This had been their entire life under the rule of Phillip Cress Sr. Firmness. Demands. High expectations. More discipline than softness. As a man, Phillip Sr. was charming. As a husband, he was loving and devoted. As a father, he had been strict. Maybe even manipulating.

The challenge to be named his successor just exposed what had been there all along.

See me? Approve of me? Tell me I'm as good as you. Tell me I'm the best of your sons.

"Now. If we are done, I'd like to bring the meeting to a close," Phillip Sr. said, his deep voice seeming to boom inside the large conference room.

"And just how long are we to remain in this holding pattern while you play with our lives?" Cole asked, ever the rebel.

Gabe envied his boldness.

Phillip Sr.'s jaw visibly tightened.

Nicolette rose with ease and moved to the door to open it. "If the family could have the room, *s'il vous plaît*," she said with a smile meant to soften her clear demand.

As everyone else left, the brothers all rose from their seats and moved about the room as if suddenly uncaged.

"So, you all are upset?" Phillip Sr. asked, remaining in his seat as he eyed each of his sons. "You choose to take umbrage like your brother? The same audacity and disrespect?"

Gabe glanced over at him from his position in front of the floor-to-ceiling window. He frowned when he saw their mother rush to his side and whisper in his ear in French as she pressed kisses to his temple. His parents always had a way of making everyone, including their children at times, feel as if they were intruding on their own little world, one meant just for them.

Most times it was cute. In this moment Gabe found it annoying. His father needed reprimanding not consoling.

"Since everyone is rooting for me to retire and fade to black, as if I have nothing to offer," Phillip Sr. said, pressing a kiss to Nicolette's palm before setting aside her hand and rising from his seat, "why don't each of you tell me why you want to be CEO?"

"I'm the eldest and the most experienced working within the company," Phillip Jr. immediately asserted.

"Sean?" Phillip Sr. asked.

"Honestly?" Sean asked, pausing in pouring himself a glass of Perrier from the bar in the corner. "I'm the star of the company. The most well-known, and my face on the company will only grow the brand."

Gabe turned, assuming he was next by order of age.

"Cole?" Phillip Sr. said.

Surprised by his father's move, he turned back to his view.

"Because you don't think I can do it, and I want to prove you're just as wrong about that as you are about plenty of things," Cole stated.

"Coleman!" Nicolette gasped at his insolence.

"Laisse-le être, bébé," Phillip Sr. said in her native tongue.

Leave him be.

Their father was as used to Cole's shtick as everyone else.

"Lucas?"

"Because you want one of your sons to step in and fill your shoes," Lucas admitted.

"Gabriel?" Phillip Sr. finally called to him.

Again, he looked over his shoulder as he slid his hands into the pockets of his pants. "To grow the company into other culinary markets that will secure the future of Cress, INC. for generations to come," he replied with ease and honesty.

Phillip Sr. nodded and splayed his hands. "And that is why Gabriel would be my top choice were I to step down," he said.

Gabe hated the pleasure that glimmer of approval from his father gave him.

"But imagine my disappointment when you mentioned to your mother and I just last week that you missed being a chef and wished you could find a way to do so in some capacity while still working for Cress, INC. A bunch of nonsense I will *never* support."

Gabe's hand tightened into a fist inside his pocket as he remembered the comment he'd made in passing to his parents. "I also said *in a perfect world*, and trust me, I know this is *far* from that," he said, unable to take the censure from his tone.

Cole chuckled. "Careful, Gabe, you'll lose the top spot and your award for The Perfect Son," he teased.

"Enough, Cole," Phillip Sr. said, his voice low but hard and unbending.

Gabe released a heavy breath, swallowing his own anger as the tension in the room seemed to roar. "But if I'm not guaranteed the position of CEO then why should I—or any of us—alter our lives on the chance of gaining nothing?" he asked.

"Why should I trust the future of the company to someone not willing to make the sacrifice?" Phillip Sr. shot back.

"Because the happiness of your sons should matter," Gabe retorted.

Phillip Sr. threw his hands up in exasperation. "Then be

happy and go cook, Gabe, but you cannot have two loves. One will always suffer."

"Good advice, Dad," Cole said suddenly with obvious sarcasm.

Everyone in the room looked at Phillip Sr. and Cole as they shared a long look before Cole turned and strode to the door. "I'm out," he said before leaving.

Gabe had found their brief exchange odd, but barely had time to give it much thought as his father stood and took his mother's hand in his and walked across the conference room, as well. For him, the conversation was not done, but for now, it was clearly over.

He was still annoyed as they all took their leave, but throughout the day, he found it hard to focus on the business proposal to present for board approval for the second CRESS restaurant in Paris.

It was a bitter pill to swallow that his parents held no regard for his happiness.

If nothing else. I've been given the freedom to do as I please and I'm grateful for that.

He lowered his hands from the keyboard and sat back in his chair behind his desk as he remembered the occasion those words had been said to him...

Monica lay on her stomach across the middle of her queen-size bed as Gabe rested on his side beside her with the dark gray satin sheets haphazardly strewn over their lower bodies. He trailed his fingers up and down her spine. He aroused tiny goose bumps across her soft skin as she gazed out the window at the stunning view of darkness claiming the Manhattan heavens as light began to fill windows of the towering skyscrapers in the distance.

The view was as beautiful as her new condo, but neither could rival her beauty when he stroked deep inside her and looked down at the satisfaction in her brown eyes.

*They'd enjoyed making fiery love. It had been a week
since they'd last sought out each other for pleasure. Although an hour had passed, they lingered in bed, still enjoying each other's presence.*

Ding.

*He bent to press a kiss to her lower back as she reached
to pick up the iPad from the nightstand.*

*"Room service is on the way," she said, looking back at
him over her shoulder.*

*Monica had purchased a condominium in one of those
buildings that was mainly a hotel but had several floors
designated for condos, combining the luxury and ameni-
ties of a hostelry with home ownership.*

*Gabe deeply massaged one fleshy cheek of her bottom
before giving it a slap. She playfully scowled and arched
a brow.*

*"Just making up for the slap you gave me earlier," he
said as she climbed from the bed nude.*

*He watched her, enjoying the sight of her soft buttocks
as she bent over to find her robe, tangled with the duvet
strewn on the floor. In the months since they'd become lovers, he'd seen more of her shy facade fade. Nearly gone
was the skittish woman who'd made it her business to remain in the background of his family's life. He wasn't sure
if it was her sudden wealth and independence or the confidence brought on by knowing he found her his best lover
yet—something he had admitted to her on many occasions
before, during and after sex.*

*"Yes, but I wasn't in the right state of mind," she said,
pulling on a floor-length white cotton robe that was innocent on a hanger but thrilling on her body.*

*He loved the way the thin material skimmed her hard
nipples and clung to her hips. He was used to lace and
silk but found pleasure every time she peeled back her*

*innocence and came alive under his touch. His arousal
stirred as she ran her fingers through her disheveled hair
and pushed the length behind her shoulders before leaving the room.*

Gabe turned to reach for the iPad to turn on the sev-
enty-inch television on the wall above the slate fireplace
positioned across from the bed. He flipped through the
channels, looking for business news but stopped at the
sight of a photo of Monica crossing one of the many busy
New York streets. He started to call out to her but stopped,
knowing she never talked about the gossip in the press concerning her and her alleged father.

The camera cut to the face of a pretty brown-skinned
woman in her seventies with reddish-brown soft curls and
a friendly expression who looked very familiar. She and
a younger woman were walking the beach as they talked.

"So, Mrs. Maynard, you are confirming the speculation
that Monica Darby is in fact your niece by your brother,
Brock Maynard?" the entertainment newscaster asked as
the woman paused to gaze out at the sun setting above
the ocean.

"Absolutely," Phoebe said, resting her hands on her
hips. She wore a linen powder blue shirt and pants. "And
she may have one of those gag orders stopping her speaking
on it, but I don't. I am proud to have her as my niece and
just wish we'd had the chance to know each other sooner."

Gabe's mouth opened a bit at that revelation. He moved
to rise from the bed and cross the room to stand before the
television. It was then he noticed that Monica favored the
woman. A lot.

"And do you care to share the real story of her birth?"

"That is a story I will only share with my niece when
she is ready to hear it," Phoebe said before turning to give

the camera a sparkling smile and a wink Gabe believed to be meant for Monica.

He glanced over and found her paused in the doorway with her hands still gripping the white-linen-covered cart, laden with the food they'd ordered à la carte from the restaurant downstairs.

She moved around the cart to reach the bed and turn off the television with the iPad. "Gabriel," she chided him, facing him with her arms crossed over her chest.

"Why didn't you just say you signed an NDA?" he asked as he retrieved the cart and removed the warmers from the plates.

She arched a brow.

"Right...because you signed an NDA."

She remained silent.

"How are you enjoying your new life?"

"It's more than I ever dreamed of," she admitted, careful with her words.

"But?"

"But you know I can't talk about it...even though I want to," she said. "I want to get out of my own head and process it all, but I can't. So just leave it be. Please."

"Seems like your aunt is more than willing to talk to you. Maybe it's time to take her up on her offer," he said, pulling the sash of her robe and letting it fall to her sides as he eased one arm around her waist to mold her body against his.

Monica released a grunt of pleasure at the feel of him as she tilted her head back and raised up on the tip of her toes to better enjoy the kisses he pressed to her neck.

"One thing I can say."

Gabe raised his head to look down at her, finding her eyes melancholy.

"If nothing else. I've been given the freedom to do as I please and I'm grateful for that," she admitted.

Gabe didn't allow his recollection to continue on to how he'd scooped her up in his arms and pressed her body beneath his as he helped erase the sadness from her eyes. The empathy he felt sent visceral pains across his chest for her. Somehow Brock Maynard had not spent one day in the life of his daughter, who'd ended up in foster care. It seemed he'd never even spoken of her existence to his lone family member until he was on death's bed.

But he had granted her money to do with as she pleased, to live as she pleased. While his father had been a constant presence in his life but withheld the freedom for him to live his dreams.

Gabe clenched his jaw at the thought of that irony and then he clearly remembered the night at the CRESS restaurant in Paris where he had reconnected with his passion for food. A joy in his life that he'd set aside for the sake of the family business. A sacrifice that was unappreciated by his parents.

Maybe it is time to do as I please and be free...

"I can't believe you made a scrapbook," Monica said to Phoebe as she flipped through the pages of newspaper clippings and prints of online articles about her.

"*A* scrapbook? I made two. That one's yours," Phoebe said from her seat on the modern sofa as she looked around at the high ceilings, stylish decor and view of Central Park via the floor-to-ceiling windows. "Your apartment is beautiful."

Monica eyed the serviced residence she purchased fully designed and furnished in subtle shades of light gray—it reminded her of the Cress home and had made her love it on first sight when the Realtor had shown it to her. "Sometimes I can't believe it's mine," she said, her voice soft as she stood up and moved about the spacious living room, touching this item and that. Artwork. Fireplace. Soft furnishings. "Everything is so different."

"Are you happy here?" Phoebe asked.

Monica leaned against the doorway of her apartment's Juliet balcony, which overlooked the floral garden of the Midtown Manhattan building. She was still trying to find comfort within her new life. Wealth brought on the expectations that came along with being on the other side of the line separating the haves from the have-nots. Being unemployed with endless time on her hands.

To think.

About the revelation concerning her father.

About the truth telling of her aunt.

About the invasion of paparazzi and gossip reporters upon her privacy.

About the identity of her mother.

And the strong and passionate skill of her lover.

The last made her smile into her glass.

I have a lover.

"Gabe," she whispered into the summer air as her entire body seemed to tingle at the very thought of him.

"What's that you said?" Phoebe asked.

Monica turned with a smile. "I'm happy," she finally answered her.

They saw each other maybe once a week, sometimes every two weeks. No expectations. No dates. No chances of mixed feelings and broken hearts. No fear of being left alone.

Or behind, she thought, thinking of her ex, James.

They knew going into it that the fire would fade and their dalliances would end without either taking offense.

It was the perfect way to have Gabe Cress without *having* Gabe Cress. It was their sexy and salacious little secret.

She could only imagine the reaction of his family if they knew—especially his mother. She'd spent five years in their home and had come to know them well. Nicolette Cress was firmly against the mingling of family and staff. Monica doubted her sudden wealth or famous father would change the fact that she would always be Monica the Maid in the woman's eyes. Mrs. Cress would never want to equate a former servant to herself. For *any* reason.

Just hope she doesn't find out about Chef Jillian, she thought with a hint of spite as she remembered the sexy note she'd stumbled upon in the kitchen.

That made her chuckle.

"All done, Ms. Darby."

Monica turned and eyed one of the building's house-keepers, standing in the living room with her hands locked in front of her in the usual gray uniform dress and comfortable shoes the cleaning staff wore. "Thank you, Olive," she said after reading her name tag.

"You're welcome," she said with a polite nod.

Monica was surprised when the middle-aged woman stopped on her way to the front door and turned.

"Yes?" she asked, feeling more like Nicolette Cress than herself.

It didn't sit well with her.

"I just noticed we never have to actually clean for you. It's always spotless," Olive said, glancing down at her shoes.

Monica knew the show of deference well. Again, she felt ill at ease at her switch in status. "I'm so used to doing it for others, that's all," she said.

"Yes, but if our supervisors were to know, they would assume the housekeeping staff is not doing a good enough job for you," she explained.

Right.

Monica gave her a soft smile. "I understand and I will try to do less," she said, knowing firsthand the security provided by having a job.

Olive said nothing else and continued out the door, quietly closing it behind herself.

Monica gave Phoebe a small smile at the long look her aunt gave her with all-too-knowing eyes.

"Give it time," she said.

"I'm bored out of my mind. There is only so much shopping and spa treatments I can do. I want—*need*—more," she said. "I've always worked. Always. I've never had a choice but to work. Even when I traveled with James, I worked alongside him or took odd jobs as a waitress or cashier to eat up some time before we were on the move to the next location."

"James?" Phoebe asked.

"Ex. Long story."

"I have plenty of those long stories in my seventy years."

"I don't have but the one, and I plan for it to be the only one," she said.

Phoebe chuckled. "Life is too long to believe you will only fall in love once," she advised with a twinkle in her eyes.

"My focus is on starting a business or nonprofit," she asserted. "Not love."

"Doing what, now?"

"I remember the fear and loneliness I felt at aging out of the foster care system and receiving no real financial assistance from the state to start my adult life," she began. "I'm considering asking my attorney, Choice Kingsley, to help me start a nonprofit to help foster care children in the same predicament."

Phoebe's eyes were sympathetic as she eyed her niece.

"That sounds like something worth investing some time, and with the rest, you give yourself room to adjust to your new life."

"You'd think after growing up in foster care and learning to adjust to different environments that I'd already know that," Monica said, coming back across the sunlit living room to reclaim her seat on the sofa across from the other woman.

Phoebe's eyes were sad, although she gave her a soft smile. "I would have raised you and loved you if I'd known, but I didn't. I swear I didn't," she said, her voice barely above a whisper.

Monica took a breath. "That's exactly why I called you, to ask the very question of just what do you know?" she said, feeling her stomach twist in knots from fear and anxiousness.

"You're ready now?" Phoebe asked.

Monica sat back against the plush pillows as she crossed one leg over the other and slightly raised one shoulder. "Someone I know suggested it was time," she said, thinking of Gabe.

"Seems like your aunt is more *than willing to talk to you. Maybe it's time to take her up on her offer."*

"This is not easy to say or admit, but it's the truth, and I always say why lie when the truth is sufficient," Phoebe began. "My brother had a taste for younger women. Not teenagers but young. I think they made him relive his glory days while he pretended his hair wasn't turning silver and things below the belt weren't quite as hard as they used to be."

Monica felt a little nervous.

"He met your mother at his favorite twenty-four-hour diner, where she was a waitress."

"How old?" Monica asked.

"Twenty."

"And he was?"

"Forty-two."

She winced. "Was he married?" she asked.

"No, but he and the singer Roz Garnet had an arrangement," Phoebe said. "They met on the set of a movie being made in Hollywood. Whirlwind. She moved back to New York to be with him. Basically gave up her career to have him."

Silly woman in love. Been there. Done that. Not doing it again.

Monica picked up her iPhone from the seat and searched for a photo of the disco singer. She found her to be a mocha-skinned beauty with curly hair and plump lips with her signature shades in place. *She's beautiful.*

"They were together but not together for years, and no one knew. They liked it that way. He left his apartment in Tribeca to her," Phoebe said. "She never had children of her own."

Monica looked up from the phone. "Is that why he didn't want me? To keep from hurting her? Was that my mother's fault? Or mine?" she asked, unable to hide her censure. "And even in his death he protected her from the truth. From me. My existence. It's pretty jacked up."

Phoebe rose and came over to sit beside her niece. "I would never make excuses for my brother's decisions. I am just giving you the truth," she implored, reaching for Monica's hand to cover with her own.

Monica withdrew it and rose to her feet to put distance between them as she felt the pain of resentment for her father spread across her chest in waves. "And the rest of the truth?" she asked, her voice hollow to her own ears. "My father turned his back on me and hid me so that his lover never felt betrayed. Now, why did my mother? Why did she desert me?"

Phoebe ran her pearl-colored fingertips through her hair as she shifted her gaze away.

"What?" Monica asked, narrowing her eyes as she looked at her.

Phoebe looked down at the floor.

"Why lie when the truth is sufficient?" Monica reminded her.

Phoebe sighed. "Your father admitted to me on his deathbed that your mother couldn't take care of you. She was alone and struggling," she began.

Monica crossed her arms over her chest and hugged herself. Preparing herself.

"He promised her he would raise you but gave you up instead," she admitted with tears in her eyes when she finally locked them with her niece's again.

Monica stiffened her back and knees to keep from swooning at her father's betrayal. It was she who broke their linked eyes as she cast her gaze down to the toes of her crocodile leather flats. "What was her name?" she asked, her voice whisper soft. "What was my mother's name?"

"That, he did not tell me."

She hugged herself tighter and raised her head just as a tear flew down her cheek. "Secrets to the very end, huh?" she asked bitterly.

Phoebe winced and rose to her feet.

Monica shook her head and held up a hand to deny her the right to come closer. She couldn't find any more words. She released a long drawn-out breath between pursed lips as she grappled with yet another loss. "Could you go, please?" she begged, feeling weakened.

"I don't want to go," Phoebe said.

Monica released a bitter laugh. "Welcome to my world.

A lot of things I didn't want to happen did," she said with a shrug and a downturn of her lips. "Do like I did and deal with it."

"I know you're angry and hurt. So am I. This man was my brother, and I would have never thought he was capable of turning his back on his own child," Phoebe implored. "I don't agree with him. I think you deserve to be recognized and embraced. That's why I let the world know you were my brother's child and I love you—"

"You don't know me!" Monica yelled, releasing years of frustration and hurt.

"I *know* that you are my niece. You are my blood. And for me…that is enough to love you on sight, Monica Darby," she said with emotion, her eyes wet from her own tears. "You have family. You have me."

Monica swiped her cheek. "You're not my mother, and even now with all the press, she didn't step forward and say *I'm your mother*," she said, drawing a shaky breath.

"But I'm your family," Phoebe insisted, taking a step toward her.

Again, Monica denied her with a shake of her head.

"Okay," Phoebe said, clasping her hands before stepping back and then turning to retrieve her clutch from the sofa where she'd first set it upon her arrival. "I'm going back to Santa Monica tomorrow. My home is your home. Always."

Monica said nothing else as she watched the older woman reluctantly take her leave. The click of the door closing behind her seemed so final. For a moment, she considered running to her aunt and begging her not to go.

Instead, she dried her tears, tucked her pain away, like she'd learned to do as a forgotten foster child, and picked up her iPhone to dial Gabe's number. He answered on the third ring.

"Gabe, I know we just saw each other earlier this week

but I need a distraction tonight. Can you help me with that?" she asked.

"You okay?" he asked.

"Nothing you can't make me forget for a little while," Monica said, longing for his presence.

"I'm on the way," he said before ending the call.

By the time she'd showered, brushed down her hair and slipped on a sheer robe, Gabe was at the door. She fell into his arms and captured his lips with her own as soon as he stepped into the foyer. With a deep moan he untied her robe and let it hang open to reveal her nudity before he scooped her body up into his arms with ease and carried her to the bedroom as she clung to him as if starved.

Seven

One month later

Gabe glanced over at Monica dressed in nothing but his tailored shirt as she leaned against the black stone counter watching him cook them dinner. He, on the other hand, wore nothing but a white apron with his buttocks exposed in the back. She gave him a mischievous look as she reached over to swat at one cheek before gripping the hard flesh in her hand as she pressed her chin into his upper arm and looked up at him.

Shit.

He couldn't look away. He felt trapped in her gaze. And when the humor faded from her eyes to be replaced with some other emotion, his gut clenched. It wasn't desire. He knew that look well. She felt more than just an attraction and might expect more from him than just carnal pleasure.

It was something that made him feel an odd mix of excitement and trepidation.

Bzzzzzz.

Thankful for the intrusion, Gabe shifted the pan of seared rib eye steaks from the heat of the Viking stove and picked up his phone from the table. A FaceTime call. "It's Cole. I was supposed to meet up with them for drinks," he said to Monica. He walked out of the kitchen and to the hall before he accepted the connection, being sure to keep his nude body out of the frame.

"What's up, Cole?" Gabe said, looking at his brother and easily recognizing CRESS X's upscale bar setting behind him.

"All your brothers are here. Where are you?" he asked, swiveling the phone to show the Cress men lined up at the copper-topped bar before his frowning face filled the screen again.

"I can't make it," he said, looking into the kitchen to see Monica glance at him before she moved to wash her hands at the rinse sink.

"Yeah, but where are you?" Cole pressed. "And with whom?"

The last thing Gabe wanted was for Monica to become a topic of discussion among his brothers. The fact she was their ex-employee would make the jokes and ribbing all the more raucous. They would assume she had been his in-house lover for the last five years. His instinct was to protect her from that. From gossip. From judgment and speculation. "I'm still at work," he lied, seeing Monica pause in drying her hands with a dish towel. "I'll catch up with y'all at the house later."

"But that's not the off—"

Beep.

Gabe ended the FaceTime call and walked back into the kitchen, setting his phone on the counter. He enjoyed the sight of Monica's smooth legs and the way the hem of his shirt fell just beneath her bottom. When she turned and caught his eyes on her, he didn't look away.

She frowned. "If you had plans, you didn't have to make dinner," Monica said, gripping the edges of the farmhouse-style sink as she leaned back against it.

Gabe used clamps to remove the steaks from the pan and set them on the cutting board to rest. He opened the top oven to remove the tray of root vegetables he'd roasted along with garlic and thyme in an olive-oil-and-lemon mixture. He took his time, thinly slicing the medium-rare steak and plating it before adding a pile of the root vegetables and garnish. Delicious and appealing to the eye.

He set the plate on the island and then poured her a glass of red wine. "I'm exactly where I want to be," he said, handing it to her before pouring himself one, as well, then touched the rim to hers.

Monica was thankful for the shade of the trees as she took her seat on the terrace of the French bistro in the middle of Midtown Manhattan. "I'll have a glass of the house white wine, please," she said to the waiter, opening the tented napkin to lay on her lap across the red wide-leg pants she wore with a matching tank and gold leather flats.

She took a sip of her goblet of ice water as she looked around at the cream-and-brown decor. The terrace was surrounded by six-foot wood panels. Above the panels, the towering skyscrapers surrounded the converted town house housing the restaurant.

She had just begun to peruse the menu when her guest joined her. "Hi, Choice," she said, rising to kiss the woman's smooth brown cheek before they both took their seats across from each other at the bistro table. "Is it hot enough for you?"

Choice Kingsley pushed her shades atop her head and set her crocodile leather briefcase on an empty chair. "Only lunch with you could get me to leave the air-conditioning of my office," she said with a smile.

A junior partner at Curro Villar and Hunt, Choice was recommended to her by Marco Villar to serve as her attorney. A work relationship had slowly become a friendship as Monica found she enjoyed the woman's intelligence and humor. She was easy to talk to and Monica considered her a godsend…and probably the first person she'd truly taken the chance on trusting.

They both ordered quiche lorraine for lunch, with Choice choosing sparkling water with fresh fruit for her drink.

"Business first," Choice said, reaching for her briefcase to remove a black file. "Your 501c3 has been officially established. Congrats on that."

Monica accepted the file and opened it, knowing the certification was only the next step in establishing her charity. It would make any money she collected as a charitable organization exempt from federal taxes. Monica's plan had been to just donate directly from her own money, but Choice had talked her into really making a go of the foundation—solicit funds, set up grants, hire small staff and maybe even a publicist.

"Now pleasure," Choice said, her fork slicing into the egg-and-bacon dish baked in buttery pastry. "How's Gabe? Or better yet how are you and Gabe?"

"Scary," Monica admitted before taking a deep sip of her wine. "We see each other more. Talk more. Call each other more. He cooks dinner. We share things— dreams—with each other. Sometimes we don't even have sex when we meet up. We're breaking all the rules we set—well, all except one. Never to spend any more nights together."

"And that scares you?" Choice asked. "Most women would give up a kidney to have Gabriel Cress in their life in *any* way."

"Most women haven't had their heart broken by both their parents when they were left to grow up in foster care without feeling seen...or loved," she said softly before forcing a sad smile to her lips at the pity in Choice's eyes.

Monica thought of Gabe lying to his brothers about his whereabouts last week and how she'd felt slighted—even though she knew she shouldn't. Somehow that conversation raked up her feelings of self-doubt. Although he was abiding by the perimeters they'd both set, the hurt little girl inside of her felt he was ashamed of his dealings with her and wanted to avoid the disdain his family would feel about him being so closely enmeshed with their former maid.

"Is he seeing anyone else?" Choice asked.

Monica's breath caught.

Is he?

"That's none of my business," she forced herself to say. To truly feel. "If so, she's doing a horrible job keeping him from my door," she added.

"Some men just can't get enough," Choice said.

"The last thing I need is more heartbreak," she said more to herself than Choice.

"You had no control growing up, but you have all of it now," Choice advised.

The waiter refilled her wine and Monica gave him a nod to thank him. "Yes, but the trick is to let my brain stay in control and not my heart," she said.

"Trust me. I agree, friend," Choice said, raising her goblet of fruit-infused water in toast to that.

Two weeks later

Gabe awakened with a start. The room was dark, and it took a moment or two to recognize the tray ceiling of his bedroom. He sat up in the middle of the bed and wiped his eyes with his hands as he yawned.

The sound of light snores caused him to freeze. He leaned over left and then right to check on the floor beside the bed. He raised the covers and lifted the pillows. There sat his iPhone, still on speaker with Monica's name across the top. He chuckled as he picked it up. They'd been talking late into the night and had fallen asleep. Something he hadn't done since high school.

He frowned and ended the call, staring off into the distance and not really seeing anything.

Monica had happened to call him to ask for advice about her nonprofit at a time when he'd been frustrated by yet another argument between two of his brothers. He revealed to her that the competitiveness in his family was tedious to him and that he desired to reconnect with his love of cooking. He was now curious why he felt the desire to share these things with her.

She had encouraged him to find a balance. To be happy with his life's decisions. Live with no regrets. Treasure his family. That exchange between them had been natural. Comfortable.

The very idea of that growing ease between them caused him to wrinkle his brow and tumble deep into his thoughts as he turned his head to look out the crack in his curtains at the streetlight outside.

Ding.

Gabe removed the glasses he used for reading and set his book down on the sofa as Monica lifted her feet from his lap so he could rise and walk over to the door. He soon returned with a tray, carrying the carafe of coffee and croissants they'd ordered. He set it down on the leather ottoman before pouring her cup first and adding the creamer and four packets of sugar she always favored.

Monica set aside the folders of materials she was reviewing of office spaces and clerical staff for her nonprofit, which she had yet to name. In turn, she added a thin layer of butter to two croissants just the way she had come to learn he enjoyed them. Moving almost in a rhythm, she handed him the croissants and took the cup of coffee he offered her. She took a deep sip of the steaming light and sweet brew.

He slid his reading glasses back on and smiled as he took a bite of the buttery pastry before taking a sip of his own black coffee. He'd come over for a lunchtime tryst that had extended to a leisurely afternoon on her sofa. Raising his arms, she slid her feet back on his lap, and without a word spoken, they both enjoyed their snack and got lost in their reading.

One week later

"My mother caught one of my brother's overnight companions in the house," Gabe said from his seat across from her at her glass dining room table.

Monica took a bite of the spinach, sausage and homemade egg pasta in garlic-tomato sauce he'd made for dinner. "Let me guess? Lucas," she said, around the food.

Gabe chuckled. "Right," he said. "Ever since the weight loss, he has been enjoying the extra attention the ladies give him."

"What did she do?" Monica asked after a sip of white wine.

Nicolette Cress was all about things being done appropriately. The facade of the Cress family and their empire always had to be of a certain caliber.

"She politely escorted the young lady and Luc to the door," Gabe said.

"*And* Luc?" Monica asked in surprise.

He nodded. "And then she proceeded to wake up the entire household and go on a ten-minute tirade about respect, decorum, decent women and gentlemen, and how none of those things were to be found in the Cress family home that night."

"But Lucas missed the speech," she pointed out.

"That was about three in the morning," Gabe said, picking up the bottle of wine to refill both their glasses. "We all heard it again at breakfast when he returned."

"Three?" Monica asked with a wince.

"You think the new housekeeper heard all the ruckus?" he asked.

"Absolutely. The vents carry plenty of juicy details," she advised him with a playful wink.

She thought of Chef Jillian's note and started to share it with him but refrained, keeping that and other endless secrets she held about the family. First, she felt it wasn't her place. Second, she'd signed an NDA. Third, she felt it would only make the strained nature of the family much worse.

Like the surveillance reports I saw in the Cresses' bedroom.

"Sometimes I forget you…"

She arched a brow as his words trailed off. "That I was the family's maid?" she offered. "Trust me, I haven't."

He set his glass and fork down as he sat back in his chair to look across the table at her. "Do you regret it?"

"Working for a living? Never," she asserted, claiming her pride in her work as a maid.

Bzzzzzz.

Monica used the hand not clutching her glass to turn her phone over on the table where it sat. She recognized the number. Bobbie Barnett.

Answer it.

"Damn," she swore.

"What's wrong?"

She shifted her gaze over to Gabe. "Two weeks ago, I hired a private investigator to find the identity of my mother," she admitted, feeling her heart pound with the force of a sledgehammer. "That's her calling."

Bzzzzzz.

His eyes locked on the phone. "Answer it," he said, as he shifted his gaze back to hers.

Strengthened by his presence, she picked up the phone and answered the call as she pushed back her chair before rising. "Hello," she said, moving across the kitchen and living room of the open area to reach the window showcasing Manhattan at night.

As she listened to the PI, the emotion in her eyes shifted in the glass's reflection, moving from fear and slight excitement to shock. Grief. Sadness. And finally they went dull as she felt a chill race over her form.

Monica closed her eyes and released short gasps as her hand tightly gripped the phone.

"Ms. Darby? Are you still there?" Bobbie said.

Monica nodded, but then remembered the woman could not see her. "Yes," she said, her voice sounding hollow to her own ears.

"I just emailed my report to you, and please let me know if there's anything I can help you with in the future."

Anger rose quickly. Irrationally. She knew it and clung to it because anything was better than yet another disappointment. "Crappy time to strike up new business, isn't it?" she asked, her tone clipped and rigid.

"Ms. Darby, I meant no harm and I am so sorry for your loss," she said, her voice soft.

Loss? Losses was more like it.

Monica ended the call and let the phone carelessly drop to the floor as she allowed the full weight and meaning of her mother's death just a year ago settle around her. Engulf her. Take her back to a time when loss was common. It all just seemed cruel. And when tears dared to well up and pain radiated across her chest, Monica used a trick from childhood to go numb. Not feel. Not let her emotions weaken her.

"Damn," she swore again, feeling her childhood trick fail.

She wrapped her arms around herself as she leaned her head against the window.

My mother and father are dead.

The hope of her inner child—the one she fought so hard to ignore—faded like a candle. For years she'd hoped they would return and reclaim her. They never had.

They never will now.

That stung.

I will never know them.

She winced and closed her eyes.

Just as I opened up to every hope of having her in my life...

One tear fell. Loss after loss after loss after loss. Like dominoes.

Father God.

"Monica? What's wrong?"

She opened her eyes and looked over at him standing across the room. Gabriel Cress. Handsome. Talented. Wealthy. Sexy. Wanted.

She cringed and closed her eyes as she held herself tighter. In that moment all she saw was someone else she would lose. "My mother died last year," she said, fighting the urge to release a long wail and give voice to the varied emotions swirling inside her.

Drowning her.

The abandonment and now the loss. Again.

And the cry came. Like a roar. Seeming to be torn from her. Echoing up to the high ceilings and bouncing off the walls. Gabe rushed to her side and turned her to pull her body close to his as he wrapped his strong arms around her. One hand massaged her neck beneath the layers of her hair and the other pressed against her back.

"Let it out. I got you. I'm here," he said into her ear. "I got you."

But for how long?

Monica buried her face against his neck and allowed herself for a moment to imagine it was forever. That he could want her in his life and not just in his bed. That she could live without fear of being hurt.

She pressed a kiss to his neck and closed her eyes to inhale deeply of his warm and familiar scent as she accepted what she had been ignoring all along. She had come to rely on him. Expect him. Miss him.

And if things did not end, she would come to love him. And then lose him.

Fear made her freeze in his arms.

She couldn't take one more loss.

"You are the last thing I need and everything I need at this moment," Monica admitted in a soft voice as she forced her body to relax as she clung to him and freed herself of him all at once.

When she felt Gabe step back from her, she took a steadying breath and looked up into his handsome face, forcing herself to do what needed to be done. "Gabe, it's over. This thing between us. It's time. It's over. It's done," she said, moving away from him.

He frowned. "What? Why?" he asked, stepping toward her.

She shook her head and held up her hands. "I'm ending it before you do," she said. "Before I get hurt. Before I lean on you and depend on you and get used to you any more than I already have."

Gabe slid his hands into his slacks and stood rigid as he eyed her for the longest time. "So, I'm the bad guy?" he asked.

"Am I wrong?" she countered.

He looked down at his feet as he clenched and un-clenched his jaw. The moments seemed to tick by ever so slowly. "We both agreed that whenever one of us said it was done then it was done," he said.

"Right," Monica said, fighting the urge to run to him and be wrapped in his arms again.

Gabe looked up and locked his eyes on her. "This is what you want?" he asked, his voice deep and serious and final.

There in the depths was an ultimatum. She knew her answer would lead to him walking out the door and never returning.

"Yes," she lied before turning her back on him and closing her eyes as she fought to do what she knew needed to be done to save herself any more heartbreak.

Monica stood by the fireplace and gripped the mantel. She listened as he gathered his suit jacket, tie, briefcase and keys, and then his footsteps echoed against the wood floors as he walked to the door and opened it. Like a fool she dared to glance back over her shoulder and saw him paused in the open doorway with his back to her. He turned his head and showed his profile. His jaw was rigid.

"I am deeply sorry about your mother," he said. "If there

is ever *anything* I can do for you to help you, just ask, and I'll get it done."

She believed him. That was the problem. He was so very easy to love.

She looked away from him.

Moments later the door softly closed behind him.

Monica released the mantel and allowed her knees to go out beneath her. There, atop the plush area rug, she curled her body into the fetal position and wept. For the mother she would never know. The father who'd abandoned her. And the love she was afraid to have.

Another loss.

At least this time it was my choice.

One month later

Gabe left the bathroom of his parents' eight-bedroom country estate in the village of Saint-Germain-en-Laye, twenty miles outside Paris, with a towel draped around his waist and another over his head as he dried his hair. Letting the damp cloth fall to his shoulders, he walked over to the large windows and looked out at the beauty of the countryside. The sun was just beginning to set and the skies were painted in dreamy colors as day shifted to night. A wind blew across the fields and sent wildflowers swaying back and forth among the emerald grass. In the distance were the red roofs of the homes in the village. Trees with leaves in shades of green, gold and claret towered, offering shade and some relief from the heat.

With approval from the board of Cress, INC., Gabe had been in Paris the last month overseeing the construction and launch of CRESS XI. At times the solace of the large country estate was haunting, but most days, he was glad to be free of the continuing rivalry among his brothers. And the work kept him busy and his thoughts occupied.

He wished he had more control as he slept. His dreams of her betrayed him.

Bzzzzzz.

He looked back over his shoulder at his iPhone on the pine French-provincial dresser. He strode across the room to flip it over and accepted the disappointment he felt that it wasn't *her* calling.

So be it.

He wouldn't be the one to make the first move. And perhaps it was for the best. What future could they have? She lacked trust and he thrived on ambition. Neither was equipped for more between them.

Eight

One week later

Monica lowered the rear window from her position on the back seat of the all-black SUV with dark tinted windows. "Gabe," she called over to him once the vehicle he exited drove away and revealed him standing on the street.

Her heart raced at the very sight of him. His shortbread complexion seemed darker. His beard fuller. His body a bit more fit in the navy long-sleeved tee and dark denims he wore with cognac oxford sneakers.

He turned in surprise and looked up and down the length of the street before he finally noticed her in the SUV parked at the curb a few houses down from the Cress townhome. He smiled and it transformed his face.

Her heart raced and her entire body went warm.

The last month without him had proven nothing except

that her feelings for Gabe ran beyond just the physical. Against her better instincts and rational thought. She was hooked. She couldn't turn him loose.

Monica motioned for him to come to her before raising the window and disappearing behind the darkness of the glass. Her eyes stayed locked on him as he strode across the street. Her entire body felt like a bundle of nerves. There was happiness to see him. Desire to have him. But also fear.

She pushed the latter away as he opened the rear door.

"I am not ready to say goodbye to you forever, Gabe," she admitted, feeling as if the moment was all or nothing.

He eyed her with such intensity.

Time slowed.

She licked at her lips, feeling as if they were suddenly dry.

His eyes dropped to take in the move she'd made in all innocence.

She gasped when he locked his gaze on hers and extended his hand. She looked down at it and then up at him before sliding hers into his.

"Get out," he said, his voice deep.

It sounded so good to her ears.

He helped her exit the car. As soon as her feet touched on the ground, he pulled her body close to his and lowered his head to hers.

Her alarmed eyes looked past his shoulder to the family's home. "What if someone sees us?" she whispered in a panic.

"I don't care."

And there, pressed against the side of the vehicle, they kissed with every bit of the hunger they felt for each other, with panting breaths and excitement beyond measure.

"What are we doing, Gabe?" she asked in between electric kisses.

He raised her chin with his finger to look into her eyes. "Taking a chance on each other."

Monica released a grunt of pleasure as she wiggled her body back against Gabe's warmth as he spooned her from behind. She had to admit that the nights he stayed over were the best. It had been a long time since she'd slept with someone, and even then, nothing compared to the security she felt from Gabe's arm stretched over her waist and one of his feet lightly resting atop hers as they slumbered. It had been only two weeks since his return from Paris, and the nights he wasn't with her, she felt his loss.

Her fear rose, but she pushed it down deep as she felt the warmth of his kisses against her shoulder. She raised her arm to stroke the back of his head before lifting her hair to expose her nape to him. He pressed a kiss there without fail, evoking a shiver. It was a sensitive spot that he'd discovered and exploited.

Monica lay on her back to look up at him. Giving him a smile, she stroked his face. "I'm glad you got rid of the beard," she said. "The shadow is much better."

He grabbed the rim of the sheet and flung it back from her body. "I like yours, too," he mused, looking down at the thin layer of soft hairs covering the plump vee.

Arching a brow, she grabbed the side of the sheet covering him and flung it toward the foot of the bed. She took in his nudity before surrounding his inches with her hand. "You could use a trim," she said, lightly playing in the soft curly bush surrounding his thick member.

Gabe chuckled. "You weren't complaining last night," he reminded her.

Monica flushed in embarrassment and playfully nudged

his side with her knuckles. "Careful. Brag about it and it might be the last," she warned.

"If you cut me off, then I'll do the same," he said, palming her intimately as he bit his bottom lip.

"Touché," she said playfully, enjoying their banter.

Gabe held her body and rolled them together until she was under him. "A quick shower and we both could be happy…and at the same time," he said with twinkling eyes before dipping his head to nuzzle her neck.

Her fingers gripped his shoulders. "Shower together, okay," she said. "I still have to get an outfit for your parents' cocktail party tonight."

"Don't stress it. You're always gorgeous," he said, sliding one hand beneath her to cup one soft and fleshy buttock.

Monica gave him an indulgent smile as she stroked his jawline with her thumb. "How about we discuss how bad of an idea me attending this party is?" she said sweetly.

Gabe released a low grunt and shook his head. "I thought we debated this enough last night," he said, releasing her to sit on the bed.

She rose and retrieved her robe from the chair where he'd knelt before her and spread her knees wide to feast. They'd enjoyed dinner at CRESS X and then she'd served up dessert.

"New day. New debate," she said as she tied the robe and turned to face him as she pulled her hair up into a messy topknot.

Gabe shifted to sit back against the headboard with his legs outstretched and crossed at the ankle. He splayed his hands and dipped his head a little as if to say "bring it."

Monica crossed her arms over her chest and bit back a smile. "Why do you want this?" she asked.

"Because I want you in my life, and there is no need to keep it from my family," he said.

"Anymore," she added.

"Anymore," he agreed.

She fell silent as she crossed the floor to stand before the windows. Monica had been witness to the Cress soirees for their family and wealthy friends. And never had she yearned to attend as a guest. Pretending she belonged.

The pretense. The facade.

The bull—

"What else, Monica?" he asked, interrupting her thoughts.

"What exactly did you tell your parents?" she asked.

"They know I am bringing a guest," he replied.

She glanced back over her shoulder. "Me?"

"No," he admitted.

"This will not end well, Gabe," she advised, shifting her gaze back out the window.

She was not surprised when he walked up behind her to wrap his arms securely around her. She leaned back against his strength.

"What's the worst that could happen?" he asked as he lightly settled his chin atop her head.

"One of them tries to kill me," she said.

"Realistically," he asserted.

She locked her eyes on his reflection in the glass. "They throw me out," she said.

"My mother? Ms. Decorum?" he mused with the hint of laughter.

"Okay…she'll politely escort me to the front door and then wish me a good evening before softly closing the door in my face with a smile," she said.

"Now that sounds about right," he said. "Raquel did not see my mother's show of real emotion until after the wedding, and she dated Phillip Jr. for three years."

"Hell, I lived with you all for five years and rarely saw

it, but if you pay close attention, she has telltale signs about how she really feels," she said.

"Like the death grip on some item while she smiles at you," he offered.

She nodded. *"Exactly,"* she stressed.

Gabe dipped his head to press a kiss to her temple before he turned her to face him. "Come with me tonight just because I want to be able to look across the room and see you there," he said in a low voice. "And there is nothing *anyone* can say or do to make me regret having you there with me."

She raised up on the tip of her toes to rub her cheek against his before taking his hand in hers and leading him to the bathroom to shower *and* pleasure each other.

But her fears and mild anxiety on the upcoming event remained right there on the surface. She couldn't ignore it. Not as they enjoyed breakfast or traveled to look at a small office in a converted warehouse in Brooklyn that she was considering using for her foundation. Nor when they enjoyed a light dinner at a restaurant before going back to her apartment to get dressed. Even up to the moment their hired car service pulled up in front of the town house.

As Gabe helped her from the rear of the SUV and she looked up at the impressive structure with its intricate detailing, she searched inside herself to see if in hindsight she had been happy during her time working there. She had. With the job had come a stability she had never known before.

"Ready?"

Monica glanced over at Gabe and then looked down at the long-sleeved silk chiffon dress she wore. With its plunging neckline, a dreamy dusty rose-and-cream print design and short flounced hem, she felt beautiful and sexy. The cut fit her small breasts and curvy hips well. "How do I look?" she asked.

"Perfect," he assured her, raising her hand in his to press a kiss to the back.

"Good," she said.

The front door opened and Cole stepped out onto the porch in an all-navy suit and tie. "I'll be there in twenty minutes," he said on his phone before ending the call.

Monica felt so nervous that she focused on each step they took, careful not to stumble in her four-inch strappy heels.

"Hello, stranger," Cole said as he reached for a gold case from his inside pocket and placed a cigar between his teeth.

"I just saw you the night before last," Gabe reminded him as they briefly tapped fists in greeting.

Cole's gaze shifted to Monica. He did a double take and then his eyes widened in surprise before dipping to take in their entwined hands. "Money and getting away from this family—well, most of us—has done you good," he said.

"Hello, Cole," she said.

He inclined his head in greeting as he smiled, then he turned and opened the front door.

"I thought you were leaving?" Gabe asked as they joined him on the top step.

"And miss Mama slip into full Stepford Wife mode? No. *This* should be fun," he said as they stepped into the marble foyer.

Gabe held her hand a little tighter.

Monica took a deep steadying breath. "No worries. I got this," she said, hoping she truly did. "Fortunately, foster care taught me how to adapt to new situations."

Delicate piano music mingling with the conversation of those in attendance welcomed them once they stepped into the living room.

"Good luck, kiddo," Cole said to her before moving past them to claim a drink from the bar.

There were about fifty people scattered about the room

with drinks in hands and fashion on display. Monica recognized many of them. And as the chatter began to die down, she realized they also recognized her—whether from her work as the Cress maid or from seeing her image exploited by the paparazzi. Either way, the stares and the looks of surprise were disconcerting.

Gabe took a step forward, but Monica felt rooted in place. He stroked her skin with his thumb, and she forced herself to move alongside him toward where his parents stood before the grand fireplace. Phillip's frown was clear and Nicolette's grip on her flute was tight enough for the skin covering her knuckles to thin.

Here we go.

"Gabriel and Monica, you're finally here," Nicolette said, with an artificially bright smile as she waved them over with her free hand.

Oh, she's quick.

Monica did not miss that she whispered something in Phillip Sr.'s ear that led him to try his best to flip his frown. His failed attempt was *almost* comical.

The chatter resumed, but they were aware all eyes were on them as they reached the couple.

Gabe freed her as he pressed a kiss to his mother's cheek and extended his hand to his father, giving him a hard stare daring him to ignore it. "You both remember Monica?" he said.

"Of course," Phillip Sr. said, leaning in to deliver an air-kiss to her cheek. "You look stunning."

"Hello, Mr. and Mrs. Cress," Monica said, hearing her own nervousness. "And you look beautiful as always."

And she did. Nicolette's rose-gold metallic dress fit her tanned skin and dusty-blond hair streaked with silver.

But beyond the beauty, in the depths of her blue eyes, Monica saw her annoyance. Her anger. Her shock. Behind the smile a million questions were flying through the woman's head. All of the who, what, where, when, and perhaps most important, why.

Of that Monica was sure. She notched her chin a little higher, pulling from the toughness she'd developed as a foster kid. *I got this*, she reassured herself.

Nicolette took in the subtle move and smiled before giving Gabe a look that promised him there was more to come later. "Enjoy yourselves," she said, wrapping her arm around her husband's to guide him away.

"Your mother deserves an Oscar," she said.

Gabe laughed. "And my father looks like he needs an enema."

"Absolutely," Monica agreed.

He faced her and reclaimed her hand.

"Everyone is staring," she whispered up to him.

"That's because you're so beautiful," he said, stroking her inner palm with his thumb.

Then why did it take you five years to see me?

"Champagne?"

Monica looked at a middle-aged woman in a gray uniform holding a tray of champagne-filled flutes. "No, thank you," she said with a warm smile.

She felt uncomfortable being served when she used to be the one doing the serving. She remembered all too well how much she hated that part of her job. She didn't doubt the Cresses' new housekeeper felt the same.

"Thank you, Felice," Gabe said as he took a flute from the tray.

"Yes, thank you, Felice," Monica said, being sure to look the woman in the eye and acknowledge her more than she'd ever been in the same scenario.

"You're welcome," Felice said with a nod and smile before moving on.

"You want something else to drink?" Gabe asked.

"Actually," she began, before reaching to take his flute and enjoy a full sip, "you know I—"

"—love champagne," they finished in unison.

But then Gabe frowned in obvious confusion over why she hadn't just taken a flute from Felice.

Monica looked about the room over the rim of the glass. Phillip Jr. and Raquel looked away when her eyes landed on them. Lucas sat beside the pianist, his eyes closed, swaying back and forth to an upbeat rendition of "You Are So Beautiful." A pair of women whose names she chose to forget but whose pretentious faces were etched into her brain gave her odd looks. She responded with a high eyebrow raise. Sean was in the center of a small crowd who looked at him in slight rapture as he spoke. And Cole, still sitting on the steps, raised his snifter of brown liquor in a toast to her, making her smile.

Felice walked up to them carrying a tray of heavy hors d'oeuvres.

Again, Monica politely declined, earning her a brief, odd look from the housekeeper.

"Mr. Cress, your father would like you and your brothers to join him in the study," she said.

Gabe nodded. "Thank you, Felice."

With one last quick look at Monica, the woman moved on about the room, offering the guests the decadent appetizers and informing each brother of their father's request.

"A family meeting midparty?" Monica asked. "I think my nose will be itching."

Gabe pressed his hand to her lower back and she felt the heat of his touch through the thin material. "Honestly? That's probably true."

She smiled to shield her nervousness as she straightened

his silk tie before smoothing her hands across the lapels of his suit. "Don't get spanked?" she lightly teased.

"And you take nothing off *anyone*," Gabe stressed.

"You're leaving me alone in the wild?" she said.

"I'll keep you company."

They both turned to find Raquel standing beside them. Phillip Jr. continued on to the stairs, where he patted Cole's shoulder on his way past him.

"Thanks, Raq," Gabe said before striding away, as well, to follow his brothers up the stairs.

"Interesting," Raquel said, raising her flute of champagne in a toast to her. "You absolutely just made my night."

"Did I?" Monica asked before enjoying another sip.

"Sometimes it's nice to see the facade of Nicolette crack just a little," she admitted. "And tonight, she is barely holding it together."

Monica eyed the woman of whom they spoke and wholeheartedly agreed. It would be clear only to those who really knew Madame Cress that the constant touches to her hair, biting at her lips, gripping of everything she touched and movement about the room revealed she was livid and probably fully in favor of her husband lambasting Gabe.

Yes. It was amusing to watch her fight like hell to keep it together.

Monica smiled into her glass.

"Shall we kill one of the elephants in the room?" Raquel asked. "Before or after?"

Monica was no fool. The woman wanted to know if her dealings with Gabe started before or after she ended working for the family. She was clear it was none of Raquel's business—or anyone else's. Her days of obligation to the Cress family were over. "After," she lied.

"Mama, I want to come to the party!"

Monica looked up at Phillip Jr. and Raquel's daughter,

Collette, standing at the top of the stairs in a shiny pink dress, a pair of her mother's heels and red lipstick smeared haphazardly around her mouth.

"Oh! All dressed for the party," she said, as everyone in attendance began to laugh.

"Let her come to the party, Raq," a woman in the crowd yelled.

"Yes, let her come to the party," someone agreed.

"Definitely not," Raquel said, handing her flute to a passing server before quickly crossing the room and taking the stairs to gather Collette's hand in her own and guide her back up to her room.

Left alone and feeling watched, Monica moved through the crowd scattered about the spacious living room to the kitchen. Jillian was wiping her hands with a small towel that she then flung over her left shoulder before wiping her sweaty brow with her arm.

Monica tapped the side of her glass with the oversize gold ring on her index finger. "Kudos, Chef," she said.

Jillian smiled in surprise. "What are you doing here?" she asked as she took in Monica's dress and new flowing waves of her hair. "Are you a guest?"

"Of Gabriel's," Monica admitted.

Jillian looked surprised, then pleased and then curious.

"Before. Once," she said, giving her the truthful answer to the elephant found in yet another room. "Lots. After."

Jillian fell silent and lightly touched her chin as she looked off in the distance.

Monica thought of the note one of the Cress family members had left for her: *the taste of you still lingers on my tongue.*

Maybe even Gabriel.

"Penny for your thoughts?" Monica said, coming into the kitchen to stand on the other side of the island.

The women eyed each other.

Jillian smiled. It was a little sad. Melancholy. "Lots. During," she admitted. "After I quit one day? None."

She understood that Jillian had just admitted to her own delicious dalliances with one of the Cress men.

"Who?" Monica asked, ready for her curiosity about the note to end.

"*Not* Gabe," Jillian assured.

"Fair enough," Monica said.

Jillian laughed a bit and turned to pull trays from both double ovens.

"Why does it have to end after you stop working here?" Monica asked.

"Different reasons," Jillian said, using silicone tongs to plate the trays of stuffed puff pastry. "Mostly because I don't think he will ever see me as anything but the cook."

Monica leaned against the edge of the island and turned her head to look down the length of the kitchen and dining room to the backyard. The sight of the illuminated water feature was soothing in that moment as her own fears surfaced. "So, can Gabe see me as more than a maid?" she asked softly, wishing she was outdoors and could hear the sound of the running water.

"It's different," Jillian said. "Money changes *everything*."

Monica looked down at the pastries. They looked delicious. "May I? I'm hungry," she said.

At that moment, Felice entered the kitchen and set her empty serving tray on the island. "Mrs. Cress would like more of the roast beef sliders," she said, her voice stiff. "Perhaps you should offer the lady one before you place them on my tray."

Monica could see the woman was offended. "Felice, I was the Cress maid before you—"

"I know. You're the talk of the party," the woman said.

"I'm sure I am," Monica said dryly.

"I *know* you are," Felice countered. "It's hard to miss when you're moving from crowd to crowd overhearing them."

"What are they saying?" Monica asked, hating that she even cared.

Jillian and Felice shared a brief look that gave the house-keeper the okay to repeat the things she couldn't help but overhear.

"They ridiculed Mr. Cress for openly dating the help," she said with reluctance.

"I'd bet good money *they* were the socialites scowling at me," Monica said, feeling annoyance.

Felice remained silent. Her reticence with Monica was clear.

"Listen, the part of the job I hated the most was serving food at parties," Monica continued, needing to explain herself to the woman. "I didn't take the food because I remember being in your position and hating it so much. I'm not comfortable being served. That's all."

Felice's face softened. "In that moment it felt like you thought my touch was dirty," she said.

"Never," Monica stressed, reaching to touch the woman's hand.

"If you are gonna move in the company of the haves then it's gonna be hard to keep the mindset of the have-nots," Felice said.

Translation: Do I belong out there with the guests or in the kitchen with the staff?

She knew where she felt most comfortable.

Felice used tongs to set an array of hors d'oeuvres on a saucer and handed it to Monica. "And you didn't hear it from me, and I will deny if asked, but that little gathering upstairs is *all* about you," she said before taking the tray of treats out to the guests.

As Jillian went back to cooking, Monica enjoyed a slider and eyed the elevator. She wiped her fingertips with a napkin and checked to make sure no one in the living room noticed when she made her way toward it. As she took it one flight up to the second floor, she *almost* convinced herself she had every right to hear what was being said about her. Knowing the elevator opened up directly into the master bedroom of Nicolette and Phillip Sr., she continued up to the third floor via the stairs, careful to make sure the double doors leading into the suite of rooms was closed.

"Is *she* the reason for your insanity lately?"

Monica winced as Phillip Sr.'s deep and gravelly voice echoed through the wood. She moved closer to the door and prayed no one stormed out and caught her.

"She's the reason I'm happy," Gabe returned.

Aw. Same.

"Happy or horny?"

"Both."

Someone laughed and Monica just *knew* it was Cole.

Silence reigned and Monica wondered what was going on that she could not see.

"There are women you wed and those you bed. Know the difference. And that goes for all of you," Phillip Sr. said.

"Don't disrespect her in that way," Gabe said, his voice hard and his anger clear. "I tolerate a lot from you, but I will not put up with that—"

"Tolerate!"

Monica jumped, feeling as if Phillip Sr.'s voice booming against the walls was enough to rattle the entire house. She moved from the door and hurried down the stairs, not wanting to hear any more. Wishing she hadn't dared to hear any of it at all.

On the second floor, she paused and pressed her back against the wall as she struggled to slow and steady her breath. Looked down upon by his friends. Judged by Nicolette. Insulted by Phillip Sr. Defended by Gabriel.

The latter made her smile.

She made her way back to the kitchen via the elevator and tried not to let her fears be exploited by her current company. But as she reentered the living room and claimed a new flute from a tray Felice carried around the room, she felt on display.

"Chin up," Felice advised.

They shared a smile.

"Aw, the new maid and the old maid have a little moment."

Monica stiffened before she turned to find one of the socialites standing behind her. She missed not one cliché detail, from her hair to her designer clothing. Those things were clearly her armor. She just wondered what the woman was hiding behind them. Possibly insecurity? That thought led to Monica giving her a pitying smile.

The young woman's face tightened in anger. "Could you fetch me a dirty martini?" she asked, her tone mocking.

Monica wasn't sure of the reason for the woman's anger with her and was bored by it and her. She took a sip of her champagne as she turned to take her leave. She gasped to find Gabe standing beside her. He pressed a reassuring hand to the middle of her back, and she felt as if he'd pushed a battery into it and given her new life.

Take nothing off anyone.

"Thank God, you're back," she said, turning to face the woman who had appointed herself her nemesis. "Suddenly the air is less vile."

The woman stiffened and released a harsh gasp.

Gabe pierced her with his grayish-blue eyes. "Go play your games elsewhere, Naomi," he warned in a cold voice.

Even Monica was chilled by it. She felt relief, like a

schoolchild saved from a bully, as the woman clenched both her jaw and the crystal flute of champagne before walking away.

"I don't belong here, Gabe," Monica said, taking a deep sip of her drink in hopes of easing her insecurities.

The behavior of his family and friends was proof that money could not buy respect. To them she was still the maid in expensive dress-up.

"I'm here and you belong with me," he said.

In his eyes she found the strength she needed. Being with Gabe meant merging their worlds and taking whatever came along with it—to a degree.

"How was the meeting?" she asked.

The light in his eyes dimmed a little. "Enlightening," he said.

"Care to share?"

He forced a smile that did not reach his eyes as he shook his head. "Not yet."

Monica reached for one of his hands and started playfully swaying back and forth as she made little silly expressions meant to lift his spirits.

He gave her a reluctant chuckle before pulling her close for a hug as he pressed a warm kiss to her neck. "Let's go," he said.

"Where?"

"You came here with me, and now I'll go wherever you lead."

Monica leaned back to look up at him. "Anywhere?" she asked.

"Anywhere," he promised.

Cloaked by darkness, Gabriel leaned against the doorway to their private overwater bungalow at the Four Seasons Resort Bora Bora. He glanced back over his shoulder at Monica, asleep in the middle of the king-size bed, before facing forward and resting his gaze on the dark shadow of Mount Otemanu in the distance. He needed the quiet and had been unable to sleep even though they'd left for their trip just a few hours after they'd ducked out of the cocktail party.

During their thirteen-hour flight, mini-chaos had reigned. Photos of them together at the cocktail party had been leaked to the press. Their relationship had become gossip fodder. The tale of a former maid, who was the secret love child of a former Hollywood star, now dating a member of the family she used to work for, seemed too salacious to be ignored. Particularly with the speculation of just when their relationship had begun.

His phone was ceaselessly ringing with calls from his family members, but he ignored them all. His disconnect from them had begun before the scandal that brought the Cress, INC. brand into the fray.

"There are women you wed and those you bed. Know the difference."

His anger at Phillip Sr.'s words rose as if he'd just heard them for the first time. He was offended by the insult, and such a mindset disturbed him—particularly coming from his father. His respect and admiration of his father's talent, wisdom and profound love for their mother had been immense. Those traits he admired were suspect with the things he'd said in that meeting. Gabe was questioning if they were different men at their core and why he'd fought so hard for his father's hard-earned approval.

He decided it was time to take his own advice.

Take nothing from anyone.

And in the silence, the answer he searched for came to him. The idea was not new, just something he had been hesitant to accept. But now he was sure.

It was time to walk away from Cress, INC. and open his own restaurant.

With one last look at the moonlight upon the lagoon, he turned and crossed the bedroom to reclaim his place in bed beside his woman. With his decision made, and feeling inspired by her strength, resilience and her kindness, even with the tough times life had tossed upon her, he wrapped his arm over her waist and finally was able to join her in sleep.

Nine

Two months later

Monica came to a stop in the hall before the frosted glass door. She reached out and lightly touched the words etched out in the film. "The Bridge," she read aloud, remembering Gabe helping her to finally choose a name for her foundation when she expressed wanting to fill the gap between childhood in foster care and adulthood alone.

And now, with the use of her inheritance, she had a small office space in a three-story building in the Dumbo section of Brooklyn and was about to walk inside and greet her small staff.

Just another new beginning. That's all. You got this, she thought to herself.

Monica worked her shoulders in the fitted jewel-neck, long-sleeved lace shirt she wore over lightweight tweed high-rise trousers with flared legs. She reached for the door knob. "Wait," she said, reaching inside her crocodile leather briefcase for her oversize tortoiseshell readers to slide on. With her sleek ponytail, she hoped they made her look older, more serious and smart.

She opened the door and stepped inside. Four women turned to view her from where they stood in the center of the large room, its four desks situated two on each side, facing each other.

"Good morning," she said, setting her purse and briefcase on one of the six waiting room chairs before moving over to each person: her two full-time employees, Kylie Branch, her administrative assistant, and Nylah Hunt, her grant writer and chief financial officer. Choice, volunteering to serve pro bono as chief counsel. And Montgomery Morgan, her on-call publicist.

She shook the hand of each one before reclaiming her original spot. She was nervous and fidgeted, sliding her hands in and out of her pockets. Clearing her throat. Moving back and forth on her heels.

Choice, who as her friend knew her trepidation so well, gave her an encouraging smile.

"Unlike myself, all of you are so experienced in your fields and I am grateful to have you here to assist me in ensuring so many children aged out of the foster care system receive the help they deserve and need," she said, hearing the slight tremble in her voice.

The women all offered her smiles.

Monica didn't reveal that she'd taken both a business and a website-development course at Manhattan Community College as a nondegree student. She hoped that, plus her two years of college, would give her better footing alongside these very competent women.

"I'm so nervous," she admitted with a laugh. "Please forgive me."

"You're doing fine, darlin'," Kylie said, holding steadfast to her Charleston accent although she'd moved to the northeast over twenty years ago.

"How about the space? Does everyone like it?" Monica asked as she looked about the office at the khaki decor with accents in coral, turquoise, citrine and gold.

"It's beautiful," everyone agreed.

She crossed the room, loving how the fall sun gleamed through the windows and lit the tiled floor as she reached the small office she'd reserved for herself. Here, the same hues from the outer office continued with a large bouquet of fresh flowers on the edge of her clear desk. She moved to push the rolling ergonomic chair out of the office, setting it at the head of the wide aisle running up the middle of the desks. "So, let's update each other before Montgomery and Choice have to go," she said, turning to close the door behind her before sitting down and crossing her legs.

The women all moved to their assigned desks, as well.

"We already have a list of ten applicants sent over from different county social service departments," Kylie began. "I've placed them on your desk."

Monica was personally funding awards of five thousand dollars each from money she'd gifted the foundation. "Reach out to other agencies in the tristate area. There are more people who need help. Let's find them," she said.

"Right away, boss," Kylie said.

Boss? I'm a boss! I like it.

She turned to Nylah.

The woman opened up a coral folder on her desk. "I think our plan should be to reach out to large companies who offer local community grants. I researched and I can meet the current deadlines of ten such corporations. I just need to adjust the grant I've already written to meet specific guidelines."

"I didn't even know these brands offered grant money like that," Monica admitted after accepting the folder and looking at the names listed.

"That's my job," Nylah said. "And I believe in what you're doing. Remember, I aged out of the foster care system myself."

Monica gave her a heartfelt smile. "Thank you," she said with feeling before turning to Choice.

"The majority of my work was done in the setting up of the foundation," she said. "I won't be here in the office, but The Bridge Foundation is a client and Monica knows how to reach out to me if a legal matter arises."

The women all nodded in understanding.

"And Montgomery," Monica said, turning to the braided beauty who looked divine in a fuchsia pantsuit with turquoise heels.

"Like Choice, I will be working from my own offices, but I agreed with Monica that we all should meet on this first day and put faces to the names," Montgomery said, giving each woman a winning smile before focusing her sharp gaze back on Monica. "We have gotten a lot of traction from the press kits that were sent out, but even more requests for an interview with you have come in."

"No," Monica said with a shake of her head.

The publicist had made it clear she wanted the still-reserved Monica to become the face of the organization. Tell her story. Try to connect with the same people she was trying to help. Try to pull at the heartstrings—and wallets—of wealthy donors.

And use my connection to my father to help promote it all.

Something the NDA would not allow. She shared a brief look with Choice, who was aware of the agreement as her attorney.

"Maybe not live interviews," Choice suggested. "But taped interviews with specific guidelines and editorial control might work best."

Monica looked pensive.

"Or speaking engagements minus Q & As," Montgomery suggested. "Especially as we gear up for the charity gala in a few months."

Monica released a breath as she turned a bit in her chair to look out the window. Sunlight broke through the towering buildings, and the skies were a beautiful blue backdrop for the concrete-and-steel structures. In that moment of quiet she was facing—and trying to conquer—her fear...

Of public speaking,

Of more public scrutiny.

Of more reminders that her father gave her away.

She tried and failed. "No," she said, forcing finality into her tone as she felt waves of relief at not stepping out of the shadows. "My intention was never to be the face or the brand or whatever marketing term it is. I just want to help foster kids, not become some pseudo celebrity. Remember for the last five years, I worked as a maid and lived seen yet not seen—if that makes any sense."

"It does," Choice said, offering her a warm and encouraging smile.

"Give me some time to adjust to everything and we'll see. Okay?" she said.

Montgomery nodded. "You're the boss," she said.

I'm the boss.

Monica glanced out the window again and smiled at the very idea of that. As they ended the meeting and Choice and Montgomery took their leave, she retrieved her briefcase from the seating area and made her way with her chair to her office, closing the door behind her. She set her things atop the desk and moved over to the lone window in the corner, crossing her arms over her chest as she looked out at the world where she was trying to carve her own little place.

Am I crazy? Can I do this?

She shifted her sight to focus on her reflection in the glass. *The only way to do it is to do it.*

Bzzzzzz.

Monica jumped, surprised by the sudden noise. She whirled to see the electric-blue light of the intercom system flashing.

Calm down, Mo.

She stepped over to the desk to press the button as she cleared her throat. "Yes?"

"Mr. Cress to see you."

Monica felt warmth as her grin spread. "Send him in. Thank you," she added, holding up her hands and grimacing before pressing the button again.

Quickly she struck several poses. Leaning against the corner of her desk. By the window. In the seat behind her desk. Finally, in the second before the door opened, she came from behind the desk and simply walked over to meet him.

"Hello, beautiful," he said, closing the door and pressing a kiss to her jawline as she slipped her arms around his waist.

She inhaled deeply of his scent and released a low moan. "You always smell so good," she sighed, allowing herself a kiss to his neck before stepping away with reluctance. "I thought we were meeting up for an early dinner?"

He gave her that look. The charming one. The one that easily beguiled. The setup before the letdown. And there had been plenty lately.

She tensed. Missed dates and rescheduling plans were becoming commonplace as he became more focused on opening his own restaurant. Securing investors. Scouting locations.

At least I hope that's all it is.

Over the last few weeks, they'd seen each other just a few times. Phone calls and FaceTime had replaced real contact. She felt the void.

"I have to cancel dinner," he admitted.

"Again," she said, forcing a smile as she glanced over at him while she took her seat behind her desk.

The energy in the room shifted. It was hard to miss. Lately it had become familiar.

"Monica."

She looked up at him.

"There was a time you encouraged me to chase my dream," he said, his tone a little hard.

"You think I *discourage* you now?" she asked. "Really, Gabe?"

He looked up at the ceiling briefly before walking over to stand beside her. He turned her chair to face him as he squatted before her and cupped her knees with his hands. "I came to tell you I am proud of you. The foundation. Your confidence. Your need to help," he said, his eyes searching hers.

Monica bit her bottom lip to keep her emotions from overtaking her. She believed every word he spoke and the look of pride in his eyes.

"The restaurant is going to take up more of my time," he admitted, reaching up to stroke her jawline with his thumb, which drew a shiver. "But I'm not going anywhere. I'm here. With you. In this. So into this. Us."

Her breaths filled the silence.

"For the first time, I want it all. The success, proving my family wrong and standing up for myself," he implored.

She turned her head to press a kiss to his hand.

"Okay?" he asked.

The breath she released was shaky. Of late she had begun to worry that Gabe had wanted their relationship once she had risen above the station of maid and they'd end once he realized that not even her sudden wealth would make her good enough for him.

What if I'd never received the inheritance? Would he have given me a second look at all?

She nodded. "Okay," she said, feeling foolish for doubting him.

Gabe felt six pairs of eyes bore into him. The den where they were seated was quiet. He didn't try to fill it. He'd said what he needed to say. Now he waited. He looked over at his father as he swirled the ice in his snifter of scotch.

Phillip Sr. stared out of the window as he stroked the hairs of his chin and silently clenched and unclenched his jaw.

"One less dog in the race for CEO then," Cole said, raising his bottle of beer in a toast and inclining his head.

Gabe looked down into the amber liquid in his crystal glass. The sound of glass crashing against the wall echoed violently. He looked up just as his father lowered his swinging arm and stared at him. The move was pure intimidation.

Gabe felt offended by it. Ridiculed. He notched his chin higher and met his father's glare with one of his own.

I'm not backing down. Not caving. Not putting your needs before mine. Not to make you proud and then fail, because there is no way to please you.

After long tense moments where it felt everyone in the room held their breath, Phillip Sr. stormed out. Gabe took a deep sip of his drink as he turned from the stunned look in his mother's blue eyes.

"No man—or woman—should divide a family," she said.

Monica.

"No woman did," he said, his voice hardened in defense of her. "It's funny that Monica was someone we all trusted in our home and in our lives for the last five years, but now that she is involved with me—"

Nicolette scoffed audibly. "Trust. More like tolerated out of necessity," she said in French.

"Penser plus haut, mère." He admonished her in French to think higher.

Her face flushed in anger as she eyed him. He was used to seeing her gaze filled with adoration, not brimming with annoyance. *"Prends tes propres conseils, fiston,"* she said, her voice soft.

Gabe swallowed her words of taking his own advice down with his drink. He turned his back on her and the revelation of her classist beliefs. He'd never realized they ran so deep. That was deeply disappointing.

"Family should be together," she said from behind him in French.

"And not at war," he countered, giving voice to his frustration with his father's controlling hand in his life.

Silence.

He turned, ignoring his brothers, to look at her.

"Your father has his reasons" was all that she said.

"And he also has sons who are grown men and deserve his respect," he said, unable to keep the edge from his tone. "Not be treated as pawns on a chessboard."

Nicolette rose and smoothed her hands over the turquoise-and-silver silk caftan she wore. She moved about the room and stroked the cheek of each of her sons.

"Nous vous adorons tous. Plus qu'on ne le sait. Plus que ce qu'on montre. S'il te plaît, n'oublie jamais ça. S'il vous plaît," she said, coming to Gabriel and patting under his chin.

"We adore you all. More than we know. More than we show. Please never forget that. Please."

And like always, his mother took her leave to be by his father's side—be he right or wrong. One thing he couldn't deny was their loyalty to each other. Even when it pitted her against her sons.

"You're a fool," Phillip Jr. said with a shake of his head as he rose to his feet and buttoned the jacket of his custom-made suit before striding to the door. "Did you really believe he would finance a solo restaurant after you stepped down from Cress, INC.?"

"And you're a bigger fool if you think I haven't already secured investors," Gabe said, his voice hard and unrelenting. "I just hoped my family would support me in this. Same way I would support any of you in following your dreams…*bro*."

One by one his brothers took their leave, most likely to seek out their parents and ensure they understood they were not in agreement with their brother. All except Cole.

"Aren't you going to kiss the ring, too?" Gabe asked, never before feeling so divided from his own family and never more determined to make his solo restaurant a success.

"There's a better chance of me kissing his butt and you know it," Cole drawled, rising from the low-slung sofa.

Gabe noticed a slow half smile on his brother's face and followed his line of vision across the wide space to land on Chef Jillian leaving the pantry to enter the kitchen.

"Now that's a behind I love kissing," Cole said.

Gabe's eyebrows rose in surprise. "*Chef* Jillian?" he asked.

Cole stopped in his tracks with his face incredulous. "Monica *the Maid*?" he shot back.

Gabe smiled. "Checkmate," he said.

He was with the maid and his brother had an ongoing dalliance with the chef. Their mother would have a conniption. Their father's head might literally explode.

"How is that going?" his brother asked, standing in the open doorway with his hands pushed deep into the pockets of his denims.

Gabe thought of Monica. The way her emotions were mirrored in her doe-shaped eyes. Be it happiness, anger, annoyance or passion. And her scent. He could close his eyes and find her in the crowd just using his nose. Or her intelligence, which he admitted surprised him when she offered such insight and unique perspective on things he took for granted. And the sex. Best ever. Period. Never had he felt so out of control in bed. And he liked it.

"Going good" was all that he confessed.

Cole nodded.

"And the chef?" Gabe asked.

Cole shrugged one broad shoulder. "It is what it is and ain't what it ain't," he said, pulling his iPhone from his back pocket.

"Careful, little brother, sometimes what you think it *ain't*, it actually becomes, and before you know it, you're in the thick of it, needing someone you didn't even know you would want," Gabe said, revealing a little more of just what Monica had come to mean to him.

He looked from Cole to the chef as his brother tapped away on the phone before lowering it to look over at Jillian. Gabe followed his line of vision, his curiosity piqued.

Jillian reached for her own cell phone. Across the divide she looked up. She and Cole shared a brief but very telling look before she typed away as she turned and walked back into the pantry, leaving the door ajar.

Ding.

Cole read the text that was clearly from Jillian in response to his, and he smiled so hard his dimples showed. "To be honest, I might just be ready for a little more than I expected, big brother," he said before crossing the den and then the kitchen. He looked around for any other witnesses besides Gabe before joining their pretty chef in the pantry.

Gabe didn't dare to think about what was going on beyond the closed door. Not at all.

"Nah," he said aloud as he crossed the den, and the kitchen, as well, to reach the elevator for a ride up to the fourth floor.

As soon as it stopped and he opened the gate, he walked over to the glass wall that ran up the entire rear of the house. Crossing his arms over his chest and spreading his legs wide, he looked out at the snow-covered backyard. The whiteness was stark and pure, particularly against the night.

Almost as pure as his intentions when he'd humbled himself and asked for his father's help in launching his own eatery. The decision to leave Cress, INC. had not been easy. Asking his father to financially back him had been even harder. Having the majority of his family aligned against him had been the worst. Still holding his drink, he turned from the view and looked around at the den, taking in the black-and-white family photos on the custom shelves and high-end tables. Memories made over the last forty years or better. Bonds being slowly shattered before his eyes over greed, forced competition and loyalty that was blind to anything but his father's wishes.

Anger and annoyance caused his grip on his glass to tighten. If he was honest with himself, there was pain and regret in the mix of his feelings. He felt foolish for even a sliver of hope that his family would support him.

Gabe pulled out his iPhone and called Monica. It rang twice. "Hey, you," he said. "You busy?"

"I can get unbusy with the right motivation," she said.

He smiled. "I'm sending a car to bring you to where I will be waiting for you," he said.

"And where is that?" she asked, her voice husky soft.

Gabe entered his bedroom suite and quickly packed an overnight bag. "It's a surprise," he said.

"Panties or no panties?" she teased.

He paused. His heart thundered. "No panties is *always* the default answer."

"Fun."

They ended the call.

He slung his bag over his shoulder and left his room to make his way back to the elevator. He rode it down to the basement, smirking a bit at how quickly he'd reverted back to his teenage days of sneaking out of the town house and avoiding his family by using the servants' entrance in the basement. He just wasn't in the mood for more confrontation. It was pointless.

Besides, he was on a mission that needed no interruptions.

Gabe stepped out and paused, looking down the hall to the quarters where Monica had once lived. Over the years, he had ventured to the cellar only to retrieve wine, and never once thought of her. For him, she'd been invisible. Someone to clean and help keep his living space orderly. Before they'd become intimate, he'd given no thought to her life outside of her part in theirs.

"More like tolerated out of necessity."

As he remembered his mother's words, he worried that maybe he was not very different from his parents.

Disturbed by that thought, he turned and made his way down the left side of the hall and past the glass door of the laundry room to the exit. He made sure the exit was securely closed before taking the steps two at a time until he reached the street. The car service he'd requested awaited him, and Gabe took a deep, invigorating breath of the winter winds as he allowed himself a look up at the town house before climbing into the rear of the SUV.

The ride was brief. Less than twenty minutes. For that, he was glad.

He spotted Monica leaving her own vehicle double-parked in front of the building. The winds whipped her hair and ruffled the ball-shaped fur she wore with jeans and thigh-high boots. She turned and smiled as he exited his vehicle with his bag in hand and stepped onto the sidewalk to pull her body close to his for a kiss. She deepened it, surprising him. As they got lost in one another, the noise and congestion of the city faded. The frigid cold and icy snow seemed to melt away. The fast-moving bodies breezing past them on the street were gone.

"Let's go up," Gabe said, breaking their connection with reluctance as he reached for her hand and led her inside the towering building.

"Up to where, exactly?" Monica asked, brushing her hair back from her face as she looked around at the modern design of the lobby.

The uniformed concierge gave them a welcoming smile and nod.

"My apartment," he finally said as they reached the set of four elevators.

She paused.

He looked at her as he pushed the button. Her expression was guarded. "What's wrong?" he asked as she took the final step to be back at his side.

As the doors slid open and they stepped onto the lift, she forced a smile, but it didn't reach her eyes. He reached for her hand and stroked her palm with his thumb as he used his free hand to press the button for the twenty-fourth floor. "What's wrong, Monica?" he repeated.

She shook her head and released his hand to wrap her arms around his waist. "Not a thing, *Gabriel*," she said, saying his name teasingly as she raised her face to press a kiss to his chin. "Congratulations on your new apartment."

He smiled, but he felt his own unease.

After the elevator came to a smooth stop and as they made their way to the apartment, he eyed her. He had come to know Monica well, and when something worried her, she became distant and quiet. Getting her to open up about it seemed to make her withdraw even more.

"This is nice, Gabe," she said, removing her coat as she moved about the furnished, two-thousand-square-foot space in the Midtown Park Avenue South building. "I didn't know you were even looking to move out from your parents'."

He eyed her as he dropped his bag on the sectional sofa, removed his overcoat and kicked off his shoes. "It was time."

Which was on her mind? That I moved or that I didn't tell her?

Monica looked over her shoulder at him as he joined her at the floor-to-ceiling windows, which were offering a spectacular view of the city landscape at night. "Are things worse with your family?" she asked.

"They'll come around," he said, dipping his head to press a kiss to her throat before he moved over to the electric fireplace to light it.

"I hope so," she said, crossing the wide-plank wood floors to stand beside him before the fire. "The last thing I want for you is to ever know what it feels like to not have family, Gabe."

He thought of the childhood she rarely spoke of and felt regret that her upbringing had been bleak at times. She wrapped her arms around him, and he looked down at her as she looked up at him. Her eyes were soft, and the flames of the fire flicked in their depths. She gave him the hint of a smile as she eased her hands under his sweater and massaged his lower back, evoking goose bumps across his skin.

Gabe felt breathless, and something profound and deep clutched at his chest as he let his eyes take in every aspect of her face. Missing nothing. Captivated by it all.

Their kisses began as light touches of their lips as they stared at one another almost playfully. They tasted of one another with deep, guttural moans of pleasure. Slowly they undressed each other, illuminated by the fire's light as night darkened their surroundings.

Gabe lifted her body up and she wrapped her arms and legs around him as he hotly licked at her mouth. The feel of her softness against him and the scent of her—that heady mix of sweet perfume and woman—lengthened his inches with hardness that rose up against her buttocks.

Monica leaned back enough to look down at him. She kissed him. Softly. With a tempting smile that he knew he would never forget, she stroked the back of his head before guiding his mouth to her breasts. With a grunt, he latched on and deeply sucked her nipple as he pressed his face into the softness and gripped her hips to guide her downward. The first feel of her heat and wetness against his tip caused him to hiss, in that hot little moment before she arched her hips to take all of him inside her.

They gasped and clung to one another.

He fought for control, not wanting his pleasure at the very feel of her intimacy gripping him to push him to a speedy end. And when she began to slowly circle her hips, sending her core up and down the length of him, he bent one leg and reached out to press one hand against the wall—looking for help to keep them from losing balance as he felt lost in a haze of passion and desire.

No words were spoken. Just panted breaths and deep gasps echoed as sweat coated their bodies from the heat of lovemaking and the fireplace. He was lost. Gone. She used her muscles to grip and release his tool as she rode him. With his free hand, he gripped her buttock as he licked and sucked at her breasts, loving each tremble and purr of pleasure he drew from her. He felt her climax nearing and took control, turning to drop them down onto the sofa, then arched his back and drove his hardness inside with swiftness and depth until soon they both cried out with a roughness that only hinted at the wildness they felt as they climaxed together.

And long after their cries subsided, their pulses slowed and the sweet addictive haze of climaxing died down, she lay atop him on the couch. His knees were bent and open as he listened to her long breaths as she slept. He turned his head to cast his gaze on the fire as he thought of that moment earlier when he had felt something profound for Monica. The captivation. The warmth spreading across his chest. Breathlessness.

He closed his eyes and clenched his jaw as he pushed away the memory and everything it could mean. A hint of feelings he was not ready to accept.

Ten

Three months later

Was it possible to truly feel like Cinderella?

Monica did.

As she looked at her reflection in the glass, she didn't notice the panoramic view of the New York skyline and Hudson River on the other side of it or the well-dressed people enjoying the colorful, carnival-themed gala behind her. The strapless white silk couture gown she wore seemed to gleam, and the Swarovski crystals sewn into a modern design across the bodice twinkled like stardust. A tight corseted waist and attached skirt gave her a buxom shape, while the thigh-high slit sexily exposed her leg. Her hair was piled atop her head, elongating her neck and showcasing her bared shoulders.

She smiled, remembering the days when she imagined the life she was now living. When she could get close to gowns like the one she wore only if she allowed herself a few minutes of folly in the closets of Nicolette and Raquel. Sometimes she felt she was in a fairy tale and someone would close the book and bring it all to an end, with her leaving a glass shoe on the stairs.

"Congratulations, Monica."

She stiffened, instantly recognizing the voice of Nicolette Cress. She gave herself one last look before turning to face Gabe's mother. The woman looked beautiful in a dark blue chiffon maxi dress with a plunging neckline. "Thank you… Nicolette," she said, never having addressed her by her first name before.

The act brought a small smile to the woman's face.

"I wasn't aware that you purchased a ticket," Monica continued, proud that she'd shown no trepidation or even the curiosity she felt at seeing Nicolette at her event.

"You captured the attention of a few of my friends who are in attendance and I thought it might be my only chance to see my son," Nicolette said, taking a sip from the flute of champagne she held as she came to stand beside her at the window.

Monica's gut clenched. "He's running late. There was a problem with the restaurant, and there's an important inspection first thing in the morning," she explained, giving her the same excuse Gabe had given her just a little over an hour ago.

Nicolette gave her a tight smile. "Never had I imagined the day I would need updates on my son from his bedmate," she said with a release of a heavy breath.

Monica's grip on her ball-shaped clutch tightened. "Bedmate?" she asked. "It seems you need an update on that, as well."

Some emotion filled the woman's blue eyes.

Monica couldn't quite place it.

"I only want what's best for Gabriel—for all of my sons," she said, her French accent heavy.

Monica used to find it fascinating. "And I'm not it?" she asked.

"Long-term?" Nicolette asked. "No."

Monica tensed, hating how the woman gave voice to her concern with such ease. Over the last few months, her relationship with Gabe had become strained as his sole focus was preparing for the opening of his restaurant. He seemed to be constantly canceling dates or showing up late, and when they were together his mind was clearly elsewhere. She told herself he was just focused on his success and things would go back to the norm, but she couldn't fight off the nagging belief the sexy playboy had tired of the relationship and would leave her behind.

In truth she had already begun to withdraw, limit her expectations and steel herself for a breakup, but she doubted he even noticed.

"Shouldn't this be a conversation you have with Gabe?" Monica asked.

"Why? When it's clear *you're* the cause for the division?"

Monica frowned, unable not to do so. "You're wrong, Nicolette, because the very last thing I want is for Gabe to be divided from his family," she said, her conviction clear in her voice.

"Yet I didn't see my son for Thanksgiving, Christmas nor New Year's Day."

"True, Gabe and I spent those holidays together, but I encouraged him to spend them with his family," she said, in truth. "Especially after the childhood I had."

Nicolette tapped the tips of her nude nails against her flute as she walked behind Monica to reach her other side. "It is your upbringing that is exactly why this *thing* you two have going will not work. Money cannot erase the indelible mark it left on your life."

"You know nothing of my life. You never cared to," Monica said, feeling offended and judged.

Nicolette arched a brow. "You were my maid, not my friend," she countered.

"And that was sufficient for me, as well, but never claim to know me. That would be a big mistake, *Nicolette*," she said with coldness.

The woman smiled, but it did not replace the anger in her eyes. "You lived and worked in my home for five years, so don't convince yourself I hate you."

"And please don't convince yourself that I was envious of you," Monica countered. "Because if it was my intention to come between Gabe and your family, then I would have revealed to him that he and his brother were under surveillance at the direction of you, your husband or both."

Nicolette looked surprised at Monica knowing that.

Monica looked down at the floor and smiled as she copied the woman's move and walked behind her to stand on her other side. "Tonight is not the night for this. After those five years working and living in your home, I know you are a woman who holds dear decorum and appropriate behavior," she said. "Tonight is huge for me and my foundation. A celebration. Not an opportunity to belittle me to my face, to judge my relationship with your son or to manipulate me into doing something that suits you. So out of respect for Gabe, as his mother, I am asking you to leave and let me enjoy the night. You're welcome to stay and appreciate the festivities, but please leave if your goal is to make me feel beneath you."

Nicolette stopped a passing waiter and set her near-empty flute on the tray. "I'll leave," she said. "You're right. I was out of line. Accept my apology for that. But still heed my warning. Anything serious between you and Gabe will not work or last."

"Have a good night, Nicolette," Monica said.

"I can see in your eyes that you know I'm right."

Monica said nothing, hating that the woman spoke to her very insecurities about her relationship with Gabe. "Good night," she repeated, her tone firm.

In the glass, she watched the reflection of the woman finally turn and retreat.

Monica closed her eyes and shook her head a little as she pinched the bridge of her nose. The urge to pull her phone from her clutch and call Gabe came, but she pushed the idea away. The disappointment of him missing most of the night stung. Truly, she didn't even want to hear his voice. Not even enough to tell him his mother had just ambushed her.

Now she really felt like Cinderella, complete with a wicked stepmother.

Just no Prince Charming.

"Ready?"

She opened her eyes at the sound of Montgomery's voice. In the glass, she shifted her gaze to the reflection of the four women standing behind her. Choice, Montgomery, Kylie and Nylah. Her team. Each had worked so hard to make the night a success. She was grateful for each one. Professional alliances had become friendships.

And even that was a sign of her healing from her past. She'd never seen the need to make friends when she'd never known when her time at that particular group home or foster family would end.

With a deep breath, she turned to face them, knowing the time had come. She had walked the red carpet. Effortlessly avoided questions about her father and about her relationship with Gabe. Pretended not to be starstruck by the long list of A-list actors and singers, celebrities, and social media influencers Montgomery and her team had convinced to attend. Greeted her guests at the carnival-style event that she'd completely co-opted from the Cress Family Foundation gala she'd attended. Made the rounds. Taken photos with the fifty foster care children who had been awarded funds to help them transition to adulthood.

And now the biggest test was next.

"Yes," she said, feeling nervous. "It's now or never."

Together the ladies walked through the crowd of the Fifth Avenue venue with its 360-degree view of the metropolis at night. After Montgomery motioned for the live band to slow and lower its upbeat music, Monica took the microphone she handed her. She looked on at the colorful lighting, abundant floral arrangements and room filled with elegantly dressed people, there to support her vision. She pressed her free hand against her belly hoping to settle the butterflies.

"Good evening, everyone," she said. "Just a quick break in the evening to thank you all for attending tonight's event and for the money we raised from your generous donations that will allow us to fund our very important effort to financially support young adults who, like myself, were aged out of the foster care system and left to figure it out on their own—a scary effort, I promise you."

She paused, hating how in that moment she would love to look out at the edge of the crowd and see Gabe standing there. Watching her. Willing her to fight her fear and press on. Quickly her eyes scanned the parts of the crowd she could see. She was disappointed but unsurprised to not see him. It stung.

"To date we have been able to assist more than one hundred such fearless people with their dreams to grow beyond their circumstances. I cannot thank you all enough for your support. I am moved beyond words and honored beyond measure...whatever the reason," she added, knowing that many of the celebrities were in attendance out of allegiance to her father and pity at her story.

Servers filed into the room, carrying trays of crystal flutes filled with champagne. Monica accepted one. "I just want to thank my entire team for their support and all of you for ensuring a successful launch of this nonprofit foundation," she said, raising her glass high in the air. "Here's to The Bridge."

"The Bridge," everyone said in unison.

She smiled, turning to touch her glass to those Choice, Montgomery, Kylie and Nylah held, before finally taking a deep sip as the room filled with applause. With one final smile, Monica handed over the microphone as Montgomery motioned for the band to resume their playing. Fraught with nerves and unsure if she'd said the right things, and wondering what these strangers whispered about her, she made her way across the room and onto the elevator to reach the roof.

The chill immediately surrounded her, and she shivered as she released a stream of breath that was visible in the frosty air. She allowed herself a moment to pretend the cold was nothing as she thought of her life just a year ago and how everything—*everything*—had changed.

"Thank you," she whispered up to the heavens.

She looked out at the city. The lights amid the darkness. The pockets of warmth in the cold. The snow blanketing the streets and the tops of the sky-high buildings. The familiar noise. She loved Manhattan. It helped to heal her. Gave her a place to finally call home.

She would love nothing more than to share this moment with—

"Monica."

Gabe.

Her heart pounded just as it did every time she saw him. She turned just as he rushed across the snow-covered roof, removing his overcoat to place it around her bared shoulders. "It's freezing up here," he said as he pulled her body into his embrace.

She welcomed his warmth but resented yet another late appearance.

"At least he showed up this time."

Gabe stiffened and leaned back from her. His eyes searched her face as he frowned a little.

"What?" she asked in confusion.

"At least I showed up this time?" he asked.

Her mouth fell open. She realized she had said the words aloud and not in her head. "Yes," she said, accepting that they were her truth and they deserved to finally be given voice.

His frown deepened as he slid his hands into the pockets of his tuxedo pants.

She stepped back from him, trying so hard not to notice how devastatingly handsome he looked in his black tuxedo. *So damn good.*

"I called and explained what happened," Gabe said before glancing up as snow began to lightly fall.

Monica did the same. "Yes, you did. You always call with an explanation…of why you're late, why you're canceling, why you're not even making plans to see me anymore," she said, as she held up a hand to let one single snowflake float down upon it. "Making phone calls is not the problem."

"What is?" he asked.

She crushed the snowflake inside her fist. "I can only guess," she said, looking anywhere but at him. "I don't know why you're fading out of this relationship, but you are. First your family and now me, I guess."

"My family?"

"Yes!" she stressed and then took a breath to reclaim her calm. "If you can cut them off and move out and be okay with not having them in your life, what does that say about your loyalty to me?"

"So now I'm disloyal?" Gabe asked, his voice low.

"And I'm divisive?" she countered.

"What?" he asked, obviously confused.

Monica knew she was all over the place. So were her emotions. Even in the storm of her anger, she knew she could find temporary calm in his arms. It would be so easy to push aside her fears and her annoyance to just get lost in him. Holding him. Kissing him.

"Deny that your family blames me for the distance between you," she said.

His eyes shifted. That was telling.

So, Nicolette had voiced her issues with me to him already.

"You have nothing to do with the way things are between me and some of my family," he said, not directly answering her question.

Gabe was not a liar.

"But I don't want you to take them for granted because you don't know what it feels like to not have family," she said, wishing the feeling wasn't so familiar to her.

"I don't want to be taken for granted either, Monica," he countered.

"Yes, but if you can walk away from them so easily—"

Gabe frowned. "You think my decision to stand independently was easy?"

She shrugged. "It seems to be."

He snorted in derision. "A lot of things aren't what they seem," he said, giving her a once-over before looking away from her.

She stiffened. "If you meant that for me, you're wrong, because I am exactly what I claim to be."

"Supportive? Understanding? Selfless?" he asked, his voice filled with censure. "You're the one in the wrong."

Monica gathered her skirt in her hands as she marched over to stand before him. "Not supportive? Not understanding? Anything but selfless? Me?" she asked, poking his chest with her index finger after each question. "Are you crazy?"

"Are you?" he shot back.

"To think you would ever see me as your equal after I was your maid?" she asked. "Yes, I just might be."

Gabe's face hardened. "I left behind the workers at my restaurant to try and share some of the night with you," he said, his tone as stiff as his face. "And you greet me with complaints."

"Not complaints. Just truth," she said, lowering her hands and balling them into tight fists that pressed the tips of her nails into the flesh of her palm.

"I don't need this shit right now, Monica! Not from you," he said, his voice rising and battling with the sounds of the metropolis, which filled the chilly night air.

"When?" she said quietly.

Gabe paused with his chest heaving. "What?" he asked, his face a mask of confusion.

"Over the last few months, you've barely given me the time of day, so when should we have talked?" she asked, remembering nights where she'd sat fully dressed and disappointed because a mishap at the site of the restaurant kept him from showing up for a date.

Gabe eyed her with intensity as he smoothed his hand over the shadow of his beard before turning to walk away from her, then suddenly turned again. "I thought you understood how important this restaurant was for me. If I mistook that, I apologize, but I won't pretend that it doesn't need or deserve my attention right now, Monica," he said.

"And I don't?" Monica asked.

Their eyes locked.

The distance between them seemed more like miles than just a few feet.

"Am I fighting a losing battle, Monica?" he asked.

She eyed him for as long as she could without feeling the urge to run to him. "Meaning?"

"My time is important, too. Am I wasting mine with you?" he asked, pausing as he raised one hand and began to tick off each finger. "I hate my family. I'm never around. I'm fading like the invisible man. I'm disloyal. What else? Let 'em roll."

Would you still be with me if I was still a maid?

She set aside her thought as some emotion flashed in his eyes. For the briefest moment she thought it was pain but decided she was wrong. Just like she had been wrong about so many things.

Like thinking this could work.

She thought of his mother—her words, her desire for them to end. Between Monica's insecurities and his ambition would Nicolette Cress whispering her objections to her son be the nail in the coffin of their relationship? She knew firsthand the Cresses were a tight-knit bunch.

She fell silent. The fracture between Gabe and his family was deepening. She felt she'd played a major role in that. She knew all too well what it felt like to be without family. That was something she wished on no one.

"If you think so lowly of me, why be with me?" he asked.

"And if I'm not making you happy, why not tell me?" she shot back.

Gabe shook his head as he clenched his jaw. "Is it possible to make you happy?" he asked.

She felt chilled to the bone by the coldness of his tone. The weather around them was warm in comparison.

"Don't be a jerk, Gabe," she said.

He scowled. "My apologies. I'll just add it to your list of complaints," he muttered as he began to pace.

"Screw you!" she snapped.

He splayed his hands. "And take the chance of you complaining about it? Hell no!" he shot back.

"You are an ass!"

He raised his hand and emphatically ticked off another finger.

She glared at him.

Gabe opened his mouth but shut it again as he rolled his shoulders, as if seeking to be tension-free. He took a large inhale and then exhaled. "What do you want from me?" he asked.

All of you.

The thought came with a swiftness and scared her. She was hesitant to reveal just how necessary Gabriel Cress had become to her. Not when she wasn't sure his desire of her was equal. "To not feel like a second thought," she said, confessing to that.

Gabe looked around at the snow falling around them. "The very last thing you are to me, Monica Darby, is a second thought," he admitted.

Her heart soared.

"But—" he stopped.

She arched a brow and tilted her head to the side as she eyed him brushing snowflakes from his shoulders. "But," she repeated to fill his pause.

"I don't know if you will ever believe that," he said, looking back at her. "And I don't know how to prove it to you. Not if it means ignoring my dreams. I want this restaurant—I need this restaurant—to succeed and that means hard work and focus."

"So if I asked you to roll it all back? Stop being so dogged in your pursuit of success, mend the divide between you and your family, find a balance between what you want and what you need…?" she said, walking over to sandwich one of his hands between both of hers.

"And if I asked you if you would ever be able to fully trust me?" he returned.

Neither answered the question they were asked.

"So you choose that restaurant over everything and everyone," she said, holding up the collars of his coat to turn her face and bury her nose against the lightweight black wool. His scent—the one she loved—clung to it.

"And you choose to hold anything and everything against me."

Am I?

Then she remembered how she'd felt all night without him there and how the lack of his presence had become commonplace. How she had begun to envision her life without him. Preparing herself for that moment when it ended and even contemplating ending it herself to avoid feeling so helpless.

To leave and not be left…

"Why did we think this would work?" she asked, her voice low.

"If you think it's not damn working, then why are we wasting our time!" he roared, splaying his hands angrily. "To hell with it if that's how you feel."

Her ire matched his. "Then to hell with it, Gabe," she shouted back.

"This is ridiculous!"

"Thinking you don't need anyone is ridiculous!"

"I damn sure don't need *this* right now."

She looked over at him as her eyes widened. "Don't let me force you to be here," she said.

He squinted as he eyed her for a long moment that seemed to tick by slowly before he turned and walked over to the elevator.

"Gabe," she called to him as her heart galloped full speed in its race to its break.

I can see in your eyes that you know I'm right.

Nicolette's words seemed to echo inside her. Mocking her.

You know I'm right.
You know I'm right.
You know I'm right.

She blinked and shook her head to free it of the woman's voice. She removed his coat and crossed the short distance to press it against his chest before releasing it without a care if he caught it or let it slip and fall. She felt his hand reach for hers and she pulled away from his touch turning her back on him. "It started on a roof with you in a tux and looks like it's ending the same way," she said with a bitter little laugh.

At his continued silence, she looked back over her shoulder to find she was alone.

Hours later Gabe sat in his apartment looking at the Manhattan skyline as he nursed his snifter of his favorite scotch as the heat of the lit fireplace warmed him. His thoughts were full and troubled.

When he arrived at her event and then rushed to the roof to find her, never had he guessed the night would end with them going their separate ways. He'd fought hard not to feel ambushed as she'd revealed to him all the misgivings she'd obviously had about him all along. His stomach clenched and his grip on the glass tightened.

He wasn't quite sure what emotions he felt swirling inside him, but anger was one. Indignation was another. For many reasons. For her lack of trust. Her belief in the very worst about him. And her willingness to end it when all he wanted was more time to make his restaurant a success—something he revealed to her early on.

Or at least he thought he had.

He released a heavy breath and took another sip.

He knew of her past, and that loyalty and trust might be issues for her—for them—but he'd never doubted that Monica would doubt him. Not see him. Not know him. Not understand him. That bothered him. He knew he had lost his focus and had become so driven that it seemed nothing else mattered but the restaurant. He'd thought she understood just how important this was to him, particularly knowing that his family had offered him no help nor support and, to him, held a desire for him to fail just so they could say, "I told you so."

He'd wanted to do anything but fail and had expressed that to her.

He'd never been one to take on a losing battle and let it defeat him.

He'd made a choice between his relationship and ambition before. Time and time again, his ambition had won. It hadn't been a conscious choice to make her feel unwanted and undesired. His desire to have her in his life had never been in question for him.

But in that moment when he'd reached for her hand and felt compelled to fight for her—to fight for them—she'd snatched hers away. He let it be. He let her be. He let her go.

Because he knew how important his success was to him. He knew there had been a choice to be made, and without her support and belief in him as an honorable, hardworking man who was driven, he had felt there had been no other choice than to tuck his head, focus on his work and get the job done. For him, he'd chosen something he could believe in. Her fears had him concerned she would never trust in him enough to not judge everything he did.

But as the hours ticked by and the truth settled in, he wasn't as sure of his choice.

Still, it had not been his alone.

She had seemed to accept that it was done and was prepared to move on.

It wasn't what he wanted. He missed her already, but he was accepting that perhaps their breakup was for the best.

He looked up at the framed photo of himself and Monica that sat on the mantel of the fireplace. They'd been skiing in Aspen, and Monica, who had felt completely out of her element, had fallen off her skis and he'd purposely tumbled down beside her and pulled out his phone to capture their laughter in a selfie.

They'd played in the snow all day and created their own heat together all night.

"Damn," he swore, setting his glass on the metal end table beside the sofa before he rose and placed the picture facedown.

Eleven

Two months later

"Monica?"

At the sound of her name being called, she turned in the lobby of her apartment building with her heart still pounding from discovering a few paparazzi following her while she was out shopping. News and rabid speculation on her and Gabe's breakup had forced them back into the public eye.

She gasped to see Phoebe rising from one of the ornate seats in the waiting area, looking pretty in coral wide-leg pants and a long-sleeved white tee. The sight of her and the obvious compassion in her eyes struck a chord in Monica as she let her shoulders slump and shook her head as emotions overwhelmed her. Phoebe gave her a smile and opened her arms wide, just as she'd promised that day in the attorney's office.

"Just know there is no deadline on when you reach out to me. Be it a day or a year or a dozen—if I'm still alive God willing—I will accept you with open arms."

In her, at that moment, Monica saw something she felt she'd never had before. Family. As she quickly crossed the divide and welcomed her aunt's embrace, she felt foolish for never fully allowing the woman into her life. "You came," she whispered, comforted by the warm pats on her back.

"You needed me," Phoebe said with a low chuckle. "Right?"

Monica nodded her head where it rested against her shoulder. "Right," she admitted.

"So here I am," Phoebe simply said.

Monica took a deep steadying breath before taking a small step back and looking at her aunt. "I love him," she admitted as tears welled.

Phoebe put a hand to her back. "Let's go up, have something to drink, and talk," she said.

"I don't have any juice or tea," Monica said as they reached the double doors of the elevators.

"Tea?" her aunt scoffed. "More like a mar-*ti*-ni."

That made Monica laugh. Maybe her first time in weeks.

As they settled in her living room and sipped on the dirty martinis Phoebe made for them, Monica felt comforted by the presence of this woman she really didn't know. "To have you here when I needed someone most makes me realize I wanted you here all along," she admitted.

Phoebe crossed her ankles and reached over to squeeze Monica's hand with hers. "When I saw the press about the breakup and saw the paparazzi hounding you again, I was determined to fly back and check on you," she said. "You looked so sad. I could see that."

"It's been two months, actually, so everyone's a little late," she said, thinking of the last time she'd seen Gabe.

"Or someone is so overjoyed it's done, they gave the paparazzi a clue."

With each day her hope that he would come and fight for her faded. Still, she hungered for him. He was in her thoughts so often. It was like nothing she had ever experienced. Nothing at all. Her love for her ex seemed juvenile in comparison.

And it was then she realized that she loved Gabe.

His strength. His passion. His intelligence. His compassion. Even his drive and ambition.

Without her realizing it, Gabriel Cress had claimed a piece of her heart, and every day she had to deal with having that love without having him.

"I was a fool to think I could avoid loving him," Monica said, kicking off the heels she wore with her wrap dress and tucking her feet beneath her bottom as she looked out the window. "No, I was a fool to think I didn't already love him before that first wild night on the roof."

"The roof?" Phoebe said before fanning herself.

Monica felt her face flush with heat at the memory.

"Tell me the story of Monica and Gabe," Phoebe said.

In an instant she seemed to remember so many moments they'd shared. Good times. *Great* times.

"I will tell you our story, even though it doesn't end well, because the beginning and the middle were amazing," Monica admitted softly, feeling her pulse race.

At times she smiled. Other times her eyes glazed over as she remembered their heat. There were many moments she chuckled at something funny they'd shared together. And then, as she spoke of the weeks leading up to the night of her charity gala, she felt weighted down by her sadness. And regret.

"You *do* love him," Phoebe said with emphasis.

Monica looked to her.

"I see it in the way you talk about him, and remember him," the elder explained. "And miss him."

"But he broke my heart. He gave up. He walked away. He left me," Monica said, working her fingers as if to remove the tension she felt rise like a wave.

Phoebe stilled the frantic movement of her hand by covering it with her own. *"Or…"*

Monica looked to her again.

"Or your time together had come to its natural end," the older woman offered. "If you spend a chunk of your life with someone and the majority is good—truly good—then you should never end it hating the other person. You move on and keep the good memories, learn the life lessons and be prepared for your next big adventure."

"Another man?" Monica asked with a frown.

"No, not always. Sometimes you discover you in a way that you've never really known yourself. Or you travel. Or change careers. Or journal. Discover religion. Or write a book—and for some, hell, read a book. Or sometimes you discover you have a family member you never knew about and wished that you had," she said.

Monica's smile to her was warm and genuine.

"Life is all about change and newness, and sometimes people aren't meant to be in your life forever…and the time you spent together is nothing to regret, no matter how it ends."

"Like seasons?" Monica asked, rising to walk over to the window and look out at Central Park in the distance. The emerald green of the grass and the bright colors of the flowers gave it an idyllic look from where she stood.

"Exactly," Phoebe stressed. "Each just as necessary as the last. Some more brutal than others."

Monica crossed her arms over her chest. She blinked

away tears that threatened to fall. She'd cried enough of them to fill a pond.

As she looked down at the street, she spotted a couple with their arms entwined as they walked and talked with each other. They laughed together before he wrapped an arm around her waist to lift her off her feet and spin her before pressing a kiss to her cheek. It was like a scene from a romance movie. It even seemed to move along in slow motion, but she knew that was her imagination at play.

How long will their season last? And how will it end? A fiery explosion or a gentle goodbye? Or will it last forever?

Gabe.

She thought of him as she had a million times over the last two months—especially at night when the world seemed quiet and there was no work at the foundation, lunch with friends or enough TV shows to keep her mind occupied. She focused on the good times they shared. Those happy, pleasure-filled memories eased her heartache. Not much. But some.

Maybe even enough to do something she thought she'd dare not.

Monica looked over her shoulder at the writing desk against the wall before she turned and walked over to it, then bent and removed a large envelope from the wastepaper basket. It was dark brown, like chocolate, with gold block letters. She licked her lips as she traced her name and address before touching that of GABRIEL. The restaurant—*his* restaurant. Not the man.

"He did it," she said, with the soft hint of a smile.

"Who?" Phoebe asked from the sofa.

Monica looked over at her as she held up the envelope between her index and middle finger. "It's an invite to his restaurant opening," she said. "It came earlier this week and I threw it away."

Phoebe kept her eyes locked on her niece but said nothing.

"I'm happy for him. I am," Monica stressed. "But I do not want to see him and the thing he chose over me. Ever. Am I wrong?"

Phoebe came over, gently took the envelope from her and set it on the center of the small modern-style desk next to a short stack of bills. "No, just undecided," she said.

True.

"When is it?"

"Next week," Monica said, digging her toes into the plush pile of the area rug. "Seems a little last-minute."

"Maybe he was undecided, too," Phoebe offered.

"Maybe," she said, wrinkling her brow a bit as she moved back to the window and stepped inside a ray of sunlight, which felt good against her skin.

Almost as good as Gabe.

Was he with someone new? Or was the restaurant his one true love?

"Well, you have a week to decide," Phoebe suggested from behind her.

Monica remained silent. Her thoughts were filled with visions of walking up on Gabe holding and kissing and giving attention to another woman the way he used to do with her. The jealousy she felt at just the idea of that was telling.

Her love for him lingered.

"What if his true intent was an invite to reconcile?" Phoebe asked.

Monica's heartbeat seemed to echo loudly inside her even as she shook her head in denial of the thought. "Hurt me once, shame on you. Hurt me twice?" she asked, using her own play on words of the popular saying. "Shame on me."

At the gentle nudge against her arm, she was surprised

to find her aunt standing beside her with a fresh cocktail in each hand. She took one with a nod of thanks. "You make a really good drink, Auntie," she said after a long and satisfying sip.

"I was a bartender in this little dive in Cuba for two years when I was deeply in passion with Armando," Phoebe said as she lightly stroked her neck and smiled at some memory before sipping her drink, giving a soft little grunt from the back of her throat.

"Armando, huh?" Monica asked, curious about the life her aunt had lived that had included a stay in Cuba.

"Yes, and Frank, and Marcus, and Harry. Just to name a few," she said, her smile widening with each name. "I've had some great passions in my life. And I gave as good as I got."

"What about love?" she asked the older woman she was quickly learning to adore.

"Love? Sometimes," Phoebe said with a little shrug. "But even when the love fades the memories remain, and that, my niece, makes it *all* worthwhile."

With Gabe there had been more good than bad. So much more. Plenty of passion, laughs and deep conversations. Travels. Adventures. Discoveries. And the sex. Their physical connection. She shook her head in wonder at the thought of the heated moments they'd shared. The things they did to each other.

But…

"I'm too hurt to enjoy the memories," she admitted.

"Of course, you are…now," Phoebe assured her. "That's the good thing about memories, because they don't go anywhere. They'll wait for when you're ready to savor them, and they'll sneak up on you when you least expect it."

Don't I know it.

"To the memories," Phoebe said raising her glass with her eyes filled with twinkle.

Monica gave her a reluctant smile, anxious for the days her recollections didn't mock her so much. "To the memories," she agreed as they touched glasses.

Ding.

Gabe sprinkled thinly sliced green onions on the short ribs braised in red wine atop thick grits made savory with French Brillat-Savarin cheese and freshly made garlic butter. He stepped back to view his handiwork as he tossed his hand towel over his left shoulder and set his hands on his hips. "Run the dish," he said with a nod, signaling the plated meal was ready to be served.

It was the last dish of the first night of his restaurant's grand opening.

"Excellent job, Chef."

Gabe smiled as he extended a hand to Lorenzo, who had humbly served as his sous chef for one more night. Together they had effortlessly served those private guests he'd invited to celebrate with him. Tomorrow he would be on his own. GABRIEL was open. "Thank you, Chef."

"It's nice to see you smile, amigo," Lorenzo said as he walked over to the leather-covered double doors to remove his apron and free his shiny ebony waist-length hair.

This time the grin was forced. "I'm okay, Zo," he lied, moving to the wash sink to clean and dry his hands before replacing the dark brown, monogrammed chef's coat he wore with a clean one.

"You can't wake a person who is pretending to be asleep," Lorenzo said, pulling on a dark blue linen jacket that matched his dark denim jeans and deep blue silk shirt.

His friend had said the Navajo saying to him many times over the last two months. "I am moving on," he insisted.

"You're going through the motions," Lorenzo insisted. "Living without living."

He wasn't wrong. The nights were the worst.

"Call her, Gabe."

His gut felt punched at the very thought of her. He shook his head. "No," he said adamantly.

Lorenzo held up his hands. "Your life," he said.

"Yes, and a new part of it starts tonight," Gabe said, glad to move on from yet another what-went-wrong conversation.

"Yes, it does. Enjoy it," his friend said before turning and leaving him alone in the small but well-stocked kitchen.

Gabe released a short but deep breath as he nodded as if he were an athlete prepping himself on the sidelines before he entered a championship game. Success or failure rested on his shoulders because everything had been his selection from the small staff, the menu, the schematics and the interior design. Every bit of it was how he wanted to be viewed as a chef to the world. More than ever before.

His sacrifice had been great and he wanted the reward to surpass that.

He needed not to feel like the biggest fool ever.

He thought of a sweet moment with Monica, laughing at something he said as they lounged in bed, but forced the thought away.

Clearing his throat, Gabe pushed through the double doors and stepped out to the front of the house. The restaurant was small and intimate with a clean and stylish decor of pale walls, dark furnishings, and bronze votive candles and floral arrangements on each of the sixteen tables. Large quarter-top windows ran across the front of the space, showcasing the brick-lined street and the river in the distance. In the deep alcove on the side wall, he'd placed the bar, with its copper background and recessed lights illuminating the array of bottles lined up on the wood shelves. He would be open for four hours, six nights a week with a focus on dinner service, offering a delectable five-course tasting menu of his choosing. He would cook what he wanted and charge a premium price to do so, with a new menu printed every night. A new inspiration every night.

Never had he felt so inspired.

He stepped deeper into the restaurant, and the applause began. With a nod of thanks, Gabe looked about the room at all the smiling faces and felt comforted that his family was among them. For a moment, he wondered if their support was more about genuine desire for his success or because he had returned to Cress, INC. in a less prominent role while making it clear he was not interested in being the CEO upon their father's retirement. He could be there only if he was out of the race. He had begun to miss his family and the great work they were doing at Cress, INC. just as much as he'd craved being a chef again.

Stop being so dogged in your pursuit of success.

Mend the divide between you and your family.

Find a balance between what you want and what you need.

What he'd once felt was Monica's ultimatum or attempt to control his life had become some of the greatest advice he'd ever received. And when he'd reached out to his parents, it was with clear intent that it was his way or no way. Finally, he'd spoken up for himself and shed the desire to be unproblematic. Having them concede to him had been shocking and satisfying. They'd missed him, as well. For once he'd thought his father saw his worth. But in that moment, he'd felt even more gratified knowing he didn't *need* their approval or support.

Still it was nice to have—

The rest of his thoughts abruptly halted as he looked

up and caught sight of Monica sitting at one of the tables near the windows. Surprise caused his heart to swell in his chest, and he felt a nervous energy course over his body as he took her in, feeling a hunger that was familiar. She wore more makeup than usual. Her smoky eyes, high cheekbones and nude glossy lips were beautiful. Her hair was pulled back from her face and behind her shoulders, framing large diamond chandelier earrings. But it was when she rose from the chair as he moved toward her that he truly felt out of breath.

The strapless black column dress was ruched at the middle, emphasizing her shape, with a hem that fell just below her knees, revealing well-toned legs and strappy heels with satin bows at the ankles.

She was stunning.

As he neared her, he saw the uncertainty in her eyes. He felt the same way.

"Hello, Monica," he said.

"Congratulations, Gabe," she said, her eyes unlocking with his to look beyond his shoulder for a moment.

He followed her line of vision to find his entire family looking at them. They all suddenly pretended to focus on their drinks and each other. Shaking his head, he looked back at her. "I can't believe you're here," he admitted, wondering if his pounding heart was as loud to her as it was to him.

"Thank you for the invite," she said.

Gabe didn't hide his confusion. "But I didn't send an invite," he admitted.

Monica frowned, then looked disappointed before her expression went blank. She looked down at her feet, then up at him. "Oh," she said before quickly turning and picking up her black-beaded clutch from the table.

"Gabe."

He looked over his shoulder to find his publicist, Frank Lawson, standing behind him.

"It's time for the toast," Frank said.

Gabe eyed two servers bringing trays of champagne-filled flutes from the bar. Just as planned. In attendance were a well-known food critic and a couple of members of the press given exclusive access to the opening. "One moment," he said without a second thought.

Frank looked concerned. "I don't know if I can hold them, Gabe," he said.

But he had already turned back to Monica, only to find she was gone. The remembered look of disappointment in her eyes fueled him as he took the few steps to yank open the copper-trimmed glass door to step out onto the street. His heart wildly pounded as he looked left and then right. She was nearing the corner to cross the street.

"Monica!" he called to her.

She stopped and turned.

The streetlamp above her highlighted the track of a tear, like the twinkle of a star. A visceral pain radiated across his chest as he rushed to her.

"I shouldn't have come," she said, raising her hand to her face.

Gabe covered it with his to lower it. He used his free hand to capture the tear with his thumb as his eyes moved over her face, taking in everything. His gaze lingered on her mouth. "I'm glad you came," he admitted in a whisper. "You coming into my life in the first place gave me the courage to do it all."

She closed her eyes and shook her head slowly as she gripped his hand and slowly removed his touch. "I came. I ate some really great food. I saw you. I said my congrats. And now I'm leaving, Gabe."

"No, don't leave me," he pleaded, not allowing shame

or ego to make him act a fool again. "The worst mistake I ever made was not fighting for us that night. Forgive me."

Monica gasped and then winced as she took a deep breath. "Gabe," she began.

"I thought you were angry at me. I thought you never wanted to see me again. I thought I hurt you so bad that I didn't have a right to convince you that I realized I love you," he said, holding tight to her hand and massaging tiny circles on the back of it as he enjoyed the simple physical connection. "*Forgive* me."

Monica kept her eyes closed as if it pained her to even look at him.

That hurt. But he understood it.

"Damn it," she swore as her shoulders slumped and she allowed her head to rest against his chest.

He rested his chin atop it. "*Forgive* me," he begged.

"Gabe."

He heard Frank behind him but ignored him as he waited for Monica to honor his request. He wanted her back in his life more than everything, and he refused to give up the opportunity to fight for her for anything.

"I was a fool, baby, please," he stressed, easing back from her enough to press his hand to her face to raise it.

Her eyes remained closed.

"Look at me," he whispered.

Slowly, she did.

It was his turn to gasp as he looked into the brown depths of her eyes and saw every bit of the love she had for him. It was pure and real…and fierce. That he knew without her speaking. It was the epitome of wearing her heart on her sleeve.

Relief coursed over him until he felt strengthened and weakened all at once.

"Gabe!"

Monica leaned to the side to look past him. "They need you back at the restaurant," she said, as she looked back up at him.

"It can wait. Nothing matters to me more in this moment than you," he said steadfastly.

She looked at him again.

When her eyes widened in surprise, he turned, as well, to find his mother guiding Frank back inside the restaurant.

Gabe and Monica looked back at each other with questions in their eyes.

Did she send the invite?

"No," they said in unison before sharing a laugh that lightened the mood.

Monica dropped her head to his chest again and settled her hands on his hips. "Gabe, I have to be honest," she began.

He stiffened.

Is she with someone else?

The thought of that was torture.

"I learned some things these last couple of months," she said, raising her head to look up at him.

He enjoyed the sight of her. His eyes wandered over her as if he were feeding a hunger.

"About myself. About love. Family. So many things," Monica continued.

He'd felt anguish when he'd thought he had lost her forever.

"I *love* you, Gabriel Cress," she stressed, tilting her head to the side as her eyes searched his. "I forgive you."

So, this is joy.

"*If—*" she continued.

He tensed again, feeling completely shaken by the emotional roller coaster. His hint of a smile faded.

"*If* you can forgive me for letting my past filter everything you did and see it all in a bad light," she said, easing her hands around his waist. "*Forgive* me."

Gabe released the breath he hadn't realized he was holding. "Without question," he said, his voice deep and brimming with meaning as he brought his hands up under her hair to hold her neck and jaw in his palms.

They stared at each other. The energy—that familiar pulse—was there as their serious expressions were replaced with slow smiles. Long, endless moments of just enjoying being in one another's company again.

This was love.

Pure and profound.

He lowered his head, giving in to his hunger, and she tilted her head up and welcomed his kisses. Slow and soft at first, with moments in between each where their lips barely touched and they inhaled of one another's shaky breaths. And when they deepened, each moaned from down within as they clung to one another, until their bodies seemed to blend.

Gabriel knew in that moment that he loved her like he had never loved before, and that she had claimed a piece of his heart that no other woman would ever be able to reach. And there was not one bit of fear in him about it. Not one.

This was love.

Why had they denied themselves for so long?

It was Monica who broke the kiss and smiled at him as she cleaned her gloss from his lips with her thumb. She slid her hand in his. "You have an opening to attend," she reminded him.

"Let's walk slow," he said with a deliberate look down at the length of him hard and pressing against his pants.

She chuckled as she leaned against his arm. "My desire is not as easy to see," she said.

"The thought of that isn't helping," Gabe said, his voice deep.

"Maybe I should put a little distance between us," she said, slightly teasing as she released his hand.

"Not too much."

"Never again," she said, stopping as they came to the front door. She held up her pinky finger. "I promise not to ever push you away and you promise to never leave. Deal?"

Gabe hooked his pinky with hers. "Deal. No fear?"

"No fear," she agreed.

When they finally walked inside, the sounds of a successful restaurant surrounded them. Conversation blended with jazzy music. Forks hit dishes and glasses touched each other in toasts. Monica made a move to reclaim her seat, but Gabe held steadfastly to her hand to guide her behind him to the center of the restaurant where his family sat.

Frank looked relieved as he motioned for the servers to bring two additional flutes.

"What made you send the invite?" he heard Monica ask his mother.

"I was tired of seeing my son miserable without you," his mother replied.

So, it was her.

He cleared his throat and stared down at his feet to gather himself before he finally looked over at his mother. By sending that invite, she had accepted and welcomed Monica into the fold. For him.

That, too, was love.

Gabe accepted the flutes and handed one to Monica before facing his guests. "I'm proud and humbled to announce that GABRIEL has full reservations for the next four weeks. Thank you for the first of hopefully many nights to come of good food, good drink and good times. This is my life's dream, and I'm honored to share this night with all of you, with my family who taught me everything I know about food, and this woman beside me who taught me everything I know about love," he said, looking down at Monica, who was already looking at him.

The night was perfect.

"To GABRIEL," Phillip Sr. said.

As everyone in the restaurant raised their glasses in a toast to him and his establishment, Gabe looked over at his father and saw pride for him in his eyes. He had grown beyond needing his father's approval, but in truth, it was an honor to have. Extending his flute, he touched his glass to his father's before then lifting it into the circle created by his family with their own glasses raised in toast.

Atop the table, he covered Monica's hand with his own and entwined their fingers.

"À la nourriture. À la vie. À l'amour," he said, leveling his eyes on each of his family members.

"À la nourriture. À la vie. À l'amour," they all said in unison.

With his thumb still stroking the back of her hand, he leaned in close to her ear. "To food. To life. To love," he said before pressing a kiss behind her lobe.

He felt her tremble. "Soon," Gabe promised.

Monica looked at him, her soft eyes filling with heat. "Another wild night like the first one, Mr. Cress?" she said for his ears alone.

His pulse raced as he chuckled. "Better," he promised.

Epilogue

Three months later

"Marry me."

Monica opened her eyes and looked up at Gabe as he paused in delivering delicious stroke after stroke inside her. She lay beneath his strong, muscled frame in the center of their king-size bed. "You're doing this right now?" she asked in between deep gasps.

Gabe kissed both corners of her mouth. "Yes," he said before deepening the kiss with his clever tongue as he resumed stroking inside her, slowly. Deeply.

She released a tiny cry, feeling his hardness pressing against her walls. Her fingernails dug into his fleshy buttocks as she took the lead and suckled his tongue into her mouth, using her hips to meet his pace.

"Wait," he gasped, stopping all movement.

"What?" she asked, pressing her head back against the softness of the pillow to look up at him.

"Don't move. I'm not ready to come. Not yet," he said, resting his forehead against the pillow beside her as he clenched and unclenched his jaw, seeking control of his body.

She smiled as she worked the muscles of her intimacy to grip and release his hard inches slowly.

He tensed. "No, Monica," he pleaded, raising his head to look down at her.

"What?" she asked again, this time with feigned innocence.

He smiled before capturing her mouth with his. "I could stay inside you forever," he said.

"Really?" she asked as she rubbed the soft heel of her foot against his calf and stroked his nape with her fingertips.

"Absolutely."

She chuckled. "We wouldn't get much accomplished," she reminded him.

"Hell with the rest," he said.

She eyed him for long moments, amazed at how freely she accepted her love for him. Her trust of him. Her desire for it to last. And how much she believed he loved her just as deeply. "Monica Cress, huh?"

"Sounds good," he said, nuzzling her neck and kissing her racing pulse as he began to roll his hips to stroke his hardness inside her again.

"Monica Darby-Cress," she sighed as she arched her back and closed her eyes in pleasure.

"That's cool, too," Gabe said, raising his head to look down at her. "As long as I can call you my wife, the name change is up to you."

Monica struggled to stay focused on his words as his lovemaking wreaked havoc on her senses. The smell of him. The feel of his body and his sweat pressed down upon hers as he made love to her slowly, his hardness filling her and slickly striking against her bud. She opened her eyes to watch his profile as he opened his mouth against her shoulder and gasped in pleasure.

"Your wife," she said, wrapping her legs around him as she dug her fingers into his back.

Gabe looked at her. "My wife," he said, with a deep thrust that caused them both to gasp sharply.

She licked her lips, feeling parched from their explosive heat. "My husband," she whispered.

He fixed his wild eyes on hers. "Your husband," he said.

"Absolutely," she said, raising her head to capture his mouth with her own.

With a primal moan, he slipped his hands beneath her to cup her buttocks as he quickened his pace inside her. Swift. Deep. Thrilling.

Monica had been sucking his tongue but freed it as she cried out. Her release came in a rush and exploded deep inside her. She gave in to the pleasure and got lost in the madness. "Gabe!" she gasped as tears welled from the passion and her love for him.

He roared in that hot second just before she felt his rod get harder inside her as he filled her with his seed. Even in the midst of her passion, with her body still trembling, she rocked her hips back and forth, drawing everything from him and evoking even more primal moans and cries. She pushed through her own weakness, brought on by her climax, and relentlessly stroked downward on his hardness until he released one last, rough cry before his entire body went slack upon her.

"Damn," he swore. "Damn."

Monica pressed kisses from his neck to his shoulder, tasting the salt of his hard-earned sweat as she enjoyed the synchronized, fast tempo of their pounding heartbeats.

"My love?" she said as she drew circles in the sweat on his back with her fingertip.

Gabe opened one eye. "Huh?" he asked, his oncoming sleep already deepening his voice further.

"Small and private wedding ceremony?" she suggested innocently, already thinking of the field day the press would have with anything else.

Gabe pressed a kiss to her shoulder, cheek and then mouth before rolling over onto his back. "Short engagement?" he countered.

Monica sat up to reach for the sheet from the floor to pull over their bodies before lying on her side and resting her head on his chest. "Honeymoon in Fiji?" she asked.

He fell quiet and she knew he was thinking of time away from the restaurant and Cress, INC.

"One week or two?"

She bit back a smile. "One," she said, knowing any time off would be hard for him to handle.

"Nah, two," he said.

She raised her head to look at him in surprise. "Two?" she said.

He chuckled as he stroked her hair back from her face. "It's my job to make you happy, future Mrs. Cress," he said.

She moved to staddle him and grabbed his hand to place them on her breasts. "Then round two, Mr. Cress?" she asked.

His eyes darkened with heat. "Your wish is always my command," he said with a roguish smile as she lowered her body so they could kiss and begin to give each other a *very* happy ending.

* * * * *

COMING SOON!

We really hope you enjoyed reading this book. If you're looking for more romance, be sure to head to the shops when new books are available on

Thursday 4th February

To see which titles are coming soon, please visit

millsandboon.co.uk/nextmonth

JOIN US ON SOCIAL MEDIA!

Stay up to date with our latest releases, author news and gossip, special offers and discounts, and all the behind-the-scenes action from Mills & Boon...

 millsandboon

 millsandboonuk

 millsandboon

It might just be true love...

MILLS & BOON

HISTORICAL

Awaken the romance of the past

Escape with historical heroes from time gone by. Whether your passion is for wicked Regency Rakes, muscled Viking warriors or rugged Highlanders, indulge your fantasies and awaken the romance of the past.

Six Historical stories published every month, find them all at:

millsandboon.co.uk/ Historical

MILLS & BOON

MODERN

Power and Passion

Prepare to be swept off your feet by sophisticated, sexy and seductive heroes, in some of the world's most glamourous and romantic locations, where power and passion collide.

Julia James
Heiress's
PREGNANCY SCANDAL
MILLS & BOON
MODERN

Jennie Lucas
Chosen as the
SHEIKH'S ROYAL BRIDE
MILLS & BOON
MODERN

Kim Lawrence
A WEDDING
at the
ITALIAN'S DEMAND
MILLS

Sharon Kendrick
The
SHEIKH'S SECRET BABY
MILLS & BOON
MODERN